A VERY NICE GIRL

A VERY NICE GIRL

Imogen Crimp

BLOOMSBURY PUBLISHING
LONDON · OXFORD · NEW YORK · NEW DELHI · SYDNEY

BLOOMSBURY PUBLISHING
Bloomsbury Publishing Plc
50 Bedford Square, London, WC1B 3DP, UK
29 Earlsfort Terrace, Dublin 2, Ireland

BLOOMSBURY, BLOOMSBURY PUBLISHING and the Diana logo
are trademarks of Bloomsbury Publishing Plc

First published in Great Britain 2022

A catalogue record for this book is available from the British Library

ISBN: HB: 978-1-5266-2895-4; TPB: 978-1-5266-2894-7; EBOOK: 978-1-5266-2893-0;
EPDF: 978-1-5266-5468-7

2 4 6 8 10 9 7 5 3 1

Typeset by Integra Software Services Pvt. Ltd.
Printed and bound in Great Britain by CPI Group (UK) Ltd, Croydon CR0 4YY

To find out more about our authors and books visit www.bloomsbury.com
and sign up for our newsletters

'That isn't the way to talk,' I said. And he said,
'Well, it's true, isn't it? You can get a very nice girl for five
pounds, a very nice girl indeed; you can even get a
very nice girl for nothing if you know how to go about it.'

Voyage in the Dark, Jean Rhys

PART ONE

ONE

Laurie was waiting tables that evening, not behind the bar, so she couldn't slip me something on the house. I was feeling rich, though, and I was thinking about buying myself another when the man sitting next to me turned and started to speak.

I saw you just now – he said. – Singing. That was you, wasn't it?

I nodded.

Yes.

I waited for him to say something else. They always wanted to say something else, the men who spoke to me. Normally something along the lines of how beautiful my singing, or I, was. Or sexy. They were normally split roughly down the middle on whether *beautiful* or *sexy* was more appropriate. Or something about how one of the songs I'd sung had brought them right back to a time when they'd done something-or-other or been somewhere-or-other, or else some story I couldn't usually follow about how my voice reminded them of their ex-girlfriend or their estranged first wife or their mother.

This man didn't say anything, though. He nodded too, and went back to studying his drink, sloshing the liquid around, looking into the bottom of his glass. I started to feel annoyed.

What did you think then? – I asked.

Yeah – he said. – It was good, I guess.

Right.

Honestly? Not my kind of thing.

Oh.

He fell silent again.

Well, why are you here then? — I asked.

I was sitting on one of those bar stools that spin round, and he put a hand on the back of it and swivelled me so I was facing the window. I was about to ask him what the fuck he thought he was doing, but when I looked at him his face was so expressionless, so indifferent to my reaction, that I thought making a fuss would be embarrassing. Anyway, I don't think I minded, not really. I just knew I probably should.

He pointed.

You see that building?

The grey one?

Yes. Now count up to the fifth floor. Got it? See the furthest window on the left? Well, that's my window. That's where I work.

Oh right — I said. — Do you come here often then?

Did you really just ask me that?

You know what I mean.

He smiled a little smile.

I come here fairly often, yes. I think I've heard you sing before, in fact. Or maybe it was someone else.

Pretty interchangeable, are we?

He shrugged.

Like I said, I don't know much about it.

So what is it you do over there? — I asked.

Know much about finance?

Practically nothing, no.

And look, you don't see me sulking, do you? Anyway, that's what I do, and today's been a late one. So to answer your original question, I'm not really here for the music — he said, like he was explaining to a child that he was too busy for finger-painting. — Don't get me wrong, I'm sure it was lovely. I'm here because I needed a drink.

Fair enough.

But I'm sorry if I insulted you.

He smiled, and looked away.

4

It normally goes something like this. Someone tries to pick you up, and either they're so stupid you have to play down your intelligence, and you keep saying – *oh really!* – or – *how funny!* – and laughing like an idiot so you don't scare them off, while really all you can think about is throwing your drink in their face. Or else they're clever, they're clever and they want to make fun of you. They want to trip you up and laugh at you, lying there, sprawled out on the floor.

But this man wasn't like either type. Not quite. I couldn't work him out. For one, he didn't seem interested in getting close to me. He had one hand on his leg, one hand on his drink. He hadn't tried again to close the space between us. If anything, he'd moved further away, and I found myself leaning in close to hear what he was saying. And his words didn't seem to have any specific intention. He didn't seem bothered about how I'd react. He was throwing them out carelessly, like someone might chuck leftovers into a bowl for the dog, just to get rid of them, not staying to see if they're eaten.

I didn't realise you were expecting effusive praise – he said. – Forgive me.

That's ok. It's just, we artists are sensitive types, you see.

Oh?

Yes – I said. – So if my audience doesn't tell me straight away that they loved it, well, I assume they hated it.

And that's an issue for you?

Well, yes – I said. – Because then I think it was probably awful, and then, well, then things start to escalate very quickly in an artist's mind. Before we know where we are, we're choked by self-loathing, telling ourselves enough's enough, it's time to give in, accept defeat, we're no good and never will be and everyone else here knows it, feeling like we've been tipped headfirst into a pit and we're trying to crawl out up the sides, even as the earth's being shovelled back in. And all this because somebody's dared to begin the conversation with a comment about the weather or the number of people at the after-party, rather than diving straight into the important stuff – how marvellous we were, which is, to be honest, all we really want to talk about.

I gave a little laugh to show I was being ironic, but he didn't seem to notice.

That sounds very tiring – he said.

Believe me, it is.

Well, let me buy you a drink, and then we can start this whole thing again.

He pointed to my empty glass.

What are you drinking?

Oh, whatever you're having – I said.

He turned to get the barman's attention, and I looked at him as he talked. He was older than me – late thirties, early forties, maybe – and attractive. Beautiful, even, as there was something curiously feminine about him, though he was broad-shouldered and had a standard issue City-boy's haircut. His eyelashes, maybe. He had lovely long eyelashes, curly and pale, like a girl's. His was a cold sort of beauty, though. Hard to know what was going on behind.

The barman put two drinks in front of us.

What's this? – I asked. Mine was different from his.

Try it – he said. – You'll like it.

And he was right, I did. It was thick and syrupy. It made my throat warm.

Now, where were we?

We were going to start again.

Right. That's right. So—

He turned his chair round so he was facing me.

So – he said. – I saw you just now. Singing. That was you, wasn't it?

I nodded.

Yes.

I hope you don't think me intrusive – he said. – I mean, me talking to you like this, when you're sitting here alone. If you want me to stop, then say. I will.

I said nothing.

He carried on.

It's just I wanted to tell you how much I liked it. Your voice, I mean. How lovely it was. Really, I mean it, it was.

I laughed.

Well, thanks – I said. – That's sweet.

No really. Honestly. I mean it. Don't laugh. What's your name?

Anna.

Anna – he repeated. – I mean it, Anna. I'm not messing around. Look, do you want the truth? I've actually heard you here before. And yes, before you say anything, yes, I know what I said. But it was definitely you, I know it was. And, well, the truth is, I liked it.

He smiled and shrugged, his eyes empty and guileless.

It's not necessarily my thing, like I said. Not something I know much about. But, I don't know, there was something about it, something about you. I liked it.

At first, I thought he was making fun of me, and I tried to arrange my face in a way that showed I understood. That I was in on the joke. But he kept talking – *I've come back a few times now, nights I thought you'd be here. I wanted to see you again* – and he kept looking at me, his eyes looking right into my eyes, not flickering down to my lips or my breasts or my legs, and after a while I became less sure of what he was doing. I didn't know what to do with my face anymore. His voice went on and on, smooth and soothing, and I stopped thinking about anything except what it sounded like, and everything else started draining away, all the feelings, all the thoughts, draining out of my body, like a tide being sucked out to sea.

He started saying something about intensity, then. Something about intensity and atmosphere – *like a magnet* – he was saying, something about magnets anyway, and about my eyes, too, he was talking about my eyes.

There's just something – he said – I can't explain it, but there's something you need, isn't there, to do that sort of thing, and I don't know much about it, sure, but I know you've got it.

But then I saw that the corners of his mouth were a bit turned up, and there was a cold, hard light in his eyes, like a schoolboy whose prank was about to be unveiled, and he finished up with — *your voice, it just, it just, spoke to me* — and he grinned, and then I knew for sure he was laughing at me, and I wanted to crawl under the table.

I picked up my drink and looked away from him.

What? — he said. — What? I tried. Was that not better?

Much — I said. — Thanks.

Hey, I didn't mean to annoy you. Don't be upset.

I'm not upset. Well done, you're good at that.

Thank you.

I nearly believed you — I said.

Who said it wasn't true?

But his eyes were laughing still.

Then he started explaining to me what his job was all about and, while he talked, I picked at a bit of skin on my thumb. I felt stupid. He thought I was vain, precious, and he was right, I knew he was right, that's why it felt like he'd held a lit match under my fingernail. I'd never liked being teased, never known how to react to it. I was one of those sensitive children who went in tears to the teacher when someone said something mean, utterly convinced of the moral rightness of the universe, thinking that people who'd done something wrong would always be held accountable.

But the way he spoke to me felt perversely good, even though it hurt, like when you scratch a mosquito bite so hard it bleeds. Something about the way he teased and diminished me, explaining things to me and saying — *have you got your head around that, then?* — and yes, there I was, playing up to it, pouting and posturing like a little girl, sick at myself, thinking — *like me, like me, like me.*

So — he said, when he'd finished. — You're not very forthcoming, are you?

Am I not?

I was doing that thing my singing teacher got angry with me about, where my voice went up at the end of every sentence, punctuated by a nervous giggle. *On the breath* — she'd say. — *Commit to it. Don't apologise.*

No. You've told me practically nothing. All I really know about you is that you're easily offended. Come on. Tell me about yourself.

I would, but there's nothing much to tell.

That defensive laugh again.

Try me.

I tried to think.

I imagined unpacking, laying out and arranging the strands of my little life in front of him, thinking – *what would he find pretty? What would he want to buy?*

No – none of it – he'd want none of it – I could tell that already. He'd find it shabby and cheap and not to his taste at all. The sort of life that's just four walls and no pictures allowed or you'll damage the paintwork and that ugly blonde furniture – that furniture that's bought only for temporary rooms by people who'll never live there. I wouldn't show him that. Finding Laurie's long hairs tangled up in my brush, and my clothes, missing, in her drawers, and only being able to spend so long in the bath before I heard our landlords, the Ps, whispering downstairs on the landing – and even when I stuck my head under, even when I ran the tap, still being able to hear them, like they were right there, like they'd crawled into the bath with me and were whispering in my ear. I imagined him rubbing the fabric of it all between finger and thumb, thinking – *no – too thin – cheap* – discarding it.

And the nights out with Laurie. I wouldn't show him them. Me and her, drifting round the butt-ends of London, cheap bars, other people's living rooms, their blonde furniture identical to ours – out of the same catalogue – all the places he'd never go. None of that. Not that sick feeling in my stomach when I was in bed and I heard the Ps moving around on the stairs in the dark. I'd hear them fingering their way around the walls – tap tap tap – like beetles in the woodwork – and not wanting to go to the loo in the night in case they were there and she'd say – *up again, are we?* That time I had cystitis and peed in my dirty coffee cup so I wouldn't have to hear her say it again – *up again, are we?* – for the fifteenth time, as she lay in wait at the bottom of the stairs like a giant snake – *can't sleep, hm?* No. None of that. I couldn't show him that.

But above all, not the ugliness of this sort of life. That wouldn't impress him. I couldn't display that to him proudly and ask him what he thought. The underwear with stains that won't wash out, the old make-up, lumpy, dried up, that won't sit flat on my skin, the heels that make a click-click sound because they need re-heeling and I'm walking on metal. And the boredom of it. The boredom of checking the money each month – *is it enough, is it not enough?* – The early mornings in the practice room singing the same note again and again – *it's not right, not yet, it's not perfect, it has to be perfect* – and walking out of there at night, how the grey streets were nothing then, because my head was filled with music, my body throbbing, humming to a rhythm of its own and everything rich with colour. He wouldn't understand that. Not the saying to myself, again and again – *this will be worth it, this bit of my life, this will be worth it, I'll laugh about this all one day* – I wouldn't show him that – not the telling myself that, over and over in that small blank room – cold, it's always cold in there – to the sadness of the sirens moaning outside the window, the constant whine of traffic, petulant, like a child who can't get her way – no—

He was looking at me expectantly, so I told him the only part I thought sounded good.

I'm not really a jazz singer – I said. – I'm an opera singer.

It was late. The bar was emptying. Laurie's shift had finished, and she came over then and hit him with her best performance, loud and brash, flicking her hair and teasing him. I thought he'd start talking to her instead, and I felt something like relief, but he didn't seem interested. He listened while she talked, with a polite listening-face glued on – the sort that looks a little pained, like she was accidentally spitting in his face.

Then he said he had to go, and we all left the hotel together. Outside on the street, he handed me a card and said – *call me, we'll go for dinner* – and I said – *ok then* – and he said – *good* – and then he went. Not towards the Tube, the other way.

Laurie linked her arm through mine and we walked to the station. It was that bit of London with all the offices where no one really lives and, even though the buildings were all lit up, the streets were empty.

Well, he was a twat – Laurie said. – Did you like him?

I don't know. Not really.

But I couldn't get rid of his image, as if it had been etched onto the insides of my eyelids, and all the time Laurie was talking, I still had his voice in my head.

On the Tube, a big group of drunk men shouted about nothing. A woman looked at her face in the screen of her phone, tugged at the skin under her eyes, trying to stretch it out.

I got my book out to tuck his card inside. Prévost's *Manon*. I was learning the role at the Conservatory, and wanted to see where the story had come from. Laurie looked at the cover.

She's a whore, isn't she? – she said. – Manon? I've read that, I think.

I don't know. I haven't started it yet.

Well, she is. Just look at the picture on the front. And anyway, men don't write books with a woman's name as the title if she's not some sort of whore, do they? Can you think of one?

Madame Bovary – I said. – She's not a prostitute.

Well, maybe not professionally, but she's definitely some sort of whore.

Anna Karenina.

Ditto.

Alice in Wonderland.

It's for children – she said. – Doesn't count.

I couldn't think of any more.

Laurie sighed.

So, Luke messaged me earlier – she said. – He wants to meet.

You won't though?

No.

She started to talk about Luke. How he'd been trying to stifle her creativity. To make her get a job. To destroy her, in other words, she said. She realised he'd been trying to destroy her. She'd told me all this before. Laurie was a writer, and she liked to narrate large parts of her life over and over again. I could never tell her anything that surprised her, because something similar had always happened to her as well, and she'd tell me about that instead.

He never said the right thing about my writing – she said. – Or else he'd say totally the wrong thing. Patronising. Things like *very nice baby, but well, I'm not quite sure about—*. So I started saying I wasn't writing even when I was, because I dreaded him asking to read it. How he'd finger the words on the page. Frown, then fake enthusiasm, like he was critiquing my sub-par arts and crafts project. It'd got to the stage where every sentence I wrote, I crossed it out, because I imagined him reading it and what he'd think about it and what he'd say. And sex always ended when he came, you know, even if I hadn't. He was one of those sorts of men. Like fuck I'm meeting him now.

She sounded hard and angry, but she looked sad, twisting the ends of her hair through her fingers. She was twenty-eight and very pretty, I thought – blonde and tall and slim – but she was worried about getting old. She'd make me stand next to her in front of the mirror so she could compare which parts of my face were smooth where hers was lined.

So, will you see that man then? – she asked.

Maybe. Should I?

I'd go for dinner. Why not? He'll take you somewhere nice. Men like that always do. He's got money – she said, putting a disdainful emphasis on the word, as if money were a sexually transmitted infection. – That much is clear.

Laurie had a proprietary interest in other people's money. She could always spot it and wheedle it out, like a pig rooting for truffles.

That – she said – was a very expensive suit. And the watch. Did you see the watch?

I shook my head. I hadn't.

I thought you said he was a twat? – I said.

So what? It's not like you have to marry him. I'd imagine he's married already. They tend to be, in my experience.

What, men?

That sort of man.

What sort of man?

The sort of man that preys on girls in bars.

Would you call that preying? I wouldn't call that preying.

No – she said. – I can't imagine you would.

He wasn't really like that – I said. – Most men I talk to in there, they buy me a drink and then they treat it like their admission ticket. Valid and ready for me to stamp. They don't come close to knowing anything about me. He wasn't like that. He—it was like he put his finger on me and pressed down on it until it hurt. Do you know what I mean?

I do. You want to fuck him because he's hot and kind of mean, and you're a masochist. That's fine, Anna. You don't need to be ashamed of that. There are worse things you could be. And God knows you need to fuck someone soon. I once didn't wear earrings for the amount of time you haven't had sex, and my holes closed up.

Thanks for that image – I said.

Any time. It's tomorrow our rent's due, isn't it? – she asked.

First Friday of the month. Yeah.

You might have to lend me some. Not much. Fifty or so. I'm short.

Sure.

I had enough. I'd done a couple of extra sets that month, and I'd just been paid. The envelope in my bag was fat.

I can give it to you now – I said.

I got the money out, handed her the notes. I never minded lending to her. She didn't ever pay me back, but she was excessively generous when she was feeling rich, insisting on extravagance and paying for everything – drinks and dinners and taxis. That's why money trickled through her fingers like water, why she always needed it, and why she was so scathing of people who had it.

She must have been worried about asking me, because she was happy then. We got off the Tube and laughed a lot about nothing the whole way down the Mitcham Road, where people clustered after dark, no matter the cold – congregating outside the grand old cinema turned bingo hall –shouting and kissing in the street – playing music from phones – queueing for the nail bar that, late at night, sold toast. Further up, though, it got quiet, and dummies stared out at us from unlit windows. Fully made-up heads in wig shops. Fabric stores, their child mannequins in satin party clothes. Laurie was getting me to sing bits of the jazz songs she liked, joining in when she knew the words – *suddenly I saw you there, and through foggy London town, the sun was shining everywhere* – and passersby stared. It was only when we turned onto our street that she became morose. She stopped saying anything and she sighed a few times and I felt this angry, sick, hopeless feeling in my stomach and I knew that she was feeling it too. She put her key in the door and she said – *this bloody fucking house, this bloody fucking life, why do we do this, Anna? I should get a proper job. I should. I will. I can't stand it anymore* – and then she turned it.

TWO

On Monday morning, I had a singing lesson with Angela. I took the Tube to Moorgate — the breed of commuter squashing onto the Northern line becoming more corporate, more expensively dressed at every station closer to the City — and then I switched for the one stop to Farringdon. Walking down Clerkenwell Road, the sky was still dim, as though lit by an energy-saving bulb, and the Conservatory was empty and quiet. Musicians weren't generally that keen on early starts, but Angela loved them. *If you can get the voice to work first thing* — she'd say — *you can get it to work whenever.*

She was in the practice room already. It was 9 a.m. and, as always, she looked ready to get on stage — silk shirt, lipstick, heels.

Nice weekend? — she said.

Not bad. I sang at one of those charity dinner things Marieke sends round. Frankie did it too.

Brave of you. They usually get you singing all sorts of nonsense, don't they?

It was ok, actually. Gilbert and Sullivan. Bit of jazz. And a few of the big opera tunes that everyone knows. Frankie had a bash at 'Nessun Dorma'. It was fun. Well, they fed us, anyway.

Angela tutted theatrically.

Christ — she said. — Totally inappropriate rep for him. Who's his teacher again? John? Did John know he'd be singing that?

Doubt it. He got through it, though. You know what Frankie's like, not much fazes him. Anyway, it was good money.

Prostituting your voices for a quick buck — she said. — Terribly irresponsible of you both. Let's see where we're at then, shall we, after all that squawking.

She played a chord and sang an exercise for me to repeat. Simple triad, open *ah* vowel, nothing special — but God, Angela Lehmann in the same room as me, hearing her sing right next to me, that voice so close — the same one I'd listened to for years, alone in my bedroom. Hers was the first voice I'd fallen in love with, discovering her recordings as a teenager, floored by the beauty of it and all that a human voice could be — its velvet intensity, so sweet and dark and rich it made me ache. As an undergraduate, I'd saved up the money, gone to London to watch her in *Tosca,* and after the show I'd waited outside the Stage Door, hoping for a chance to talk to her — it had started to rain, though, and she hadn't come out.

I'd always wanted to study at the Conservatory, knowing she taught there, but it was a vague fantasy — like how a child might say they wanted to go to space when they grew up. I didn't apply at undergraduate level, too intimidated by the lengthy audition requirements, the jargon on their website — they wanted singers who were *artistically truthful*, they said. *Versatile. Musically excellent. Vocally prepared for the demands of professional training.*

I ended up at a small performing arts school out of London, and I stayed to do postgraduate there when they offered me a bursary. In my final year, I applied for the Conservatory's opera school programme, with no expectation that I'd even be called for audition, but I was — and, in the email, I saw that Angela would be on the panel. Over the course of a week, they'd hear hundreds of singers, most of whom were already studying at the Conservatory or at another major college, British or international. From them, they would select just twelve for their two-year opera school programme — the final and most prestigious step in a young singer's training. My chances of acceptance were, I knew, practically zero.

Stepping off the train in London, though, I felt oddly confident. I breathed, and the city rushed in. It filled up my lungs and fed my blood, made me new, and there was my future, stretching out in front of me, bright and unbroken. Mine to walk into, and I did, out onto the stage to audition, totally sure of myself. It was a certainty I'd only ever felt while singing – like the space was mine and, in it, I could do anything – and after I'd sung, Angela smiled and said *brava*. Later, it was her who called to say I'd got a place.

And I was wondering – she asked – if you might want to learn with me? I'd like to teach you, if you'll have me.

So I was moving to London, city of superlatives – the best singers, the best directors, the best opportunities. I floated through the last few months of my masters, barely noticing it all – the end of year opera in the community centre, no budget, wearing our own clothes as costumes and improvising with props from home – my final recital in an over-lit church hall, half-full.

In my first lesson, Angela sat me down.

Now, I'm sure you were the star where you've come from – she said. – And you're not going to be the star here, at least not for a while, and that will be hard on you, I know. But you're responsible for your own future, Anna. The voice is there and it's got something special to it, or you wouldn't be here. But no one's going to make allowances for you being behind. The rest is down to hard work – she said, and then she smiled. – But well, I love a wildcard. We'll show them, won't we?

Since I'd started last month, I was almost always first in, getting to the Conservatory an hour or so before classes began. Walking through the corridors at that time – past the noticeboards announcing instruments for sale, language lessons, flats to rent – most of the practice room slits were dark. The occasional snip of light, a snatch of a violin sonata, a singer sirening up a scale, but otherwise silence. It was my favourite time to work. An hour alone with my voice, before the day started properly and I couldn't come up for air. Standing in front of the mirror, straightening shoulders and massaging jaw. Leaving this world and going into a new one, one I liked better. Bringing it in from silence, starting with the breathing, then gently into real sound, until there's my voice again, exactly as I'd left it. Repertoire. Building a piece from the ground up. Sing the notes to *La*, then work with the text – translate it, write the phonetic notation above, practise on the vowels, get the line, then add in the consonants, but don't let them break it. They're the foundations. But then, add the walls, the colour, the furnishings. Shape the piece into a space I can inhabit, a room I can walk through. Practise until I can't get it wrong. Get it into my body, imagining the notes replicating themselves in my cells, so that I'm living the music and not just singing it. Looking inside myself for images, for memories that make me feel the way this text needs me to feel, and then turning myself inside out so they colour my song – because singing is not ventriloquism. To be a character is not to speak their voice through your body, their dead words on the page, but to zip yourself into their skin, to animate them with your own voice, to breathe new life into their words.

That day, I'd taken Manon to my lesson. I was covering one of the final years for the December opera scenes show.

It suits you – Angela said, when the hour was up. – Some roles fit your voice exactly, and this is one of yours, so enjoy it.

I knew what she meant. The music felt to me like an old jumper, comfortable to slip into, moulded to the shape of my body.

She's a brilliant character – I said. – I've always loved her.

Me too. None of the men know what to make of her, do they? Seductress or ingénue. Passionate lover or money-grabbing whore. But you need to understand her, of course. Don't just learn the notes. Make sure you know the woman properly too.

While I was packing away my music, Angela told me about when she'd done the role. A very famous tenor had played her Chevalier.

Many years ago, this was – she said. – I'd be stretching the boundaries of credibility playing a teenager now, even by opera's standards. Anyway, this man hugely fancied himself, thought he could do no wrong on stage, and he used to kiss me with tongues, even though I kept telling him not to. Said it was the only way he could get into the part. So one night, when he stuck his tongue in my mouth, I bit it. Actually made him bleed, which I felt quite bad about, I didn't mean to do it that hard. Right before his aria too.

What did he do? Was he angry?

Well, he never did it again, let's put it that way. Not that I'd encourage you to assault your colleagues necessarily, but sometimes needs must. Are you doing anything nice tonight?

Kind of — I said. — I'm having dinner with this guy I met last week. At the hotel bar I sing at, you know.

It had taken me a long time to construct the message to him. I felt awkward committing to a tone, knowing I was making myself into something he could reread, but when I sent it, he replied straight-away and suggested Monday. It would have to be lateish, though, because he couldn't get out early. He named a time, a restaurant. Offhand, like he was arranging a business meeting.

Oh, good girl — Angela said. — Go and have a love affair. Get some life experience. Something to sing about.

Angela was one of the few people I knew who used phrases like *love affair* non-ironically.

Well, I'll do my best — I said.

The rest of the morning was acting class with Stefan, who always wore a long black coat and called everyone, unsmilingly, *my friend*. We took turns walking into imagined spaces with purpose, while he leant against the wall at the back, watching.

Where is she? — he asked. — How does she feel? How old is she? Is that clear from what she's doing?

At lunchtime, I realised I'd left my sandwich at the Ps', so I sat drinking boiling water. Beth — who, by virtue of being the only mezzo in my year, got cast in everything — asked why I wasn't eating. I said I was doing a cleanse.

Ooh, interesting — she said. — I've never done that before. Is it a vocal thing? Maybe I should try it.

Early on, I'd heard some singers discussing a postgrad who'd complained about having no money — *it's like she thinks she's special* — and I wasn't about to make the same mistake. Being health-obsessed was fine though. Encouraged, even.

In the afternoon, I did some practice by myself, and then it was general rep class with Marieke, the Head of Opera. The class took place in the concert hall, no windows, nothing lit up except the stage. The hall could seat hundreds, but the class was only my year, the twelve of us clustered in the front rows, making notes and nodding along to everything Marieke said, trying to make her like us.

I was glad I wasn't signed up to sing. I was distracted, wondering why I'd agreed to meet him — a man who was probably at least a decade older than me, and who I almost definitely disliked. *It might be awful* — I'd said to Laurie, when I was contemplating cancelling. *Yeah* — she said. — *Well. So might everything.*

Marieke was in a particularly pedantic mood as well, and so no one was allowed to sing more than a bar or two before she stopped them. An illustrious career behind her, she had only recently become Head of Opera, and was terrifying with it. In the space of a minute, she could flip from being charmingly whimsical — dancing around, waving her arms, or making you pretend to be a tree — to scathingly annihilating your character.

It was Natalie's turn for deconstruction. She sang twenty seconds of music, and Marieke stopped her.

The text is all over the place — she announced. — Double consonants everywhere. All over the place. Diphthongs. Diphthongs. Why are you doing all those diphthongs?

She covered her mouth with her hand, as if physically pained.

Why? — she said.

Natalie seemed about to speak, which would have been a mistake. Marieke's questions were nearly always rhetorical, and she disliked her performance being interrupted by people trying to answer them. Luckily, before Natalie had the chance, she began to speak the text herself.

E pur così in un giorno perdo fasti e grandezze? — she declaimed, in an accent more Italian than the Italians could ever dream of emulating. — *So, in a day, I have lost my glory and my greatness?*

That's what we're aiming for — she said. — Like that. Do it like that.

E pur così—

No, no, no – she interrupted, despairingly. – Not like that. Like this. *E pur così, E pur così.* Am I speaking a foreign language?

One of her favourite jokes. We all tittered obediently.

She let Natalie have a stab at singing again, interrupting every other note so that the attempt became garbled nonsense. Natalie's face began to give a much more convincing picture of Cleopatra's abject despair, though. Perhaps this was Marieke's aim all along.

Who told you to do an appoggiatura on that? – she shouted. – An appoggiatura is a *lean*. Expressive. Why would you do a lean on a name, hm? Well, I mean, of course – she conceded – there are *some* circumstances where you'd lean on a name, but THIS ISN'T ONE OF THEM. Stop it. I don't like it.

Or – you *did* say you'd taken this to your Italian coach, didn't you? Or didn't you? Well, for God's sake, take it again.

Or – that note should be connected to that note. Well, it should all be connected really, but we'll do what we can in the time.

Or – that word is *important*, Natalie, so make it important. It's an active word. Do you know what I mean by an active word? What then? Well, don't say yes if you don't. This isn't primary school.

Natalie agreed that it wasn't, and Marieke dismissed us all, yawning, like when a cat unexpectedly tires of playing with a mouse and lets it go without eating it.

I had an hour before meeting him, so I went to the cafeteria. Sophie, the final year I was covering in *Manon*, was sitting by herself, and I went to join her.

Oh, you're still here – she said. – Do you have a rehearsal tonight?

No, I'm waiting to meet someone.

Oh right. I've got extra coaching – she said, in a way that strongly suggested this was a better use of time. – Tim managed to fit me in for an extra slot. I'm doing this *Così* external, and the recit's killing me. He's great with recit.

She tipped her head over to one side and pulled it with her hand. I heard her neck crack.

So, how are you finding Manon? – she asked.

Every time she spoke, she seemed to gesture outwards, as if everyone wanted to hear her and that was fine by her.

Yeah, it's going well – I said.

This was the first set of opera scenes since I'd started, and I hadn't been given my own part, only the cover. It was hard not to be disappointed.

You're a soubrette though, aren't you? – Sophie said. – I mean, I thought you were? Aren't you finding Manon a bit big? It's so unhelpful the way they do that here. Give people roles they wouldn't in a million years sing in big Houses. It's as good as useless for your CV, isn't it?

It's not really big for me. I've learned the arias before.

At the last place you were at?

Yeah.

You know, lots of the girls in my year were saying it was amazing you got in here. When we saw the list I mean, not that you're not good – she said quickly. – Of course, I don't mean that. But that place you were at before was barely even a conservatoire, was it? Everyone was saying you must be exceptional. Before you arrived, I mean.

Well, thanks – I said, although it wasn't quite a compliment.

Over the past month at the Conservatory, I'd learned that getting my place wasn't a guarantee of success, as I'd stupidly thought. It just meant I was now in the running, as opposed to being nowhere. We had to audition for everything, even internally, and there weren't enough roles for us all. Everything was a competition, and I wasn't winning. Going into class when it was my turn to sing, I often had to visualise that moment in my audition, Angela smiling and saying *brava,* because I felt nothing like these singers. They spoke another language, talking about people I didn't know, companies I'd never heard of, external auditions that had been and gone without me getting the memo.

Sophie had lost interest in me. She'd gone back to massaging her jaw.

The voice isn't particularly happy today – she said.

I didn't yet talk about my voice as if it were a separate entity. I made a mental note to start.

Larynx is tight – she said.

She let her tongue flop out of her mouth, and began to chew on it.

I waited for him for what felt like a very long time.

Long enough to hang around outside for a bit, hoping he'd show up. To get too cold to stay there. Long enough to humiliate myself on the door, having to deal with the woman who'd watched me waiting.

What's the reservation under?

Max, I think.

Nothing in that name. What's the surname?

Um—

Having to find his card in my book, where I'd used it to mark my place, to check. Long enough, then, for her to fully assess the situation, to change the way she smiled at me. To glance down at the ripped lining of my coat when I held it out to her, and take it with an expression of polite distaste, like a doctor attempting to seem neutral about her patient's pot of bloody urine. Long enough to wonder what I was meant to drink, to pick a glass of wine at random from the middle of the list and drink it – too quickly – and then to think – *it'll look bad if he turns up and I'm sitting with an empty glass* – and order another. Long enough to become angry. To wonder where the fuck he was and why he hadn't told me he'd been held up. To think about leaving and then to remember that, if I did, they'd expect me to pay for the wine.

He was twenty minutes late in the end, but he walked in like someone who was right on time, giving his overcoat to the woman, having a joke with her, both of them laughing, no rush to get to the table.

When I didn't stand up, he squeezed my shoulder and sat.

Sorry I'm late – he said. – I was on a call with a client in New York. He's needy. I couldn't get away.

It's fine.

Then, remembering I'd meant to be arch – but didn't you say you're kind of important?

23

Did I? – he said. – That doesn't sound like something I'd say.

I think that was the subtext.

A slightly bemused smile, and there was a pause. It went on a bit too long, and I drank my wine to hide my face.

So – he said. – I take it you've been here a while?

I went to a Catholic school. Inbuilt sense of guilt. I'm incapable of being late.

What the hell was I talking about? He was looking at me like I was a bizarre performance art piece, strangely entertaining, but hard to say what it was meant to be about.

It's a rehearsal ethic thing as well – I said, trying to add something that made a bit more sense. – If you're not there when the director wants to start, you won't get hired again.

So you were being serious?

Serious? About what?

About the opera. You said you were an opera singer.

Of course I was being serious. What, you thought I was lying?

No, not lying – he said. – It surprised me, that's all. You don't look much like an opera singer to me.

What the fuck's that supposed to mean?

Everything I said was coming out wrong, every intonation flat and off, like an automated message. He laughed.

Wow – he said. – I don't know. Just that you look quite young, I guess.

I'm twenty-four.

Well, yeah. Isn't that young to be a singer? I knew someone who sang opera for a bit, till she had kids. She trained for years, I think. But maybe she wasn't very good.

I'm still training too. I'm a student.

Oh, I see – he said. – So you didn't mean professionally.

My body tensed with defensiveness, as though he'd pushed me.

Well, I guess it all depends on what you mean by *professionally* – I said. – I sing in front of audiences. Sometimes I get paid, sometimes I don't, because what artist doesn't love working for free for exposure, after all. So yeah, maybe I don't fit your exacting definition.

I was trying to match the sort of person I remembered him being, trying to be cold, dry in the way Laurie could be, but he just looked confused. He wasn't that person anymore, and it threw me, like when you think there'll be another step at the top of the stairs in the dark. You stumble. You feel the world lurch.

I don't remember you being this aggressive – he said. – Last time, I mean. Maybe I caught you on a good day. But anyway, you're right. I have no imagination.

I couldn't think of anything clever to say to that, and then the waiter came over to take our order. He was flirty with Max, teasing him about keeping me waiting, and Max was going along with it in that indulgent, we-both-know-I'm-humouring-you sort of way. I dug the spike of my heel into the fleshy bit on the top of my other foot. *Get a hold of yourself. Stop being a bitch. He doesn't like it.*

When the waiter had gone, Max, casually, as though we'd only just sat down, asked if I'd been to New York. No, I said, I'd never really been anywhere. He told me he used to live there, still went quite a bit for work.

It's a bizarre place – he said. – You really can do whatever you want. Whenever you want to, I mean. It's a bit like what you think being grown up will be like when you're a kid, and then you grow up. Find it's much more boring. There was this one time, February—

The waiter brought a bottle of wine, a fresh glass for me, topped us both up. I stayed quiet and listened, because that seemed safest.

A group of us were out after work – he said – and talk turned to summer. Everyone got nostalgic, and this one guy there, he said he knew of a rooftop bar. Heaters. The grill on all year round. So it was 2 a.m., but we all got a cab there, and suddenly it was summer. Exactly like a summer night, the smell of meat in the air and the heat on your face.

It's funny – he said. – You can always tell who's from New York and who's visiting, because the visitors all shuffle round looking upwards. They're like kids trying to find their parents in a crowd. I was always a bit like that. Never got over them, the buildings, even though I was there for years.

Would you live there again?

I don't think so. I had the chance to quite recently, actually. Turned it down. I grew up in the country. I don't want to be in a city forever.

He started telling me a story – when he'd first moved to London, days pre-Google Maps, how he'd tried to walk from Edgware Road to Edgware, thinking they must be close – and I began to relax. I realised this wasn't some sort of test. He wasn't trying to catch me out, trip me up. He was trying to entertain me. He was even, I thought, trying to impress me, and then the waiter brought our food and topped up our glasses, and I felt very happy suddenly. I allowed this new version of him to be superimposed on the last, so that this became all he was.

When did you move to London? – he asked.

Not long ago. Summer. I started at the Conservatory in September.

How are you finding it here?

Yeah, it's ok.

Ok? Where are you living?

With this couple, the Ps. They rent out the rooms in their attic. Laurie's there too. You remember Laurie? You met her last time.

The waitress?

She's a writer, actually. Mainly theatre, she's had a couple of short plays put on, and she's writing a novel now. But, yeah, that's how we know each other. We met at the Ps'. She broke up with this guy she'd been living with for years. Just before summer. So she moved there same time as me.

So you girls live in a literal artist's garret? – he said. – How romantic.

He was smiling and, without knowing why, I found myself describing the house to him. All the details I'd thought would repel him.

Well – I said. – Romantic's one word for it. So, they have this old cat with sticky fur who keeps peeing in my shoes. And all the cupboards are full of old cards. You know, like birthday cards,

26

Christmas cards, congratulations-on-your-new-baby cards, dating all the way back to the seventies. And me and Laurie's rooms were storage before we arrived. They didn't really bother to clear them, just moved the stuff onto the landing, so it's full of boxes. Abandoned kitchen utensils. Ripped bedding. Rolled-up rugs. A rocking horse. We tried to move them once, kept tripping over them in the dark, but underneath the first box we picked up was a pile of writhing moths. I mean, a literal pile. You could pick them up in fistfuls.

He laughed, and that made me feel good.

What are they like? – he asked. – The Ps.

What are they like? Well, they sleep on a mattress on the floor. I went into their room once when they were out. It's like a crack den – stained sheets, bottles of rum on the floor – but she's got a wardrobe full of beautiful clothes, Mrs P. Silk dresses, cardigans from agnès b. I don't know when she ever would have worn them, but I guess they must have money. The house is pretty big too, but we're not allowed in most of it. They don't exactly go out of their way to make us feel at home. Don't like us using the kitchen much. And they've told us not to fill the bath higher than a certain point. After we've used it, Mr P creeps in there and checks where we filled it to, and if he thinks it's too high, he comes up and shouts at us when we're still in our towels. Oh, and they keep all the windows shut all the time. They're sealed round the sides with masking tape. I think they believe in poisonous spores or something.

Another bottle of wine appeared. I hadn't noticed him ordering it. He'd stopped laughing now, and he looked at me, suddenly serious.

But how do you feel about it? – he said.

What do you mean?

Well, it sounds awful. I mean, how do you feel about having to live like that?

And he seemed to expect so completely the truth that, barely stopping to think, I found myself handing it over. I told him about Mrs P. How she would talk at me for hours, worrying away at disparate strands of conversation – her children, her bank's reduced opening hours, the school up the road and how rough it was these days, her health problems, and how the schedule on Radio 4 kept changing for the worse. How I'd stand there, watching the minutes tick by, feeling like she was collecting up time, pouring it into a hole she'd dug in the garden. I told him about the evenings with Laurie. The hours spent Googling, scrolling through endless images of rooms to rent, but how nowhere we could ever find was even close to as cheap as the Ps'. I told him about the Mitcham Road. How every time I breathed, I imagined it all layering up in my lungs like sand at the bottom of a test tube. How all the streets off it were the same as ours, the houses going on and on as far as you could see, all exactly the same. You walked down them, and you could see in through windows, and there were beds everywhere. Beds in the front rooms. Beds by windows which opened right out onto the street, so that you could look in and see people lying there in their pants. Beds barely concealed by grubby net curtains. Beds in basements with bars across the glass. How I hated it. I told him how I hated it. All those beds. All those people. Thinking how little space a person could take up. It made me want to scream.

So what is it you want then? – he said.

What is it I want?

Yes. Why are you doing it? What's the game plan?

Oh, I don't know – I said. – I guess I'd like to cobble together some sort of little career eventually.

I don't believe you – he said.

What do you mean, you don't believe me?

I mean, I think you're being disingenuous. Do you know what I think?

No. Please. Enlighten me.

I don't think you'd settle for a little career, Anna. You don't strike me as that sort of person. You've got drive, I can tell. You shouldn't do it down.

Then he started asking me questions and, while I talked, he sat, unmoving, and listened to my answers. He wasn't the sort of man who needed to nod to show he understood. His energy was narrow, focused on me, like he was shining a light in my eyes, and I felt that same intense concentration of performance – only this space matters now and nothing else.

He asked me how I'd got into opera, and I said that, well, singing was natural, wasn't it? Everyone sings. All children sing, before they get self-conscious. I used to sing to myself after the lights had gone out at night, try to remember the words of songs I knew. I was quite old before I started learning properly, before I thought what I'd do with it, but once I did it seemed obvious. Because a vocation is a fact. It's something you know to be true about yourself, like your name or the colour of your hair, even when you're sure of nothing else. He asked how I was paying for it all, all the training, it must be expensive, and I said that it was, but my fees were paid – scholarship – and rent was cheap. I did things here and there for cash, some choir work, the jazz – Laurie'd found me the job, she'd been waitressing at the hotel bar for years – that paid ok. I muddled along. But it could be lonely, I said. It could be lonely. No one was here to make friends. The other singers, they were assessing you all the time. Is she better than me or worse than me? Threat or not threat?

And what about money? – he said.

What about it?

Do you ever earn any, I mean? This all sounds like quite some process to go through to never get paid.

Oh, but an artist doesn't do it for money – I said. – She does it for love.

That sounds sustainable.

The waiter had taken our plates away, though I don't think I'd eaten much. I got up to find the bathroom. The restaurant floor was vast, a maze of tables and chairs, dark panelled walls, soft lighting.

The bathroom, madam? – a waiter intercepted.

He pointed to a door of dark wood, unmarked.

Through there.

I felt dizzy, but it wasn't unpleasant. The world seemed softer, more welcoming. The dizziness smoothed the sharp edges, and I had that feeling you always get after a few glasses of wine – like nothing else matters, it doesn't matter about tomorrow, there's always tonight. I washed my hands and looked at myself in the mirror and I thought my face looked softer too, and my eyes were black and bottomless.

When I got back to the restaurant, I found he'd paid the bill. I said thanks, and he said thanks for coming, and we were helped into our coats.

Out on the street, we stood close together and he looked down at me and smiled. This had all been an elaborate anecdote and he was about to tell me the punchline. It was a predictable one, I already knew how it would end, but I'd pretend to be surprised, because I knew he'd like that better.

But he just said — are you heading to the Tube? It's quite a nice night. I can show you a more scenic route if you like.

Sure — I said.

We turned down a backstreet. It was quiet out and empty. The street was narrow and, when you looked up, the buildings seemed to go on forever, all glass and concrete, and when you looked down the road there were more and more of them, bisecting the sky at odd angles, like a pop-up book not fully opened, so that all the bits of cardboard overlapped. He walked a little bit away from me, his hands in his pockets. He was treating me suddenly like I was a distant relative visiting London, pointing out street names, saying they were like a fossil record, what it used to be like round there.

Angel Court — he said. — That was the sign of the stationers. There's still an angel on a building somewhere.

He couldn't find it, though, and I was half listening to him, half feeling like I'd just auditioned with my most difficult aria — not a note-perfect performance, perhaps, but it had been emotionally true — and the panel had smiled and said — *no thanks. Who's next?*

I said — so do you live round here then?

About five minutes that way.

What sort of building is it? One of the new ones?

A few years old. One of the towers.

I didn't know anyone actually lived here. I thought they were all owned by Russian oligarchs.

Well, they mainly are. When you look up at my building at night, most of the lights are off.

It must be weird being right in the centre like this.

I'm used to it. I'm only here in the week, anyway.

What about the weekends?

I've got a house just outside Oxford. Near where I grew up.

Oh, right.

I remembered then what Laurie had said.

So you're married?

He laughed.

Um, no – he said. – I'm not. Why? Are you?

I just assumed. Sorry.

You assumed? Can I ask why?

Well, you fit the profile, I guess. House in the country. Flat in the city. Your job. Your age.

My age?

I couldn't work out if he was amused or offended.

How old exactly do you think I am?

I looked at him. His hair was the sort of blonde that could be mixed with grey and you wouldn't be able to tell. He had little lines around his eyes, the corners of his lips. I liked them. They were the right sort of lines. They showed that he smiled more often than he frowned, on balance.

I don't know exactly – I said. – But the sort of age where it's not unreasonable to assume you'd be married.

You should meet my mother. You'd have a lot in common. I'm thirty-eight. So, you know, not quite past it yet, but I appreciate your concern.

I was worried I might have insulted him – he didn't say anything else – and then we were at the station. He'd walk away from me, rejoin the masses of faceless, suited men. I wouldn't see him again. I hadn't been what he'd thought I might be.

He said goodnight and went to kiss me on the cheek and I – why? – wanting to make this unambiguous, I suppose, something that couldn't be taken back or explained another way, pulled him down towards me and kissed him properly. I clung onto him. Eyes shut, the blackness spun. There was a loud noise in my head, like a plane taking off, and it took a second – a minute maybe – I have no idea how long it took – for me to realise he wasn't quite resisting, not quite, but he hadn't kissed me back.

I let go.

Well, goodnight, then – I said.

Night, Anna. Get home safe.

The last image I had of him was of his smile. He was smiling when I turned away, but more to himself than at me, like he was remembering something funny from earlier. Something he wasn't going to tell me because he didn't think I'd get it.

THREE

So we were in Paris — Laurie said. — Me and Luke. And before we went, all my friends were like, *oh my God, he's taking you to Paris, he's going to propose, he's definitely going to propose!* And I was like, do you honestly think I'm waiting for that? For him to propose to me? Do you really think that — what? — that the only reason we're not married yet — ignoring everything I've ever said I believe about anything — is that he hasn't asked me? Because that's what all women want, whatever they say, and even if they really do think they don't want it, that's just because they don't yet know what they want?

She pulled a book off the shelf.

Look — she said. — This was published last month. Unbent spine. Not read. But, so, they actually come in here, or what? Why haven't they cleared it out?

It's really not that different to the rest of the house — I said.

The Ps were out, and we'd gone to their daughter's room. It was still crammed full of her stuff, even though she'd moved out years ago. Laurie stood, studying the mess of books on either side of the boarded-up fireplace, and I sat on the bed. There was an empty condom wrapper on the bedside table.

Do you think that's left over from a teenage assignation? — I asked. — Or does Mrs P bring her lovers here?

Please stop it — said Laurie. — Please don't say *Mrs P* and *lovers* in the same sentence.

Sorry.

She put the book back on the shelf, and began to pick through a pile of clothes.

Anyway — she said. — So on the last day we went for this walk. Got lost. Ended up miles away from anywhere on a bridge. There was loads of traffic, but an, I suppose, alrightish view of the Eiffel Tower somewhere over the water. And there was this woman in a wedding dress, having her photo taken up against the view.

She extracted a dress and held it up against herself in the mirror — Peter Pan collar, faux-naïf, not her thing at all — threw it back on the pile, went over to a different one. The room was full of clothes, disparate towers of them, some as high as our waists, half of them still with tags attached. Long strings of beads, dreamcatcher earrings were interspersed in the piles. Jelly shoes. Suspenders. Unopened bottles of Jo Malone perfume. We topped up our wardrobes from the room whenever the Ps were out. I smelled of English Pear and Freesia now, sometimes Grapefruit. Laurie favoured Pomegranate Noir.

I was thinking she had this massive bridal party — Laurie said. — Because there were all these other women in white standing around, holding their skirts up to keep them out of the grime. But then I realised that — no — it was a fucking queue. They were all separate brides, waiting to have their photos done in the same fucking spot.

On a main road?

Well, I guess you wouldn't be able to see that in the photo. Anyway, I noticed they were all Asian, and when I pointed this out to Luke he said — *well, yeah, it's quite a common thing in China, isn't it? You get married there, then come to Europe for location wedding shoots.* And then — what with that, and with my friends going on about him proposing — well, anyway, I started thinking about weddings and capitalism and the commodification of love, and I know I shouldn't have, it was bad of me, but I brought it up with him. We had this big argument, actually. Him saying he'd had enough of waiting for me to sort my life out.

Wait, he said what? To sort your life out? Seriously?

Yeah. He said that he'd been waiting for years for us to have some sort of future together. How he felt like he was watching me, every day, destroy that with all the inconvenient things I wanted for my own life. Ok, he didn't actually say that, I'm extrapolating. But what he did say, what he did actually genuinely say was – *you know you can't talk like that, you can't talk about money like that, like it's so far beneath you, when I'm paying for our relationship.* Paying for our relationship. And I said – *well what exactly do you mean by that? Do you think our relationship's like a handbag? A mini-break?*

And what did he mean?

Fuck knows. All he said was – *I don't buy handbags.*

A pathetic response.

Well, exactly. Anyway, it's fine. Maybe it took that trip, the brides, to really get it. Things had been bad for ages. Those last few months together, we'd be sitting on the sofa, watching TV or eating dinner or whatever, and I'd find myself scanning the shelves, thinking about which of the stuff was mine, what I'd have to take if I left, you know. How many boxes I'd need.

You can't have taken much – I said.

Laurie had even less stuff than I did.

Well, most of it was his – she said. – I've always tried not to have many things. A point of principle, saying I don't need stuff, which is stupid really, because nobody cares. But I guess I did want to make that point. That my life's not centred around things, you know. I'm not structuring my life around acquiring things. It's not my aim.

Nobody cares how you present yourself though – I said. – Not like the girls in my year. They act like, because I don't own outfits specifically for auditions, or go with them to Pilates classes at their swanky gym every lunchtime – which, by the way, costs £90 a month, I checked – I can't be that serious about singing.

Well, yeah, theatre people don't care if I look a bit scruffy, I guess. But my uni friends do, trust me. They all feel terribly sorry for me, I can tell, not having a proper job like them. Like it's a sort of embarrassing illness. Best not to mention it. No one even asks me that *what are you doing at the moment?* question anymore. They find it too awkward. You know, back in final year, when everyone was applying for jobs, they all kept asking me what I'd do. There was something I found perversely entertaining about it, not getting a proper job like I was meant to. Watching them all start to earn money – and I mean, really, a lot of money, a stupid amount of money, some of them – take expensive drugs every weekend, go on ridiculous holidays, buy property – and me be left behind. I'd make them feel uncomfortable at social gatherings by talking about how little I earned. It made me laugh. Still does.

Only because you think something will change – I said. – You wouldn't find it funny if you thought it was for forever. You always think, don't you – I do, anyway – that something will happen. I don't know what exactly. But something will happen, and you'll have a different life.

Laurie sighed, came and sat on the end of the bed.

Yeah, I suppose I think that too.

Things are important – I said, thinking about my parents. The objects in their house they guarded, like flames they'd cup their hands around. The decades-old clothes. The mugs with the handles glued back on. The chair with the legs that fell off. You had to make sure not to sit on it, but they wouldn't get rid of it. It made up the set.

You can say they don't matter – I said. – That you don't need them. Expensive objects and lovely clothes and beautiful rooms with high ceilings. You can say they don't mean anything, and that's partly true, of course, but not completely. You need some things. Some things are important. They make you feel like you're a person living, not still sealed up, packaged—

Like the Ps' daughter's Christmas gift set – said Laurie, prodding with her toe a never-opened body lotion collection that had wormed its way out of one of the piles.

Well, yes – I said. – Like that. Things show people who you are. You can wear clothes that express your personality, surround yourself with objects you think are pretty. Without that, you're still a blank, not defined. You're still sealed and packaged, waiting for the plastic to be cut off your face.

You should work in marketing – Laurie said.

What I didn't point out was that she was only willing to live a life of poverty so far. Even her destitute writer look was carefully constructed, and she certainly didn't dress like that when she went out. Most of the money she did have, she spent on beautiful clothes. *It's not worth buying things that won't last* – she'd say in, I imagined, an unconscious imitation of her mother, and sometimes then I could see behind her skin the sort of person she could have been, or might become still.

Talking of things – she said – I'll take this one to wear tonight. Don't you want anything?

Nothing I haven't fumigated first. Not after the flea bites.

Fair.

We went back upstairs. Laurie started to get ready.

Sure you won't come? – she said.

I can't. Can't really drink. Rehearsal first thing.

Laurie was always going out. She'd grown up in London, and she could look right anywhere – a nineties night at a sticky-floored club in Clapham or a poetry slam in a basement bar in Shoreditch or a party on a Notting Hill rooftop, the parents' house of a very rich friend of a friend. Before I moved to London, I imagined it would be one discrete place with one particular quality. I thought that quality would stick to me, and I would automatically become the sort of person my parents meant when they talked, disparagingly, about *Londoners*. But the London Laurie showed me wasn't one thing. It was messy and incoherent and chaotic, always expanding, and I remained exactly the same. Sometimes I loved it, feeling like nothing was set, always the potential to play a different part. Other times, chatting to yet another man I'd never meet again in yet another bar in yet another bit of London I couldn't name, I'd feel like the city was a maze. Laurie was leading me round and round the edges, but I couldn't find the centre.

Are you working at the hotel tomorrow, though? – I said. – I've got a free day on Friday, so I could come? Once your shift's over?

Do you think I haven't noticed how much keener you've been to hang out there lately? – she said. – I've noticed.

I don't know what you're talking about – I said primly, though she was right. Even Malcolm the Manager, who normally encouraged us to stay drinking after our shifts had finished – the only way to guarantee there'd be two women there at any one time – had started making snide remarks. *Enjoying my liquor are you, girls? Trying to pick up more fancy men?*

Well, don't expect to ever hear from him again, that's all – Laurie said. – Men just disappear. They disappear. One minute they're all *I've never felt this way about anyone* and the next they're sending messages that say things like *I'm really busy, but maybe we could have coffee at 4 p.m. next Sunday* and you say *ok then, let me know* and you never hear from them again. And it's London. It's not like you'll ever bump into them. They could have died for all you know, except they haven't, they're just fucking someone else.

I changed the subject. Asked her where she was going, who'd be there.

After she'd left, I went to my room and pulled the curtain across the glass. It wasn't late, but it was already black outside. It was nearly November now, and the night came sooner every day, until it felt like it might keep on like that, coming sooner and sooner until it was dark all the time. Laurie was right. I was being weird. Maybe because it was always dark, because it was cold, but I'd let him take up too much space in my head. I'd imagine him witnessing me be attractive or impressive in some way, until I started to bore myself. Letting all those synapses connect in my brain by turning it into narrative, making it real by repetition, letting it grow and harden there until it became part of my story. I'd try to picture where he spent his evenings. With a different girl, maybe. One who knew more precisely how to strike that note I aimed for – somewhere between *take me seriously* and *really don't*. The sort of girl who takes taxis when it's raining and who drinks cocktails with unpronounceable names that taste of money. Whose laughter has an edge of cruelty. I'd see him quite clearly, talking to this girl. How she excites him, and her indifference. And then a man would come into the bar, a man who could be him, and I'd feel – sharp and automatic

– a hot thrill in my gut, before I'd see I was wrong and feel faintly silly. I'd sit on the Tube and get my phone out, look again at the message I'd sent him. *Thanks again for dinner* I'd said, and he'd replied *my pleasure*. I'd read them over and over, those two words, and I'd try to find a meaning where there wasn't one.

Laurie was wrong, though, because the next time I sang, he was there. He came in towards the end of my set, sat at a table in the corner. I tried to keep going like I hadn't seen him. I kept singing, swayed my hips, shimmied my shoulders, half enjoying that he was there, watching how everyone watched me, and half feeling like a puppet on a string, jerked around, mimicking natural movement, but never quite right.

When the set was finished, I went over and said hi. I thought he might stand up, kiss me on the cheek or something, but he didn't move. He looked at me, smiling a bit, and I suddenly thought, fuck, maybe he's not here to see me. He came for a drink, hoped I wouldn't bother him, or had forgotten I existed at all. But then he said – so, I suppose you're expecting me to say how good you were?

An opportunity for me to be funny. I fumbled with it for a bit, then dropped it on the floor.

Well, of course – I said. – Why do you think I came over?

He smiled, and I was sure he knew how much I'd thought of him.

Shall we go? – he said.

I only realised outside that I hadn't asked him where.

It had been raining. The City could have been a film set, the pavements all washed clean and ready to start again, and no one else there. That feeling like we weren't really outside, just somewhere that looked a lot like it, and you couldn't believe there was a sky up there. You'd look and look and never see a star.

He didn't try to chat, and so I talked about nothing, scared of silence. About jazz. How it made me nostalgic. A false kind of nostalgia, though. It made me miss things I knew I'd never had. Worrying then that sounded too intimate, trying to make it into a joke – like how the smell of Christmas trees always made me miss the Christmases of my childhood, I said, even though I knew they'd always been shit. I could hear my voice going on and on, and I was thinking *God, why am I being so boring? Why can't I think of anything interesting to say? Why hasn't he said anything?* But he just smiled, walked a little bit away from me, hands in his pockets.

This way – he said.

He guided me onto one of the backstreets, and then he pushed me up against the wall and started to kiss me. I forgot everything I'd thought to say. It was like a convincing argument that wiped my mind of how to answer back – there was just the heat of his mouth, his fingers wrapped around mine, the roughness of knuckles pressed against brick. Pulling away from me, his smile was knowing, all *see what you made me do*, and I wished I'd had a drink. He had. I could taste it on his tongue.

He said – *come on* – and I followed him into a building on the corner. His apartment block, though it took me a moment to realise. It looked like an office. Glass onto the street, man in black behind a desk, bright lights.

In the lift, he kissed my neck, undid the buttons on my coat. He put his hands inside my shirt. I felt drunk, even though I wasn't, that same giddy recklessness. We got out at the nineteenth floor, all softly lit like an upmarket hotel, and that same sterile smell you get in hotel lobbies. He opened the door to the flat, let me go ahead of him, and then there was the view. Impossible to ignore. The walls were glass. The city drew me towards it, and I went to it, looked out. London in miniature from up there. Glowing dome of St Paul's, disparate clusters of skyscrapers, the dark slash of river.

I turned round. He was leaning on the back of the sofa, watching me.

Aren't you meant to stand behind me and point out what I can see? – I asked. – Put your arms round me so I can follow the line of your finger? I assume that's the point of having a flat like this.

That's London – he said.

He hadn't switched the lights on, but the light from neighbouring office blocks fell on the kitchen counter, the table, the bed. It could have been moonlight, but it was too white and it came from everywhere. It showed me that the flat was small. Only one room really – a dividing wall between sleeping and living space, no doors.

He said – *come here* – and I went to him. He pulled my shirt over my head, undid my jeans. He didn't do the coy stages of undressing. He got all my clothes off so quickly I almost laughed, and he said – *something funny?* – and I said – *no, nothing* – and tried to do that face he did where it looked like he knew something I didn't. I went to undo his shirt, but he held both my wrists, pulled me up against him, so I could feel the roughness of his jacket on my skin, kissed me for a long time, and then he let go and looked at me. He didn't pretend not to be looking, like most guys my age did, as though they saw so many naked women it wasn't really interesting. I sat on the bed. He stood there, taking off his jacket and tie, unbuttoning his shirt, and he really looked.

Then he came over, started to kiss me, pushed me backwards onto the bed. There was something that felt perverse about it all, and I realised that, when he spoke to me, he used his normal voice. He hadn't gone totally silent, or started talking in a pseudo-sexy whisper that sounded like he didn't mean what he was saying. He meant it. He said – *get on your knees, turn over, touch yourself* – conversationally, like he was talking to me in a bar. At first, I was so focused on looking like I was enjoying it, I thought I wouldn't be able to. That I wouldn't be able to stop thinking – about how he responded to me, about finding that sweet spot where I was concentrating enough to be able to come but not concentrating so much that I'd act like he basically wasn't there, about the hum of the fridge on the other side of the room, and what I'd find to say to him when the lights went on. But he was persuasive. He pulled everything out of my grasp, bit by bit, nothing left to hold onto, so that for the first time I could remember, I didn't have to imagine something else to be excited.

Afterwards, I lay next to him, watched the rise and fall of his chest slow down. His eyes were shut, but he rested his hand on my thigh and stroked my hip with his thumb. I didn't shut my eyes. I looked at him, at his face, down at his body. I wanted to fix an image of him in my mind, in case this was the last time. The stillness of his mouth, his long fingers, neatly cut nails, the scar on his shoulder, a faint tan line across his hip.

I thought he might be asleep, which is why I said – *can I ask you a question?* – but he was awake, so I had to ask it.

Last time—

I wasn't sure how to finish the sentence.

I thought you weren't really interested in me like this – I said, eventually.

Was that a question?

Why didn't you try anything, I mean?

Try anything? Like what?

You know. To sleep with me.

He laughed.

Can I not take a girl out for dinner without trying to fuck her? – he asked. – Is that not the done thing with you young people?

No – I said. – Not really, actually.

Thanks. I'll bear that in mind in future. Anyway, call me old-fashioned – he said – but you seemed rather drunk. I don't think you can be too careful about that sort of thing these days. Why? Did you want to?

God, no. I'm a woman, remember. I hate sex.

Certainly seemed that way.

On his way to the bathroom, he flicked a couple of switches by the bed, and the whole flat lit up tastefully. I could see it properly then, how smart it was – dark wooden floor, neutral furnishings, a strip of kitchen, all stainless steel and black marble, running down one wall. I could have believed it was another empty apartment, bought off plan, sitting here to sprout money – except for the jacket discarded on the sofa, the tie hung over the back of one of the chairs, the mug, the plates, stacked up by the sink. I felt a stab of tenderness for him, here alone.

It was nearly one. I thought he might expect me to leave, but when he came back, he didn't mention it, so I went and brushed my teeth with my finger, tried to get my make-up off with soap. He'd put boxers and a T-shirt on, so I asked if I could borrow something to sleep in, but he said — *no, I like you like that.*

We were both in bed when he said — I actually had been going to suggest you came back.

What?

Last time. I was going to ask you back. Follow up on your incredibly subtle hints about wanting to see the flat.

I was just making conversation.

Sure. Anyway, then you, well, then you asked if I was married. That kind of threw me.

I felt like when you go out with bare arms on a bright spring day, overconfident. By early evening you're cold to the bone. I stayed quiet.

What I said wasn't exactly true — he said. — I am married. Technically. Separated. In the process of not being married anymore.

I noted that he couldn't quite bring himself to say *divorced*.

I see.

My life's not exactly simple right now — he said. — And honestly, when I first met you, I didn't realise how young you are. At dinner, you just seemed so unjaded and nice.

Nice?

He laughed.

It wasn't an insult, Anna. Don't be offended. Anyway, I was trying to do the right thing, believe it or not. Didn't want to get you involved. But I found myself thinking about you. I enjoyed your company. I thought, well, why shouldn't we have some fun. If you want to, that is.

He switched off the light.

I just don't want to mislead you — he said into the dark. — About what I can offer you. Because honestly, right now, it isn't that much.

He said this casually, almost ironically, like he was talking about someone else, and that's how I knew he meant it.

When I woke in the morning, he was at the table on his laptop. He didn't offer me coffee or ask how I'd slept or get back into bed with me, but out on the street he kissed me for longer than he needed to. He said — *I'll see you soon.*

His flat was a short walk from the Conservatory, but it was hours before class still, so I went home to change. Everything on the Mitcham Road seemed greyer than usual. The yellow Snappy Snaps and the blue bank and the red postbox were muted and dull, like a photograph discoloured over time. Faded formalwear hung limply in dry-cleaner windows, and piles of once bright clothes, dumped outside shut charity shops, turned dark in the drizzle. Nothing kept its colour here.

Back in the house, Mrs P was in the kitchen. She was sitting at the table, looking fixedly at the door, like an actor waiting for a cue that hadn't come. She never seemed to be doing much. Her impulses were all negative. She'd come into a room and say — *it was so cold in there* — or — *I could hear next door's telly through the wall* — and then she'd stand and look at you, like a cat who's just come in through the cat flap and can't remember why.

Morning — I said.

I started to boil the kettle.

You weren't back last night, now, were you? — she said. — Just come in? Enjoying yourself, haa?

She often punctuated sentences with a bleating laugh. I wasn't sure if it was a nervous tic or if it expressed something in particular — sarcasm? disapproval? — but it didn't seem friendly. She'd say things like — *the prices are going up in Sainsbury's, aren't they? And then who knows how I'll afford to do my shopping, haa?* — and she'd stare at you like she thought you were to blame.

I had a nice time — I said. — Thanks.

I was saying to Mr P, where's Anna? I said, and he said, well, it's Thursday, doesn't she work on Thursdays? And I said, yes, but she'll be done by now, surely, and he said, well he didn't know then, because it's not like you to be out late, is it? Not like that other one, hey, because who knows where she ever is, haa?

She stared at me with big curious eyes. She was oddly childlike for someone who looked so unlike a child. She couldn't hide emotion.

I opened the cupboard to find the coffee.

And where's the other one? – she said.

Laurie? I don't know. Still asleep, I'd guess.

Are you leaving then, haa?

Yeah, I've got classes. I'll just drink this first, get changed, then I'll go.

Mrs P kept her eyes on me to check I wasn't using her coffee. That wasn't something I'd do. Her coffee tasted of dust. All the cupboards were filled with layers upon layers of half-empty packets of food, and the small table was piled high with browning back copies of the *Daily Mail* – good for mopping up cat sick, Mrs P explained. The fridge and all the cupboards had children's drawings Blu-Tacked onto them, some so faded they were almost blank.

You really should be turning the kettle off at the switch when you're done – Mrs P said. – Mr P and myself keep meaning to say.

Sorry.

And you'll be wanting to cook for yourself tonight, I suppose?

I don't know. I suppose so. I haven't properly thought.

Well, then, what'll I tell Mr P then, haa?

I don't know – I said. – Tell him I haven't properly thought.

She nodded.

You haven't properly thought – she said. – Ok. I'll tell him that.

FOUR

After that, I saw him once, sometimes twice, a week. We didn't make plans in advance. He was bad with messages. If I texted him, asked when he was around, most often he wouldn't reply. He teased me when I got annoyed.

I'm a different generation to you, remember? – he'd say. – Not into this whole constant communication thing. You'll have to cut me some slack.

He'd text me on the day, and say *tonight?* Sometimes, if I had plans I could rearrange, I would, or I'd say, *yes, but it has to be later. Rehearsal, can't change it. I'll come over when I'm done?* But sometimes it didn't work out. He'd say he was tired, couldn't stay up that late, or he'd say *no, it's fine. I've made other plans.* I felt I'd lost something, those nights, wondering what he did instead. I'd keep my phone in my pocket through rehearsals, hoping it would buzz.

Some nights, when we did manage it, he'd take me out. He took me to the sorts of places I'd never been before, restaurants with thick white napkins, real art on the walls, not prints. He'd get me to try things – a type of fish, the wine from a particular grape. I'd feel his eyes on my throat as I swallowed, and then he'd smile at me, like he'd said something clever and was waiting for praise. He was the performer then, wanting audience approval. He was like that when we went out – magnanimous, ready to entertain. He knew something about everything. Whenever a subject came up, he could tell me about it. He always had an anecdote ready and he could always make me laugh.

Sometimes he was different, though – moody, prickly, teasing. Once, he made fun of me because I pronounced a politician's name wrong. He said – *of course I wouldn't expect you to know much about the real world, you artists* – and I felt like he was sort of joking, but sort of not. Overcompensating, I made a grandiose statement about art being all about the real world actually, far more so than banking, and he found that hilarious. He wouldn't let it go, and even after he'd got bored of it, the whole evening tasted of that to me, that flavour masking everything else, like a dish with too much salt. Another time, I made a throwaway comment about how, when I was at school, I'd wanted to sleep with a teacher – not a specific one, just generally, as an idea – and he looked at me like I'd confessed to fucking his mum, and said – *that's disgusting* – and I went to the toilet and cried. I splashed my face and redid my make-up, and when I got back he was kind, pretended not to notice. It was all stupid stuff like that, but it had me trying harder and harder to get the reaction from him I wanted, making me feel I wasn't good enough and that was why, making me think *if only I could –*. But then the next time he'd be back to normal, and I'd wonder if I'd overreacted, imagined it. People are like that, aren't they, like optical illusions. Once you've got them in your head one way, it's hard to tip them over.

The places we went to were expensive, so expensive that looking at the menu made me feel a bit sick, but he always paid. He was one of those men who pays when you're in the toilet, very discreet, something they teach them to do at boarding school, Laurie said. I'd say – *I'll get it next time* – and he'd say – *sure, whatever* – and then the next time was the same. We both knew I couldn't afford it anyway, so before long I kept quiet.

Other nights, he finished late, or I did, and I went straight to his. In some ways, these were the nights I liked best. I came to love his flat. How we were suspended up there, nothing to get in, nothing to hurt us. How you could see the tiny people through the glass, the tiny cars, but there was no sound, like watching the TV on mute, and I never got bored of looking. I loved the thick cream towels, their identical shade of bland. His huge bed. How there'd always be a bottle of wine in the cupboard to open. Those evenings were endless and sweet and full of possibility, everything easy, nothing hurried or complicated, nothing a problem. He was kinder than when we were out together, not trying to entertain me, quieter, somehow. He wanted to know everything about me. He asked me questions and listened properly to my answers, and I felt I could say anything to him then, when we were in bed. Like all the words were mine, and I would never run out.

I told him about being a teenager and learning to sing. The guy who ran our school choir thinking I had talent, finding me a singing teacher who said my voice could be operatic if I trained it properly. How the strangeness of that appealed to me, though I knew next to nothing about it. It seemed like something that couldn't be confined, I told him – an antidote to the identikit boxy houses in our town, to the grey sky, and nothing beyond the borders but the long grey roads and the grey fields. To a mother who would sit in the front room, watching for me when I came home after dark, running through all the awful things that might be happening to me. A mother who never slept – who I'd hear wandering round all night, pulling out plugs, checking the window bolts, opening doors and shutting them.

With the guys my own age I'd dated, I skimmed over how much work singing involved, how little in the way of conventional fun I'd had as a teenager. The hours spent practising, listening to operas, looking up the translations online – finding that, while they were in languages I didn't understand, they told of emotions that I did, or wanted to – devouring books about opera singers, listening to all their recordings, writing down their advice in my notebook. But Max was impressed. He said I was one of the most focused people he'd ever met, the most serious. It was a rare quality, he said.

I didn't tell him that sometimes at the Conservatory it felt like I was drowning. He saw my acceptance in London, like I had, as the happy ending to my story, the culmination of years of work. I loved too much that he saw me as successful to correct him, but I did tell him about the time, early on, when my year had all gone out for dinner. I'd seen the prices on the menu and ordered a starter as a main, drunk tap water and, at the end, one of the other singers had said – *let's just split the bill*. How now, whenever they went out, I made an excuse. I told him I worried sometimes that having online banking on my phone had done something physical, irreversible to the way my brain was wired. How I found myself unconsciously going to check it, sometimes twenty times a day, even though I knew I was expecting no money in or out – a nervous tic, feeling like if I didn't keep looking at the number, it might all disappear.

He seemed impressed by these stories too. He would never be able to live the way I did, he said. I was brave. He teased me for always wearing the same two bras on rotation, kissed me where my hipbones jutted out – *I guess I need to take you for more nice dinners,* he said – called me his dark-eyed bohemian.

I tried to collect information about him too – after we'd had sex, when he was affectionate and sleepy. He was someone who could talk a lot. We'd have these long conversations at dinner, and I'd go away feeling like I was close to knowing him. Then I'd look back and think, well, what had he actually said? What had he given me? Nothing much. Nothing concrete, anyway. So I'd press him, those evenings in his flat. I'd collect up his facts and then afterwards, when I was alone, I'd try to arrange them, to fix them into a narrative.

I asked him about his family.

A father – he said. – A mother, a brother.

Older or younger?

Older.

Surprising.

Really?

Yes.

They were very similar growing up, he said. They liked the same things. The same sports, the same subjects, the same girls. But his brother was always that little bit better than him, and his parents encouraged the competition. His dad did anyway. Never intervened when they fought, said it was good to learn you needed to be strong, or else to have a better way to win an argument. I said – *and how do you feel about that?* – and he laughed and said – *what do you think? Damaged beyond repair, my love* – and I was too distracted by him calling me that to ask him anything else.

He was born in London, but his family had moved to the Cotswolds when his dad retired. He'd retired young, or rather, retired from his job. Was still on various boards and that sort of thing. I had no idea what that meant, but I acted like I did. I asked about his mother too. I wanted to know what she'd done, and he said – *she had us, two boys, she brought us up* – in this tone of creepy reverence, and I thought – *oh God, here we go, right-wing mummy's boy* – but the next moment, I wasn't so sure. He told me that he used to say to friends – *don't worry about taking your shoes off, we have these carpets that dirt doesn't stick to*. He only realised years later that she used to run after them with the hoover. He described a dinner party his parents had once, she'd spent hours cooking, and his dad turned to her after the first mouthful and said – *duck's a bit fatty, isn't it, Jane?* How he'd tease her for spending her allowance too quickly. How she'd often be on the sofa, all the curtains drawn at 5 p.m., kids' TV on, saying – *but I've been working all day, that's why. I'm so tired.*

Is she very beautiful? – I asked.

That's a strange question – he said. – I have no idea – which seemed to me a strange answer.

He said to me once – I feel like you're trying to create a tragic backstory for me. An abusive father, perhaps. A history of mental illness or sexual assault. I'm sorry, Anna. You're going to learn in time I'm really not that interesting.

But he was to me.

All those evenings we spent together, through all these conversations, he never mentioned his wife. I didn't even know her name, so Google wasn't much help – though, trust me, I tried. If he'd talked about her, she might have occupied less space in my head. I might not have wondered if she looked like me or different, if he'd laughed more when he'd been with her, if she'd ever spent time in this flat.

Then there were the other days – most days, I suppose – when I didn't hear from him at all. I'd be in the practice room, phone face up on the piano, and it wouldn't light up. It would get late, and I'd go home alone. I found it harder and harder to go back to the house. I'd go upstairs to my room and, standing there in the doorway, I'd feel like a hand was closing over my throat. The ceiling always seemed lower than I remembered, and the walls were closer together. The objects all seemed different too. I was sure Mrs P went in there and touched my stuff when I was out. It absorbed her look and threw it back at me. Little things started bothering me out of all proportion. When the knob of the wardrobe came off in my hand, I threw it at the wall. When one of the lights on the ceiling blew — one of those flat ones — and I couldn't get the cover off to change the bulb, I sat down on the floor and I cried. I'd tell myself — *well, it doesn't matter, because so much of me is there with him, not here*. It was always strange, then, to go back to his flat. Every time, it was as if I'd never been there before. I could assert no permanence. He was fastidious. I never found a hair of mine in his comb or wound up in the metal of the plughole. The sheets were always clean and fresh. I tried to leave a toothbrush in the bathroom once and he ran after me down the hall and said — *here, this is yours, don't forget*.

I never asked when I'd see him again. I let him kiss me goodbye, and said a breezy — *well, see you, then*. I didn't make any demands on him, emotional or otherwise. I was casual, non-committal, the sort of girl he wanted me to be. But not really — no — not really. Inside, I was trying to attach myself onto him with enough hooks, like a burr, so he couldn't just pick me off.

And sometimes I thought it was all about sex. For me, I mean, as well as for him. Because I would do anything he wanted. I had no sense of possessiveness over my body with him. I wasn't shy. I let him turn me over and over, take my hands and press them against the wall, up above my head, pull them behind my back, push my legs apart or draw them together. I let him touch whatever part of me he wanted. There was excitement in that, in knowing I would do anything. He'd say to me — *I've never been with a girl who's as open as you before* — and I'd say — *well, why not? I like sex. That's not so strange, is it?* — and he'd give me this look that I read as admiration and say — *you'd be surprised, actually, you'd really be surprised.* That made me feel good. I loved being watched by him, when I was on top of him, or when I was leaning over him to drink some water, or when I walked naked across the room to the sink. I was used to seeing my body as an instrument, but seeing it through his eyes, it was different. It could excite. I was powerful. Looking at myself naked in the mirror, I'd try to see it how he would. Not how I used it to make sound — the expansion of the ribs and the release of the stomach to engage those support muscles — but the curve of my hip, the narrowness of my waist, the dark shape of my nipples. I thought about my body a lot, that first month with him. I started shaving parts that it had never occurred to me before to shave. I spent a lot of time in the bath.

Sometime around the end of November, the sky was always white, and the leaves had all turned to mush in the gutter — cereal left to soak in milk too long. We were lying in bed, and I said — so are you still incapable of loving anyone, or what?

I don't really know why I said it but, if I had to guess, I'd say it was because I'd just worked out why he always put his clothes back on after sex. I'd assumed he didn't want that sort of casual intimacy with me, but then I realised — little things — how he didn't really eat carbs, went to the gym all the time, often dropped into conversation how fit he'd been not even that long ago — that he was self-conscious. I liked that. The imperfection in his body and that he thought I might care.

That evening, for the first time, he didn't bother. He went into the bathroom, and — well, maybe a part of me thought he was more likely to tell the truth naked — when he got back into bed, I said — so are you still incapable of loving anyone, or what?

I was trying to be light-hearted, but it came out high-pitched, desperate-sounding. He turned on the pillow to face me. He looked a bit alarmed.

I didn't mean me — I said quickly. — To clarify.

Right — he said.

I was just making conversation.

Well, I don't think I said I was incapable of loving anyone – he said. – Did I?

You did. Something like that, anyway.

I wouldn't go quite that far – he said.

He laughed.

It's really not that dramatic.

He didn't say anything else, but I felt like I was close to making him so, for the first time, I asked directly. I asked when his marriage had ended.

Summer. Just before.

That's recent.

I know. I said it was.

Does she, I mean, where is she? Did she not get the house in Oxford?

She's in New York.

Why?

She's from there. That's where we met. She went back.

Oh.

Being in possession of some of the facts almost told me less than if he'd told me nothing at all. It ruined New York for me too, knowing she'd always been the unspoken part of his stories. I'd had vague fantasies he might take me next time he went, but I didn't want to go anymore.

Do you see her when you're there? – I asked. He'd been three times that month.

Sometimes.

Feigning indifference, I said – do you still want to be with her?

No, it's not that. It's more, you know when you have a plan. You've seen, or rather you've imagined that your whole life is going to turn out one way, and then suddenly it doesn't.

Well, you probably don't know, actually – he said. –You're probably too young.

For a second, I felt a jealousy so white and sharp it was like a hot needle under the skin. In that moment, I hated him.

Well, it's all a learning curve, isn't it? – I said, thinking – *reduce her, cut her down*.

Oh, yes? I forget how wise you are. What is it you've learnt then, in all your extensive experience?

I thought. I thought how sudden, how unpredictable that shift could be – that shift from desire to contempt. You think you want someone, spend all evening with him, meaningful glances, suggestive conversation – a sweet game, and you know how to play it. And then, how rarely that translates into something physical that's good. Sometimes even the moment he kisses you, you know it won't, but you do it anyway. No matter how little attraction you find you feel, or what he looks like, back at his, with the lights switched on. Why? Too embarrassing not to, I suppose. You follow the script, and then it's always too real. Just bodies. No one for a while, not since I'd moved to London. Bored of the performance, I suppose.

I've learnt that choosing a partner based solely on physical appearance is actually a really valid method – I said.

I'll take that as a compliment.

You?

He thought for a little bit.

I guess I've learnt what real pain is.

But he said it laughing, like he was making fun of someone else, and he pulled me on top of him.

Stop talking now – he said.

I had a lesson with Angela late the next day. I was learning Rusalka's aria to add to my audition rep. Rusalka, the water-nymph, obsessed with a human prince. Ready to give up everything for him – her immortality, her voice – to become human for him, although they've never spoken. The aria's beautiful, rich with sweeping phrases, full of longing. Rusalka sings to the moon. She asks it to tell the prince she loves him.

Angela wasn't happy with my final phrase.

It's a great top note – she said. – But the B flat isn't the end of the line, is it? Sing through it, Anna, don't give up.

I sang it again, tried to see the breath, to imagine it unspooling, spinning out in front of me.

Better – she said. – Don't think you can pack up and go home once you've done the high notes. We care about expression in this business, don't we? How you tell the story, not how impressive your top is – although we care about that too, of course. Now, have you noticed how you're sticking your jaw out on the B flat? Let's try it again, but this time, look in the mirror. Put your finger on your chin so you can feel it.

Angela never let me get away with anything. She'd make me do it again, stern and serious, until finally, incredibly, she'd beam at me and say – *yes, like that, wow, that's exactly right* – and I'd be high on elation. I loved my lessons with her, feeling I was being unpicked and resewn, put together better. She helped me to interpret snippets I picked up from other singers too, things I didn't want to ask them for fear of looking stupid. Yes, she told me, it was a good idea to wear clothes that covered your elbows and knees if you were auditioning for Michael – his tastes were pretty conservative and he found women generally irritating so, yes, best to be on the safe side. No, of course you can apply for the Martignargues Festival Academy with me as your reference, even though we've only recently started working together, and don't listen to anything Beth says anyway, she knows that's not true – she's trying to put you off. A compliment, really. She sees you as a threat.

I sang through the phrase again, my finger on my chin.

See what a difference it makes to the sound? – Angela said. – Much freer. Practise it like that. It's something you do to make it feel safe, holding onto it like that. It's a habit. You can break it.

She said we'd finish there, and I started putting on my coat.

Talking of bad habits – she said – how's the jazz singing?

Angela was very scathing about the jazz. Whenever I sang in English for her, she'd pounce triumphantly on any word I pronounced with the slightest hint of a dropped T or an American accent. *You see?* – she'd say. – *That's what jazz teaches you.*

It's really not that much – I said. – A couple of times a week. It's fine, I'm being careful.

Well, so long as you're always singing with proper technique, not crooning. I might do a spot-check one day, turn up unannounced to make sure. Might get to meet that boyfriend of yours too.

Angela was very interested in Max, and always asked how things were going. I enjoyed talking to her about him. It was hard to with Laurie, because Laurie was only interested in the bad parts. She loved the bad parts. We'd spend whole evenings dissecting why he never talked about his wife – *ex-wife, you mean,* I'd say – *well, no, not legally,* she'd say – or why he hadn't replied to my last message, and while it was fun at the time, I'd be left feeling miserable. I'd say – *of course, I'm only telling you the bad parts. I haven't told you the good parts because other people's happiness is boring* – and she'd say – *oh, yes yes yes, the good parts, spare me.* Unless the good parts were about sex.

He's really not my boyfriend – I said.

Isn't he? What is he then?

I don't know. It's complicated.

Bloody men – she said. – They love to make things difficult, don't they? But, well, the romantic lives of performers are never simple. Best get used to it. I think he's good for you, anyway. You seem more confident. The voice sounds great, too.

Thanks – I said. – But I can't imagine you'll be meeting him anytime soon.

We'll see.

By the time I got to the station, it was rush hour. The packed Tube always made me think of an exercise we did in movement class – walking and then running, all of us in the same tight space, careful never to touch. Sometimes we did it with our eyes shut. *An instinctive awareness of other people* – our teacher would say. – *How far away from you they are. The direction of their bodies in relation to yours. It's the key to stagecraft.* But the key to the London rush hour was the opposite. Learning to have strangers pressed up against you and not to respond. To ignore the bodies too close.

I was nearly out of money for November, but I hadn't eaten, so I went to the reduced aisle in Sainsbury's. I used to make a vat of something on Sundays and eat it all week, but the Ps complained.

Said I was taking up too much room in the fridge with my big pots. They didn't like me using the kitchen every night either, though, and so my diet was becoming increasingly weird. Cheap staples – rice, pasta, couscous – that I could cook quickly before they had a chance to come in, to ask when I'd be done, standing by the hob until I left. Tins of sweetcorn, chickpeas, baked beans. Whatever looked ok that had a reduced label on it that day – sausage rolls, bagged salad, cottage cheese. It had become a point of pride, not caring about whether the stuff I was eating tasted nice, just thinking about cost. I only ate good food with him.

I bought a reduced picnic quiche, and had it with some leftover rice that tasted a bit funny. When I'd washed up the bowl, I went to my room and started to work on the Rusalka. The house was dark – I thought I was alone – but after five minutes or so, there was a knock on my door, and there was Mr P. He was wearing grey Y-fronts and a white shirt, unbuttoned. He had skinny legs, but the rest of him was pudgy, and his clothes stuck to his still damp skin.

Sorry – I said. – I didn't know you were here.

I got home early – he said. – The house was empty and I thought to myself, I thought, I know what I'll do. I know what I'll do now it's quiet, now that everyone's gone. Because that doesn't happen too much these days, as I'm sure you must know. I'll have a long bath, I thought. A really long one, a deep hot bath, where you just lie there until your fingers turn pruney and the water's gone cold, like how you used to do when you were little. Or, at least, how I used to, anyway. And so I ran my bath and I got in it and I was just lying there – I didn't even hear the door, didn't hear you come in – I was just lying there and then, and then, and then this noise started up, this noise, and at first I had no idea what it was. I thought it was coming from next door, you know, maybe a power tool, they were drilling, something like that. But then it went on and on and it got louder and it got higher and then I realised what it was. That's Anna, I thought, isn't it? That's Anna singing.

I—

And at first I just lay there, you know how you do, and I hoped it would stop. I thought, it can't go on for much longer can it, not like this, that would be crazy, I thought. That would be — excuse me — *inhumane* — excuse me, my dear, but it would. But I was wrong. It did. It kept going. And I tried running the tap. I tried sticking my head under the water, but I could still hear it, and there wasn't even a proper tune — he said. — I mean, there wasn't, was there? What was that? There wasn't even a tune.

That's because I was singing the same few bars — I said. — I'm sorry, I—

There wasn't even a tune — he said. — And then, well, then the bath stopped feeling warm and comforting, you know. You know what it's like — have you ever got that? — when you suddenly become aware of what a bath really is. That you're lying in a soup of your own filth. That's why the water's grey. So I got out.

I'm sorry — I said. — But I did tell you when I took the room that I sang.

You did. But there's singing and there's singing, isn't there? — he said.

Well. Yes. I suppose that's true.

He started to button his shirt.

A couple of days later, I met Max out. He asked how my day had been.

I ate a sandwich on the train — I said. — And it was lunchtime, not rush hour or anything. A normal time to be eating. The train wasn't crowded, and I had twenty minutes to get from college to a rehearsal, so it was the only chance I had. Anyway, I noticed this man sitting opposite me staring, like he found it kind of disgusting. Then he got his phone out, held it up to me, and he took a photo.

It had happened hours ago, but I was still angry. Angry with him, angry with myself. I'd been mortified. Had said nothing.

Really? — said Max. — Come on. Why would he do that?

Well, I don't know. Because he found the sight of a woman eating disgusting, I guess. Because men seem to think that women don't need to eat or that, if they do, they should at least be too ashamed to do it in public.

He laughed.

Oh, really? That's what men think, is it? Well, thanks for letting me know. I guess we should skip dinner in that case. I wouldn't want you to disgust me.

He was looking at me indulgently, like my anger endeared him.

Seriously – I said. – I'm not making this up. There's a website of it, or there used to be anyway. Men take pictures of women eating in public and put them up. Shame them for it. Honestly. It's a thing.

Ok – he said.

What do you mean *ok*?

I mean, ok. I believe you.

I could tell he didn't really though, and I was about to say something else, but he called the waiter over. Then I didn't bring it up again, because he was in a funny sort of mood. Cold. Drinking wine like water. Starting anecdotes, discarding them.

Actually, it doesn't matter – he'd say. – Forget it.

I tried to break into him, but he wouldn't let me. Every subject I raised, he toyed with for a bit then pushed to one side, until eventually I couldn't think of any more words. None that would interest him, anyway. We didn't stay out long.

Back in the flat, he poured himself a drink. I sat on the sofa, but he didn't sit. He went over to the window. Sighed. Leant on the glass. A heaviness between us that wouldn't lift.

Max? – I said. – What is it?

He didn't turn around.

What? – he said.

What is it? What's wrong?

Wrong?

I thought he was going to say that nothing was wrong, or else say nothing at all, but then there was a dull thud – he'd hit his fist on the glass, like he was trying to break out – and he turned back towards me, exhaled loudly.

I'm just so fucking bored – he said.

I thought about the silences at dinner, my inability to hold his interest.

Bored?

At work.

Oh.

I'm fucking crushingly bored of my job – he said. – That's what's wrong.

Oh. Why?

Why? Well – he said – some days I can get wrapped up in the fun of it all – because it can be fun, there are parts of it that are fun – and sometimes that's enough. But other days, days like today, I'm just so fucking bored of it. When what you're doing doesn't really mean anything in the real world, not to most people, doesn't have any fucking impact on anyone. You know, I was thinking about walking out today. Genuinely. Not even quitting. Just walking out. Fuck, I mean, I was never going to do this forever. That wasn't the plan.

Well, what was the plan? What was it you wanted to do?

He didn't say anything at first, went back to the kitchen, topped up his glass. Every movement was harder than necessary – the weight of his step, how he slammed the bottle back down on the counter – but his voice stayed quiet and cold. It frightened me. I'd never seen him angry.

I don't know – he said. – The plan? I never knew what I wanted to do. That was the problem. Generically clever with no plan, so I did what all generically clever people with no plan do, and I went into finance. And then there was the recession and that was that, I couldn't leave. No other jobs.

But you could leave now?

He carried on like I hadn't spoken.

I'll never forget this – he said. – When I first started, this one night, it was about three in the morning. One of the other guys said – *if you were going to kill yourself, but you had to do it without leaving the office, and without jumping off anything, how would you do it?* And you know what the strangest thing was? It was that no one else found the question strange. They all seemed to have given it some thought. Had answers prepared. I knew then that I had to get out, and now, it's – what? Fifteen years. Fuck. That was fifteen years ago. And I'm still doing that same fucking thing I never even wanted in the first place.

He never normally swore, and it sounded odd in his voice. Not like punctuation, but violent, like he really meant it.

I guess you'd be ok for money for a bit? – I said. – If you quit without something else lined up? So why don't you take some time and figure it out?

You don't ever leave without knowing what you're moving onto, Anna. That's suicide.

Well – I said – you've got the best job of anyone I know, if that's any consolation.

That wouldn't exactly be hard – he said. – But it's sweet of you to say.

He was leaning, his outstretched arms resting on the kitchen counter. I couldn't see his face. There was a silence and I felt sick, wondering what he might say next, thinking about how inept I was at comforting him, when suddenly, wonderfully, he laughed. He came and sat next to me on the sofa, put his arm round me.

You know what I've always wanted to do? – he said. – This fantasy I've always had? I've always wanted to grow my own food. Live somewhere where I can be self-sufficient. Keep chickens. Bring up kids in the country. It's kind of why I bought the house in Oxford, I suppose. Moving more towards a life like that. But maybe I should just do it. Stop thinking about it. Just do it.

That sounds nice – I said, thinking – *but what about me?*

He took my face in his hands, kissed me then with unexpected tenderness. It disarmed me, like his anger had.

You know, I admire you – he said. – You know that, don't you? I admire you. For knowing what you want. Going after it.

Well, I present a good front – I said. – Don't be too impressed. There's an awful lot you wouldn't admire. The navel-gazing. The complaining. The hours spent in class talking about which muscles you use to stand on one leg. How much later than you I get up.

That is true. You are exceptionally lazy.

This stung – I hadn't expected him to agree – but then he pulled me on top of him. I sometimes forgot how attractive he was, because it wasn't so much that I responded to. It was how he inhabited his face. The curl of the lip, the raise of an eyebrow, that look of clear intelligence or amusement in his eyes. Only sometimes, like this, I'd really look at him, see him again as if for the first time, and remember.

He started to kiss me, and I was entering that space between where thoughts and words are, when he stopped.

Anna – he said – I feel I should ask. What is it you want from this?

What do you mean? From what?

From this. Us. This.

What do I want? – I said. – I don't know.

I didn't know what he wanted me to say.

Well, I thought we were having fun, weren't we? – I said. – Seeing how it goes. That's what we said. I don't want anything else.

It's just, you're so kind to me – he said. – I don't want to hurt you.

Please. Don't flatter yourself.

He laughed and, in his voice, I heard relief. The right answer, then.

I just wouldn't want to think I was stopping you from meeting someone else – he said. – If you wanted to. If you met someone.

I don't want to – I said. – I mean, I haven't. I haven't met anyone.

Ok, well, good. I'm glad. Because if you had I'd have to fight him. And I'm really too old for that.

I thought you didn't care.

Who said that?

That night, he turned towards me in his sleep, and a thought came into my head. It was shameful, and I would never repeat it to Laurie. To any other woman. I was right – I thought – I was right – I don't want anything other than this. And why, after all, did I ever think that I did? Why did I ever think I wanted something so spectacular – that I was deserving of something so special in my life – when what makes me happy is so ordinary, so entirely banal? This – this – that it is me he reaches for in the night, unconsciously. The feel of his arm, heavy, across my back in the dark.

FIVE

After German rep class, I went to the cafeteria with a few other singers. I saw the email notification when I glanced at my phone.

Subject: Your Martignargues Festival Academy Application.

I didn't open it. I already knew what it would say. *Not quite what we're looking for. Try again next year.* The autumn term was audition season, when summer festivals heard singers for chorus and small roles, and young artists programmes chose next year's intake. Everyone was caught up in the general hysteria of applications. For weeks now, all anyone had wanted to talk about was who'd got a recall where and who was on the panel for what and how many extra coaching sessions they'd booked and how much their new headshots had cost.

So far, everything I'd applied for, I'd been rejected from outright, without audition.

But how am I meant to show them I'm good if they won't even hear me? – I'd complained to Angela.

Well, next year, you'll have some better roles on your CV – she said. – And you'll have worked with some directors they've heard of. Be patient, Anna. And for God's sake get some proper headshots done.

So I said sure, fine, I would, but I knew I couldn't afford to. Though I hadn't yet attended an audition, I'd spent most of my money that month on them. Lots of companies charged fees just to process your application. I hadn't been able to apply everywhere

I'd wanted, and so every *no thank you* email was not only a rejection from them, but a missed opportunity elsewhere.

I turned my phone face down.

Natalie and Rose were talking about a London festival's chorus auditions, while Frankie looked through his *Manon* score, stayed quiet. He was that rarest of things – an attractive tenor with a genuinely beautiful voice. He seemed to get cast in everything just by showing up, and had no need himself for one-upmanship.

Well, actually I just spoke to Richard – Natalie was saying. – He asked if I could prepare one of Silvia's arias too. It's just for cover, but they do proper cover performances, you know, so that would be amazing. But the audition's on Friday. God, I'm so stressed.

Oh wow – said Rose, not trying too hard to sound convincing. – That's amazing, love. Congrats.

Well, let's not get too excited. He wants to hear me, that's all.

Natalie and Rose had both gone all the way through at the Conservatory – junior school, undergrad, postgrad, opera school – and were allegedly best friends. They were always in each other's profile pictures on social media, and they'd blow kisses to each other and shout – *love you* – across the cafeteria when they went off to their separate lessons. I found it hard to believe they liked each other that much, though. They looked very similar and had the same voice type, so they were always after the exact same parts. Their suffocating friendship – they lived together too – seemed to me more a convenient way to keep an eye on each other. Natalie had said to me early on, cosily conspiratorial – *you know, Rose's teacher has a reputation for being incredibly pushy. Back when we were auditioning for postgrad, Rose didn't even make it through to the second round, and he complained and made them hear her again. That's why she's here.*

Are you auditioning for them too? – Rose asked me, trying to find someone else who wasn't favoured by Richard, whoever he was.

No, I didn't apply.

Oh, really? You should have done. Marieke and Richard are friends. He often uses her singers.

Natalie examined the selection of food on offer that day, declared it all way too stodgy to sing on, and they went off to the Japanese restaurant down the road. Frankie shut his score.

You still sulking? – he asked.

No, no. All good – I said. – I understand. Alexander gets off on humiliating women. For him, the greatest tragedy in opera is that there's any need for female singers at all.

Alexander gets off on humiliating everyone – said Frankie. – So don't think you're special.

I'd forgotten to tape my music together for the pianist in German rep class, and Alexander, who demanded that everything went exactly his way, had spent the first ten minutes shouting at me. *Amateur! You fucking amateur! How's he meant to turn the fucking pages then?* He hadn't let me sing.

Frankie tested the temperature of his cup of boiling water, poured in salt from the shaker.

Remember first week? – he said. – When he told me he couldn't take me seriously while I was wearing patterned trousers?

He had a point there, though.

Frankie couldn't reply. He'd taken a big mouthful from the mug and was gargling.

You know, I've received four rejection emails this morning – I said. – Four. It's a personal record.

He spat into a glass.

You still care about rejection emails? I've got a special folder for mine. Might turn them into a performance art piece when I'm famous. You'll have to toughen up.

I'm tough.

He held the glass up to the light. You could see all the bits from his tonsils and teeth floating around in the water.

You're all mushy on the outside, Anna – he said. – Like a peach.

Do you have to do that?

I'm getting ill. It's the Britten Comp final in two days.

Wait, you got through? That was one of my rejections.

Don't sound so surprised.

I'm not – I said. – Of course you did. You know it's because you're a tenor, right? Only two of you applied.

I know it's because I'm exceptional.

Ahh, opera school. The only place in the world where they need quotas to make sure there are enough below par white men.

Don't be jealous, darling – he said. – It doesn't suit you.

Frankie called everyone, male and female, *darling*. I wasn't sure if his mannerisms were unconscious imitations of the guys around him, who were almost all gay, or – more cynically – whether they were deliberate affectations. It didn't hurt for the men in charge to assume you liked men. It didn't seem to affect Frankie's standing much with women either. Two months in, and he'd had sex with half the postgrad girls already – a fact which made them all very angry with each other but not, it seemed, with him.

Well, maybe you shouldn't have got wasted last night then? – I said. – Just a thought.

He'd left class twice to vomit.

God, please don't go all moral on me – he said. – I thought you were different.

What, from all the other girls?

From all those precious sopranos who never drink, anyway.

I drink – I said. – But not if I've got something important coming up. I do notice a difference. I wish I didn't.

Well, you should come out next time. It'd be fun.

He turned on his phone torch, and got me to shine it down his throat to check for pus.

Nothing?

Nothing – I said. – You're all good.

On my way to my singing lesson, I opened the email. I'd been shortlisted for the Martignargues Academy. The audition was in six days' time, and it was in Paris.

Of course I want to do it – I said. – But I don't have any money.

No one has any money – said Angela. – You're a singer, not a management consultant. Best get used to it.

But I'm not using that expression as a turn of phrase – I said. – Not like Natalie, who says she doesn't have any money, then shows up to class after lunch with shopping bags. I mean, I literally don't have any money. I don't have the money to go to Paris next week and to stay in a hotel and also to pay my rent and to eat. That's what I mean when I say *I don't have any money.*

She looked at me like I was being deliberately perverse, and I felt a hopeless rage. I'd expected sympathy.

Well, what about your rent? – she said. – Is that negotiable?

Negotiable? No, of course it's not.

And who said anything about a hotel? It's an audition, not a mini-break.

But I can't do it in a day. They've given me an early morning slot. What I was wondering was, well, can you talk to Marieke for me? Get the department to lend me the money? I'll pay them back.

For an audition? – she said. – Afraid not. Everyone's got auditions all the time. It wouldn't be fair on those who are paying their own way, not to mention we'd soon be bankrupt. Anna, come on, this is the Martignargues Festival, isn't it, not some silly choral society gig. I had Sophie in here this morning, crying over her rejection, and – though she'd kill me for saying it – she's five years older than you. This was her last chance, the age limit's thirty, and she's tried every year she's been here. Honestly, you'd be mad not to go. Is it that you don't want to? Is that it? Don't feel ready? Because, yes, there's work to do, but by next summer—

What? Of course I want it.

And I did. You have to want every audition you go for, of course, or there's no point, you won't stand a chance. There'll be someone else who's just as good but wants it more, and they'll get it instead. It sounds obvious – you have to want it – but I mean want it want it, need it, so that your want for it is physical and painful and constant, like too-tight shoes that make you cringe with every step. You won't get it, of course. Most people, statistically, don't get it, but no matter, you'll deal with that later. And some auditions, it's harder to make yourself care about than others, but with this, I didn't need to try. It was six weeks next summer in France – masterclasses with top singers, recital opportunities, concerts with major conductors. From the moment I'd read the email, the need had bloomed under my skin like a fine web of nettles, and I could feel it with every breath, with every movement, sharp and sweet.

Of course I want to fucking go – I said. – I'm not insane.

Angela did a performative intake of breath. Angela, who was quite happy to tell lengthy stories about who had slept with whom on what production, and why exactly that famous conductor hated that soprano, had very clear ideas on what constituted unprofessional behaviour. I'd crossed a line.

I'm sorry – I said. – I'm upset.

She sighed.

Look, Anna. God knows I know how tricky it can be for you young singers, but you invest in this career. You get out what you put in. You know that.

I said then that I'd find a way to pay for it, and she said – perfect, of course you will. What is it they want then? Two arias? Something in French? It's Paul on the panel, isn't it? He'll love your Rusalka. And what about that sexy bit of Poulenc?

We started to work.

I felt stressed at the idea of spending any money, so I walked home after class. It was a cold, clear evening and – crossing over Waterloo Bridge, looking at the immensity of the river stretched out on both sides, its blackness streaked with reflected light – I was surprised to find myself happy. It was my favourite part of London, the part where I felt I could see all the city at once, and it belonged to me, or I to it. I walked over to South Bank – where the trees were strung with blue lights, and Christmas market stalls lined the river – and through the crowds of people enacting festive rituals. I'd done it. It was the audition I'd wanted the most, and I'd got it. There was no reason not to be happy. As I walked, I decided on a strategy. The cost of my rent would cover it completely, so asking Mrs P seemed simplest. If she'd let me pay a week or two late, I could do it. I'd ask

Malcolm for extra shifts to make it up. Skip lunch next week. Walk back every day.

My optimism lasted until I reached Vauxhall, when I realised I was nowhere close to home. As I headed further south, the roads became broad with traffic, and no one was walking for fun. The streets had no coherence round there, like a jigsaw puzzle put together with pieces from different boxes. Huge dark Victorian houses – the sort that characters in horror films wander into blithely, right before they're disembowelled – grimy windows, net curtains turning grey with pollution. Low-rise council blocks with concrete balconies. Chunks of street cordoned off, new buildings shooting up behind screening – *Luxury Apartments, 24-hour Porters, 80% Already Sold*. Gambling shops. Tile shops. Dog grooming shops. Gyms with floor-to-ceiling glass, revealing young professionals in Lycra doing squats.

It took me two hours to reach my Tube stop, where a makeshift Christmas tree stall had sprung up on the pavement, and pedestrians veered into the beeping traffic to get past. Walking had been a futile gesture anyway. I would have had to do it every day that month to save the money I needed.

I found Mrs P in the kitchen, where 'Driving Home for Christmas' was on full volume. She had the cat on the counter, and was brushing him. There were clouds of hair pluming upwards, landing in an uncovered dish of lasagne.

Back then, haa? – she said. – We've been meaning to talk to you, Mr P and myself.

Oh, really? What about?

About the cooking. You've been cooking, haven't you? The two of you? With onions?

Onions? – I said, stupidly.

You have. You have, or the other one has. We don't want any cooking with onions here. Understand? No onions. No garlic. No spices. They get in the walls, see. They get behind the wallpaper. And then how will we ever get them out?

I glanced at the walls. They were splattered with years' worth of stains. The paint was all peeling.

I don't know – I said. – I'm sorry. It won't happen again. But actually, I wanted to ask you something too.

There was an unintended edge to my voice – confrontational, defensive – *stop it, make her feel sorry for you, she likes you, more than Laurie, anyway.*

Hm?

She let go of the cat, and I told her about the audition.

And I was wondering – I said. – I know it's a lot to ask, but I'm a bit short this month. Could I maybe pay the rent a bit late? I could get it to you in a week. Or, well, maybe if we said two, that would be safest.

It's Friday the rent's due – Mrs P said.

Yes, I know – I said. – What I meant was—

Mrs P opened the cupboard above the hob and started pulling stuff out – half-empty packets of pasta, flour, bulldog clips, writing icing, the tubes all crusted. She extracted a wodge of paper and peeled a sheet off the top.

Here – she said.

The cat had started to eat the lasagne. She pushed him off the counter and put the paper down on the sticky Formica.

Look.

She pointed.

I looked. It was the tenancy agreement, and her finger was pressed to the amount.

The first Friday of the month, haa – she said. –That's this one.

Yes – I said, feeling like a weight was crushing my skull. – Well, ok then, never mind.

On my way upstairs, I found the cat in the corridor, scratching at the living room door. I opened it a crack and let him in, then shut it.

Upstairs, I sat on my bed, and looked at my phone – that word, *Home*. I hadn't returned my mum's calls from the day before. I'd been on my way to the practice room the first time she'd rung, so I'd ignored it, planned to call back when I got there. But the second she hung up, she tried again, and then I knew she wouldn't have anything good to say – she never did, when she rang over and over like that – and I couldn't face it. Put my phone on silent, watched it on the lid of the piano, lighting up and going dark again. Twelve missed calls in total. When it seemed she'd given up, I texted to say I was in class, would call back later. I put it out of my mind and, guiltily, forgot.

The phone rang for a long time before she picked up. Calls were an event in my parents' house, and not one they enjoyed.

Hi – I said. – It's me.

IT'S HER – she shouted to Dad. – IT'S ANNA.

It's late to call – she said to me. – What's wrong?

What? Nothing. It's not late. It's nine o'clock.

It's nine thirty.

Right. Sorry – I said. – And look, I'm sorry I didn't call you back yesterday. It was—I've been busy. Was there something you wanted to talk about?

There was a pause, the sound of a chair scraping. I imagined her in her yellow dressing gown, sitting down at the kitchen table. She seemed very far away. A memory from my distant childhood.

I wanted to check when you were coming home for Christmas – she said. – But I asked your dad and he told me, so it's fine.

Oh right, yeah not for a couple of weeks. The 22nd, I think it is. I've booked my train.

I was pretty sure she was lying. She never wanted anything that straightforward when she called repeatedly, always something obscure, unpredictable. She'd demand that I go through all my toiletries and throw away the ones that contained parabens. She'd try to make me promise never to use the Central line, because she'd read an article saying it was dangerous. She'd have heard something on the radio about revenge porn, and she'd be in tears, begging me to reassure her I'd never sent naked photographs to an ex. Then the next time we spoke, she'd be cold and we'd pretend it hadn't happened.

You know, I saw your nice friend Tara yesterday – she said. – In the supermarket. Did you know she's had her baby?

Yeah, we're in touch. She sends me photos.

Sweet little thing. Tara seems happy.

She does, doesn't she?

Mum had always disapproved of Tara, particularly when we got older and she fell in with – so Mum saw it – the wrong crowd. She suspected, correctly, that Tara encouraged me to drink and make out with boys, and she blamed any aspect of my behaviour that she disliked on Tara's influence. That was until Tara had moved back to the safety of the village, got married absurdly young, had a baby. Then she'd become *your nice friend Tara*.

What are you guys up to then? – I said, trying to make neutral conversation.

We're halfway through an episode of *The Wire*.

Oh really? I wouldn't have thought you'd like that.

It's ok, we've got the subtitles on. I should go and tell your dad to switch the TV off actually. We've got it on pause and you know that's not good for it.

Don't worry, I'll leave you to it. But actually there was something I wanted to ask you first.

I told her about the audition, what a good opportunity it was, that it was a big deal to even be heard.

And the thing is – I said – it's in Paris, and I have to make my own way there. I need to stay in a hotel too. And I can't afford it. If you lent me, I don't know, I think a couple of hundred, I could do it. I wouldn't ask, it's just it's really important.

She took a breath and held it.

Mum? – I said.

She exhaled.

It's in Paris? – she said. – But you've never been to Paris before. Not since we went that time when you were little. And never alone. Do you even know what train you'd get? Or which hotel you'd stay in? Which area? It's not as simple as just turning up somewhere, you know, Anna, and expecting everything to be ok. That's not how the world works.

It was impossible to get her to focus on the right things. It was like taking someone to a window to show them the glorious view, and having them watch instead – obsessively – the progress of a fly on the glass.

It's—I can ask my teacher about that sort of thing, Mum. Or the Conservatory. It's fine, honestly, you don't have to worry about that. Look, I know it's a lot of money, but I'll pay you back. I promise.

There was a silence. It was stupid to have told her.

I'll have to discuss it with your father – she said, her voice thick, like she was close to tears, and she hung up.

I started listening back to my lesson, until I heard myself tell Angela I'd find a way to pay. She said – Of course you will.

My room seemed suddenly unbearable. Plain, blank walls, low ceiling. Blonde furniture. Wardrobe put together so the doors didn't meet in the middle. Fine layer of dust that covered everything no matter how often I cleaned. Traffic grating past outside, jarringly predictable, never quite in the distance. I stuck my headphones in, immersed myself in *Manon*. Act One. She tells the Chevalier she loves pleasure, well, that's what her father's said anyway, that's why she's being sent to a convent. As if pleasure is the worst thing in the world a woman could want. As if pleasure – knowing what it feels like, how to get it – is straightforward in itself for a woman.

I started to sort through the pile of clothes on my floor.

I didn't hear Laurie come in, but the next time I turned round, she was sitting on my bed. Her mouth was moving. I took my earbuds out.

Engaged to her boring chubby boyfriend – she was saying. – Like that's something to celebrate.

Sorry – I said. – Who are you talking about?

Keep up. Amanda. My schoolfriend. You know, the one who says things like *it's so great having you as my friend, you're the only place I get my culture from*. As if culture's a vegetable. Once you've had the recommended daily amount, you get a free pass on all the other crap you eat.

Snob.

Don't pretend you're not. Anyway, she's engaged. She told us tonight. And then everyone started talking about all the weddings they'd been to and which aspects of other people's weddings they wanted to buy for their own weddings and which they'd thought were shit. I've spent all evening talking about other people's flower arrangements. Women are genuinely pathetic, aren't they? It's literally no wonder men are still in charge of everything. They deserve to be.

I'd got to the bottom of the pile. All the clothes that far down were covered in sticky cat hair. I threw them in my laundry bag, and sat on the bed.

Maybe – I said – you need to accept that women are free to make their own informed choice to buy into the patriarchy. That perhaps that might even be a feminist act, you know – the freedom to collude in your own oppression?

I do sometimes think I'm too good for this world – Laurie said.

She picked up the pad of post-it notes on my bed. Listening back to my lessons, I sometimes scribbled on them things Angela had said and stuck them on my mirror. *It's not the job of the singer to please the audience* – I'd written. – *Truth comes from the inside.*

What the fuck does that mean? – Laurie asked. – Oh, and Mrs P's spitting, by the way.

Why?

The cat got shut in the front room. He crapped all over the sofa.

Oh really? – I said. – How funny. I wonder how on earth that happened.

Laurie smirked.

I like it when you're bad.

Do you like it enough to lend me money?

How much?

Quite a bit. At least 200.

I would if I could – she said. – But I can't.

You do owe me. I lent you last month.

Is cuntwad teaching you to be a baby capitalist, then? — she asked, sweetly. — Are you going to start charging interest?

That shut me up.

She went over to the mirror, put her face up close to the glass, and she started pulling out the grey hairs at her hairline. They caused her untold despair, though I could never see them when she tried to point them out.

Why do you need it? — she asked.

I told her about the audition.

I asked Mrs P if I could get out of the rent this month — I said.

Seriously? I bet that went well. But why don't you ask cuntwad? Easy. He'd spend £200 on a stripper of an evening, so why not on you?

Can you stop calling him that? — I said. — You've never even met him. Not properly.

I thought we were in agreement about the whole him being a cunt thing, though.

I'd made the classic error of sharing far too much with Laurie at the beginning. I was now unable to erase her comprehensive mental catalogue of his every possible character flaw.

Well — I said. — We're not anymore.

You know you don't have to fall in love with him because you're fucking, right? — she said. — Thank God. Sex is actually pretty banal, whatever you might have learnt in romcoms.

Is that what Oscar tells you? — I said, faux-innocent.

Oscar was Laurie's new boyfriend, though I wasn't allowed to call him that. They were sleeping with other people, or he was anyway, because he didn't want to be That Guy, he said. The sort of man who claims ownership over women. He thought that we should all be able to give sex freely, as and when, and until we can learn to live by that principle we're all still slaves to the patriarchy. Still trying to control women and their desires, no better than the men who used to put their oversexed wives and daughters into asylums and call them hysterical. Or something along those lines. Laurie explained all this to me when they first started seeing each other, and when I raised some queries, she said I was both old-fashioned and repressed, which I suppose was probably true.

Oscar's a revolutionary — Laurie said. — You could learn a lot from him. He rejects the system.

Is that why he lives in a flat his parents bought him?

Laurie snorted.

It's a fucking nice flat — she said.

Anyway, I'm not in love with Max.

But you like him now, do you? — she said, with pointed emphasis, as if to like someone was a particularly perverted sex act.

Yes. I like him.

Why?

I tried to think of the right words. I could say — *he's a warm sort of person, it's like being under a spotlight when he looks at me, and everything I say matters, is heard, is important* — or I could say — *he's cold and cool, when I'm with him I'm fixed into place, calm, and I just have to stay there, and everything's good.* But neither would be right, not exactly. I couldn't fix an image of him in my mind. He was blurry round the edges. I only knew how he made me feel — like my life had been very small and narrow and I hadn't even known it. Like I'd been walking round and round and round in a room with blank walls and I'd thought that was everything, but he'd opened the door for me and outside, outside there was—

He's nice — I said.

He's nice? — she said. —You know what your problem is? It's that you're too busy worrying about what other people think of you to work out what you think of them.

I asked her then whether she didn't think it was maybe unfeminist to care so much about ageing, and she told me to shut the fuck up.

Mum left me a voicemail while I was in class. She said they couldn't lend me the money. It was too much.

And Anna — she said. — Your dad and I were talking and, well, don't you think it's maybe best if you sit this one out, anyway? It seems a bit much they expect you to pay all that money just to go for an audition, and to travel all that way as well, and you've only just moved to London really, and –

She was trying very hard, I could tell, to sound casual, reasonable, but I wasn't fooled. When I was a child, she taught me to understand the world like she did. There were things that were safe – our village, our street, our house – and things that were not safe – a broad and nebulous category, including, but not limited to, the germs on other children's hands, stains on bus seats, instant messaging apps, unwashed fruit. For a moment, I imagined Paris as she would – poorly lit side streets, random shootings, an unnavigable transport system, predatory men. I listened to the end of her message, then I deleted it. I emailed the festival and said I'd be delighted to attend.

In the evening, I had a *Manon* rehearsal, the first Stage and Piano in the theatre. The performances were in just over a week. I sat at the back in the dark, watching Sophie sing.

Isn't that a waste of time? – Max asked, whenever I had cover rehearsals evenings he was free. – You don't get to sing? Not ever?

I tried to explain that it was important. Manon was a big role, I said. Learning to cover was an important skill. I talked about it like being given the part was an achievement, made it sound like all the first years were only covering, not wanting him to suspect there was any difference between me and the other singers. My disappointment I kept to myself, though secretly I thought he was right. It didn't feel important. Walking into the Conservatory's theatre – that vast space, bigger than anywhere I'd ever sung before – and heading straight to the stalls to sit in silence. Spending hours writing blocking in the music for a scene I'd never act myself. Watching Frankie and Sophie annoy the director by giggling over the kiss.

Max was in the gym when I arrived. It was on the twenty-first floor, and there was a pool there too. I sometimes came and swam when he had work to do, and I always had it to myself. I'd asked him once why there was never anyone else there. Overseas investment, he said. As far as he knew, only him and one other guy had bought in the building and actually lived there too. The other flats were rented to City workers who were rarely there, always in the office, or else they sat empty, accumulating money.

The gym was separated from the pool by a glass screen, and I could see him in there, doing deadlifts. He put the weight down, picked up his water bottle, and then he saw me.

I knew he was still looking at me when I took off my coat and jumper. Then I unzipped my boots and peeled my tights off, and I pulled my dress over my head. I sat on the edge of the pool with my legs in the water. The longest wall was made of glass, and the city glinted away outside, curiously sterile, curiously unreal, like an image on a screen. I knew I had to ask him now – now I'd said yes. I slipped into the pool and swam the length underwater, eyes shut, just kicking my feet, my arms by my sides. When I felt the wall, I turned over and swam back. He was sitting on the edge.

Exhibitionist – he said. – You know there's CCTV here, right?

It's exactly the same as a bikini. Anyway, you love it.

So will Muhammed, I'm sure. How was the rehearsal?

It was ok – I said. A little pause, then – but today hasn't been great.

Why's that?

As soon as I started telling him, I found myself playing the victim.

I'm just so angry – I said – and upset. It's such an amazing thing to have been offered, and I can't do it because of the money. The best people don't get stuff. The richest do. It's stupid.

Yeah – he said. – Still, there'll be others.

Other whats?

Other opportunities. Other auditions.

I guess – I said. – Not quite like this.

I floated on my back and kicked off from the side.

Bikinis don't go see-through – he said.

The water went all the way up to the window. It felt like if you kicked too hard you might tip down into the city below. He didn't say anything else and I realised that, really, truly I'd never thought I'd have to ask him, that's why I hadn't planned anything to say. I thought all I'd have to do was mention the audition and – the way he threw money around, like it was just paper, I'd seen it – he'd offer. I held my breath and put my head under the water, floated there suspended, until I ran out of breath.

When I got back to the edge, he was stretching his calves, both arms out straight, palms on the window.

Max? – I said.

He didn't turn round.

Yeah?

I don't suppose you could help me?

Help you? – he said. – With what?

With the trip, I mean.

He turned round, but he stayed standing.

I just thought – I said. – I thought that—

I trailed off.

You just thought what? – he asked.

I couldn't work out if he genuinely didn't know what I meant, or if he wanted me to say it. I affected confidence, made myself speak as though saying lines someone else had written.

I thought you might be able to lend it to me – I said. – The money. For the trip. I'd pay you back as soon as I could. A week. Two, tops.

He stood without moving, looked at me like he was trying to work something out. Didn't speak for a second, and then he said – you want me to give you money?

No. Not give it me. Lend it to me. I'd pay you back.

Another pause and then, inexplicably to me, he laughed. I wanted to slip back under the water.

Well, ok – he said. – Perverse to give up on your dreams over something so tiny as money. It's no problem. You want money? You can have it.

A little inflection of irony when he talked about my dreams. I tried not to notice.

Thank you – I said.

I'll book it when we're back upstairs. You can stay in the hotel I use for work.

I'll pay you back. I promise.

He shrugged.

Sure – he said.

I hung onto the side of the pool, kicking my legs and biting the skin of my nail, until I looked down at my hands and saw how awful they were, like those bodies of drowned corpses you see in crime series. The bitten skin round the nail all swollen up with water. He put his phone on the bench, kicked his trainers off, then he came and dangled his feet in the pool.

Are you really sure it's ok? – I said. – Honestly, I'll pay you back.

It's not a problem. Stop worrying. Are you all prepared?

Kind of. I'm doing Rusalka's aria.

Rusalka?

She's basically the Little Mermaid.

Fitting – he said.

It's quite big. Not really my *Fach*.

Not really your what?

My *Fach* – I said.

That sounds rather rude.

I wrapped my arms around his knees.

Much more boring than that, I'm afraid – I said. – It's how you describe the weight of a voice. Certain *Fachs* play certain types of character. Which kind of makes sense. It would sound stupid to have a big wobbly voice sing a young ingénue, for example. But yeah, my teacher knows one of the panel. He casts light apparently. She said he'd like it.

What are you then?

I'm between two. I used to do soubrette parts, but now I mainly do lighter lyric ones.

Which means?

Soubrettes are children or sluts – I said. – And light lyrics are the younger, more pathetic romantic heroines.

Sounds about right.

I wouldn't have thought I was strong enough to pull him into the water, but I was.

In the moment when his head went under, there was time for me to wonder why the hell I'd done that and whether he'd be angry. He surfaced and he didn't splutter or cough or do any of the cartoon things people are meant to do. He just said – *you can be such a fucking child sometimes* – and he didn't smile, and I thought – *fuck, fuck, fuck* – but then he kissed me. He tasted of chlorine and sweat.

The hotel he'd put me in was by the opera house and, after I'd checked in, I went to look at the building. Ornate, greying in the middle of a major junction, like a wedding cake left to moulder on a skip. I walked past the tourists sitting outside cafés, where they breathed in traffic, trying to pretend that this was glamour, this was Paris. Past a little girl, big white bunny in her arms, standing on the pavement, waiting to cross. It wasn't what I'd imagined. Not the France of the art-house films Laurie made me watch, though I knew she preferred *Love Island*. There was a metallic taste in the air, and I wrapped my scarf tighter round my mouth, headed back to the hotel. Ordered room service, then felt guilty when they asked if they should charge it to the same account. *Yes please* – I said, and then thought – *well, he'd want me to eat*. I ate in bed, watched an impenetrable game show – contestants, all dressed as mice, trying to get through an obstacle course, while being chased by a bull – and then I slept early, no dreams. I woke up scared.

The audition was in an opera house building, close by. I worried I'd be intimidated by the setting, even though they'd hear me in one of the rehearsal spaces, not on the main stage – but I felt ok when I got there. The pattern of auditions is always the same. You follow the routine, and the routine makes you calm. The person on reception took my name. The usher led me down a long corridor to the windowless warm-up room, left me for twenty minutes, then came back to get me. Led me through some more corridors until he stopped, knocked on the door, and a voice said – *send her in please* – and then – steady breathing – stand tall – shoulders back —— I walked into the room.

The panel were at the back, lamps lit over notes.

Name?

Anna.

What will you sing?

Rusalka's aria. 'Song to the Moon.'

Mouth so dry I'm sure I won't get a note out. Starting to think those thoughts that are death to all singers – *what if what if what if*. Breathe. Try to see what's inside me. My muscles, my ribcage, my diaphragm, this alive body and how the breath turns into sound, the lips move, the tongue, to form a language I've never spoken but can sing. Piano starts, and all that practice kicks in – easy to block the panel out once I've started, the way I've learnt how, because if you sing for your audience – look out at them, try to reach them, to touch them with your song – you'll never make something real – you must go inside instead, and bring them to you – and then I'm there, inhabiting the space I've built again. Remembering what Angela said – *Rusalka spends most of this opera in silence. Sing this like it's the last thing you'll ever sing.* So I sing about when the moon's so big it's fake in the sky, and the still water like a black sheet of glass. About wanting something, wanting something, wanting something more than anything, wanting something so much that the hurt of it's like a physical pain, someone pulling your hair or scratching their nails down your back.

Over to the panel for questions and then – *thank you so much for coming, Anna. We'll be in touch* – and me shaking their hands and feeling this sweet, sweet relief because, by the way that they smile, you can always tell if you've got it.

Back in London, the sky was heavy and white, like being trapped in a windowless waiting room, waiting your turn to be anaesthetised. His flat was always nice though, especially once it was dark out, all the buildings lit up.

Well, congratulations – he said.

Thank you.

They'd offered me a place right after the audition. I'd got the email on the Eurostar back.

He took my coat, hung it up in the wardrobe – full of suits, all of them black or navy, shirts still in their dry-cleaner wrapping, white or blue or pink. He didn't seem to have any other clothes.

So what did you think of Paris?

I've been before – I said. – A long time ago. Yeah, it was ok, I didn't see much of it. Do you like it?

Well, the Parisians always pretend not to understand my French – he said. – Even though it's pretty good, though I say so myself. But a couple of times, I've made a small slip – got the gender of a noun wrong or used slightly the wrong form of the past – and the person I was talking to acted like they had literally no idea what I meant. Like it made no sense at all. So I suppose Paris makes me think that all national stereotypes might be true. The fur coats as well. The poodles. But yeah – he said. – It's ok. I got some champagne, by the way. I put it in the freezer a while ago. It should be cold.

Oh, thank you. You didn't need to.

We're celebrating, aren't we?

He opened the bottle, poured two glasses, and we sat on the sofa to drink. He asked me about the audition, what the festival involved, why it was important, and I enjoyed telling him about it. He held my hand on his leg while I talked, stroked the backs of my fingers.

When we'd finished the glass, he said I should top myself up, he was going to take a shower, hadn't had time to after the gym.

Sure – I said. – But Max, by the way, I did mean it when I said I'd pay you back. For the trip. I haven't forgotten.

I'd already started trying to get the money. I'd emailed Marieke, asked her to put me forward for any other charity dinners that came round. I'd skipped lunch and taken a couple of rolls of toilet paper from the Conservatory bathroom. At first, Laurie and I had used the Ps' loo roll, but then Mrs P said we consumed wasteful quantities. To be fair on her, if Laurie ran out of tampons before her period ended, she'd often stuff a wodge of it down her pants instead of buying another pack, and I'd taken to doing the same. Mrs P now hid the roll in her bedroom, only taking it to the bathroom when she needed it.

Max had stood up. He was looking at something on his phone, distracted.

What? – he said. – Oh. Don't worry. You actually don't need to. I go to Paris a fair bit for work. I expensed it this morning.

Really? Isn't that kind of unethical?

That sort of money's a rounding error to a bank, Anna – he said. – You shouldn't worry so much.

He went to take a shower, and I got the champagne out of the fridge, topped up my glass, then I took the cork off the kitchen counter and put it in my bag.

He was only in the bathroom for a minute, and then I heard him say *fuck*, and he came back. He'd taken most of his clothes off, was in his underwear.

Can you – he said. – Do you mind – there's a—

He looked like he might be sick.

What? – I said.

A spider – he choked out.

A spider? Wait. You're scared of spiders?

He sat on the sofa, took a deep breath, like someone who's just witnessed a traumatic accident, trying to erase its afterimage.

Nobody needs that many legs – he said.

Are you joking?

What? Of course I'm not joking. Why would I be joking? Look, no, it's – can you – do you mind them?

No. Not really.

Please – he said, glancing back at the bathroom. – Do something with it.

Ok.

It took me a second to even see it. Back wall of the shower, about the size of a two pence piece. I nudged it to crawl onto my fingers, cupped it in my hand.

What have you done? – he asked. – Did you kill it? Are you sure? Is it definitely dead?

I'll put it out.

He looked at my hands and realised what I meant.

Fuck – he whispered. – You're insane. There's a mad woman in my flat. What's wrong with you?

It's tiny.

He was staring at me, transfixed, like I was a toddler holding a gun. I was rather enjoying it.

Can you open the door for me? – I said, calmly.

Don't move. Stay there.

There was a narrow balcony at one end of the room, but even when it was nice at ground level, it was too windy at that height to use it. He slid the door open and ran back to the sofa. I tried to deposit the spider onto the balcony edge, but it was swept out of my hand.

Has it gone? – he asked, when I came back.

All gone. Can it survive the fall, do you think?

Who cares? Let's hope not. Wash your hands before you come anywhere near me.

I rinsed them in the kitchen sink.

I wonder how it even got up this high – I said. – What it thought it was doing. There can't be much to eat up here.

Human flesh – he muttered.

Don't be a baby.

I went to him. He pulled me onto his lap.

You're being very mean – he said, petulantly.

I traced his collarbone with my fingers.

You've got goosebumps. You really are scared, aren't you?

The door was open. I'm cold.

Sure.

One fell on me once when I was in bed – he said.

Fell on you?

It suddenly appeared on my chest. I can't have been older than, what, six, and there it was. It was huge.

Maybe you were just very small. But what do you mean, it fell on you?

What do you mean, what do I mean? I mean it fell on me. From the ceiling.

But I don't think spiders can fall, can they?

You know, Anna – he said. – It's not very nice to make fun of people for their phobias. Fear isn't all that rational. Though, frankly, there's nothing irrational about hating spiders. Have you seen those close-up pictures? All those eyes.

Yes, I know, darling. Very scary, aren't they?

He looked up at me, and his face was so serious, I started to laugh, and then he was laughing too. I crawled my fingers up the back of his neck, and he jumped, which made me laugh even harder. He grabbed my arms and pinned me to the sofa. I tried to kick him off, both of us helpless with laughter, and then he said – God, this is turning into a John Lewis Christmas advert.

Wrestling with a semi-naked man? – I said. – I'm not sure those are adverts you've been watching.

Fuck off. I'm going to take a shower.

Well, make sure you're careful in there. They tend to come in pairs, I heard.

His weight lay heavy across my body, and he held both my hands in his.

You're horrible – he said, his mouth right next to mine. – I hate you.

No you don't – I said.

SIX

The next week, Marieke called me out of class. Sophie was ill, she said, wouldn't be doing Manon that night, and I'd be going on instead. It was nearly the end of the afternoon. Sophie would've spent all day, face hovering over a bowl of boiling water and towel round head, breathing in steam. Testing the voice and still finding it gone. If you had to miss a performance, then this one – the last night, the one Marieke invited her contacts to – was the worst one to choose. Marieke was still talking – saying they'd actually thought about cutting the *Manon*, but it was Frankie's only scene and there were agents in and he was very upset, of course, poor thing, but wasn't it a wonderful opportunity and wasn't I lucky. And I was agreeing with her, smiling, saying I was grateful, registering that this was a threat from her, and knowing I had to be good or else, but not really paying attention. That one thought – tonight, tonight, three hours' time, I'm on tonight – filled my head, no room for anything else, and excitement dropped into my gut like a pebble in water, its ripples spreading out and out and out.

I had plans with Max that evening, so I messaged to say I couldn't make it. He called me, and when I told him about *Manon*, he said he'd come.

Really? – I asked. – Why?

It wasn't that I minded, more that I couldn't imagine it. Him and singing didn't slot together in my mind. They were two tunes played by hands that never crossed.

He laughed.

I'm insulted you seem so surprised – he said. – It sounds important.

Well, it kind of is – I said, not wanting to disappoint. – But it's only a scene.

I'll come. I'm curious. Wouldn't you be?

Curious. A cold word, emotionally empty. An uncomfortable flashback to a time early on – him lying on the bed, propped up on elbows, watching me undress. Me walking over to him, kneeling, legs either side of his legs. Him still fully clothed, not looking into my face, but down at my body – exciting at first – but then this cold detachment in his eyes, like he wasn't looking at me at all. Not moving to touch me, but staying like that, lying back, looking down at my body. Trying to make him – kissing him – tracing the shape of his lip with my thumb – taking his earlobe in my mouth – biting – kissing his neck – unbuttoning his shirt and sliding my hands inside – undoing his belt – trying to push him backwards, but him stronger than me, propped up, this little smile – something like amusement, like he was waiting to see what I'd think to do next – a purely academic interest – and I hadn't come up with anything very interesting yet. And feeling suddenly like – if it kept on like that – if he kept looking at me like that – I'd hit him round the face or, far worse, cry. But then he'd stopped. He'd put his hands on my thighs and turned me over. He'd pressed my arms above my head and kissed me back, and I'd forgotten about it till now. Until he'd said that word.

I'm curious – he said. – Wouldn't you be?

I suppose so.

I put him out of my mind. There wasn't time. Three hours till curtain up and there was too much to do. There was going to Wardrobe and having the costume pinned. There was seeing Angela. Her warming up with me, going over the hard bits, giving me the pep talk. There was making sure I ate something early, so I didn't have to later, and drinking constant sips of water. Sitting in a dark practice room, stretching, trying not to stress that I'd had some wine last night, hadn't slept much, telling myself that it wouldn't make a difference, it would be fine. There was Frankie talking me through the bits they'd changed in the blocking, asking me was I sure I'd got it all, was I sure, did I think we should go through it again.

And all that time, there was Manon – and not Sophie's Manon, but mine, the woman I'd created, who I dared to hope might be more real. Always, in my head there she was – and not just her text and her music, but her laugh – the one she does when she's not actually happy – her knowing smile that drives him mad, the way that anger makes her quiet, her desire – and all these were like secrets between us, me and her – she was whispering them with hot breath in my ear and I couldn't stop myself from smiling.

Then there was only an hour to go, and backstage was all noise. Lip trills, arpeggios, bits of arias, that same phrase – the one that caused panic – sung over and over again. There was overspill from the dressing rooms, people coming out to escape the thickness of hairspray in confined spaces, or to get away from the soprano – the one who thought she was better than them – pointedly singing bits of their part. It was hard to pick your way down corridors. They were littered with broken furniture and costume racks, with discarded props from previous productions, with half-clothed sing-ers lying, hands on stomachs, to breathe.

There's no glamour backstage. The money goes into front of house, the bits the paying public see. Backstage it's all long corridors, bare walls, concrete floors and exposed piping, fluorescent strips of light. There's something here, though, that's better than out there. Something alive. It zips – electric – between you and every other person whose eyes you meet. You feel what they feel. It's in the walls as well. It's in the concrete floors. It's in the costume you put on, the tag sewn inside with the names of the people who've worn it before. This energy, this intensity. It tingles in every cell. It prickles your skin. It pulses somewhere deep, somewhere right in the core of you. And you feel sure suddenly that this is what it is to be alive – that normally you're not, and now you are. Nothing can match it – this excitement – this knowing that, just beyond those walls, are people who've come here to hear you. Who won't interrupt you, but listen. They're not interested in perfection, these people, although you intend to be perfect. What they want is for you to say something real. Something with meaning. Something that changes how they see and think and feel, even just for a bit. You can do that for them. Everything out there will turn on a single moment, and no one controls that but you.

I was sharing a room with the girls in *Figaro*. Doing our faces in the bare-bulbed light, they unpicked their year one by one. *You know, Sophie's got laryngitis* — they were saying. — *She's been singing on it all week. She went to an ENT today, and he says there's damage already.* Foundation first, not leaving any gaps, like white-washing a wall — blank and neutral surface to colour. *Frankie says she's a nightmare to act with. Did he tell you she wouldn't let him kiss her? Made him put his thumb over her lips and suck instead. Wasted opportunity. I'd kiss him, given half the chance.* Blusher, colour in the eyelids, thick lines, layers of lipstick. Make-up for the audience members at the back. Close up, we were parodies of women, but from there, it looked natural. Natural to us was to them a child's drawing — round blob for head, no detail in face, blank and smooth and eyeless. *You know Sophie's a born-again Christian. She's been revirginised. Revirginised? Yes, revirginised. She's a born-again virgin. Don't ask me how the fuck that works.* Getting into costume. Helping each other with zips and buttons. Painting concealer onto spots on backs. *Have you seen Amy? She's fucked up that top C every night this week. Apparently, she's so nervous she's been throwing up all day.* And I was part of the gossip too, the first year cover. People dropping by to have a good look, to check if I was scared. They'd seen me sitting through rehearsals, pencil and score in hand, but they hadn't heard me do it. I was up last. When I went on, they'd squeeze into the wings to hear. They'd want to know if I was any good.

And then it was 7:25. Beginners to the stage, and the chatting stopped. One of the girls sat on the sofa and ate an apple with eyes shut. The other lay on the floor and muttered to herself — *I am a singer I am a woman I am strong I am nervous I am calm I am free I am —.*

I leafed through a programme, and saw the insert announcing the cast change. *Due to illness, Sophie Mitchell is no longer able to —.* I closed my eyes, ran over my words, once and then another time and then another.

Then the girls were on for *Figaro* and I was left alone. For the first time since he'd called me, I thought about Max. How he'd be sitting up there already. How he was about to hear me. A stab of nausea, like a trapdoor in my stomach had opened, but I was strict with myself. I wouldn't be distracted.

And then we were called to the wings. Darkness. The scene before ours finishing and the audience applause. Frankie's breath in my ear, deep and heavy, and the dampness of palms as he touches my hand and says — *have fun out there* — and me — *you too*.

I know what they've been told about Manon, what's written in the programme — that she's run away with an impoverished Chevalier. Thought that love alone could sustain them, but she soon finds she wants more. She craves excitement, wealth, beautiful things. Enter the rich de Brétigny, who wants Manon and, if he can have her, will give her everything she desires in return. But there's a catch — Manon must not tell the Chevalier that his own father, who disapproves of their relationship, has arranged to have his son kidnapped that night. She must let him be taken, and then she'll be free. So, in this scene, right before the Chevalier's kidnappers are due to arrive, she's alone in the little room she shared with him. She has to decide between the two men — whether to warn the Chevalier and stay with him, or to let him be taken.

It sounds ridiculous in summary. Most opera plots do. It says nothing about her, the woman she is, and it's my job to show them. I don't become Manon, and she's not me, but something in between — two sheets of film placed one on top of the other, which make a new image. She makes me the thing I've never been, and I give her what I know, and together we'll peel off the skin and show what's inside.

*

And it's time. Resettling of audience behind curtain. Silence. I'm cued. Deep breath. Curtain rises, music starts, and I step out, on, into the light.

Manon enters, upstage right. She stands, looking into the room.

There's nothing romantic here – the narrow bed, the traffic outside, the grey light that illuminates the dust in the air. No, nothing romantic, but it made me happy once. I love him, I do love him, I still love him, but my love for him is like the snatch of a tune heard from someone else's window. I recognise it, it makes me sentimental, but I couldn't say why. And to think, anyway, to have ever thought that here we could keep love alive. Keep it urgent and sharp, next to this – this – the never having enough money, the adding it up, the checking the amount, the this-much-for-the-room and this-much-for-the-food and then nothing's left. Love, which struggles for air at the best of times. Love, which begins with – *I'll never, I always, I've never, always always, for the rest of my – yes – the rest of my life till I die –* and drifts – yes, even at the best of times – to petty squabbling over toilet brushes and to whose turn it is to and to why can you never and to bodies that function but don't excite.

Manon moves upstage left and sits on the bed. She fiddles with the tassels at the edge of the blanket.

And I'd thought he had more to give me, but we're just these four walls. We can't afford to go out. It didn't use to matter because our bodies were enough, but they're not anymore. Not when the sheets smell of damp because there's nowhere to dry them, and not with the bathroom right next to the bed, so I can hear him in there, pissing and coughing up phlegm. He sits in bed at 4 p.m., watching me dress. He's bored. He goes to the supermarket and comes back. He throws his coat over the back of the chair and leaves all his shit – keys, wallet, phone – on the surfaces I've just cleared and he switches on the big light even though he knows I hate it – seeing into all the crevices of the room, their ugliness, and how the dust gathers.

Manon moves to upstage centre, and looks around the room.

But that other man promised something different. This room seemed smaller with him in it. He stood, taking it all in, and I was ashamed of its shabbiness. I felt everything diminished, reduced by his eyes – but not me. When he looked at me, I remembered what it was to feel wanted, to feel like anything could happen. I saw that my life was just these four walls, and he'd offered to open the door. And I won't be made to feel bad – for wanting the things that make life good. For wanting beauty when I'm young. For wanting people to admire mine while I have it. Because one day it'll go and the rest of my life will be without it.

She moves to the little table centre stage.

But I'll say goodbye to this now, because I loved it. There was fun in it once, having nothing. Goodbye to our little table – big enough for us, we sat so close together. Where we made those plans we knew would never happen, so we could say – *yes, me too, I want that too.* Goodbye, little table. We only had one glass. Drinking, I'd search for the imprint of his lips, and him for mine. I was happy here once.

Manon is crying, as the Chevalier enters upstage right. She runs to the mirror to check her face, and he comes up behind her. He puts his arms round her, his chin on her shoulder.

He asks why I'm crying, and when I say I'm not, he doesn't push it. I think less of him, unfairly – how stupid to just believe me. But I'm more loving to him, not less, more affectionate – not sure if I'm trying to distract him, or wanting him like this one last time. Holding his hand and smiling at him as he talks. And I do it so right that I start to believe it, so that when he kisses me, I'm right back there to that first time, when I thought – irrational, instinctive, like a drug that would send me mad – *I will give up everything for this man, everything, if I can't have him, I'll die.* And so the knock on the door is almost, but not quite, a surprise. And when I hold him back and say – *no, don't answer it, don't go* – I couldn't say for sure if I mean it.

Curtain down. Silence, and half the lights blocked, like a big shadow's fallen. And then the applause.

Frankie squeezed my hand and whispered – *fucking hell* – and the curtain came up for the bow. The audience were giving us back noise, not silence, now. Looking right out at them like that, I saw how many there were. Sweet relief I hadn't thought it before. I came forward to bow and then him, and then together, and he pushed me forward again though I tried to make him come too. We ran into the wings but the clapping didn't stop, and we were pushed back on. Daring to think – *so it was good?* – and then, as the applause kept on, like a tide that doesn't ebb but keeps on coming, a growing certainty – *yes, it was good. It was really fucking good.* Coming off, still hearing them out there and the other singers gathered there clapping too, asking them in confusion – *is there a company bow then?* – not understanding what they were saying above the noise – *go back on, go back, they're still clapping.* I tried to pull Frankie with me, but he was shaking his head and pushing me, so I went out alone. I realised suddenly what was happening – that they were all clapping for me – and I was invincible.

Afterwards, Marieke came backstage with the director and they did a little speech. *Special congratulations to Anna for stepping in* – she said – *and for doing such a marvellous job* – and everyone stamped their feet. They'd brought a few bottles, and paper cups were passed round of something warm and fizzy. Getting out of costumes, doors left open, people wandered in and out, half-dressed, hugging and saying – *well done* – or pointing out where they'd messed up and asking if we thought Marieke had noticed. I looked in the mirror. It was like my eyes were trapped in someone else's face, under someone else's heavy lids and stiff lashes, blinking away, and for a second

– breathing slowing, adrenaline dropping – I wanted more than anything to sleep. But then I finished my glass, and I had another, and Frankie came to find me – *how's the superstar then?* – all touchy-feely to show everyone else we were pals – joking with me about how kissing on stage was much better unrehearsed, felt real – and we picked over the scene, where it was best – and suddenly I was happier than I'd ever been before, knowing that this was the only way I wanted to live. This, this sort of life, where every nerve in my body was alive. How it was always different and never knowing how it would be, and then it happening, and being able to say – *that was me.*

SEVEN

On my way up to the theatre bar, I worried he'd be conspicuous. I imagined everyone wondering who he was – expensive suit, struggling to affect an interest in the arts. I shouldn't have worried. Most of the men were in suits, and I couldn't even see him. Laurie was there though, at the bar with Oscar, and I was about to go over, when I was grabbed – *you were Manon, weren't you? I just wanted to say* – and then I was part of the dance, one person moving, another taking their place. These were not the sorts of people – pearl necklaces, silk shirts – who'd normally listen to me. I baked in the heat of approval, heard my voice changing to more closely match theirs. Marieke found me too, once she'd stopped holding court, performatively intercepting the important people, who'd go away from her looking dazed, having promised to part with large sums of money for the Conservatory, trying to wipe the imprint of her lipstick off their cheeks. She said to me – *congratulations again, Anna. Let's chat next week* – and Angela engulfed me on her way out of the door, and told me she was proud.

I felt a hand on my shoulder, then, and there he was. I was shy, like I'd told him an intimate secret and had no idea how he'd react.

I was waiting for you outside – he said. – I called you. I thought you'd left.

Sorry. I thought you knew I'd come here.

Why would I know that?

Did you enjoy tonight?

I did.

Right. Well, good.

Then he said – no, really. I did. You were great.

Thanks.

I mean it, you were. I was pleasantly surprised.

I'll take that as a compliment.

It was a compliment. I didn't know exactly what to expect. Standard-wise, I mean. On the way here, I suddenly worried you might be awful and I wouldn't know what to say. So how good you were was – yeah – it was a pleasant surprise.

Well, that's very sweet of you to say.

He laughed.

Don't sulk – he said. – You know you were good. A lot of opera's very silly, though, isn't it? I liked your scene, but what was the point of the one with the flowery hats?

Laurie and Oscar found us then, and she threw her arms round me.

Babe – she said. – There you are. Been trying to get to you all night. This place is chock-a-block with cunts.

Max looked slightly taken aback.

Max – I said. – Remember Laurie? You met her before. And this is Oscar.

Oscar was dressed all in black, like an overgrown crow.

They've been giving me free drinks – he said. – Tactics. They assume you're part of the band if you wear all black.

Him and Laurie had clearly had quite a lot of free drinks. She embraced me again, nearly pushing me over, and said, with the earnest intensity found only in the very drunk, slowly and pedantically – *you were incredible, Anna. I mean it, no, I mean it, honestly. You. Were. Incredible.*

Oscar started to ask me how I felt about reproducing the works of dead white men – *is that something you find you can live with? Morally, I mean* – and then Frankie came over. He said that the singers were moving on to somewhere down the road.

Shall we? – I asked Max.

He made a face and said he was tired, but I didn't want to go home. Performing was a drug. Once you slept, it wore off. And I felt cheated, I suppose. He'd been nice, but not in quite the way I'd wanted. The buzz had diminished. I needed another hit.

Please come – I said. – Just for a bit. I'm going to go.

Ok – he said. – For a bit.

We went to a members' club in a townhouse. Frankie got us in. The other clients were men in their fifties, who all turned round to stare, but the proprietor – there were photos of him stuck on the walls, anyway, arms round various men – came over and shook Frankie's hand. He brought us a couple of bottles of wine, which had the logo of the club printed on the label. It didn't exactly taste like wine, but it was good.

Laurie and Oscar disappeared off to a dark corner booth, and it looked, from her spiky gestures, like they were arguing. Max was talking to a singer in the year above whose name I couldn't remember. She kept fiddling with her hair and touching his arm, and he was standing very still, smiling. He could always do that, stay still and have people move towards him. I wasn't jealous. It's depressing to be with the person no one wants to flirt with, the one who skulks in corners at parties and isn't desired. I liked knowing other people wanted him too.

I stood with Frankie and a few girls from the year above. They would have ignored me if we'd passed in a corridor the day before, but now they treated me like one of them. Normally, someone could say to me – *no, don't be like that, be like this* – or – *you're that sort of person, aren't you?* – and I would try to change myself entirely to fit their idea of me, sure they must be right. But this version of me – the post-show version – seemed clearly defined, immutable.

After a bit, Max and the girl came over. She said she was leaving.

Already? – Frankie asked.

I've got an audition on Saturday. I can't drink.

For Nigel? So do I. It's not stopping me.

Well, that's going to be your problem, isn't it, sweetie – she said.

She hugged everyone and we did the round of congratulations again. When she'd left, we started talking about covering. I'd never done it before, I said. One of the girls told us about a show she'd been in where almost everyone was fucking in some combination, and they'd all given each other laryngitis. On the first night, only the covers were fit to go on for every major role.

The director couldn't bring himself to watch it – she said. – He sat backstage with earplugs in and a bottle of whisky.

Everyone was being loud, interrupting each other to tell their own stories, and I was too. Someone else said to me – *I can't believe that was a cover performance, Anna* – and we all started complimenting each other. We all meant it. The post-show buzz makes you love everyone, and they love you too. Max was very quiet though, asking people polite questions, then falling silent. It started to annoy me. I wanted to show him off, for him to be charming in the way I knew he could be. I'd say – *Max, tell them about that client you used to take to the opera. This is a good story* – but he'd just shrug and smile, and someone else would soon interject.

After a bit, he went off to the bathroom, and when he got back, he sat with Laurie and Oscar instead. I followed.

That's what I think most men don't understand – Laurie was saying. – That it's possible for women to have sex and literally feel nothing at all, just a kind of vague discomfort, like having a smear test.

Have I joined this conversation at the wrong time? – I said.

Max was smiling, but I wasn't sure what his smile meant. Oscar was blank and inscrutable, like a chalkboard wiped clean. He was very pale and thin. He didn't have the energy for facial expression.

I was telling them about this guy I slept with once – she said. – He asked me if it was arousing to put a tampon in. I couldn't stop laughing. Him imagining women all over the country shoving cotton sticks up their cunts in toilet cubicles, overcome with lust.

I once dated a guy who thought you stuck sanitary towels onto your body, not your knickers – I said. – He took me correcting him quite personally.

Laurie choked on her wine, then she started telling us about the fancy dress parties they'd had at university.

Fancy dress — she said. — What it meant was we'd dress up as whores. And don't get me wrong. I'm not using that word, *whore*, in a sex-worker-phobic kind of way. I'm using it because that's what they would have called us. The guys, I mean. The themes would be things like CEOs and Corporate Hoes. Jocks and Cheerleaders. Pilots and Slutty Air Hostesses. You get the idea. All not-so-subtle code for — *guys, wear whatever you want, and girls, dress like whores.*

I glanced at Max, but he wasn't looking at me. I started to feel a numbing dread. I put my hand on his hand under the table and stroked his fingers. He took it in his and held it still.

That's how they get you, isn't it? — Laurie said. — Men. When you're young enough to not know what's normal. I'd check to see the other girls were smiling, then I'd smile too. We weren't really friends, the guys and girls in my group, not really. Rivals, more like. There was always some sort of stupid competition between us, which of us was the most popular, had the most fun, that sort of thing. And the girls always lost, even when they ostensibly won, because we all know what you call a girl who has that sort of fun, and the guys never hesitated to call us it. When someone calls you a whore, that's just the end of the conversation, isn't it? There's nothing you can say back to that. It's — what's it called? — performative? — something like that — like I love you, I hate you — the fact of saying it makes it true. I never stopped to wonder why it was such a bad thing, or why the same men who were perfectly happy to fuck me now seemed to despise me.

I think you're being unfair — Oscar said.

Oh, you do, do you? — said Laurie. — He thinks I'm being unfair — she said to me.

I've never called a woman a whore — said Oscar. — I've never even called a woman a girl.

Don't you love it when men look at you like that? — Laurie said to me. — That kind of *who? me?* look. *Surely you don't mean me?* Because he's a man, you see, he assumes I'm actually talking about him and not men in general. It's impossible to have a philosophical discussion about anything without him taking it personally. I'm getting another bottle.

She went to the bar.

What's wrong with her? — I asked Oscar.

She's working through some shit — he said. — She's having a hard time understanding she doesn't own me. I'm trying to teach her that's learned behaviour, you know. Social conditioning. Not natural. We're getting there. It takes a long time to process this stuff. It's so engrained.

Max had got his phone out and was looking at an email. I squeezed his arm.

It's late — he said. — Let's go.

I felt a spike of irritation. He couldn't even pretend to have fun.

I need to talk to Laurie — I said.

She brought the wine back to the table, and we went to the loo. There was only one cubicle. We took it in turns to pee, and then we both put on my lipstick.

Well, he hasn't got any more interesting, has he? — she said.

Is everything ok?

Apart from Oscar being a little cunt, it's all great, yeah. So we had one of our meetings earlier today, you know —

They had regular meetings where they told each other about the other people they'd slept with, and how they felt about it. It all seemed quite time-consuming to me, but I guess neither of them had proper jobs.

And anyway, he told me he'd had sex with Maya. You know, my friend Maya. And what is fucking me off most about this is that he won't even admit that that's against our rules. If he could own up to having fucking—

Someone started banging on the door.

Fuck off — she shouted. —Yeah, to having fucked up. If he could just own up to that, I might forgive him, but as it is — WE'RE COMING — as it is—

She trailed off and she pressed her lips together, studied her face in the mirror.

Let's go – she said.

The volume in the bar was turned up. The singers were drunk. Snatches of *Madama Butterfly* and *Così* floated up from the general babble. Post-show, it was acceptable for singers to suspend the rules, to forget about protecting the voice, to get wasted. The adrenaline added into the mix made that almost inevitable. I was sober, though, feeling I was still in the middle of a performance, alert to manoeuvre round the tricky corners.

In the booth, Oscar was showing Max his photographs of Laurie. She often posed for him. There was one of her leaning against a brick wall holding a spatula, blood running down her leg.

I call this one Crimes Against Humanity – Oscar said.

Another of her crouching naked over an egg in an egg cup.

Battery Farming – he said.

Max was studying the pictures closely, but he didn't comment. I asked Oscar what sort of art it was, and he said it was a departure from his normal style. He was an auto-artist, he explained. He photographed his own hair, his own skin. He photographed his own faeces. He was interested, he said, mainly in himself. That was the auto bit. And of course, he said, so were all artists. What was so revolutionary about his art, he said, was its transparency. He was attracted to the immediacy of photography, exact representation, no fucking around on a canvas. That sort of art was dead, he said, dead and buried. That was why he was going to be a photographer.

What, when you grow up? – said Max.

No, when I've finished my PhD – said Oscar smoothly, oblivious to tone. He started explaining his PhD. It was on false footnotes in literature.

You know – he said. – When a writer uses a footnote to refer to a fake book, or else the footnote sends you to another footnote in the same text which then refers you back to the original footnote.

Max asked him the exact purpose of his thesis, but he pretended not to understand the question. He went to the loo and he didn't come back.

Anna tells me you're writing a book? — Max said to Laurie.

Oh, she did, did she?

She did. What's it about?

I can't imagine you'd find it very interesting — she said. — It's a feminist deconstruction of the relationship between men and women in the internet age.

It does sound interesting. What do you mean by *feminist*?

What do you mean what do I mean? — Laurie said, looking at him like she wanted to rip his face off.

I just mean it's quite a loose term, isn't it? It seems to mean basically anything these days. Just anything a woman does, like that model who rolled around naked in ravioli on Instagram. That was meant to be a feminist statement, but surely it was kind of the opposite. It seems more like a brand name, is what I mean. A slogan a marketing team can slap onto something a woman's done to make it more sellable.

Sellable? — Laurie spat.

Yeah, I mean, it's quite a fashionable label these days, isn't it?

Well, men still find it easier to get published than women — said Laurie. — So, no.

Oh, do they?

Yes — she said. — They do.

You know, Max comes from quite close to where your parents live — I said. — He's—

The thing about male writers — Laurie carried on. — Men. Is that they write any old shit and then they shout about it and shout about it and shout about it until someone listens to them and it gets published. They bash it out like a wank and expect you to lie there and let them splurge it all over your tits.

Yes, well. I can see that might be — he paused — Disheartening.

Every time she said something vulgar, I saw a twitch of distaste on his face, and I knew she saw it too. That's why she kept doing it, so that she could say afterwards — *oh, so he's the sort of man who doesn't like it when a woman says* cunt. *Of course he is.* I had so wanted Max to like my friend. To be impressed by her, and for her to like him too. I wished he'd stop smirking at her, like she was an amusingly naughty child who ultimately wasn't his problem. It would be nice if she'd stop behaving like one too.

So you're a banker then, are you? — she said, with a poisonous grin. — Are you one of the ones responsible for the recession?

No, that's traders — Max started saying, but then a group of singers came over and stuffed themselves into the booth, and we were all squashed up together.

Anna — he said. — Come on. Let's go.

Well, give me a minute to say bye to people.

I turned away. I could see him out of the corner of my eye, not even trying to talk to the person next to him, and I thought — *good*.

The whole palaver of how great everyone had been started again, but by now everyone was too loud to be coherent. A boy kept starting to tell a story, making everyone stop talking to listen, and then he'd collapse into hysterics, too overcome, unable to continue. A girl who clearly wanted him tried to match his laughter. A couple of the others started singing showtunes, and one of the girls from my dressing room knocked an entire glass of wine on my lap. She leant across the table and grabbed me by the shoulders and said — *oh my God I'm so sorry I'm so sorry you're so incredible I love you so much.* I could see, up close, that her powder had settled into the creases of her skin, and her lipstick didn't follow the lines of her lips. When she changed her expression, you could only just trace the movements of her real face underneath the mask, almost imperceptible, like when you see someone's bones slipping under their skin.

Max squeezed past everyone and put his coat on. He leant over to me.

I'm leaving — he said. — Are you coming?

I suddenly felt very tired.

Where's Laurie? — I said.

I don't know. I haven't seen her.

I found her in the toilet, throwing up.

Oscar left — she said. — He left. With another girl. One of these singer cunts. The little prick.

I'd rather thought that was the point of their arrangement, but I kept that to myself. I pulled her up, and she leant on me, heavy and slack.

I need to take her home – I said to Max, once I'd got her back to the bar.

He looked at her and then at me.

I'll come with you – he said. – Make sure you both get home safe.

You can't. We're not allowed.

I can't imagine she can walk – he said. – Can you carry her?

So we left. On the way out, I looked back into the bar. One of the girls was sitting on Frankie's lap, feeding him vodka from the bottle. He'd fixed her with this expression he had, focused and determined, like a GPS-enabled drone. Someone had smashed a glass and was trying to pick the shards out of their bleeding hand. Someone was crying.

On the street, Max hailed a black cab and I gave the driver our address. Laurie fell asleep almost straight away, her head on my shoulder.

Max said – so that's your scene, is it?

I wouldn't say that – I said.

He didn't comment on the house – not on the smell of overcooked meat in the hallway – not when I used the torch on my phone so we didn't trip, illuminating the shoes, the old newspapers, the handbags that were dumped on the stairs – not, when he deposited her there, on Laurie's eccentrically untidy room. His silence embarrassed me, made me think he found it worse than I'd ever imagined he would. I told him my room was next door, I'd be there in a minute, and he went.

I put Laurie to bed in her clothes and made her drink a glass of water, then I went to find him. He was standing by the window. I thought he'd be looking at my stuff – the photographs I'd stuck on my wardrobe, the books on my bedside table – but he didn't seem interested, like he'd taken it all in already, and dismissed it. There seemed to be much less space with him there, and I felt very cold suddenly. I realised I was shivering. I went over and pressed my cheek into his back, put my arms round his waist. I wanted his comfort. When he turned towards me, I kissed him, and he let me for a bit, then he pulled away.

Can I stay? – he said. – I know you're not allowed, but I've got to be up in three hours. I can't face going out again.

Stay.

Let's go to bed.

Not yet.

I laced my fingers round the back of his head and tried to pull it down. He held my wrists.

You're drunk – he said.

I'm not.

He let go of me, sat on the bed.

I need to sleep – he said.

He shut his eyes, leant his forehead on his hands.

Come on, Anna. I've got a long drive tomorrow. It's going to be fucking dangerous as it is.

A drive? Where are you going?

Home. My family.

Were you planning to tell me?

Which part of it? That I'm going home? It's Christmas. You're going home too.

I didn't say anything, not sure exactly which part annoyed me.

What is it? – he said, a nasty edge to his voice. – You're offended I didn't ask you? You want to meet my parents? Is that it?

He presented this like it was an entirely crazy suggestion.

Well, why not? – I said.

It's three in the morning, Anna. I've been up since five. Can we please just go to bed.

What the fuck's wrong with you?

Wrong with me? Nothing.

His blankness nourished my anger.

You've been weird all evening – I said. – Trying to ruin things for me. Is this about Frankie, is that it?

Who's Frankie?

The guy in my scene.

Isn't Frankie a girl's name?

Because I had to kiss him. Is that it?

He started unbuttoning his shirt.

Please stop acting like a child – he said. – I'm really tired.

There was nothing I could think to say that wouldn't underline his point.

He sighed.

Ok, if you want the truth – do you? – really? – well, fine. If you want the truth, I hated how you were tonight. In that bar. That love-in. All that self-congratulatory aren't-we-so-great-and-isn't-what-we-do-so-important thing. I thought you were a more serious person than that.

Well, I'm really sorry – I said. – I'm sorry I wasn't how you liked me. Forgive me. I'll make sure to be exactly what you want in future.

I'm sorry – he said. – Look, that came out wrong. I get it. You put more than two thesps together and it turns into a performance. I remember that from uni. I've just never seen you like that before, I suppose. You've never seemed like that sort of person.

I hated him then. I hated him for studying the version of me that other people liked best, putting a line through it.

That girl I was talking to at the beginning – he said. – The one who left early. She told me she'd talked to some directors and stuff right after the show. She'd put the time in, got some people's contact details, been offered an audition by some guy, just by being switched on like that, by looking out for herself—

Well, good for her – I said. – You know she's four years older than me? Slightly closer to your age actually. Maybe you could fuck her instead.

He made a little move to stand up, and I thought for a crazy moment he might hurt me, and I wasn't sure I even cared. But whatever he'd been going to do, he changed his mind.

You're being ridiculous – he said.

You didn't have to stay. You didn't even have to come.

But I wanted to.

He held an arm out to me, touched the side of the bed next to him to tell me to sit. I slid down the wall and sat on the floor. Ignored him.

You're talented, Anna – he said. – That's what I'm trying, very badly, to say. Seriously, you are. I know that I know pretty much nothing about it, but even I can see that. You stand out. You're someone people want to watch. I was actually really impressed. I just think it would be a tragic thing for you to waste that. You see so many people with talent do nothing with it. Just mess around, you know. Those sorts of people tonight. People who get distracted. Lose their focus.

I know more about this than you – I said. – They're not just a bunch of wasters, those singers, they are focused. But tonight was important. Hanging out with them like that – it was important. Successful singers need to be liked. They need to have contacts.

Yeah, but those people aren't going to help you. They're your competition. And come on, you want me to believe they're serious people? Those singers? Or people like Laurie? What is it she even does? Has she ever actually written anything? She's not a serious person, Anna. And you're different when you're with her, you try to be like her. Please, whatever you do, don't see her as a model for success. Someone who's too busy getting drunk and complaining about how unfair everything is to play the game. Her need, that unhappiness she has with herself, it radiates off everything she says and does. Can you not see that? It's exhausting. I'm exhausted. It depresses me to think of you here with her.

You don't know anything about it – I said. – How dare you think you can tell me what to do, who to be friends with, when you won't even be with me properly. What's wrong with you?

He looked at me. He didn't say anything. There was a pause, and I thought he might get up and leave, but then he said – right, so that's what this is about.

It has nothing to do with that – I said.

Anna. Look, I thought we'd – I mean, we've talked about this, haven't we? I thought you understood that—

Fuck you – I said.

But the words sounded empty and stupid, and he looked at me with sad, tired eyes, like I'd disappointed him.

He said – come here – and then he said – please.

I went and sat next to him, feeling like a child in the aftermath of a tantrum that's fuelled itself, exceeded the bounds of its own logic. That same sense of incoherent shame. I let him put his arms round me and pull me to him and kiss me.

Let's go to sleep – he said.

I woke to the shape of him dressing in the grey of the room. I hadn't heard his alarm. I was about to ask him – *what time is it?* – but I stopped myself. I wanted to see how he'd wake me. If he'd kiss me, say my name, shake my arm. I could measure from that how angry he was. I shut my eyes.

I must have fallen asleep, because when I opened them again, he was gone. It was light outside. He'd left a box on the bedside table, with a note on top. It said that he hoped I'd slept well and that I felt better this morning. This was my present, he said, to open at Christmas. He'd let me know when he was back.

I looked at the box, and all the rage I'd felt the night before came back. What exactly was it he expected? That I'd put it under the tree, open it on Christmas Day in front of my parents? They'd say – *oh, that's lovely, who's that from?* – and I'd say – what? – I'd say – *oh, just a friend?* – I'd say – or – *some man I'm fucking?* Or did he think I'd open it alone on Christmas morning? Alone in my childhood bedroom, I'd open it and think of him? Feel grateful to him? Miss him? Was that it? Was that what he wanted? Fuck him – I thought – fuck him with his I'll-let-you-know-when-I'm-back. Fuck him with his opinions.

I opened it. It was a bracelet, fine gold chain, a charm hanging off it – a little disc with the letter A engraved. I rubbed the roughness of it between finger and thumb. It was the same bracelet you see dangling off every other girl's wrist on the train. I imagined him giving instructions to his secretary, very discreet, I'm sure she always was. The initial, an attempt to make it personal, which somehow made it more generic. The boxes of bracelets in the department store, and the woman in her pencil skirt and blouse, thumbing through them, the different letters, at the end of her lunchbreak. How many of them would she have bought, over the years, I wondered. Different letter, same product. It said nothing about me.

I leant over the side of the bed. The floorboards had a little gap between the slats. I dangled the bracelet between finger and thumb, and fed it through.

Laurie wasn't in her room, so I went downstairs. I heard her voice in the kitchen. The Ps were both there, standing, and Laurie was sitting at the table. Her face was grey.

What's going on? – I asked.

We've been telling her – Mrs P said. – Mr P and myself. We've been telling her that we've had enough, haa. We're not going to take it anymore. We shouldn't have to take it. Not in our house.

We want you girls to leave – Mr P said. – Enough's enough.

Take what? – I said.

All that getting in late – Mr P said. – All that waking us up. All that going to the toilet in the night. The cooking. The long baths. All that singing.

We're very sorry – I said. – We'll be better, we promise. Won't we, Laurie? We won't disturb you anymore.

And last night – Mrs P said, ignoring me. – Last night, that was the end, wasn't it? That man. In our house. What do you think this is, haa?

She must have seen him on his way out. Peered at him as he passed her bedroom door. Poked her head through the gaps in the bannisters as he was creeping down the stairs.

I'm sorry – I said. – I didn't know we couldn't have guests.

Guests! – Mrs P said. – You think I don't know what sort of girl entertains a man like that? With a suit like that, haa? Now, I might be old-fashioned, but there's a word we used to use for girls like you, and I'm not having any of that in my house.

But—

I took you girls in out of the goodness of my heart—

Well, I mean, we are paying rent – I said.

And it just goes to show what I always say – and I always want to be proved wrong, but I always say it – that you can't trust people, can you? You can't trust people.

We'll let you stay until the New Year – Mr P said. – Because it's Christmas.

They stood looking at us until we left.

Laurie came up to my room with me.

Well, I hope you're happy – she said.

Whose fault do you think it was we had to come back here?

She answered with icy silence.

Let's not argue – I said. – Please.

We got into my bed, and then she cheered up.

You know – she said. – Mrs P said appearances were deceptive and you're no better than a common hussy.

She didn't.

You know she did. But we'll find somewhere better, I promise. And so that was the grand man, was it? The great romance of the century? I mean, my memories of last night are a little blurry, but seriously? He's such a cliché, isn't he, Anna? Things didn't work out with his wife, so he's fucking a child. Original.

I'm not a child – I said.

You know what I mean.

Well, no, I don't actually.

He seems so desperate to prove himself, doesn't he? – she said. – It's tedious.

Wanting to show Laurie that my understanding of him was better, more nuanced than hers, I said – there was this one night, a couple of weeks ago. He knew I had an early start, a rehearsal in the morning, and it was late already, but we had sex anyway. And then afterwards, he made me come again. And then even after that, he went down on me again. And then, yeah, I think another time, I kind of lost track. It was so late at night, and it didn't even feel good by the end. It actually hurt. I mean, talk about proving yourself. That had nothing to do with me, did it? My pleasure. That was all about him.

I thought Laurie would laugh, but she didn't.

But why didn't you say something? – she said.

I don't know. I didn't want to offend him, I guess.

Jesus – she said. – That's so fucked up. Are you ok?

It really wasn't like that – I said quickly, regretting I'd told her. – Anyway, I take your point. I've had it. Enough.

Well, good for you. I'm proud. Personal growth, and all that.

She looked like she was about to say something else, but then she saw the box and reached for it.

Ooh. What's in here?

Nothing – I said.

EIGHT

I spent the week before I left for Christmas trying to distract myself.

I distracted myself with packing, or thinking about it. Throwing things away. Laurie had convinced me to get rid of half my stuff. She didn't identify as a consumer, she said, she identified as a human. The less she bought into consumer culture, the more human she felt, the more free, and I would too, she said – though I suspected that, really, she just wanted me to take up less space when we moved. Anyway, getting rid of stuff hadn't made me feel free. I'd barely even noticed. Just sometimes, I'd open a drawer and be surprised to find it empty.

I distracted myself by ushering for Conservatory auditions, next year's intake. Meeting the singers at reception, showing them to the warm-up room, standing outside the door and hearing them sing. A million sopranos who looked just like me.

And then the ultimate distraction. The day before I left, Marieke called me into her office. They were casting me as Musetta in *La Bohème*.

Of course, we don't normally use first years for the big roles – she said. – Not for our main productions. You'll have a cover who'll be properly rehearsed, and if we don't think you're up to it by March, she'll step in. But the Director saw your Manon, and he's keen to have you.

The fog of purposelessness lifting, the cycle of creation starting again. Getting the score out of the library, seeing the notes on the page and thinking what I'd build.

Back home, though, it was harder to distract myself. The nights were so dark there and so quiet, no traffic, the birds only singing at the right time of day. Mum's hands were cracked, her knuckles raw with washing, and Dad moved round her, silent and obedient, always careful not to get in her way, like a good but dull child. Everything I did, she observed – *you're not going to cut that with that knife, are you? You're not going to use that towel, are you? You're not going to put that cup on the table, are you?* – until I grew uncertain, became worried instinctively about things I knew didn't matter. It was hard not to let Max fill my head then, a favourite song I'd play over and over and over. I tried to stop myself. I went for long walks. Watched TV with them in the evenings. Practised at the upright in the hall, trying to find a way into Musetta, that carefree woman who wants everyone to look at her. She seemed unimaginably different from me – but not really – not really – because that super-sexy aria is a front, isn't it? He doesn't notice her anymore. That's what it's about. She's in pain. I used images of Max to make her come alive, and tried to frame them in my head as memory, not hope.

On my first night back, we sat at our places for dinner and Dad poured us some wine. A treat because I was home. They didn't normally drink.

Cheers – he said. – Nice to have her back, isn't it?

Mum nodded.

Thanks – I said.

After that, they made conversation as though I'd never left and had nothing new to tell them. We talked about the Christmas films we'd watch, the end of term panto at the school where Dad taught geography, who Mum had bumped into in the street earlier, when we should decorate the tree. I'd drunk the best part of the bottle by myself before Dad said – so how are you liking it in London then? Changed your mind yet?

I hadn't been gone twenty-four hours, and already I missed the rhythms of the city, its beat and its breath – the smell of Tooting market, spice and meat – the night bus with Laurie, being swung through the streets, like we were on a fairground ride, too quick round the corners, and all the bright lights outside – the Polish supermarket I went to sometimes, odd comfort in unfamiliar products, in the sound of a language I knew nothing about.

It's always new — I said. — You could walk all day and never get to the edge.

Why would you want to do that? — Mum asked.

Never mind. No, is the answer. I haven't changed my mind.

You're getting by ok? — Dad asked. — With money?

Fine, yeah.

How much is it you're earning?

My parents didn't see money as private, I suppose because they'd never had much of it. Growing up, I always knew exactly what things cost. School trips, cake and hot chocolate after swimming, new shoes. The shopping list for the week was always stuck on the fridge, the price next to each item, and they'd total it up before the big shop, go to the supermarket with the right amount of cash. Dad still got paper copies of the phone bill. He'd highlight the calls he considered excessive, pin it to the corkboard in the kitchen.

Well, it varies — I said. — Not the same each month. Enough, though. You don't need to worry.

Mum was looking out into the garden, face carefully neutral, like she thought any engagement with my life in London might be mistaken for approval.

So, do you not want to hear about my course then? — I asked. I still entertained a vague hope, I suppose, that if I expressed what I did in the right way, it might inspire enthusiasm.

Dad said, well, yes, of course, and I started telling them about *Manon*. The scale of it, the prestige. I wanted to show her something she'd have to look at.

It was in the Conservatory's theatre — I said. — And we had a proper orchestra, not just a piano, even though it was only scenes. The biggest audience I've ever sung for, too, and I thought I'd be really scared, but actually there wasn't time to get nervous. I only found out I'd be performing on the day. And Marieke — she's the Head of Department — she was really impressed. They've given me a main role in the next full opera, which is a big deal for a first year.

The director they've got in is pretty well known. He often works with Conservatory students again once they've graduated, so it's really good for him to know me, and—

But why didn't you tell us? – Mum said. – About the show. We would have come.

Well, I only found out on the day. You wouldn't have made it down on time.

Your dad could have driven us.

It's quite far.

Even so.

The truth was, I hated my parents coming to hear me. They always focused insistently on the wrong things – how long it would take to drive there, how much the tickets cost, whether there'd be an interval to go to the loo – and the whole experience was diminished, became mundane and ordinary, and then I'd feel guilty for thinking that, which made it even worse. Mum would always get upset, and we'd have an argument about something stupid – whether I'd been short with her when I left dinner to warm up, or whether I'd put my dirty shoes in the same bag as my clean clothes when I'd changed into concert dress. I wasn't ever convinced they enjoyed the music either. They never said much afterwards, and their compliments were always things like – *that was much better than that last one you did* – and I'd petulantly say – *why, what was wrong with the last one?* – and Mum would tell me to stop being such a diva, and we'd drive home in silence.

Well, I'm sorry – I said. – Next time.

There was a little pause.

It's so quiet here – I said.

I noticed Mum was looking at me in a funny way.

What?

You talk differently, that's all.

What does that even mean? – I said, but she'd already stood up to clear the plates. I realised – a habit with her watching me, automatic – I'd spent so much time cutting my food up small, I'd barely touched it.

*

Mum must have spoon-fed me until I was at primary school, because I remember it. My chair turned to face her, the clink of metal on teeth. Even when I was older, she still cut all my food up into bite-sized pieces before she gave me the plate. The same in my lunchbox. Sandwiches with crusts removed, sliced into fingers. Grapes peeled and cut in half. Cereal bars taken out of their packets, divided into squares and wrapped in clingfilm. Food had to be made safe, she said, and so I should never eat at a friend's house. A few times – when their dinner was too tempting, or I was too embarrassed to say I wasn't allowed – I did anyway and, back home, I'd have to force down another full meal so she wouldn't know. *Why aren't you eating?* – she'd say anxiously, when I could only pick. – *What's wrong? Are you ill?*

She had worked as a nurse before I was born, and everything was a potential symptom. My body was an object of constant scrutiny. Every morning before school, she made me sit on the bottom step so she could take my temperature. She combed my hair several times a day to look for lice, plucked out bits of fluff and examined them. She weighed me on Saturday mornings, increased or reduced my food intake if the number didn't please her. She sat with me when I was in the bath and checked my skin for marks.

To keep my body safe, there were many rules. I wasn't allowed to turn on the TV by myself. I wasn't allowed to climb onto a chair to reach a high shelf or to use any knife, not even a blunt one. I wasn't allowed to boil the kettle or touch my face or eat fruit with my hands. I wasn't allowed to climb trees. I begged for a bike, but she said no. I wasn't allowed to use toilets outside our house – not even the school ones – unless I promised to hover without touching the seat, and I wasn't allowed to wear my uniform at home. She made me take it off in the hall as soon as I got back, so she could put it straight in the wash. I wasn't allowed to sleep over with friends or to go to birthday parties with activities she considered unsafe – paintballing or rollerblading or Laser Quest. When we took trips – which wasn't often – she didn't let me talk on public transport. She forbid me from touching poles on trains or from pressing the bell on buses. Sometimes she wouldn't press it either, and so if no one else wanted to get off, we'd miss our stop and have to walk back.

The routine examinations of my body were connected to the rules, I knew that. If I didn't follow them, my body would be damaged, and my mum would be able to see that the moment she looked at it – though it wasn't always clear to me how. Sometimes the connection between an activity and the potential harm it might cause was obvious. Other times, I wasn't so sure, and she never provided much explanation, not even when I asked, she'd just say – *it's not safe, Anna*. Those rules were the most frightening – the ones I didn't understand. They meant I couldn't trust myself to read the world properly. I didn't seem to know instinctively what was dangerous, what could cause me harm, make me ill. I needed her to tell me.

Other children didn't live by the same rules as me, but I didn't doubt my mum, not when I was little. She took more notice of me than my friends' mums did of them. More notice than Dad took too. He was home from school late most days. Sometimes, when it was just me and him, I'd ask him a question he'd think was clever, and then he'd get down an atlas or draw me a diagram to explain, but mostly he'd read his book and I'd play by myself. Mum gave me all her attention. She bought me lovely presents and baked my favourite biscuits and gave me the most elaborate hairstyles. Twenty minutes before I had to leave for school, she'd sit me on her bed and braid it tightly, and when I stood up, there'd be bits of my hair, broken off, all over my skirt.

But the new restrictions brought in for my teenage years – no shaving, no make-up, no social media, no staying out late – clipped my fledgling attempts at adulthood and marked me as different. For the first time, I examined the rules. I looked them right in the face and saw them for what they mostly were – pure, irrational fear dressed up as reason. I began to flirt with hazards. Said I was going to someone's house, then got the bus into town instead. Smoked in the woods with Tara until I was sick in the bushes. Lost my virginity, age fifteen, in an upstairs room at a party – someone's older brother, back from uni – watching the luminous hands on the bedside clock tick round, trying to think of an excuse to leave by 10 p.m., when my dad would be downstairs to pick me up.

My attempts at rebellion were tentative, though, and short-lived, largely because I didn't really enjoy them. I felt too guilty, like I was doing something horrible to Mum, knowing how upset she'd be if she found out – and, anyway, I was afraid too. Fear had become instinctive to me by then, even though I knew it wasn't rational, like the automatic dizzying rush looking down from a height though there's no chance of falling. At parties, I often pretended to drink. When guys who didn't go to my school asked for my number, I'd give it to them with one digit wrong. Whole evenings could be ruined for me by friends taking photos and putting them online – I'd stay up all night afterwards, typing my name into Google, checking that nothing came up.

At weekends, often, even while I resented her for it, I preferred to stay home and be a child with Mum, just like she wanted. *Why would you go and see that film? It had terrible reviews* – she'd say, if I asked to go to the cinema with friends that evening, or – *I didn't think you even liked Rachel, why would you want to go to her party?* – and it was easiest to agree. Instead, Saturday nights, in our pyjamas by 6 p.m., we'd divide up packets of Haribo, making sure we each got the exact same number and type of sweets, and then we'd watch reruns of *Blind Date* – her favourite programme, she'd taped every episode when it was on in the nineties. We'd sit with our backs to the TV so, like the contestants, we couldn't see the men, and at the end we'd pick with them, which one we liked best. Dad would come in while we had our faces buried in the back of the sofa, were giggling about one of Cilla's smutty jokes, and he'd say, bemused – *you're both completely mad.* Back at school on Mondays, though, all talk was about that weekend. If someone asked me – *what did you get up to?* – I'd say I'd had family commitments or too much work or I'd been unwell, that's why they hadn't seen me out. I'd feel then like life was happening somewhere far away from me, and I wasn't even sure I knew what it was.

When I was seventeen, my form tutor asked if I'd thought about university.

I want to do Italian – I said. – Maybe Spanish as well.

I had no particular reason for this, just that studying languages brought into my mind an image of endless space – cafés outside, a blue sky, no walls. It seemed the antithesis to my parents' house. It was only by leaving, I thought, that I could become a different person – someone who wasn't afraid.

My form tutor taught music, and he told me I should join the choir.

We're doing Spanish folksongs – he said. – Improve your language skills. Good settings, not too hard. You'll like them.

Maybe – I said.

Something for your application too. You don't do enough outside school, do you? Universities want to see other interests as well, you know, not just grades.

So I said fine, I'd try it. I'd played the piano a bit as a child, could read music already, and I'd always liked singing, even though I hadn't tried properly for years – only hymns in assembly, some carols at Christmas. I went along to the first rehearsal, expecting to be bored, so how much I enjoyed it was a surprise. It lit up some part of my brain I'd forgotten about – the part that lets you play with pieces of plastic moulded into humans for hours when you're little, absorbed totally in their stories you've imagined.

A few weeks in, the teacher asked if anyone wanted to have a go at the solo part and, without stopping to think, I put up my hand. I sang it through, and he asked me to do it in the concert. On the day, everyone seemed to expect me to be afraid, but I wasn't, not really. I liked that I could do something that made other people scared. I liked discovering that I – who teachers often had to ask to repeat my answer several times, my voice was so quiet – could fill a room with sound.

*

I sat cross-legged on the sofa, picking the toffees out of the festive selection and throwing the wrappers in the fire. Mum was just back from her last shift before Christmas. She'd started working as a ward clerk when I was a teenager. Oncology department at the local hospital. I could never tell if this was an odd choice of job for her, or the perfect one – a way of keeping everything that scared her within sight and controllable. I imagined her clean and ordered days, making sure everything was in the right place, a stickler for the rules, all visitors directed to the hand sanitiser.

She was sitting on the floor, stapling Christmas cards onto lengths of ribbon.

He's shown me the ones that are meant to be funny – she said. – But they don't make sense to me.

Dad had got into YouTube. He was at the kitchen table with his laptop, letting the videos autoplay.

He trusts Google – she said. – Google always finds videos he likes, he says.

She looked up at me.

Stop doing that, Anna. There's plastic in those.

Sorry.

She tied the ribbon she'd finished round a picture hook and hung it off the mantelpiece, underneath the framed photographs that were nearly all of me. Me smiling in my uniform, my graduation picture, a blown-up copy of my most recent headshot.

She cut another length of ribbon from the reel.

So what happens next year then? – she asked.

What do you mean?

When you finish your course? You're not really planning to stay in London, are you?

But I don't finish next year – I said. – It's a two-year course. There's another year after.

She definitely knew this, but regularly pretended she didn't.

Seems like a lot – she said. – After all those years you spent in that other place too. Five, wasn't it? Could have become a doctor in that time.

That's an original remark, Mother.

Still. Have they not taught you to sing yet?

This was how Mum dealt with things outside her experience. By acting like they were stupid, made no sense at all. I tried not to show my irritation.

Well, that's not really how it works – I said. – Opera school's more about professional development anyway. Learning roles and that sort of thing. Not technique.

But so what will you do after?

I'll probably apply to some young artists programmes. A few opera companies have them.

More training?

Not really, no. You get a salary, and you do covers and small roles. They're proper contracts. Or I might get cast – maybe in bigger roles – without that. Marieke's well connected. If she likes you, she introduces you to people who'll hear you. Helps you out. So it all sort of depends.

And she likes you?

I think so.

We were quiet for a minute. I picked out the purple chocolates and arranged them in a ring around the box.

And have you met someone? – she asked, in a tone of such forced casualness, I realised this was what she'd wanted to ask all along. – A boy?

For a moment, I considered telling her about Max. About his job, about his flat, about the places we'd been together. I wanted her to see how far away I'd gone. How I was too far now – could she really not see that? – to ever come back. She ripped one of the cards off the ribbon and repositioned it, and I thought of the night when he'd held my arms up above my head and said – *don't move* – and he'd bitten the soft flesh just above my hip, and moved down to the inside of my thigh, and it had started to hurt too much, so I'd reached to cover it and he'd said – *I said don't move* – how shame had fed perversely into desire, and the bruises that flowered there.

I haven't met anyone, Mum – I said. – I'm very busy.

I tried to prise my fingers off the memory.

I saw Tara on Christmas Eve. She took the baby's hat off and smoothed his tufts of hair, put him on her lap so he could bang the table.

God – she said. – Look at you. I'm so jealous I could cry.

Really? Why?

Just a vibe you've got. Freedom. That sexy little outfit.

I didn't think this could possibly be sincere. I was wearing leggings and one of Laurie's jumpers I'd accidentally packed, which said *dump him* on the chest. Tara had barely looked at me, anyway, distracted by holding her hand against the baby's red cheek, checking if he was warm.

Well, thanks – I said. – I try.

I'd known Tara since primary school, and we'd stayed friends all through our teenage years, even though she was much more popular than me. Her parents were permissive and often absent – the dream combination – so she'd hosted regular parties. She kissed me at one of them once, when we were fifteen or so. She wanted to make some boy notice her. I thought about it for nights after, that kiss – the warmth and softness of her mouth, the taste of her dad's rum. I thought I was in love with her. Cried at her indifference. I think I probably was a bit in love with her, or in love with her life. Everything seemed to come easily to her. She did well at school, had lots of friends. We'd often talked about living together in London one day, so I was disappointed when she chose a uni close to home so she could visit her boyfriend every weekend. When she moved back right after graduation to be with him.

The baby stretched his hands towards me.

He's very pretty – I said, then thought she might have rather I'd said handsome.

He is, isn't he?

The baby made us strangers. We were meant to talk mainly about him, I understood that, but I didn't know the right questions. I ate the cream off my hot chocolate with a spoon, and she told me about feeding and sleeping and weaning. The baby was a cult she'd joined, and I had to pretend I didn't remember what she'd been like before.

So, tell me everything – she said. – Give me news of the real world.

She said it kind of mocking herself, but I felt like she must be semi-serious, and I didn't want to make her feel bad. So I told her about London, about Laurie, I touched on Max, but everything in the negative. She made sympathetic noises at me while trying to stop the baby from eating her spoon, and I started to feel depressed.

She gave him to me to hold while she went to the loo. I turned him round to face me. His pupils were so big they took up most of his eyes – that look most babies have, totally open, totally guileless, though I suppose that's actually what babies are, and not just a look – the way he let me hold him, how he reached out to grab my hair and face. I wondered at what stage, biologically, that became more harmful then helpful. When he'd start to pull away and scream when dumped on the lap of a stranger. I was glad when Tara came and took him back.

By evening, the horror of nostalgia had got the better of me. The rituals I expected would tap into some deep childhood feeling now felt meaningless to me, though I still insisted on performing them, like an actor reading through a play to an empty hall. I made cupcakes and drew Christmassy things on top of them with writing icing. I spent an hour washing up, making sure nothing held any traces of use, and I wondered who would eat them anyway. I went for a walk with Dad. Because I couldn't see his face properly in the dark, I said – *how's Mum doing? Is she ok?* – but he acted like he didn't know what I meant. He climbed into a neighbour's garden and cut some holly off their tree. I remembered one year, Christmas Eve, he'd stopped me suddenly in the street, and said – *shh, listen* – and then there were bells, crisp and sharp in the darkness, like the crunch of ice underfoot. We went home and started watching *It's a Wonderful Life*, but in one of the breaks, there was an advert shot at Highbury Fields, and I'd already said – *oh that's not too far from where me and Laurie are moving* – before I remembered I hadn't told them yet. The TV was put on mute. Mum asked me question after question – *what happened? Anna, come on, I know when you're lying. Did something happen? Where are you moving? Why? Do you know that area? How long's the walk from the station?* – which descended into an argument that made so little sense I couldn't get any hold on what she was upset about to reassure her. In the end, she said – *fine, of course, you do what you want, anyway, you always do* – and I went upstairs. I had a box of matches from a restaurant I'd been to with Max. I lit one and let it burn down, then I lit another and then another, until the box was empty and my room filled with smoke.

On Christmas Day, I heard from him. A message saying *Happy Christmas*. And I was happy, even though I told myself not to be, until I read it again and thought that maybe he hadn't sent it just to me. Maybe he'd sent it to all his contacts, although that didn't seem like the sort of thing he'd do.

Then there were more rituals. Church with my parents. The new priest got people to stand up and talk about their presents, then tenuously tied that to God, and Mum got angry with me when I was snide.

He's a lovely man – she said.

Christmas lunch had become quieter as each grandparent had died, and now it was just us. I noticed that my parents didn't talk to each other much, addressed most of what they said to me, and I wondered if they spoke at all when I wasn't there.

After lunch, I sang some carols, and Dad had drunk a couple of glasses of wine, so he got sentimental. We opened presents under the tree. One Christmas, Mum told me not to touch the fairy lights – they were electric, she said, and that meant they could kill you – but then one day, alone in the room, I touched one. I couldn't stop myself, wanted to see what would happen. I spent the rest of Christmas terrified, wondering how long it would take to die.

Then there was the heaviness of Christmas afternoon, like a Sunday that wouldn't end. We half-heartedly played Scrabble, the only game that really worked with three, and none of us liked it.

I drafted messages to Max — some funny, some flippant, some flir-
tatious, some emotional, some cold. I realised that none of them
could get out of him what I wanted him to say, so I deleted them.

Then it was the nothing days, and then I could leave.

Let us know when your opera is — Mum said at the station. —
We'll come.

I will do — I said, knowing even as I formed the words that I
wouldn't. I was exhausted. It was exhausting, being around someone who watched you every moment, but didn't approve. A few
times over the past week, she'd left the room for a minute, and I'd
realised — a habit I hadn't known I had, until I started to sing — that
I'd been holding my breath.

They stood on the platform, and I got on the train and found them
again through the window. I felt guilty almost straightaway, looking
at them from a distance, and thinking about the stocking Mum still
put at the end of my bed, the dessert wine Dad got because I liked
it, my new jumper that exactly matched my eyes, and wondering
why, when it would cost me so little now, I found it so hard to be
kind. They waved and the train pulled away.

There were two women opposite me, discussing why they no
longer looked in mirrors.

If there's a mirror in a lift — one of them was saying — I go in backwards. And of course, it sometimes means you miss if you've got
toothpaste on your face, but on the whole — she said — I find it's worth it.

I put my headphones in, listened to the playlist for a recital I was
doing. There was perverse comfort in learning these stories of pain
and betrayal, imagining yourself at the centre of something tragic.
It made my decision less clear. Well, you can excuse basically any
form of bad behaviour, can't you, any mistreatment, if you've learnt
everything you know about love from art. This woman pursued him
— this one stayed with him, even though he hurt her, though he
treated her badly — she wanted him even though he didn't really
love her, or loved someone else as well, because — listen — listen to
her feelings — hear how strong they are.

NINE

The first thing I noticed back at the Ps' was how strongly their house smelled of cabbage. I couldn't remember if it had always been like that. Maybe I'd gradually got used to it until I didn't smell it anymore, like how when you swim, you're cold at first, and then you're not. Body and water become the same. Maybe I'd started to smell like cabbage too.

The house was dark, but I could see a strip of light under the door at the front and I could hear that the TV was on. I knocked on the door and went in.

Sorry to disturb you – I said. – I just wanted to say I'm back.

I had to lean round the Christmas tree to see them. They'd put it right at the entrance, in front of the sofa, so that the door brushed against it when it opened, and all the bells jangled. It was huge, and thick with ornaments – red and blue and pink and yellow and gold tinsel, several clashing strings of multicoloured lights, a sea of gnomes.

Which one of you is that then, haa? – asked Mrs P, without turning round.

Her and Mr P were sitting on the sofa, watching *Bridget Jones*. They were on the final scene – the bit where it's snowing and she runs down the road in her pants. Mr P leant forward and pressed pause, but they didn't take their eyes off the screen.

It's Anna – I said. – Sorry, I also wanted to check you'd got my message? When I said we're leaving on the first? Is that ok?

Mr P started picking through the bowl of chocolates on the table. He extracted a purple one for himself, and he handed Mrs P a blue. She unwrapped it and sat poised to pop it in her mouth.

The new girls're in on the third — she said. — So make sure it's all cleared out, right, all your things gone. The first, haa? Doesn't give us much time.

Mr P pressed play, and I went upstairs. It was dark all the way to the top of the house, and my room had that cold feeling of abandonment, though I hadn't left it long, as if it knew. I emptied out the rucksack I'd taken to my parents' place, dumped everything on the floor, and I opened my wardrobe and pulled out all the drawers in the dresser, started throwing my stuff on the bed. The dresses I'd worn with him, this one he'd said he liked. I went out onto the landing to find the cat. I wanted to cry holding him, but he struggled free. He'd never liked me much.

The next day, Laurie came back. It was New Year's Eve, and we were going to a party at someone's house — one of Laurie's friends she said I'd met before, but I couldn't remember.

She sat on my bed, drinking wine from a mug and pulling the hairs out of her nipples with my tweezers.

That seems like a lot of effort — I said. — Given that your hair's blonde anyway. I really don't think men notice that sort of thing.

I don't give a fuck what men notice — said Laurie. — Men literally never notice anything. And anyway, you're the only person who's seen my nipples in weeks.

Well, thanks — I said. — I'm flattered.

Heard from cuntwad, then? — she asked.

Not really, no.

Big surprise. Not going to bail on me tonight to see him, then?

Not tonight. Not ever. I told you.

Easy to say when he hasn't asked you. He's not even in London, is he? Do you even know? He hasn't told you, has he?

Is there a particular reason you're being like this? — I said. — Or have you just missed me?

I was dressed and doing my face in the mirror. Laurie kept insisting she was ready too, but she was wearing only her bra and dotty pyjama trousers.

So, when I went home – she said. – I brought these chocolates back. A big box. Just to be nice. Nothing special. And when I got them out, my mum kind of grimaced and was like – *where did those come from?* – and when I said I'd bought them for us, she didn't say anything, she just picked them up and looked at the ingredients, and then she said – *packed full of additives, aren't they? How long do you think they've been on the shelf for, hmm?* – and then she said – *well, the thing is darling, we already have chocolates, so it was very kind of you, but I really don't know what we're going to do with them.* And my sister wouldn't eat them because she's apparently now allergic to dairy. And her kids couldn't eat them because they're not allowed sugar, not even at Christmas. And every time people came round, my mum got them out and put them on the table, right next to her homemade truffles and the selection she'd got from this hamper my sister'd bought from Fortnum & Mason, and she said – *oh, and Laurie got these* – with this forced smile, like I'd just done a really shit performance on the recorder and she was hoping that everyone would have the sense not to hurt my feelings – and they all said – *oh lovely* – and then didn't eat them. I ate the entire box myself. The bourgeois cunts.

Laurie put a lot of effort into pretending not to be rich. Her accent gave her away though, however much she tried to finish words early. She hauled herself off the bed and went to put on a dress.

So that's why you're in a bad mood? – I asked. – Because of the chocolates?

You can be very basic sometimes – she said. – Oh, and when she was driving me to the station earlier, my mum said that they'd talked about it, and they were willing to pay for me to freeze my eggs if I didn't meet someone soon. Late Christmas present. I started talking about climate change and overpopulation, and she said she knew I only said things like that to annoy her, and that, anyway, it wasn't attractive to always have such strong opinions about things, and it wasn't any wonder I didn't have a boyfriend. Next time I say I'm going home, remind me not to. Please. For the love of God. Just say *don't*.

I sometimes wondered if Laurie made these stories up entirely. I'd met her mum. She'd taken us both for lunch when she was in London. She'd seemed nice enough.

Laurie topped up the mug and we finished the wine, our different coloured lipsticks making smudgy prints on either side of the rim. By the time she was ready to go, she was drunk. She linked her arm through mine on the way to the Tube.

Isn't it funny? – she said. – I love you so much. I love you probably more than anyone else in the world. Isn't that strange?

She looked a bit teary, and I felt bad for thinking mean thoughts.

Some time before midnight, a group of us went outside to try and see fireworks. We couldn't – they were all too far away – but we heard the bangs. It would've been too cloudy to see them properly anyway, and it wasn't really dark, London never is. The sky was grey and flat, and a couple of Chinese lanterns floated aimlessly across it, made fuzzy with cloud, their light gone out.

The party was in a big house a long walk from any station, and I didn't know many people there. A handful of Laurie's theatre crowd – mostly actors who'd been in her plays at uni – a few others by sight. I hadn't worked my way into that group. It was hard to join in with their sort of social life if you had any other commitments, the evenings that started whenever – none of them had much else to do – and meandered on to whenever too. I never really knew what they were talking about, either. They all had a habit of starting sentences with – *of course* – and then going on to say something that I would never in a million years have thought. Things like – *of course, if we take as a given that all human experience is fundamentally solipsistic, theatre with dialogue becomes inherently nonsensical.* The more obscure or controversial what they were saying was, the more they acted like it was obvious. The first time I spent an evening with them, it took me so long to work out what any of them meant, I barely said anything at all. Laurie said afterwards – almost impressed, I think – that they'd found me aloof.

I'd been stuck chatting to Mil for the past hour, both of us scanning behind the other one's head, looking for someone to save us. Mil was Laurie's friend from uni – a theatre director, doing quite well for herself, but she never put on any of Laurie's plays, which caused tension. She was relentlessly serious and rarely engaged much with anything I said, letting me talk, and only occasionally exclaiming – *now* that's *interesting* – almost, it seemed, in surprise. I'd come outside hoping to find Laurie – I'd lost her early on – but she wasn't there. She'd been courting oblivion all night. I'd never seen her drink so much. As soon as we'd arrived, she'd got this hard, determined look in her eye, and the next time I bumped into her, in the queue to the toilet, she was drinking wine out of a pint glass and asking the girl next to her if she thought it was unfeminist to like being spanked.

Outside, a guy started talking to me. I hadn't met him before, I don't think. I didn't catch his name because I wasn't really listening, though I guess he probably told me. He was new in London, I think he said, or maybe I said I was. Someone started a countdown to midnight. When it got there, we all hugged and someone started singing Auld Lang Syne, but no one really knew the words so it petered out quite quickly, and we all went back inside. The guy asked me if I wanted another drink and I said sure.

Back inside, people kept arriving. Things were starting to deteriorate. I wasn't sure whose house it was – it seemed too nice to be lived in by anyone at the party, and no one there appeared to care what happened to it. People were smoking, letting ash drop down the crack between the sofa cushions, or tapping it into the vase by the window. Someone had lit a bunch of candles – the main lights were off – but they hadn't bothered to put them in holders or on coasters. Wax dribbled down onto the table, the carpet. The table was sticky with fluids, and glasses had been discarded round the edges of the room, stacked up against the walls. They kept getting kicked over in the dark and so the floor had a slight crunch to it, as glass ground into carpet. If you didn't look too closely, it felt like walking on snow.

I went and sat on the arm of the sofa. There was a long, theoretical discussion going on – something about art and sex and exploitation. Every time I thought they'd finished, someone else had something to say – *that's not sexual violence, unless you think that sex is inherently violent and misogynistic, which is apparently a fashionable thing to think these days* – and so on it went. It was like being on an endless, monotonous journey, no view from the window.

I checked my phone and, seeing there was no message from him, I knew how much I'd expected one. *So I was right, then* – I thought. – *If I move one step away, make it anything but easy, he won't follow.* It didn't feel good being right. There was a message from Laurie though – *I've left* – she wrote. – *With Jack. Still got it.*

I wrote back – *still got what?* – but she didn't reply.

The discussion was still going. I considered leaving, but I didn't want to go back to the Ps' alone, to wake up in the morning and have things be the same. There was a little table by the sofa with a candle. I stuck each of my fingers into the melted wax to make little finger hats. I prodded the index finger of my right hand in deeper, so it was touching the wick, and I held it there. It took me a moment to notice it hurt.

When the guy I'd met outside came back with my drink, I finished it quickly and smiled at him.

That was nice – I said.

He asked me if I wanted another, and I said – sure.

We went to the kitchen together. There was no one in there, and the main light was on, just a bare bulb, so you could see all the crap piled up in the sink. He went over to the table and started picking up bottles to find out how much was in them, his feet squeaking as he moved on the lino. I sat on the floor, my back to the counter.

Here we go – he said.

He'd found vodka and some sort of mixer, not much left in that bottle. He sat down beside me and topped up my glass. He started to talk. He worked for a start-up, he said, but he was really creative.

Really creative? — I asked. — Or creative, really?

What's the difference? — he said.

Whenever I finished my glass, he filled it up, more vodka than tonic, undrinkably strong, though, somehow, I drank it. He looked at me drinking and smiled approvingly, like I was a child eating up all my vegetables. One of those men, then. One of the ones who wants you to drink as much as they can make you. Doesn't back himself. Quite sweet, I suppose, in a way. He wasn't bad looking. He was wearing an awful shirt, but he smelled nice. I thought — well, who knows, maybe he could make me happy, why not, it can't be that hard. We kept drinking. He was telling me about his ex-girlfriend and some holiday they'd been on in Spain and how she'd kept their dog when they broke up and he missed him the most. We finished the vodka, and the only bottle left with anything in it was Baileys. He said he'd sort something, and he tipped it into a pint glass, nearly up to the brim.

I'm not drinking that — I said. — I'm not twelve.

It's fine. Trust me. I'm not done.

He topped the rest up with milk from the fridge.

Well, that's much more grown-up — I said.

It's a White Russian.

It's really not — I said, but I took a sip, and it tasted good.

Stomach lining, see? — he said. — I'm looking after you.

We passed the glass between us, and he explained to me his idea for a novel. It was about passengers in a Tube carriage, he said, connected by chance events. He thought they'd all have the same birthday too, though he wasn't exactly sure why. I was starting to feel quite drunk, and I think he was too. I saw that his leg was touching mine — it hadn't been the last time I'd looked. He put his hand on my hand and said — *what did you do to your finger?* — and even after I told him, he left it there. Then he stopped saying anything and I knew he was trying to work out if he'd done enough groundwork to kiss me, and so I kept talking, on and on, brightly, about nothing, because – because – well, because he would kiss me and then he'd say – *let's go back to mine* – and if I said, if I said – *ok, sure* – because I might, after all, why not, I was young, wasn't I, I could do it – if I said – *ok, sure* – well then, what next? His flat. He worked for a start-up, right, so it would be one of those personalityless newbuilds, lingering smell of fresh paint, recently unpackaged carpets, like a school building after summer holidays. I'd stand in his kitchen, not able to say anything that would change things, anything that would make him go – *oh* – just on and on like this, my worst, my most insincere self, and that would be what he wanted. Next – his unloved little boy's room – the having to pretend to enjoy the fumbling I wouldn't even feel, and how his breath would taste when the milk went sour – how he'd get on top of me and my legs would split apart like a chicken being carved and I'd look up at his ceiling, at the fine, long crack that arched there like a smile.

Hey, is that your phone? – he said. – Do you need to get it?

What?

I fumbled to find it in my bag, then stared at it. It was Max.

Anna – his voice filled the room. – Where are you?

There was noise in the background, and I heard him say something to someone, and then the sound of him walking and it was quiet.

I'm out – I said. – At a party.

I was worried.

Why?

Because you didn't pick up.

Yes – I said. – I did.

No, before. I've called you more than once.

Oh right. I didn't hear it.

I moved the guy's hand off my leg and stood up.

Where are you?

What? I told you. I'm at a party.

No. Yes. I mean, where, where are you, whose party, where is it?

His intonation was off, stresses in the wrong places, like English wasn't his first language, and I realised he was drunk. I didn't think I'd ever known him to be drunk before, not properly, and I liked it, it made me smile — that weakness in him, knowing it was me that he called.

Friend of Laurie's — I said. — Somewhere east. Nothing special.

I started walking out of the kitchen.

Are you leaving? — the guy said.

Who was that? — said Max.

Friend of Laurie's.

I pushed past the people in the hall, and went and sat at the top of the stairs.

Are you drunk?

What? No. Not really. Are you?

You never said anything about the bracelet. Did you like it?

Sorry, yes. Yes, I did. It was nice. Thank you.

Why haven't you been replying to my messages? — he asked.

Your messages? Well, I mean, you've hardly sent me any.

He laughed.

Are you feeling neglected? — he said.

What?

I'm back next week.

I remembered the line I'd rehearsed.

I don't think I should see you again — I said.

Oh, really? — he sounded amused. — Can I ask why not?

I just don't — I whispered.

Well, that seems a bit childish, doesn't it? Shouldn't we at least discuss it?

I didn't say anything.

He kept talking — *were you not having fun?* — he was saying. — *I thought you were. And I know that last time was a bit, well, not so much fun, but look* — and while he was talking, I saw the guy downstairs come out of the kitchen and say something to the people in the hall. They shrugged. He was looking for me. I crept up onto the landing.

Next week – Max was saying. – Anna? Are you listening? I'm back next week. Let's meet then.

And I said – ok then – because was he not right to want more for me than this, I thought.

You will?

Yes – I said. – I will.

I felt this great sense of relief saying it, like I'd spent the past couple of weeks trying to stuff myself into a box, to pull the lid over my head, and I'd only just realised that I was suffocating myself and I'd let myself out.

Max? – I said. – Max, I—

He'd already gone.

The next morning, Laurie came and got in my bed.

Might as well get used to it – she said.

We were moving into Mil's place, and she only had one room free, so we'd be sharing. Cheaper that way, anyway, so it wasn't all bad. My stuff was packed into two suitcases by the door, and Laurie had squeezed hers into a case and two backpacks. She pulled my duvet up to her chin. Her eyes were rimmed with red and she smelled of wine.

How was your night? – she asked.

Fine.

I hear you ran out on Gus.

How do you know that? I mean, it's also not true. Ran out? What does that even mean?

People talk – she said. – He's a nice guy. I can give you his number. You should just have a drink with him, have some fun, it'll be good for you. You have to move on sometime, you know.

Maybe – I said, because I knew she was trying to be helpful, but I hated the clinical way people talked about moving on, like it was purely anatomical. Fuck someone else – a quick, routine operation, no side effects – then you'll be well again.

I didn't want her to press any harder. I tried to distract her.

So, who the hell's Jack then? – I asked.

You get to a point – she said – where you stop wanting sex to be a competition, who cares the least, you know. If you manage to make the other person think it's you, then you've won. I think I've got there. I've had enough. It's boring. It's exhausting. I'm tired. You'll see when you get to my age.

You're really not that much older than me.

You'll see – she said again.

So, how do you know that Jack – it is Jack, isn't it? – doesn't care?

Because he's engaged to someone else. Jess, her name is.

Oh. Where was she last night, then?

Is that really the first question that occurs to you?

Kind of. I was just wondering, you know, logistically, how that worked.

Laurie gave me a scathing look. Her eyelashes and eyebrows were pale, almost white, and what with that and the pink tinge round her pupils, she looked very vulnerable all of a sudden, like a newborn mouse.

She was in South Africa, I think. With family. That's where she's from.

Oh, right.

God, I'm embarrassing – she said. – I'm so embarrassing. When I think about myself, I'm embarrassed.

Not as embarrassed as him, I'd imagine.

Well, thanks. That's sweet.

I meant, I'm sure he's embarrassed about himself. Not that he's embarrassed about you.

Right.

We lay there for a little bit without talking.

We should really try to leave – Laurie said, eventually. – Before they kick us out.

Can you help me with something first?

I showed her where I'd dropped the bracelet. Thirty minutes later, coat hanger and chewing gum, we had it. I fastened it round my wrist.

That's pretty – she said. – I don't think I've seen it before.

I don't know. Yeah, maybe you haven't.

I went over to his early in the evening, around six, but it felt much later than it was. I was singing at the hotel that night, so I couldn't stay long. I'd been in bed with a cold for half the day and, by the time I got up, it was already dark. I tried to put concealer on the dry bits round my nose, but that made it look worse, like paint flaking off a rough wall.

When he opened the door, he pulled me in and kissed me.

Fuck, you're cold – he said.

I put the backs of my hands on his cheeks.

Don't – he grabbed hold of my wrists and held them behind my back.

Ow – I said. – I'm ill. You have to be nice to me.

We'll see – he said.

But he was. He ran me a bath, and he sat on the lid of the toilet and talked to me while I lay in it. He didn't seem about to mention last time, so I said – *things got a bit strange, didn't they?* – and he just said – *it's ok, let's not talk about it* – and I said – *ok* – because I didn't really want to anyway. It seemed a long time ago now, and irrelevant, like looking at a photograph you can't remember taking.

The lighting was low. I could see the ripples of water reflected on the ceiling. It was very calm and quiet in there, like being in a high-walled garden, no one to look in. I kept the bracelet on and dangled my arm out over the edge of the bath. He reached out and stroked the inside of my wrist.

Pretty – he said.

Where were you when you called me? – I asked.

When?

New Year's Eve.

Oh right. I was with a group of friends. We rented this house in the country. We do it every year.

That sounds fun – I said. – Which friends?

Not people you know.

I meant, how do you know them?

Oh, I see. Oxford. We were at university together.

I found it hard to see him in the context of an everyday life. To imagine his friends. In a way, I liked that about him, it made him more interesting, anyway. It's always disappointing seeing people in context – the tedium of their specifics, their banal connections with other people. They become like everyone else. He never was.

In bed, he spread his fingers out on my stomach, round my neck, on the insides of my thighs – his hands on me were erasure, wiping my skin clean, and soon my mind was dark and my body empty, only the parts he was touching lit up.

Afterwards, the city glittered outside the window like a million pairs of eyes and we were quiet. He never shut the curtains. They were too far away to see, he always said, and anyway, who cares if they do. He got up and took his laptop off the table, then came back with it. I liked watching him work, found it kind of fascinating – that he did something so important, so lucrative, and all of it was on that little screen.

I've got a couple of emails to write – he said. – I won't be long. Get yourself a drink.

It's ok. I have to go anyway.

Why?

I told you, didn't I? On the phone. I'm working tonight. My set starts at nine.

Oh right. Do you have to?

Do I have to what? Start at nine?

No. Go. Do you have to go?

Well, kind of. Yes.

He was frowning at something on the screen, then he turned and looked at me.

But what about your cold? – he said.

What do you mean, do I have to? You know I have to. I said I did.

Isn't it bad to sing when you're ill? – he said. – Given that jazz isn't good for you, anyway.

You sound like an American Puritan.

You know what I mean. For your voice.

I'd told him that Angela disapproved of the jazz, thought I should quit. It was sweet he remembered.

Up to you, obviously. But surely, they can find someone to cover if you're not well? It's not really worth it, is it?

I suppose – I said, imagining it, going out in the dark, walking over there, vocal warm-ups in the toilet – there was nowhere else to do it – being frowned at by the guests when they came in to pee, a bar full of suited men talking over me all evening, late home, the Tube.

Shouldn't you prioritise your actual career? – he said.

Well yes, but the thing is, I need the money.

How much would you get?

I told him.

That's nothing. Really, Anna, it's not worth it. I'll give it to you.

He reached down, found his trousers on the floor and pulled out his wallet. Then he counted out some notes and put them on my stomach. I could see them move up and down as I breathed in and out.

I heard my voice saying quite clearly – no – don't – and I was sure I'd said it out loud, but then I saw my hand reach out and take the money, and I saw myself stand up and find my handbag and tuck the money inside, and I knew that I hadn't said anything at all.

I won't make you sing for it – he said. – Total vocal rest, that's good for you, right? You don't even have to talk. Actually – he said, shutting his laptop screen, leaning over and biting my nipple – I'd prefer it if you didn't.

PART TWO

TEN

Half of January, he'd been in New York. He was just back. I wanted to stay in, but he wouldn't.

Cabin fever – he said.

He was leaning, palms flat against the window, forehead rested on knuckles, looking out. It was strangely quiet. You couldn't hear the rain, but you could see it, smashing against the glass, and the buildings opposite were fuzzy – pencil sketches half-erased by an ineffective rubber. It was nearly February now, and it had been like this for weeks, end-of-the-world weather that threatened never to end. I sat on the kitchen counter, circling my ankles, hearing them crack.

I've booked us somewhere – he said.

Cabin fever? You've only just got back.

He tipped his drink down, crunched on the ice, put the empty glass in the sink. Then he came and stood between my legs, hands on the outsides of my thighs. He looked very tired, with a thumbprint of blue bruised under each eye.

My hotel room was identical to this flat – he said. – Different view, that's all.

Did you not have a good trip?

It really wasn't that sort of thing.

Well, what about the evenings?

There weren't any evenings – he said.

This didn't seem to me to make a huge amount of sense, but I didn't push it. I wrapped my legs round his waist. I liked relearning him – not being able to picture him when he was away, not quite, and then seeing him again. The thrill of finding in his face all I'd seen there before. I nudged him closer with my heels, kissed him, and I tried not to wonder if he'd seen his wife in New York, if I'd be able to tell that by the way he tasted. I'd promised myself not to ask. Anyway, he tasted the same.

I've got a dress you left – he said. – I'll find it.

We'd had movement class that day. I was wearing old leggings, one of his shirts.

He poured himself another drink, and then got the dress. He sat on the bed and watched me change.

How are things in the house? – he asked. – Girls still driving you mad?

It's ok. Well, sharing a room with Laurie isn't ideal. I've had to sleep on the sofa a few nights you've been away. She's seeing some-one new.

Again? She gets through them, doesn't she?

She sees sleeping with lots of men as a feminist act – I said. – Although it mainly makes her miserable.

He laughed, and I felt disloyal.

Well, I hope she changes the sheets – he said.

Not every time. But she uses condoms. She's against the pill.

Anna, that's disgusting.

Using condoms?

What? No. Not changing the sheets.

Well, I guess so – I said. – But the washing machine's pretty much always on with other people's stuff, and there's no outdoor space to hang them so they stay damp for days. And anyway, I wear pyjamas.

God, I'm glad I'm a grown-up.

Fuck you.

I threw the shirt I'd taken off at his head. He lassoed me with it and pulled me onto his lap, then he kissed my shoulder blade and did up my zip.

You seem happy – he said.

You sound suspicious.

He laughed.

I am suspicious. I hate it when you're happy.

Then he said — *we really should go* — but he said it like he didn't really mean it, and he started kissing the back of my neck, and then I wanted to make him pleased with me.

I have some news, actually — I said. — Max? I went by the hotel before coming here. I quit.

He stopped kissing me, and I turned to look at him. I felt like I'd given him a present — something I'd thought carefully about, spent a lot of time in choosing — then seen that flicker on his face, almost imperceptible, the moment before he smiled, that showed he didn't really like it.

Oh — he said. — Really?

I waited for him to say — *that's great* — or something like that, but he didn't say anything, and then he said — *I don't understand. Why?*

Well, you were right — I said. — About it being a waste of my time. I'm free now. No more pointless late nights being hit on by wankers.

He raised an eyebrow.

No offence — I said. — You know what I mean. Time to concentrate on singing. Real singing. More free time too. You always say I'm too busy — I dared to add. — More time to see you.

Well, that is good — he said.

I stood up, then realised I had no reason to be standing.

Did you not think I should quit? — I said. — You kept saying I should.

Ever since I'd told him how much I got paid, Max had become increasingly critical about my job. Early January, before he went away, he turned up a few times, listened to my songs, watched as I self-consciously tried to be nice — like I was meant to be — to the men who spoke to me after. His presence embarrassed me, knowing what he thought of it all, and Malcolm found it hilarious too. *Does your fancy man take a cut of your earnings, then?* — he said to me once. I pretended not to know what he meant.

Max started to put on his coat.

Well, I certainly didn't think you should be doing that, no – he said. – But look, we're going to be late. Let's talk about it there, shall we?

It was still raining, so we got a taxi to the restaurant. We'd been there a few times before. It was off a quiet square, right in the middle of the City. Hidden. You'd never find it by chance. It had handwritten menus that changed each time we were there, and the manager knew Max by name. When we arrived, he came over, effusive, shook Max's hand and led us to our table.

Is this alright, sir?

It was next to a family – mother, father, two little girls. January tans, that spoke of wealth and winter holidays. The littler girl wore an alice band and a velvet dress, the bigger one, skinny jeans, a crop top that revealed her perfect pre-teen tummy. I expected he'd ask we be moved – that he shared my view on children and nice restaurants – but he said – *perfect, thank you* – and I saw him smile at them.

He hadn't mentioned the job since we'd left, and I wondered if I'd imagined his reaction. Once we'd sat, he started chatting about the square we were in, how the buildings all used to be part of a monastery before Henry VIII took them, used the church to store his hunting stuff.

Sensible man – I said. – I hate churches.

You hate them? That seems extreme.

My parents are quite religious. Well, my mum is anyway. Church every Sunday when I was little, enough to put anyone off. And Ella – one of my flatmates – she went to a convent school in Ireland. Sounds like the stuff of nightmares. She said they had to write these letters when they were thirteen or so. Letters to their future husbands, explaining why they'd saved themselves for them.

And did it work? Did they save themselves?

Well, she didn't. But lots of her friends did, apparently. Some of them, the ones who were really devout, they used to have anal sex instead, when they started dating boys. They couldn't keep them interested forever by rubbing their dicks through their trousers.

And anal sex isn't really sex, that's what they thought. They thought they were still virgins. That God wouldn't mind.

The girls I lived with loved Ella's Catholic school stories. They'd all laugh, and then they'd say – *yes, but of course the point is* – and we'd talk about the evils of organised religion, or how definitions of virginity were inherently patriarchal.

But he didn't laugh, he said – maybe keep your voice down a bit – and he glanced pointedly at the children.

I wasn't speaking loudly – I said, but then I wasn't sure if that was true. I could hear everything they were saying, now we were quiet.

The father offered the older girl a sip of his wine, and she took it, made a theatrical face, opening and shutting her mouth.

It's not even nice – she said. – And, like, so bad for you.

I would never drink – the younger one said. – Never ever.

My body is my temple – the older one said.

Mine too. My temple – said the younger.

I raised my eyebrows at Max.

I think they're probably fine – I whispered.

I broke off a piece of my bread roll and bit it, but it tasted like battery acid, so I put the rest back on my plate. I was using that bitter nail varnish, the one to stop you biting, and it infected everything I touched. I kept forgetting.

But, like – the older one said – all you can do is live your best life. And consistent bodily abuse is just, like, so damaging to personal growth.

Well, yes – the mother said. – I suppose in a way that's true, but –

Max looked at the bit of bread I'd put down. He always made a thing about me not eating enough, pressed me to eat more, though I suspected he actually liked it, and it wasn't true, anyway. I just never wanted to be too full when I knew he'd see me naked later. He didn't mention it now though. He took a sip of his wine instead, and said – *I'd love to be religious. It must be amazing. Believing that whatever happens, you'll be ok* – and then our food arrived.

So, about the jazz thing – I said.

Yes, I was going to ask.

The way he was looking at me, like I'd done something silly – not even something important – just something silly, made me suddenly want to stab my knife into his hand.

We've talked about this – I said. – You thought it was a waste of my time, and you're right. I'm sick of getting back late every night, never doing enough practice. And when you were away, Marieke offered me a really good external – a couple of days workshopping with a composer, potential to be cast in the finished opera, well-paid work – and I had to say no, because Malcolm wouldn't give me the time off, so she gave it to someone else. Angela was really annoyed with me, said I'd get a reputation for being unreliable, and that Marieke might not ask me again. The other singers don't have to deal with this stuff. They take the best opportunities when they're offered them, never mind any other commitments, and you have to be like that – single-minded – to be successful. Plus I've got all these auditions coming up – auditions for good stuff, I didn't even think they'd hear me – and rehearsals for *Bohème* will be starting soon. I need more time to focus. It looks like I could actually be getting somewhere. Way before anyone would expect, given my age, Angela said.

I was showing off, trying to make him find me impressive. I hated myself for it. The more I spoke, the less true it all sounded.

And I don't understand why you're being weird – I finished. – Given that you were always scathing about my job anyway.

I'm not being *weird* – he said, with a little inflection, to show this was not a word he'd normally use. – And I'm sure you're right. I was just going to ask if you'd thought about what you'd do instead? For money, I mean.

Well, I did extra shifts in January. I have my deposit back from the Ps too, because Mil didn't need one. And my rent's so cheap now, because of sharing, I've barely spent anything all month. I've got enough saved.

Well, but the thing about money, Anna – he said – is that, when you spend it, it goes.

I am aware of that. Thanks.

I just don't think there's anything romantic about not having any money, that's all – he said. – I don't buy the myth that the struggling artist makes – what? – the best art? The most moral sort? Do you? Surely the struggling artist is the one who gives up. Sure, don't do the jazz if it gets in the way. But have a plan B.

Well, I do have a plan B. I thought I'd take a couple of months to get through these commitments. I've just about got enough saved for that. And then I'll take on more choral society work. Maybe some teaching.

Isn't that the same sort of thing though? Casual work. Don't you need a longer term plan?

I have a longer term plan.

What's that?

To be an opera singer.

There was a little pause. He seemed to be considering whether to speak.

But do people make whole careers doing that? – he said eventually. – Most people who try it, I mean? I know that some people do, but surely they're the minority. Pretty exceptional cases, right? I wouldn't want you to end up like Laurie, that's all. Running around, earning bits of money here and there, never secure. You wouldn't want that.

What is it you'd have me do then? – I asked.

He shrugged.

It's obvious you're talented – he said. – Of course you should give it a proper go. But be clear-sighted, is all I'm saying. Keep your options open. It's a mistake to be passive about your future, Anna. To assume things will just work out.

I tried to explain to him then that if I spent my life trying to sing, never earning proper money, but still able to do it, I didn't think I'd mind about anything else. I'd be happy. But while I was saying it, I felt fear spread out inside me, stretch and curl itself around my organs, and he said, gently – but I don't think that's true, is it? I wouldn't say you're happy now. Are you? Living in that house? Sharing a bed with your friend? Would you want that sort of life forever? Don't you want your own home one day? Children? A family?

I don't know – I said.

And then I tried to explain to him that I thought money was liquid, unpredictable. Not something to hold onto, useless to base your life around. You needed it, but only like you needed air. Not to accumulate. And he laughed and said – *well, I think you're being a bit disingenuous, Anna. You like nice things* – and then the waiter came over with the dessert menu, and everything I could think to say would have seemed ironic, so I said nothing.

But as he was asking for the bill, I thought – he's wrong though, isn't he? It does make sense, what I said. The sitting in this expensive restaurant, eating dishes with names I can't pronounce, and the shivering under the duvet with Laurie, how cold her feet are in bed, not wanting to turn up the heat – both of them come naturally to me, familiar and easy, neither state more me, nor closer to my core.

It's ok – I said to him, trying to make light of it. – I know you don't think my work is important.

It's not that I don't think it's important, Anna – he said. – It's just, if you're not making any money from it, I'm not really sure you can call it work.

You have to live every day of your life – the older girl was saying to her parents.

But what exactly does that mean, Jessica? – the mother asked.

Duh – the younger one said. – It means you can't not live it.

He was nice to me all the way home, affectionate, trying to make me laugh. He knew he'd upset me. Because I'd missed him – missed his mouth and his skin, the muscles in his back, the things he whispered – I didn't stop him when he kissed me, when he unzipped my dress. I let him distract me. But afterwards, he slept, and I couldn't. Awake all night, thinking about what he'd said – *but don't you want your own home? A family?* – *a mistake to assume things will just work out* – thinking – how much have I got, how long will it last me, and then what, and then what – thinking – I'm going to be one of those people, aren't I? One of those people whose lives don't work out – thinking –

But I must have slept eventually, because when I woke, he was in the shower. I lay there for a second, listening to the water, and then I opened his bedside drawer. It was still there. The stack of notes I'd seen a few weeks ago, looking for a charger. Several stacks, actually. Different currencies. I took out the one of sterling, and started thumbing through it. I hadn't planned it, I didn't really know why I was doing it, but suddenly, there I was, watching my hand as it peeled off the note on top, reached for my bag, tucked it inside. I was wondering if I could get away with taking more, when the water went off, and I thought – *just what the fuck do you think you're doing?*

I put the bundle back and shut the drawer, made a coffee and drank it looking out of the window. You could see some people in the office blocks, standing with their mugs, looking out before the day started, or already at their desks, typing away.

Now, don't laugh – he said.

I turned round. He was wearing powder blue jogging bottoms, tapered at the ends, and an oversized baggy sweatshirt, brand name scrawled across the chest.

Wow. You look like a fifteen-year-old at a skatepark.

That's the look I'm going for.

Not going to lie, I find it oddly sexy.

Is that your thing, then?

Apparently. So, what's this? Has the mid-life crisis just hit?

He took my coffee out of my hands and started drinking it.

Meeting with a sports brand this morning – he said. – They're interviewing a few banks. The Head of Department's told us to wear their clothes.

Is that normal?

Well, you have to make your own fun, don't you? Normal? I wouldn't go that far. Boarding school then Oxford then finance. None of them are normal.

You've literally just described yourself.

I have more life experience – he said, in that way he had of making the most innocuous statement sound suggestive.

Then he said he needed to leave, so I got dressed, and we went.

In the lift, he said – do you actually not want a child?

What?

Last night. You said you didn't know if you wanted a family.

Why are you asking?

Just wondering – he said. – I do. Want a child, that is.

You'd probably want to call it something like Cecil though, wouldn't you?

Cecil?

Something like that. Traditional and wanky.

I have a cousin called Cecil.

No you don't.

Honestly, I do. My mother's sister's child.

Is he traditional and wanky?

I suppose you could say that.

The lift stopped in the lobby. We stood at the glass door, looking out onto the street.

Something wrong? – I asked.

Yeah. I'm genuinely embarrassed about going out dressed like this.

Trust me, it's much less embarrassing than what you normally wear.

Suddenly serious, he said – look, Anna. I feel bad about last night. I was thinking about it this morning. You're right. Why shouldn't you have the chance to make a go of it? See if you can make it into something? A couple of months to focus. I get it. It's an investment.

Well, thanks.

I can see how tough it is. What you're trying to do. I just don't want you to have to worry, that's all.

He kissed me on the street, and then he was absorbed into the stream of suited men, and in my hand was left, like a magic trick, an envelope. It was full of cash.

*

I had to get rid of the note I'd taken. I could feel its presence, nagging and constant, like the gnawing drag of tummy ache. I went into Costa and bought a coffee and a croissant, then I got some water and some gum as well, another coffee, and then it was gone. I had French language class in an hour, but I was still tired, and it was an elective anyway. No one would notice if I didn't go, I thought, so I headed home to nap.

Our new place was on a road of warehouse buildings, which Laurie described as either in Harringay or in Islington, depending on who she wanted to impress. Some of them, like ours, had been converted into overpriced apartments, and others were boarded up, or had steel netting across the windows, *Units for Let* signs outside. *Yuki's Day Nursery* was written in chalk on the window of one, and a phone number, though I'd never seen any children.

When I let myself into the house, there was no one downstairs. I took out the envelope and counted the money. On the bus there, I'd decided I'd give it back to him, but then I saw how much it was, thought how much time it would buy me, and I knew I couldn't. I sent him a message, thanked him and said I would pay him back.

I went upstairs to take a bath, but it was full of clothes left to soak and the water was red.

One of my first mornings in the house, I'd seen that Sash had blood on the back of her trousers.

Oh, I don't use tampons — she said, when I pointed it out. — I free bleed. Tampons are capitalist. You shouldn't have to pay to have periods.

Then Ella interjected to tell Sash off for using the word *period*. *Period* was a male scientific term, she said. It implied an end point. Menstruation, on the other hand, was all part of the constant female bodily flow that men were so threatened by and thus tried to control.

Well, but period doesn't mean *end point* — said Sash. — It's from the Latin, meaning *cycle*. So, kind of the opposite, actually.

What, and Latin's not the language of the patriarchy? — said Ella.

Anyway, living in that house I soon discovered, as I'd always suspected, that menstrual synchronisation was a myth. The bathroom always smelled sharp and sour, the sink, the bath, full of bloody items left to soak. They'd spend hours scrubbing stains out of their clothes, though often they'd try for a bit, then give up, throw them away, buy something new.

You shouldn't be squeamish about menstrual blood — Mil said once, when she saw me moving a cushion to cover a stain on the sofa before I sat down. —That's the patriarchy speaking. Blood is sterile. Well, kind of. And it's frankly archaic, isn't it? Controlling fascist crap. Telling women where they can and can't bleed. Get out of our vaginas, you know. Hands off. Anyway, it's only furniture. My dad can buy a new bloody sofa if it means so bloody much to him.

ELEVEN

A week later, we were having one of our house nights in. Attendance was compulsory. The house was Mil's experiment in communal feminist living, and we all had to follow her rules – a sign that we shared the same vision. We'd take it in turns to cook, and then dinner would invariably lead to a discussion of issues. Whether pornography was inherently misogynistic, the pros and cons of women-only shortlists, why straight white men didn't care about climate change.

That night, prompted by an afternoon with Laurie at the sexual health clinic, where I'd had a coil put in, we were discussing the ethical issues surrounding contraception. A few weeks before, a condom had broken with Max, and I'd gone to Boots for the morning after pill. The pharmacist asked me if the sex had been with a boyfriend.

Um – I said. – Well. Kind of.

Why do they even ask you that? – I said to Laurie later.

Curiosity, I guess. Can't see it makes much difference either way.

I'd felt sick the whole day afterwards from being stuffed with hormones, and the incident had spooked me – made me think how little it took for your body not to be yours. Max had always complained about using condoms anyway, but I didn't want to go on the pill – I'd been on it before, and it dried out my throat, made the top notes harder – so I decided to get a coil.

That night, though, I told the girls that I was morally against the pill, and they approved.

I find it incredible – Mil was saying – that men still expect women to be on the pill. That when you ask them if they've got a condom, they're all like – *oh, but you're on the pill, aren't you?* – kind of incredulous, as if it's your duty as a woman to make your vagina as welcoming as possible, just in case some random man might want to enter it.

Also – said Sash. – When a man's, like, that fucking blasé about condom use, you just know he'll give you something nasty. No one thought women would be taking the pill forever. When it was first invented, I mean. It was a stopgap, until they came up with something better. Something with fewer side effects. But no one actually gives a fuck about women's health, do they? We've known for years it's not healthy for women to—

I take your point – Ella said. – But, honestly, I think that the word *healthy* puts a value judgement on health that seems to me unhelpful and exclusionary.

Laurie looked at me, her eyes full of meaning, then she smirked and glanced studiously away. She pulled out a strand of her hair and stuck it into the candle on the coffee table, watched as the flame zipped up it and blackened into a ball.

Society's obsession with health as something, what, something desirable? – Ella said. – Some sort of achievable goal for everyone? I'm sorry, but that's just so ableist. I'll never be 100 per cent healthy, you know, because of my sensitivity to gluten. That's something I've come to terms with. But having *healthy* rammed down my throat as this kind of super-desirable-life-goal thing doesn't help. Can you not see that saying everyone should be healthy is just the same as saying that everyone should be thin or everyone should be rich? What about the people who can't be those things? What about the people who don't want to be those things?

Sash looked like she was being forced to drink bleach, but she stayed quiet. Another of Mil's rules was that we let ourselves be called in for our unfeminist behaviour, rather than called out. This essentially meant you had to sit there and take it while everyone bitched about you, before saying wholeheartedly and unreservedly what a very bad person you were.

After Sash had apologised and promised not to put the burden on Ella to educate her in future, Laurie and I went upstairs. We could hear them arguing all the way up the dangerously impractical spiral staircase. The house was all exposed brick and steel, stripped floor-boards, underfloor heating that seemed to breed moths. It belonged to Mil's parents, and I knew from looking it up on Zoopla that it had cost a lot of money.

We really need to get the fuck out – said Laurie.

Well, they're your friends. I thought you liked them.

I lay down on our bed. The pain in my stomach was still there, as though someone was blowing up a steel balloon inside me, almost imperceptible at first, and then bigger, bigger, forcing my organs out of the way, and then it popped – sweet relief – until they started to blow up another. I was glad Laurie had come with me to the clinic. I'd waited hours to be seen, and the waiting room was bleak. Big screens looped music videos – bikini-clad women gyrating sexily – and flow-charts warned how, even if you've only slept with one person, you've probably, by proxy, shared germs with thousands. Laurie kept me entertained. We filled in a whole stack of feedback forms, pretending to be different people. We guessed what STIs people thought they might have by how miserable they looked. We took as many free condoms as we could from the condom buckets, trying to be subtle, taking it in turns to appear like we were looking at the noticeboards, then casually lifting a handful on our way back to our seats. After they'd put the coil in, I had to sit back down on my blue plastic chair, head on knees, and wait for the feeling – like someone was dragging a net through my insides, skimming off scum – to pass. I was glad she was there then too. She said – *God, you really do love drama, don't you?* – but she got me some water, and then she called us a taxi, even though I said I could walk, and she insisted on paying.

She lay down on the bed next to me.

Is that what you're wearing tomorrow? – she asked, noticing the dress hanging on the back of the door.

I'd used some of Max's money to buy it. An investment. I had three important auditions that week – two for chorus jobs, one for a small role, all proper paid work, and nothing smart to wear.

It is. It's new.

Show me.

Did you watch your mum getting ready when you were little? – she asked, as I got up to put it on. – I always liked that. Not knowing where she was going, but thinking that was what it was to be an adult. Putting on nice clothes to go out. Do you remember that?

Well, mine never really went anywhere – I said. – There was nowhere much to go.

I watched myself in the mirror, stepping into the dress. It was simply cut, and it fitted my shape exactly. I was so used to seeing myself in the clothes I always wore, but that dress made me think – underneath our clothes, we're all just bodies, all the same, and you can strip us down and dress us up in something quite different and then we're different too.

Did she have lots of friends? – Laurie asked.

My mum? Not really. I guess that's why she was so into me.

I'd told Laurie about my mum. She loved to psychologise, using my childhood to analyse the sort of person I was now, but I was never convinced her conclusions were right. I'd spend hours trying to understand the psychology of characters I played – to construct backstory and use it to explain present motivation – but I found it hard, often, to relate that to myself. Inside, I felt like a big, still pool of water. I could swim down and down into it, but I'd never see the bottom.

My mum had hundreds of friends – said Laurie. – She went out all the time. Only when I was little, though. She stopped working when she had my sister, but she knew loads of cool people from before. Her and her friend had started this fashion brand. That's beautiful. Turn around.

I stood on my tiptoes so she could see what it would look like with heels. I'd done the same when I showed it to Max last night. Him behind me, his arms round my waist. Us both looking at my reflection. Worried he'd be annoyed I'd spent his money on clothes – it was important to look right for auditions, I said, that's why – but he didn't seem bothered. He liked the dress, it was a good choice. I needed to smarten up, he said.

You know, I've always wanted to be a patron of the arts — he said.

Seriously?

Sure. Spending your money on beautiful and useless things. It shows you've made it, right?

I started telling him to go fuck himself, but he put his hand over my mouth, and laughed into my hair — *I'm joking* — he said, and I bit his hand, but he didn't let go. He pulled me towards him, so my body was right up against his. *Careful* — he said.

Really nice — said Laurie. — How much was it?

I can't remember. Not much. Why did your mum stop working?

Not sure. I've never really asked. Can't imagine my dad made it easy for her, though. He's not the world's most enlightened man. Easier for her not to, I suppose. But I don't think it was ever her plan. To stop, I mean. She was ambitious.

That's sad.

It is. Anyway, she had all these beautiful clothes and she'd get invited to parties. I used to lie on her bed while she got dressed in the clothes, put on lipstick, perfume that didn't smell like her. She always had this kind of nervous energy when she was getting ready. Like there was something in her that was trying to get out. Dad hated it, I think. They always used to argue on those nights, but I found it fascinating. Seeing her how I guess she used to be. As I got older, she went out less and less, though, and then — I don't know exactly when — but she stopped altogether. I'm not sure why. The invites kept coming, for a bit anyway. I remember, because she'd stick them on the fridge, so she must have liked them. But the clothes had stopped looking right on her, like they'd been made for someone else. I think she worried about what she'd say to people too, though I don't know if I realised that at the time or later. I think she worried they'd ask her what she'd been doing with herself. That she wouldn't have anything to say to impress them. Then she tried to kill herself. Have I told you that before?

Seriously? No you didn't — I said. — You never told me. That's awful. I'm sorry.

Yeah, it wasn't great. I was about fifteen. I found her when I got back from school. That's what I never really forgave her for. She knew I'd be first home.

She looked at me and laughed.

You really don't need to do that face at me – she said. – I'm fine. It was a long time ago and, anyway, it's not like she managed it, is it? But I hated her for ages after that. That tedious predictability, you know. Woman uses her energy to turn against herself, not to make things better. Original. I lost all respect for her. I wanted her to get a grip.

She was lying on the bed, but she suddenly sat up.

Hey – she said – were you there yesterday in the kitchen when they were all talking about their pubic hair? You know they all pay thirty quid a month to have it all waxed off? All of them. And all of it. Ella was saying how it's really honestly not at all about men. It's about her. She just doesn't find it comfortable having any hair. When she has it, she says, she's aware of it all the time.

God. Imagine what amazing acts of greatness I could achieve, if I wasn't constantly aware of my pubes.

I know, right. Must be nice.

Two pieces for the first audition, and one of them must be Mozart, that evil genius who writes the simplest of music to reveal all your flaws. If any of the voice doesn't work, those spare phrases will show it, and if it's all there, perfect and beautiful, you'll finish and your audience will say – oh, Mozart, isn't he great – never mind the singer.

Smiles all round, the panel are friendly. It's early in the day. They're not bored yet.

We'll hear the Mozart first, please, Anna. Whenever you're ready.

The Trojan princess is my Mozart of choice. Ilia, who's not allowed to love the man she loves, is betraying everything she's ever known by loving him, but she can't not love him, how can she not. I start to sing, and it's one of those days where everything works, it barely feels like singing, the music comes not out of my mouth, but from every pore of my body and the tips of my fingers, and—

Sorry, we're just going to stop you there — they say. — We're a little short on time, but thanks so much for coming.

Try to be friendly and grateful in case they ever agree to hear me again. Walk out, telling myself it's about my height, or the colour of my hair, not that I'm bad, just they want something different. Try to let go of the wanting, or find somewhere else to put it. That was Tuesday.

The one on Wednesday's in some cold church hall. Can only find the child loos before, the mini loos with mini doors that adults can look over. There's blood in my knickers and rusted down my leg. Body still in shock, then. Trying to expel foreign object. I spit on toilet paper and try to wipe it off my thigh, shove a wad in, but my dress is tight and I'm sure they can see. Church hall, overly bright, where they do Sunday school, posters up with drawings of Noah's ark, the Garden of Eden. Fluorescent lights, too much scrutiny. A mistake — approach a top note wrong, don't dig down, and it's not attached to me, floats off somewhere, and I see — in the too bright light — everyone write something down.

Then it's Thursday. Early evening. Recital room not in London. Two hours and too much money on the train. The runner comes to the warm-up room.

With careful use of the passive, he says — I'm really sorry, but the timetable's been messed up.

Messed up?

The panel think they've heard everyone, but there's still you to go. If you come with me now, I'll ask them to hear you.

Down the corridor, he knocks, says — just wait outside — and then I hear him in there, explaining. They're annoyed, don't want to stay, then eventually one of them says — well, where is she? Is she waiting? You'd better send her in.

I go in, and as soon as I open my mouth, one of them gets his phone out of his pocket and texts. The other one looks at me for a bit, then stares out of the window. My head flips between Ilia and the man on his phone, the man looking at the trees, like a TV being flicked between two channels.

Well, thanks — one of them says, and there's silence.

You look lovely — Angela said, when I arrived for my lesson. — I like your earrings.

Don't worry, I'm not that fragile. You don't need to be extra nice to me.

When I'd got my rejection emails, I'd sent Angela a melodramatic text. *Courage!* — she'd replied. — *We'll talk on Monday xxx*

I do like them, though — she said. — Did your man give them to you?

He did, yeah.

He'd bought them for me in Spitalfields Market one evening when we'd gone together. He'd wanted a specific type of lamp for his house, thought a guy he knew of there might have one, but he didn't. We'd wandered around for a while, stopped in front of a case of art deco jewellery. *What do you like?* — Max had asked, and I was hesitant, not wanting to pick out something he'd find vulgar, unable to predict his taste, but when I pointed to the earrings, he said — *good choice*. I'd worn them every day since. They seemed a seal of his approval.

Well, lucky you — Angela said. — Hang onto him. Between you and me, a wealthy partner's the most useful asset a young singer can have. Now, tell me about the auditions. How did you feel about how you sang?

I shrugged.

Fine, really — I said. — I sang fine, I think. That wasn't the problem.

But, Anna, that's the only thing that matters. If you do twenty auditions, singing to the absolute best of your ability, you might expect to get one, and don't even bother trying to guess why you didn't get the others. That way madness lies. You have to be tough, you know that. What's wrong? It's not like you to be defeatist.

Nothing — I said, though I felt inexplicably close to tears. — I think I'm just tired.

We spent the lesson working on *Bohème*, and afterwards Angela gave me a hug.

You're doing really well — she said. — Honest. There's nothing in it for me to lie to you.

Thank you.

You've got to find a way to deal with rejection and not let it break you. Not to lecture you. But this is an overcrowded industry that doesn't want you, Anna. That's the sad fact of the matter. You need to keep fighting it yourself, because no one else is going to do it for you. The only people who truly care if you have a career are you, me, and your mum.

When I was eighteen, and I told Mum I was applying to music college, she said — *but what about university?* — and then she said — *we can't afford to pay for that sort of thing, Anna, you know that.* When I told her it counted as a university degree, I could get a loan, it was obvious she was disappointed.

My mum really doesn't care that much — I said.

Well — said Angela — there you go.

In the evening, Max took me out for dinner. I hoped he'd forget to ask about the auditions, but he brought them up straightaway. I said they'd gone ok, but I hadn't been offered anything.

That's a shame. Why not?

I don't know. I sang well. I just wasn't what they were looking for, I guess.

It's interesting, isn't it? — he said. — When I'm hiring people, so much of it's down to how they come across. How they talk. How engaging they are. How much you like them. It's often not the person who's best on paper.

What's wrong with how I come across?

What? That's not what I meant. Nothing. Well, I have no idea. I've never seen you audition. Something to think about, though, I guess.

I felt he was studying me too closely, appraising my worth, like I was a piece of jewellery he was considering buying — holding it up to the light, checking that the stone was flawless and how much it sparkled, wanting to know he'd get back more one day than he'd put in.

But then he said — there'll be other auditions though, other opportunities. It's partly a numbers game, right? — and I thought I'd been unfair, thinking badly of him.

He was in a good mood. He'd spent the weekend in the Oxford house fitting the kitchen.

By yourself? — I asked.

A lot of it. There's a guy who helps me with the parts I can't do.

I'm impressed. I'd always thought you were hopelessly impractical.

He paused with his wine glass half raised to his mouth, and he gave me this look that made me think, I am lost, so laughably far from in control of this. That made me think how naked I was under my clothes and how it shouldn't be allowed, him looking at me like that, not here, not in public, where anyone could see.

I know you've never thought that — he said.

He took a sip of his wine.

I've always wanted to build a house from scratch — he said. — Maybe one day I will. But this seemed close enough for now.

I'd like to see it.

I couldn't at all imagine what it was like. Old. New. Bare, white walls, clean lines, empty of clutter. Wood panelling and antique furniture. I had no idea and it seemed important to know, thinking it might help me to place him. I'd hinted a few times that I wanted to come, but he was always vague.

It's still a mess — he said. — Not ready for guests.

You saw my last place — I pressed. — I'm sure it's better than that.

He laughed.

Marginally, yes. Anyway, I spend most of the weekend working on it. You'd be bored. I'm sure your weekends in London are much more fun.

I'd taken to inventing details of my life apart from him, embellishing how exciting the parties I went to were, and how varied and interesting my social circle. I wanted him to think my life was rich and full, that he was the afterthought, and not the other way round. The way he was smiling at me now made me sure that he knew.

He could see exactly how my weeks gathered round him and how, when he was gone, whatever I did seemed empty and sucked clean of colour.

I said – well, yes, probably – and changed the subject.

We'd nearly finished eating, when a woman came up to the table.

Max, it *is* you – she said. – I kept saying it was. We were sitting back there. We're just leaving.

She gestured to a man standing at the door, holding her coat. She was perfectly put together, like a Playmobil with plastic clothes designed to snap exactly round her body. White tailored dress and dark boxy jacket. About the same age as Max.

Hi. I didn't see you.

So, how have you been? It's been ages. How's everything?

She looked at me, and I smiled, but he didn't introduce me.

Fine – he said. – I've been good. How are you both?

Really good. We're moving, actually. Out of London. Hitchin.

That's nice. Well, I hope it all goes smoothly.

And how are you? – she asked again, when she got nothing more from him. He'd adopted an expression I recognised well, mouth a grim line, questions met with frosty chippings, like they were being hurled at a wall of ice and couldn't break through.

Nothing much to report – he said.

She glanced at me again, but he just smiled.

Well, it was nice to see you – she said.

They looked in at me through the glass as they went.

Who was that? – I asked.

Helen. I haven't seen her for a while.

He paid the bill, and said – let's go for a drink.

I didn't really want to. I wanted to be back in the flat with him, his skin on my skin, his voice in my ear, the way it sounded when we were completely alone. It was the woman, I think. I felt we were threatened somehow. But he was tense and quiet, and I didn't want to say no to him, so we walked to a pub round the corner. It had been raining all day, and the greyness still hung in the air.

God, London's depressing – he said.

It's the rain. It'll be spring soon.

It's the flat too. It depresses me.

I love your flat.

It's ok – he said. – It's just not a real place.

I imagined putting the key in the door, opening it and there being nothing there. A ledge. A drop. The street, nineteen storeys below.

We were outside the pub, when his phone buzzed in his pocket. He took it out and glanced at the screen.

I have to take this – he said.

He handed me his wallet.

Get us both a drink.

The pub was by all the offices, and it was full of men. One of them started talking to me at the bar. He was young, and his City suit didn't look quite right on him, like he'd borrowed it from his dad. Idle chat. He offered to buy me a drink, and I said I was ok thanks, I was with someone, he was outside. He said something surprisingly funny, I laughed, and then the barman came back with my drinks, and I saw Max standing by the door, looking at me. I said – *well, it was nice to meet you* – and he said – *you too* – and I left.

Who was that? – Max asked.

No idea. Just some guy. Everything ok?

What?

The call.

Oh right. Yeah. Work.

He said he'd get us a table, and I went to find the bathroom. When I got back, he smiled at me like he knew something I didn't.

He was staring at you, you know – he said.

Who was?

That guy you were talking to at the bar. He was staring at your bum as you walked past. It wasn't subtle.

How charming. I didn't notice.

He was looking at me in a way I didn't understand. He was smiling, but his eyes were hard.

Do you like him looking at you? – he asked.

Like it? I don't know. I feel neutral about it, I guess.

Why do you like it?

I said I felt neutral about it.

Sure — he said. — So why are you smirking?

Am I?

You are.

I laughed.

Well, I guess it's always nice to feel desired, isn't it? I like seeing that other people want you too. When other women look at you. It feels like a compliment to my taste.

You don't get jealous, then? — he asked.

The nights I'd spent torturing myself with the idea of his wife — the most perfect woman alive — the ins and outs of the life they'd had together — the one I couldn't even imagine, let alone match.

Of you? — I said. — Not really.

Why not?

I guess I'm not a jealous person.

I had this girlfriend once — he said. — She used to make us try to pick up other people. We'd go clubbing, or to a bar, and we'd let people chat us up, dance with them, even kiss them sometimes, she wasn't too bothered. And then at the last minute, we'd find each other. Go home together instead. The sex afterwards was—

He laughed.

Well — he said — I guess that's why she liked it.

I managed to remain blasé.

She made you, did she? — I said.

Well, I was quite into it too — he said. — At the time.

He put his hand over mine, and then he said — is he still looking at you? — in this low voice, like he was suggesting we go and fuck in the toilet.

I glanced up. He was sitting with a group of guys in suits, a couple of tables behind us. He caught my eye. I wasn't sure if he'd been looking at me the whole time, or if he'd just happened to then.

Kind of — I said.

Max started to run his nails over my knuckles.

Would you? — he asked.

Him?

Yes.

I looked again and he saw me looking.

Theoretically? – I said. – Or actually?

Either. Both.

I didn't know what he wanted me to say.

Maybe theoretically. He's not bad-looking. Actually? Well that would be quite impolite. I'm here with you, after all.

Sit next to me then.

What?

Move your chair.

Seriously?

Seriously – he said. – I can't relax, knowing some guy's checking you out behind my back. Sit next to me.

He was still smiling, inscrutable.

Are you being serious?

You think I'm joking?

I stared at him.

What's wrong, Anna? – he asked. – Do I not give you enough attention?

I looked up, and the guy saw me looking. He gave me a confused smile, and I looked away. Max raised his eyebrows, expectant, and I moved my chair. He looked at me for a second, and then he started to laugh.

Fuck – he said. – You do know I was joking, right? You can sit wherever you like. I really don't care.

He was still laughing, and I felt like an idiot. I wanted the other guy to think I'd had a proper reason for moving, so I put my arms round Max – and then, because I didn't know what to say, I was really all over him, running my fingers through his hair, kissing him, putting my hands on the insides of his thighs. He told me to stop.

We left after one drink. The rain had started again and, once we were off the main road, he pulled me to him and he kissed me, rough and hard, like he wanted to hurt me. It was a short walk back, and we

didn't say much. He didn't touch me again, but he looked at me –
when he held the door open for me, when he stood opposite me in
the lift – with that careless, knowing smile he had. The one that said –
I know everything you've ever wanted. There's nothing you can keep from me.

In his flat, he pinned my hands to the wall, leant his arm flat across
them. He undid my jeans with the other hand and pulled them down.
He pushed my legs apart with his knees. He fucked me like he was
trying to get at something right in the heart of me, or to eradicate it
completely. I didn't try to push back against him, because I knew he
didn't want me to. He was stronger than me, anyway. I didn't try to
do anything. I thought that what he was doing to me probably hurt
– the weight of his arm on my wrists, his fingers wrapped round my
hair, how he pulled my thigh up round his waist, his hip bone crushing
my hip – but I wasn't sure. The pain of it, or what might be pain if it
wasn't good, fixed me, open-mouthed and heavy-breathed and stupid.

He put his hands round the backs of my thighs and lifted me. He
carried me to the bed. I lay on top of him, hearing his heart slow
down. He shut his eyes, and I rested my chin on the back of my hand.
I traced the line of his collarbone, the scar on his shoulder. I wanted
him, always. I wanted to have him. Only right afterwards, like this, I'd
sometimes think – *well, that's what it is then, that's what it's like, I don't need
him again* – but then, always, it would start up again, the dark beat of
desire – the way he smiled, or how, wherever he touched me, I could
feel the tingle of it through every cell or, leaving his flat in the morning,
the smell of his hair, his skin, unexpected, on the collar of my coat.

His eyes were still shut, but I didn't want him to sleep. I often
wanted to tell him I loved him at moments like this, not necessarily
because it was true, but because he'd have to say something back.
He couldn't ignore it as a statement. He'd have to react.

Tell me something – I said, hoping for a confession.

He opened his eyes.

Like what?

I don't know. Anything. Something I don't know about you.

He thought for a second, then he said – I used to steal things
from supermarkets.

What, when you were a kid?

No. Quite recently, actually.

What do you mean by stealing? Shoplifting?

From the self-checkout machines – he said. – It's easy to do.

By accident? Everyone does that. I wouldn't call that stealing.

No, not by accident. I don't mean by accident. I mean, I'd scan something that was the same weight as something more expensive, then take the expensive thing instead. Scan ham, take steak.

A true motto for life.

He laughed.

Are you being serious? – I said.

What do you think?

But why?

I don't know – he said. – Because it was easy.

I turned my cheek flat on his chest, so I could smell the warmth of his skin.

Who was that woman? – I asked.

What woman?

You know what woman.

Helen? – he said. – No one. A friend of my wife's.

He was looking at the ceiling, not at me.

I never liked her much – he said. – What about you? Have you ever stolen anything?

You – I thought, but I knew that wasn't really true, so I said – *no, nothing important* – and I pressed myself to him and kissed him. I thought – *my poor broken boy*. Just flashes of it, sometimes. The little ironic inflection on *my wife* and how he still called her that. How he wouldn't look at me when he spoke about her, had never said her name. I'd think then, in those moments, that he'd been unhappy for a very long time, perhaps more unhappy than he knew. He'd said to me once – *it's funny, looking back on the things you've had, knowing you'll never have them again* – and I knew he meant her. I thought – *but you could have that again. You could have it with me, and I would be better* – but all I said was that, yes, I knew what he meant.

TWELVE

The Director didn't bother to introduce himself. He strolled into the space, casual, like he might have come to borrow a music stand. He leant against the piano and looked at his watch, stared out of the window. A minute or two passed, while everyone kept chatting, and then he shouted that the rehearsal was meant to have started by now and could we all please kindly shut the fuck up and stop wasting his time. The Shock Factor. The cast fell instantly silent. The Director was a pro. He knew exactly how to work a room.

Let's all get to know each other a bit then, shall we? – he sneered, then he began to shout instructions. – Pair up. One of you lead. Choose an emotion. Show the other person that emotion. No talking. None at all. If you're being led, watch closely. Sense the feeling. Feel it too. Once you've got it, swap. That's it. Let's go.

In silence, we paired up and decided who would lead. Most did so by pointing, mostly to themselves.

This is an exercise in empathy – the Director tutted performatively, as he stalked round the room. – Pay attention to your colleagues. This isn't fucking mime.

I was with Frankie. We looked into each other's faces for what felt like a very long time, then he gave a little smile and seemed confused. I tried to seem the same. The Director stood and stared, and nobody moved.

What emotion was that meant to be? – I asked, when he'd finally moved on.

Wasn't I following you? – said Frankie.

So just so we're clear – the Director said, when he'd seen each pair. – I don't give a fuck about your process. That's your job, not mine. So sure, you're at music college, but let's get one thing straight – I'm not a fucking teacher. A show – he said. – Now, that I can do. I can give you a show. But the process is yours. I don't do tears. I don't do personal lives. I don't do backstory. I don't do excuses. I just do the show. Do we all understand?

Everyone nodded to show they understood.

But the one thing I will say is this – he said. – Some of you, by the looks of things, really need to get a fucking process. There will not be one singer on my stage who shakes their fist to show they're angry. Understand? Who cries to show they're sad. Think, all of you, please, about how real people behave in the real fucking world. Look. Pay attention. Watch. It's only people pretending to be angry who shake their fists. Manipulative cunts cry. Do some research please – he said – on human fucking nature.

That night, I watched Max closely. He was cooking, and I sat on the sofa and watched him, casual, cross-legged, book in hand, trying to look like I wasn't. I watched him light up his phone on the kitchen counter, and scroll, checking something – a recipe, perhaps, though I'd never seen him use one. I watched him look up and stare at the window, like he'd had a thought, something important, maybe, something he'd forgotten to do. I watched him run his hand through his hair, drink some wine, glance back down at his phone. I watched him stir the pot and taste the end of the spoon, rest it on the edge of the lid so as not to dirty the counter. I watched him look over at me and I smiled and pretended to read. Max couldn't show me how people behaved when they felt certain things. I was still stuck the other way round – trying to work out from how he behaved what he felt.

I tried to make my look objective.

There he was, standing under the halogen lights that picked out the grey in his hair and the lines in his face. He was a middle-aged man, I told myself. That was all. A middle-aged man, standing in his kitchen, cooking me dinner. But my look wouldn't stay cold. I couldn't be detached. Because I loved that he was worn, that he'd been in his skin for longer than I had in mine. I loved that we'd stopped going out all the time, that he'd started to cook for me. That he wore an apron and didn't get why I found that amusing.

I watched him as he put the lid back on the pot and adjusted the heat.

I watched him as he came over to the sofa.

He pushed me backwards, and he bit my lip. The spice on his tongue burned.

Stop looking at me like that – he said.

It was funny, actually, because I'd only noticed recently how much he looked at me. Well, had I only just noticed, or had he only just started? I don't know, but every time I looked, he seemed to be looking. He watched me all the time – while I was getting dressed, or putting on make-up to go out. He'd say I looked pretty. That he liked my eyes, dark like that. I felt very cool and calm in those moments, like he was fixing me into place, and all I had to do was stay there and let the world happen round me, and then I'd be perfect. He'd do up the clasp of my necklace, and he'd rest his chin on my shoulder, look at me in the mirror. Or he'd be lying back on the bed, propped up on his elbows, and he'd watch me, moisturising my legs after I'd showered, or brushing my hair. Sometimes, he'd look and he wouldn't say anything, and sometimes he'd say – come here.

I craved his look, and when I was away from him, I missed it. I'd started to feel about other people's eyes on me the same way I felt about most of their conversation. The evenings I'd spend without him, talking to someone who didn't ask me the right questions, and so I'd say nothing of interest, and I'd know they thought me boring. There were lots of evenings without him – he was away a lot – and I'd go home feeling colourless, like if you held me up to the light, you'd see right through me. But then he'd come back, and I was animated by his eyes. I blossomed and was real and what I did mattered. If he liked something about me, then I liked it too.

But if someone looks at you that closely, studies you like that, with that intensity, they'll see the bad things too, not only the good. His eyes weren't always kind. There were things about me, more and more things, that I wasn't so sure that he liked. Small things.

He didn't seem to like that I was busy. When I had rehearsals late or concerts, and I'd go round afterwards to his, he'd be reading or sitting at the table on his laptop, and I'd feel bad, knowing he'd been waiting. Feeling he was lonely. He'd say, with that smile he had, inscrutable – *don't worry, I'm happy just hanging around here, waiting for you to make time for me* – or else he'd be cold with me, a little distant, and I'd spend all evening trying to warm him up. It was difficult to find the time to meet. I never understood his schedule, but it was inflexible. He'd suggest Tuesday, and I'd tell him I had a concert, and he'd say casually – *oh well, never mind, but that's the only time I've got for the next couple of weeks*. So I found myself moving things around, stopped doing the gigs that didn't pay so much. It was funny, once I started really scrutinising my diary, examining my commitments, I realised how many of them were unimportant, how few were actually, truly fixed. Easy to feign illness at the last minute or to say I'd got a better offer, always another soprano willing to take my place. He never asked me to cancel – it wasn't that – but I suppose I started to think he was right. It was mostly underpaid casual work, not helpful to my career, and anyway, I'd rather see him.

He didn't like me being on my phone. When it rang and I picked it up, or when I messaged someone back, or when we were talking and neither of us knew the answer to something and I went to Google it. Laurie got angry with me about it once. She'd been calling me all evening, was upset about something, and I'd seen my phone light up on the table, and had turned it over. When I said the next day that I was sorry, I'd been with him, she said – *oh right. So he doesn't let you pick up calls now, does he? Sounds about right.* Laurie liked to read everything Max did as an attempt to negate my personality, but she was wrong. He'd never stopped me from doing anything. He didn't even ask me not to. It was just this feeling I had, sometimes.

Something in the way he looked at me. This feeling that I wasn't quite right.

Other things. Expressions that he said I'd picked up from Laurie. Using *fucking* as an adjective, for example, which I'd never used to do, he said. It was always a joke, making fun of me, not serious, but – how cold he could be, hard and blank, and then he'd laugh and say – *God, Anna, relax, I'm joking* – but it didn't always feel that way. One time – I think we were talking about how all artists are a bit inward-looking – he teased me for being self-obsessed.

Have you ever noticed – he asked – how many of your sentences start with *I*?

No – I said, stupidly. – I haven't, actually.

He found that hilarious, and even more so that it took me a second to work out why. Some evenings, when I was tired, I didn't trust myself to speak much at all.

He didn't like it when I was on my period. I'd been spotting almost constantly since I'd had the coil put in. Laurie told me to masturbate – she said it got the blood out faster – but after trying, in a joyless panic, to make myself come in the ninety snatched seconds I got alone in our room, I concluded that, anyway, she was wrong. When I told him I was still bleeding, he'd say – *I honestly don't care about that sort of thing, Anna. I'm not a teenager.* But afterwards, little things – the way he glanced at the sheets or got up straightaway to shower – I could tell that he did.

And then the way that he watched me – when I was brushing my teeth, or trying to get the lid off a jar, or checking I had all my stuff before I left – felt unfriendly. His eyes made me clumsy, breaking mugs by putting them too close to the edge of the table, or spilling coffee down my top. It was like he didn't believe I could navigate the world, and the less he believed it, the more difficult I found it to do. Then he'd call me an idiot and he'd call me a child, and he'd say it affectionately, teasing, but sometimes in those moments I wasn't even sure he liked me. The way he looked at me made me sure that he didn't.

Once, my mum called, and I saw him glance at my phone when it lit up, and I said – *stop being so fucking controlling* – and I picked it up and talked to her, and afterwards he said – *please don't say that to me again, Anna. You know it's not true and it's really not nice.* I felt bad then. And another time – the time that made me most ashamed – I'd had a bad day, and he made a comment about me putting the spoon I'd used to stir my tea down directly on the counter and, overtaken suddenly by an impulse to hurt him, I said – *is this how you used to talk to your wife? Is that why she left you?* – and I saw his face close off like the blinds had been pulled down behind his eyes. He went and sat on the bed, his back to me, and I knew he was furious, followed him, fired up for confrontation and, to my absolute horror, I saw he was crying. And I said that I was sorry, I was sorry, I hadn't meant it, it was wrong of me, I didn't know what I was talking about, I was sorry, please forgive me. I would have said anything, I think, to make him stop.

And other times, I'd make fun of him, call him old and crotchety, unable to accommodate anyone else, and he'd laugh, and it was like watching a statue come to life. Then I'd think I'd been unfair, looking for the things in him I expected to see – the things Laurie said about him – and not seeing him at all as he was. Because that wasn't what he was like, not really. Times when I'd feel he was looking for flaws in me, he'd suddenly smile. He'd suddenly say to me – *I'm really glad you're here* – or even – *you're so beautiful* – when I was thinking about something else, doing something innocuous, not trying to be beautiful at all. He could be sentimental. He'd play me a song he liked and he'd pull me up off the bed, put his arms round my shoulders. He'd rock me, a half sort of dance but barely moving, his cheek on my cheek, his breath hot on my ear, the city, our audience, looking in through the glass. Or he'd lie with me on the sofa and we'd make out like teenagers. I'd try to unbutton his shirt, or go to take off his belt, and he'd stop me. He'd say that, no, he just wanted this. He'd make fun of me when I tried to pin him down about the future. I'd ask, in a tone I hoped was casual, when exactly he was planning to leave London for good, and he'd say — *I'm here right now, aren't I? Tonight, I'm here with you. That's what I'm thinking about, not some theoretical point next year.* And in those moments, I'd think he was right, what was the point of worrying? I'd try to drink as much of it in as I could – the feel of his hands and the smell of his hair, the way he smiled – like this had some special meaning for him and not just for me. He'd tell me I was lovely, and that I should stay always exactly as I was right then. He'd say how London bored him, he'd stayed too long, he said, longer than he'd ever meant to, but it was more fun now with me here. He'd call me *my love*, although he'd never say he loved me.

I was emptying an envelope of cash to put in my drawer, when Laurie came into our room. I'd thought she was out.

What have you done? — she asked, merrily, when she saw the money in my hands. — Have you killed someone?

She must have really looked, then, seen how much there was, the cash I was holding, the pile on the bed. She sat.

No, but really — she said. — Have you?

Drugs. More lucrative. How come you're not at work?

Shift got pushed back. I didn't realise you had so much saved? — she pressed. —You said you were struggling?

Well, I was.

You were?

It's – well—

I couldn't think of a plausible excuse so, casually as I could, I said — Max lent it to me.

She looked at me like she didn't quite understand what I meant.

Hang on — she said. — So that's where you're getting all your money from? I knew he was probably paying for stuff, but – what? – no – not since you quit? All this time? He's been giving you cash? Seriously?

Well, not all—

And what exactly is it he expects in return for that, then?

He doesn't expect anything – I said. – He's just helping me out.

And he didn't. He'd never asked me for anything. Only once, it had felt strange – late at night, had to get up early, remember thinking – when I was nearly asleep and he started kissing me – thinking about the envelope earlier that evening, thinking that maybe I owed him. But very quickly, I dismissed that thought – it wasn't true. That wasn't why I did it. Women had sex when they didn't want to all the time – I certainly had in the past – nothing to do with money – and, anyway, I enjoyed it once we started.

You can cut the moral act – I said. –What about that time you went out for dinner with a different man every night, so you didn't have to spend anything on food for weeks? You tell that story like you're proud of it.

That's totally different.

Why? No, it's not.

There was no expectation. I never saw most of them again. Only if I wanted to.

And anyway – I said. – Anyway, it's not where I'm getting all my money from. I've got savings.

This wasn't true. He'd been right. The money had gone quickly, much more quickly than I'd ever thought it would.

He just lent me a bit this month – I said. –That's all. I was short after those auditions. I'm going to pay him back.

A bit? There must be – what? – I mean, literally how much money do you have there?

She started thumbing through the notes on the bed.

A grand? It can't be much less than that.

She suddenly laughed.

Fucking hell, Anna. I hope you know what you're doing.

It's nowhere near that much.

I looked down at our duvet, the faded rosebuds with lacy trim.

And it's really not that unusual – I said. – It's not unusual for people in the arts to be supported by their partners. I'm pretty sure half the singers at the Conservatory are. Or by their parents. I don't know how they'd do it otherwise.

Oh, so you're supported now, are you? I thought you were going to pay him back?

I am.

Then she said gently – but anyway, Anna, he's not your partner. I mean, is he? Are you even actually together? In any definable way? Has he told anyone about you?

She knew she'd got me there. I had no idea. The few times I'd brought it up, as nonchalantly as I could, he'd been kind, reasonable, indescribably vague. I couldn't bear it, so I stopped asking.

Come on – she said. – Do you honestly not find this strange? Do you not think that, you know, if he actually wanted a relationship, he'd be looking for someone a bit closer to his own age? Someone who wants to start a family soon, and all that sort of thing?

You're being remarkably conservative – I said. – For someone who claims to be so alternative.

Yeah, but he doesn't claim to be alternative, does he? I'm being realistic. That's surely more what he's looking for – sensible, success-ful woman in her thirties to have kids with? Unless – well – unless, of course, he's got all that already.

She looked at the time on her phone.

Anyway, I've got to go – she said.

My response to anger was never to be angry. It always hurt, made me feel bad, wanting to make things better, even though I didn't think she was right. I saw her glance down at the money again, and I remembered one time a few months ago. She'd found a fifty pound note on the pavement, and she'd come to meet me at the Conservatory, taken me out for lunch. *You don't keep money that comes to you like that* – she'd said. – *The universe wants you to spend it.*

Do you have enough this month? – I said. – Do you want some?

She made a noise that could have been a laugh, but it probably wasn't.

Really, Anna – she said – I'm good.

THIRTEEN

I was waiting to go into my lesson when his name flashed up on my screen.

Anna – he said – there's something I was hoping you could help me with.

I'd been running through a difficult phrase in my head, trying to remember how it should feel. His voice snapped me out of it. He'd never called me from work before.

Oh really? What's up?

It must have been about eight thirty this morning – he said. – I was nearly at the office, when this guy came jogging past in workout gear. Lycra, trainers, little cap. So far so normal. But then he got closer and I saw what he was holding. I'd thought it was an energy drink or something, you know, from a distance, but I was wrong. It was beer. An open can. He was jogging carefully, arm outstretched, so it didn't spill. Running or Going for a Run?

It had started in a restaurant a couple of months back, these games we played about people. I'd seen a girl who looked like a teenager holding hands across the table with a middle-aged man.

Relative or Lover? – I'd asked him.

Relative. Surely Relative.

I don't know. Does anyone hold hands with their dad like that?

We'd invented lots of categories since then. Crackhead or Jogger. Pregnant or Fat. European or Going to a Roller Disco.

It's a tough one – I said. – Did you actually see him drink it?

No. But if he wasn't drinking, then why was it open?

Stayed up all night at a workout-themed party? – I said. – Realised he was late for work? Ran out, still holding his last drink?

We should discuss this in more detail. Come over tonight.

Tonight, I can't.

Why not?

I've got an audition.

An important one?

Kind of, yeah.

It was for a well-known small company. A good role, but it was a pay-to-sing – always enough young professionals out there, desperate for experience, to make that viable as a business model. Cast members rehearsed full-time, so you couldn't do it if you had a job, but they also had to make a donation towards production costs. Not an insignificant amount, either. I wasn't about to tell him that.

What time? – he said. – You can come over after.

It's in the morning. It's just I need a good night's sleep.

Your idea of the morning? Or everyone else's idea of the morning?

I don't remember the exact time – I said, which wasn't true. It was at 2p.m.

Sophie came out of her lesson, and Angela stood waiting at the door.

I have to go – I said. – I've got class.

Well, let me know if you change your mind.

Will do.

I hung up and said – sorry, hi – to Angela.

How are you then? – she asked, when we were inside.

Fine, yeah. Well, I'm a bit annoyed.

I'd got into trouble at the Barbican Library during my lunch-break. They'd caught me photocopying an entire score, told me off for breaching copyright laws, made me give them the pages.

But everyone does it, don't they? – I said. – It's hardly like the composer's still alive. And who the hell can afford to buy a full score every time they need to learn a role? Well, maybe someone like Beth can, but—

I realised Angela wasn't engaging.

What? — I said.

I just got a call about you.

Oh, really? Who from?

Alexander. He called to say you've missed two of his classes in a row, and didn't tell him you weren't coming. One of them you were meant to be singing in. He'd been going to recommend you for an external, he said, and now he's not anymore. Doesn't want to work with you. He was actually all ready to tell Marieke. Come on, Anna, don't look so surprised, you should know by now how sensitive he is. Anyway, I managed to stop him. Said I was sure you had a good explanation. So do you?

I, yeah — I said. — I do.

A couple of Alexander's classes had been moved to the evening at short notice. The first night, I'd already made plans with Max, didn't want to cancel at the last minute. The next time, it was the only evening he had free that week. I figured it was only a class, not a rehearsal or anything, it didn't matter that much. I'd forgotten it was my turn to sing.

I had to work — I said.

Work? What sort of work?

At the hotel.

I thought you'd stopped doing that?

Well, yeah. I had. I mean, I have. But I was short of cash this month, and so — yeah — I took on a few shifts. I'm sorry. The change was so last minute, I lost track of what week I was singing in, and I forgot to tell him, and — it won't happen again.

Well, you need to go and apologise — she said. — He's very upset. You can't get this sort of reputation, Anna, not to mention that if Marieke gets wind of you not singing when you're meant to, she might not pass you this year. You shouldn't need me to tell you this. Now, let's not waste any more time, let's work.

We went through Zerlina's arias for the audition. Angela was more critical than usual, stopping me after every note, and snapping when I, unable to do what she wanted, started to giggle uncertainly.

We'd eliminated that habit, hadn't we? – she said. – *Please let's not go backwards* – and I realised how annoyed she was.

By the end, I felt like I'd been turned inside out, and she said – the voice sounds tired. This is tomorrow, this audition? Do you have anything on now? Well, good. Go home and rest. Lots of water, lots of sleep.

It was starting to get dark. I'd never had Angela angry with me before, and I suddenly couldn't bear the thought of going home alone. The packed bus back, turning the wrong way for life from the station – away from the high street, past the McDonald's drive-through, the row of beauty salons that always looked shut, and then the long walk down endless residential streets – pebble-dash terraces, drab colours – all exactly the same. Back in the house, there'd be no hot water to take a shower – none of the girls went to work in the conventional sense of the word, so they were often around all day, taking leisurely baths. Sash had met some guys who'd started a pottery collective in the warehouse next door, and they were coming over that night too. They'd be in the sitting room, thudding about till 5 a.m., snorting coke with the special metal coke straw Sash favoured – she considered herself an eco-warrior, and plastic was bad for the oceans. The pot of food I'd made to last the week would most probably be finished already, because we weren't allowed to stake a claim of ownership over replenishable items. It was one of the house rules. *It all evens out in the end* – Mil would say, as she sent you out to buy her expensive OGX conditioner, or ate the last of your soup.

I sent Max a message and said that I'd come, but could I stay asleep after he'd gone in the morning. He texted me back, *sure, fine*.

I didn't think you'd want to go out tonight? – he said, when I'd taken off my coat.

I don't.

So why are you dressed like that?

Audition clothes – I said. – So I don't have to go back in the morning.

The role was Zerlina, one of Mozart's coquettes, so I'd borrowed a dress of Laurie's and was wearing high heels. An opportunity to show the panel you looked right for the part.

He put his hands on my shoulders and held me at arm's length, studied me for a second, then he smiled.

When I suggested you might want to smarten up your image, this wasn't quite what I had in mind – he said. – Is this really the sort of thing girls wear for auditions?

What's wrong with what I'm wearing?

Nothing. Nothing at all. I like it very much, in fact. Wondering if I'm in the wrong industry, that's all.

He went over to the fridge.

What are you drinking?

I can't drink tonight. My voice is feeling a bit tired actually, so I probably shouldn't talk much either.

Fun evening ahead, then. You sound completely insane, you do know that, don't you?

Perks of dating a singer – I said, then I thought, idiot, why did you say *dating*, and I started blathering about how I was actually quite chilled out, some singers carried portable steamers around with them and wouldn't go into air-conditioned buildings and drank so much water they needed to pee every thirty minutes, but he just laughed and said it was fine, we didn't have to talk.

He ordered excessive amounts of fancy-looking Asian food, and I took my dress off and put on one of his shirts. We started watching a documentary. He'd been looking out for when it would appear on Netflix for ages. It was about a guy who'd built a log cabin in Alaska, and lived there by himself for decades. He'd done all the footage himself, setting the camera up, then getting into the frame, demon-strating how he fished, constructing kitchen tools out of scraps of wood. I didn't understand half of what he was saying, but it was soothing – like listening to people speaking in a foreign language, just enjoying the intonations of speech. I shut my eyes.

The buzzer to the flat went, and he got his phone out of his pocket and paused the TV.

Here – he said, passing it to me. – Choose something else.

I thought you wanted to watch that?

He got up to answer the door.

You're literally falling asleep – he said. – It's somewhat interfering with my enjoyment.

Honestly, I'd rather watch this than have to make a decision you might judge me for.

I thought that might be the case. That's why I'm making you do it.

He grabbed his wallet off the table to tip the guy, and went to the door. I started scrolling down the Netflix homepage. I heard them exchange pleasantries, then he put the takeaway containers on the coffee table, a couple of plates, some serving spoons. He said – *help yourself* – and went back to the kitchen to top up his glass.

I reached his viewing history. The last thing he'd watched was *Up*.

You're full of surprises – I said, when he'd sat back down.

What?

There was a moment – maybe I only imagined it – but a moment where I thought he was angry. He took the phone out of my hands and looked at the screen.

I meant, I didn't have you down as someone who watched kids' films?

He seemed confused, and then he smiled.

Oh – he said. – That was my nephew. My brother's kid. They were over at the weekend.

I didn't know you had a nephew.

I do. Two, in fact.

I tried to slot him into this new scenario. Max, the favourite uncle, carrying the boys on his shoulders, or running around with them in the garden, kicking a ball. It wasn't hard to imagine, but the two boys I conjured up looked too much like him.

Do you have children? – I asked, in as conversational a tone as I could manage.

I don't – he said, but something about how quickly he answered made me sure he was lying. It was only a second though, and then he laughed and said – do you not think that's something I might have mentioned? – and I told myself not to be crazy.

What are they like? Your nephews. Do you like them?

Like them? – he said. – What sort of question is that? Of course I like them.

I shrugged.

Children are just like any other people, right? – I said. – I assume there are some you like and some you don't.

I think you tend to like ones you're related to.

Really? I wouldn't know.

Narcissistic Only Child Syndrome. Anyway, *Up*'s not really a kids' film. It's good. Emotionally devastating.

Emotionally devastating?

It is. I cried after those first ten minutes. Apparently everyone does. You know, the bit where they fast-forward through the couple's life, from when they're children up until she dies.

Seriously?

Is that so hard to believe?

You being emotionally manipulated by a children's cartoon? Kind of, yeah.

Technically an animation – he said. – And either way, it doesn't matter, because it's psychologically accurate. The idea that people spend their lives chasing something big and ambitious. They don't realise until it's too late that they were happy all along with normal.

Well, yes, I suppose – I said. – If you're happy to stay second-rate.

He took a sip of whisky and put the glass on the table, then he leant over and took my face in his hands and he kissed me. He tasted of smoke and citrus, and his mouth was cold, and then I felt a trickle of liquid in the back of my throat, the acrid burning of 40 proof. He was laughing in my mouth, and I tried not to swallow, but he kept his lips pressed to mine, and I had to or I'd choke. I tried to push him off, but he was on top of me, crushing my spine into the back of the sofa, pinning me down by my shoulders, and suddenly I couldn't breathe, I couldn't speak, and so I pushed and pushed and

I tried to shout and I flailed my arms, and then he jumped up, his hand cupped round his cheek, and I realised I'd hit him.

Very quietly, he said – what the fuck's wrong with you?

He took his hand away and his cheek was smeared with blood. I couldn't understand it. It was like a stage trick, and I was amazed by how realistic it had been, wondering where the blood had come from, and then I saw my hands. My costume ring. The sharp bit. I looked up at him, and on his face was pure, white anger, like he hated me. It was such a shock that I started to laugh.

You find it funny? – he said. – Seriously? What's wrong with you?

What's wrong with me? What's wrong with me? You were hurting me.

You hit me – he said, his voice still quiet, but steely, like a thin, precise blade. – Do you actually think that's ok?

You were hurting me – I said again, but I sounded too loud, hysterical, in the silence of his flat.

In what way was I hurting you exactly, Anna? We were messing around. You didn't have to fucking hit me.

I could still taste the whisky, and I imagined it drying and taking with it all the moisture in my throat. But if I said that, he'd think I was mad.

I didn't mean to hurt you – I said. – I was trying to make you stop.

He was looking at me like I was making no sense at all, and then he went into the bathroom and I heard the water from the shower. I could feel my heart fluttering like it was trying to break out through my ribs, and my limbs all felt too big and not attached to my body. I wished he'd shouted. I would have understood shouting. The quiet, I couldn't understand.

He was in there for a long time, and then I thought he must be waiting for me to leave. I'd taken his shirt off, was putting my own clothes back on, when he came out, towel wrapped round his waist.

What are you doing?

Leaving.

I sat on the bed to put on my tights.

Why are you leaving? Don't leave.

You're angry with me.

I'm not — he said. — I'm not angry anymore. I know it was an accident. Anna? Are you listening to me? Don't leave.

He pulled me up off the bed, and he wrapped his arms round me. His chest was still damp, and he smelled clean and fresh.

I hurt you. I didn't mean to hurt you.

He put his hands on my shoulders and said — look, look at me, see, it's really nothing, it was just a shock, that's all. I'm sorry I was angry.

And I looked up at his face and he was right. Now that he'd cleaned it, it really was nothing. It was barely even a scratch.

I woke up tired, and he was gone. There was an envelope propped up on the bedside table, written on the front, in his touchingly childish writing — *Good luck with the audition. Get a taxi.* I opened it and counted the money inside. It would have paid for a taxi to France. I added the amount to the list I'd started on my phone, which I showed him periodically, saying — *look, see, I know exactly how much I owe you. I'll pay you back* — and he always said — *sure, whenever, no rush* — and I wondered if he had any idea how much he'd given me over the last month or so. Looking at it now made me feel a bit sick.

I lay in bed for a little while. I had a few hours before the audition, and I knew I should get up and do a proper warm-up, but that didn't feel important. Tiredness, maybe. I made coffee, opened all the curtains, and took it back to bed, drank it, staring out at the white sky, the fluorescent lights of office buildings. Then I opened his bedside drawer and took out the stacks of cash, started looking through the papers underneath. I knew that going through his things wasn't exactly moral, but it didn't feel like that was what I was doing. The stuff seemed too impersonal. I didn't know what I was looking for, anyway. Evidence, I suppose, though evidence of what, I wasn't sure. Something I could fix him with — turn him into a butterfly pinned on a corkboard, a beetle trapped in a glass, hold him still, stop his wings from flapping. But I didn't find anything like that. Documents from work that I didn't understand, lots of figures on them, paper-clips, expired visas, biros printed with the names of different hotels. Nothing with emotional content. I got up and opened the drawers in the wardrobe. Nothing much in them either. Underwear, belts, a jumper I'd never seen him wear. A bag was hung on one of the hangers, and I opened that too. Some documents in a plastic folder. A couple of letters. One of them was still sealed, but the other was open. A bank statement. I looked through it, but it didn't tell me much. The only thing that really surprised me was the amount he'd been paid that month. I checked it three times to make sure I'd read it right.

I was about to put it back, when I noticed it had been sent to his house in Oxfordshire. I took a photograph of the address, then I sat down on the bed and typed it into Google, found out how much he'd paid for it and when. April last year. So they'd chosen it together. Lived there together, perhaps. I'd never asked. And did he not want to disturb the memory of that, like when a parent leaves untouched the room of their missing child? Was that why he wouldn't let me go? I found out how many bedrooms and how many bathrooms it had, but there weren't any photos. I looked it up on Google Maps, and then I tried to switch it to Street View, but it was off in one of those unphotographed bits, and I could only get as far as the bottom of the road. Then I had to get up and take a shower. I was going to be late.

The audition was at someone's house, which was odd. Trying to cut costs, I suppose. It was further out of London than I'd planned for, and the house was so big, it took me ten minutes to find the way in. A woman answered the door.

Hi, I'm Anna — I said. — I'm a little late, I'm sorry.

Anna, welcome. You're our 14:03? Don't worry, we're a touch behind too.

She led me into the kitchen, which had tiled floors, oak surfaces and lots of copper pots hanging above a chopping island, like an American farmhouse.

If you could wait here until the warm-up room's ready for you –
she said. – Oh, and I don't think you've paid your audition fee yet,
have you?

I found Max's latest envelope, pulled out a couple of notes and
handed them over.

There was a girl, about my age, sitting at the kitchen table, flicking through a score. She'd highlighted her text in pink.

I sat.

Zerlina? – she said.

Sorry?

You're trying for Zerlina?

Oh right. Yes. You?

Same – she said, lips slightly pursed, as if to say – yes, I *thought*
so.

The ones who talked to you before auditions were always like
this – smiling mouths and hard eyes – because it was never really a
chat, not really.

She shut her music, and started to ask me questions.

What's your name? – she said. – Anna? Hm. Anna. I don't think
I've seen you around before, Anna. Not much on the London singing circuit, hm? What's your surname? I haven't heard of you. Oh,
new in London? Well, sort of new. That would be it then. Are you
studying here? Oh *really*? Interesting. How old are you, if you don't
mind me asking? Sung this role before? The full role, I meant. Sung
with the company? Do you know the MD then? The director? The
repetiteur? Well, who *do* you know exactly? Which companies *have*
you sung with? I meant in London. And who's your teacher, anyway?

She listened carefully to my answers, and then she nodded and
turned away. She got out a brush and ran it through her long blonde
hair, flicking it first this way and then the other, flick flick flick, trying
to work out which side it looked best flicked on. She dabbed on a
bright red mouth, checked her teeth in her hand mirror and smiled.
She pulled off her trainers and picked up her tote bag – name of
an opera festival printed on the front – took out some Louboutin
shoes, patent leather, high but undeniably classy. She stood up and

stepped into them, and then she sat back down, opened up her score. She didn't look at me again.

Anna? – our hostess poked her head round the kitchen door. – The warm-up room's free. If you'd like to come this way.

I followed her upstairs.

Through there – she said. – I'll come and get you when they're ready.

The room was small, with lots of clashing florals – floral wallpaper, floral throw on the sofa, floral curtains. It was very warm. I took off my jumper. I hadn't noticed it so much downstairs, that clammy heat you get in old people's houses – heat needed to toast those who never move, like lamps to keep lizards warm.

I went over to the window. Huge landscaped garden, some construction at the end of it, a pool house maybe. I felt no urgency. The pre-audition high should have hit me by now, but it hadn't. I stood there, looked out at the improbably green lawn, the designer cat picking its way across the garden wall. A couple of weeks ago, Max had made a comment about art being less important to a country than politics. I'd tried to explain why I didn't think that was necessarily right.

He said – but what you're saying is so obviously not true, Anna, it's hard to believe you believe it.

He said – but a large part of what motivates an artist is what they personally want, right? There's something fundamentally selfish about that, isn't there? Something arrogant? You're saying, the world's not good enough for me. You're saying, I want a different sort of life. Yes, maybe there's some external benefit, but it's secondary, right, to what you personally want?

I'd been offended, and he'd said then that he thought we were having a theoretical discussion, he hadn't meant me, and I shouldn't be so sensitive.

I remembered that, standing, looking out of the window. I thought about what he'd said, and I knew he was right. This wasn't important. This little company. Their little performances in a room above a pub. Their chi-chi Islington audience, there for the interval wine, and so they could say — *oh yes, we saw that*. I wasn't even sure that it was important to me. It felt pointless, actually, auditioning for a role I'd have to pay to do, imagining his face when I told him that and what he'd say — *but aren't they meant to be paying you? I thought you said they were a good company? But, so, how does that work?*

The woman hadn't told me how much time I had, probably twenty minutes, not long left now. There was an odd pleasure in not warming up. A perverse excitement in being bad. I'd felt it as a child — when the teacher told us to get out of the swimming pool, I'd dive under the water and hold my breath, look up at the wobbly shape of her standing over me, know I was in trouble. I'd feel this excited sting between my legs, though I wouldn't have known then what it was, just that I liked it. I looked at my watch. Ten minutes had passed. I was running out of time.

I stood in front of the mirror, struck a note on the upright, and started to sing. As soon as I opened my mouth, I wished I'd gone into the Conservatory first thing, actually done some work, instead of wasting my time going through his stuff — looking for evidence — for fucking evidence — for evidence of what? I didn't even know. I was tired, and my voice felt unwieldy, like a too large parcel that didn't fit under my arm. I looked at myself in the mirror, and saw that my heels were too high. They hadn't seemed it yesterday, but looking at them now, undeniably, they were. Too high and trashy looking, particularly with that dress, I'd have to put my jumper back on, never mind the heat, because I wasn't like that girl downstairs — that girl whose clothes just worked, who was whole and complete, just one thing, while I was made of all these different parts that didn't fit together.

I was warming up the scale but I still wasn't in my voice, I was standing outside it, and I looked into my face and saw that my eyes were wide and black, and I realised, suddenly, horribly, that I was frightened. Not standard pre-audition nervous — those nerves you can use and channel into energy — but frightened. Fully, bodily, Run Away frightened. It tingled through me. It paralysed my throat, as if someone had put their fingers round my neck and squeezed.

Something gave way. The note split, it broke in half, it stuttered, faltered, then it stopped.

There was a knock at the door, and the woman stuck her head in.

They're ready for you – she said.

I wasn't sure how long she'd been outside. My heart was beating in my throat, high, too high, like if I opened my mouth I might vomit it out.

They're just through that door there – she said. – Knock and wait, and they'll call you in.

I stood outside for a second, breathed, then knocked, but nobody answered.

I knocked again, and I waited. Still nothing.

I knocked a third time, and then I was worried they hadn't heard, so I pushed open the door and went in.

The space wasn't big. A grand piano filled most of it, rug on top, piled with scores. There was a sofa on the opposite wall, four men squashed together, looking too large for the room, like adults trying to squeeze into a child's playhouse. They were all wearing suits, although one of them had discarded his tie and undone some buttons, and another had taken off his shoes. He was sitting in mismatched socks.

I realised why I hadn't heard them say *come in*. None of them could speak. They were all helpless with laughter.

The Shoeless Man had his head on his knees, hands interlaced over his skull, shoulders heaving.

The Tieless Man was swinging his tie over his head like a lasso, hitting the Pink-Shirted Man with it, while he snorted and gasped and squirmed *stop it mate, hey, hey, stop it.*

The man in the middle sat with legs wide open, forcing the others into the corners. He looked to his left, and then to his right, and he smiled. He was, I knew, from Google, the Man in Charge.

Hi – I said. – Sorry, I did knock. Are you ready for me?

The sight of me made whatever they were laughing about funnier – they seemed to enjoy an audience – and I worried that it was my outfit, or – worse – that these rooms weren't well soundproofed and they'd heard me warm up. I was about to say I was sorry, I didn't feel well, I was going to have to leave, when the Man in Charge said – *you're Anna? Well, come on in* – and without me wanting them to, my limbs obeyed.

Sorry about them – the Man in Charge said. – They're just – they're just—

He collapsed into childish giggles.

The room was oddly shaped, and there was nowhere obvious for me to stand. I ended up slightly too far from the piano, and slightly too close to the men. I said hello to the pianist, and she smiled at me, as if to say – *sorry, tough luck, you're on your own.*

Most of the men were trying to control themselves by now. The Tieless Man was biting the back of his hand. The Shoeless Man was doing performative deep breaths. The Pink-Shirted man had gone pink himself with embarrassment. But the Man in Charge looked right at me, laughing openly, tears running down his cheeks. I wanted to cover myself with my hands.

Part? – he asked.

My throat was dry. It took a couple of goes to speak.

Zerlina.

Ok, right – he said. – So, Anna. We'll start with 'Batti Batti', and, and, hang on—

He snorted with laughter, got out a handkerchief and blew his nose, wiped his eyes.

Ok, so, what I want you to do, right, yeah, is to sing the aria, ok? Ok, and – ha – and – and while you're singing, I want you to look at me, ok? And what I'm going to be doing is – I'm going to be sort of like, waving my arms around –

He jiggled his arms in the air to demonstrate. The other men snickered.

And I want you to like, follow my arms, cos I'll be showing you what I want you to do with it, you know?

Sorry, I don't quite – you're going to conduct it, you mean?

No, like, I'm going to show you how to interpret it? Ok? So if I wave my arms higher like this, that might mean I want you to be a bit, like, brasher, right? And – look, I just want to see how you take my direction, ok? Be creative.

Um, right – I said. – Ok.

Auditions are artificial. The panel's always too close and the room's always too bright. You have to block that out. You have to picture the scene very clearly, make it feel real. But I couldn't. I was staring at the Man in Charge, his cold blue eyes and the open amusement in his face, and I heard, somewhere very far away, the pianist play the opening chord. He made a stabbing gesture to tell me I was meant to come in. She played the chord again, and then a third time. I stood there. Everything was quiet in my head.

They were laughing at me, now. I was sure of it. Not laughing in general, but laughing at me.

I turned to the pianist.

I'm really sorry – I said. – Could we start again?

She played the chord, and this time I came in, but the fear stayed. It normally went. It normally went when you started to sing and realised it was going to be fine, but this wasn't going to be fine. My voice was thin and wispy and sticky, like candyfloss. The more I tried to grab at it, the more it came apart.

But what if I am not to blame?

I'd spent hours in the practice room working on these phrases.

What if it was all his doing?

The intention behind them, the changes in mood, hours and hours spent crafting Zerlina's pleas, her interjections, her accusations. But I was staring at the Man in Charge and he had some very different ideas to me, and the more I tried to follow his movements, the more my voice detached, floated somewhere away from me up there on the ceiling like a lost helium balloon.

I tripped and stumbled through the opening recit, and launched into the aria. The Man in Charge waved his arms at me emphatically, like I was the entire section of a symphony orchestra playing wildly out of time, about to lead the performance to catastrophe. The room was getting smaller. Sweat pooled at my collar and pricked round my hairline. The walls were closing in, really close now. They were crushing my head, squeezing my lungs, they were about to force the organs out of me, and the men were on the sofa, somewhere over there, watching, laughing, because really it was too funny – haha – watching everything be squeezed out of me like this. With every note, thinking, *that's it, I have to stop, I just have to stop, I have to stop and say I'm sorry and leave*, but you never stop, you never stop, those are the rules, whatever happens, you look like it's right, you keep going. And then there we were at the end of the aria, and I almost didn't want it to end because once it stopped I'd have to say something, or maybe they'd say something first, and I wasn't sure which would be worse.

The pianist didn't bother with the final bars of music, stopped with me. Nobody moved. Nobody said anything.

I swallowed. My tongue was too big for my mouth.

Well, thanks – I whispered, and I turned to go.

Hang on a minute – said the Man in Charge.

I turned back.

Zerlina's got another aria – he said. – Have you prepared that too?

Um. Yes. I have.

We'd like to hear it.

I thought – *he can't be serious. You should turn and leave*. But I heard myself saying – ok – because those were the rules. As long as he waggled my strings, I'd keep dancing.

So, what we'd really like with this one – he said – is to know what you're like on stage. Tell us. What's it about?

Well, Don Giovanni's just beaten up Masetto – I said. – That's Zerlina's, I mean, my fiancé. And I'm trying to cheer him up, you know, to make him feel better.

Well, yes – the Man in Charge smirked. – You could put it like that. So, what we'd like you to do is pick one of us to act with you. Decide on your Masetto.

Sorry?

We've had all our Zerlinas do the same – the Tieless Man said.

Right.

I scanned the sofa. I remembered that the Pink-Shirted Man had looked embarrassed, so I pointed to him.

The others roared and whooped.

No way! Again! – the Shoeless Man shouted.

Every time! – said the Tieless Man.

What's he got that we haven't? – the Man in Charge sneered.

The Pink-Shirted Man put a chair in the middle of the room, and sat down.

Ok – the Man in Charge said. – Let's just run the aria, shall we? And while you're singing, we want you to improvise. Whatever comes naturally. Whatever Zerlina would do.

The pianist played the intro, and as I started to sing, felt the shake in my legs, the flutter in my voice, I was suddenly reckless. Hysterical, almost, with how bad this was and thinking, well, it couldn't be worse. The Pink-Shirted Man was looking at them, not at me, and I could see them smiling at each other, so I thought, *if this is what they want, they can have it.* They wanted to see what I'd do, thought I'd be too shy to do anything, and that that in itself would be funny. Because it's meant to be sexy, this aria, she's meant to be seducing him, and we were nearly at it, the bit where she says *I have the best medicine for you, Masetto. I carry it with me always, you can try it if you like, here, here it is, feel it beat, touch me here.* It's right there in the text. She makes Masetto grope her breasts. The guys were giggling like schoolboys, and the Pink-Shirted Man still wasn't looking at me, he was smirking at them, so I sat on his lap. Someone whistled. I grabbed his head and turned it to face me. *Feel it beat, touch me here.* I took his hand and pressed it to my chest. I could feel my heart going thud thud thud through his fingers. He grinned at me and, up close like that, I could smell the booze on his breath, and then I had this feeling, this sudden mad feeling like I might do anything – exactly like last night, Max pinning me down, that exciting, terrifying, out-of-control *fuck, was that me, what the fuck did I just do* feeling. The blood on his face, afterwards. His hand cupped round his cheek. The way he'd looked at me. It was like that now again, like I might do anything. I might slap him. I might dig my nails into his cheek and gouge them down. I might kiss him. I might bite down on his lip until I had his blood, sharp, in my mouth.

The Pink-Shirted Man shouted – fucking ow.

He prised my fingers off. I hadn't realised how hard I'd been gripping him. There were deep grooves on the back of his hand from my nails. No one was laughing now.

FOURTEEN

Back home, I'd already put my pyjamas on, got into bed, when I remembered I had a rehearsal. I checked my phone. Four missed calls from the Director, and two from Frankie. I texted them both saying I was ill, but I didn't hear back. I curled up under the covers.

I'd had bad auditions before, of course, everyone had. I'd forgotten words. The panel had been rude or just not interested. I'd cracked notes, or I'd got to the high bits, the bits that were meant to be impressive, and they hadn't worked. I'd had auditions where I'd got to the middle of the piece and wanted to stop. I'd had auditions where I'd barely managed to get out of the building before I cried. But I'd never been afraid, not like that. I'd stumbled somewhere on my way into that room, lost my footing, was still falling. I couldn't imagine opening my mouth again to sing.

I must have fallen asleep, because the next thing I knew, I was in a dressing room. It was nearly time to go on stage, but I couldn't remember which opera I was in. They were calling me over the tannoy. I hadn't warmed up and so I tried to sing, opened my mouth, took a breath, and – nothing – nothing – I couldn't make anything come out. I tried to hum. I tried to lip trill. I couldn't make a sound, and then I woke, and it was dark outside. My throat was so dry I couldn't swallow and the sheets were damp with sweat.

It was just before six. I had a text from Laurie, saying she hoped the audition had gone well. She was staying out that night but she'd see me tomorrow. There was one from the Director too, which said – *VERY late notice*. I thought about calling Angela, telling her what had happened, but I thought she was probably still annoyed with me and, anyway, I knew what she'd say. She'd say — *well, everyone has off days, you can only learn from it and move on.* When I described how they'd behaved, she'd say — *it doesn't do to be shy and uptight, Anna. Not in this industry. There simply isn't time.* She'd be right, and it wouldn't make me feel better.

Instead, I called Max. He picked up after two rings.

Anna? I'm at work.

I know.

Is something wrong?

Can I see you? Tonight?

What is it? — he said, impatient, angry even. — Has something happened?

I'd let myself imagine he'd drop everything, come straightaway. He'd be loving and sympathetic, gentle, and in his arms, with his voice in my ear, I'd forget.

I'm upset — I said. — The audition today went badly. I just wanted to see you.

I heard him say something to someone in the background, and I wasn't sure he'd even been listening, but then he said — look, sure, let's do something. I'll let you know when I'm done here, ok? Then you can come over.

Can you come here instead? Laurie's out.

A pause.

Please — I said. — I'm not feeling great.

Text me your address then — he said, and hung up.

A couple of hours passed. I thought about trying to tidy the room, but it was mostly Laurie's stuff and, anyway, there was a part of me that wanted him to see it at its worst. To see the distaste on his face as he stepped over Laurie's pants on the floor. A perverse part of me that wanted his pity.

My phone rang and he said he was outside. I went down to let him in, and he kissed me with cold lips.

Did you find the house ok?

Evidently. I got a cab.

He took off his shoes and hung his coat on a hook by the door, then he introduced himself to Mil, who was in the kitchen. It was a quality in him I always admired, was jealous of, actually – how he made himself comfortable anywhere, that casual ease he had. They chatted for a bit about the house, the neighbourhood. I stood there awkwardly, not contributing much, until Mil asked if we wanted some food, and he said – *Anna's not feeling well, actually, so we'll leave you to it* – like I was the outsider, not him.

We went up to my room.

There's a lot going on here – he said.

I sat on the bed. The room was small, so it was pushed up against the wall, and I'd drawn the short straw side-wise, had to climb over Laurie if she went to sleep first. Max picked up a framed photograph of me and Laurie, taken at a party right after I'd met her last summer. I'd felt lucky being there with her, I remembered. Lucky I'd ended up living with someone like her, just by chance – the sort of person who can make anything seem fun. The light in the photo had bleached our hair and our skin, so we looked far more similar than we did in real life. He looked at it for a while, and then he put it down without saying anything. He touched the edges of the colourful cloth draped over the dresser, pulled at a thread. He picked up tubes of Laurie's make-up, littered on the surfaces, opened them, twisted a lipstick till the colour popped out, then twisted it back. He picked up a notebook on the desk, and flicked through it. It was Laurie's and definitely private, but I didn't tell him to stop, because he'd barely looked at me since he'd arrived, and it made me nervous.

He came over to me, lay on the bed, pressed his hands into his eyes.

What's wrong? – I said.

Nothing. Strange day. When I got in this morning, they'd cordoned off the lobby. The department on the third floor were swapping with the traders on twelve. The guys were moving their stuff in boxes. All the floors have a corridor that looks out over the lobby. There's a safety rail, but you can climb over it, and one of the traders had jumped in the night.

That's horrible.

He'd been having a bad time for a while, apparently. Family problems, and then his deal was going wrong and he was losing the company loads of money – I mean, millions, he was losing us millions of dollars – and I guess he'd had enough. But you know the worst thing? The worst thing is that everyone carried on trading. They didn't call an ambulance until people started to arrive in the morning. I wouldn't have done either, if I was them. You can't. The markets don't stop because someone's killed themselves.

Who did they swap with?

What do you mean?

The traders. Who was on the third floor?

Oh, I see. Risk Management, I think.

Is that a joke?

No – he said. – It's not.

He still had his eyes shut. I could see the thin white line on his cheek where I'd scratched him.

Anyway – he said. – It made me think.

About what?

About how many more decades I want to give them. That's what it made me think about.

He opened his eyes and looked at me.

And so what about you? – he said. – Very dramatic. Summoning me here. What's wrong?

Dramatic?

You sounded upset.

I started telling him about the audition, but it sounded trivial, and I didn't know how to tell it, how to get his sympathy and still sound good.

Well, it's a learning experience, isn't it? – he said. – What can you do to make sure it doesn't happen again?

I don't know.

He looked at me, pensively.

There've been a few like this lately, haven't there?

Not really. What do you mean?

A few auditions you haven't got.

I guess. But there are always auditions you don't get. They were nothing like this.

You've seemed tired lately – he said. – Quiet, you know. Stressed out.

Really?

He looked around the room, and then he said – to be honest, I'm not surprised. That this sort of thing is happening, I mean, with you living here. How can you sleep with Laurie here too? Or relax? Or practise? Can you practise here? I assume you can't, not with all these people on top of you.

He was right, I couldn't, but this wasn't what I wanted to hear. I wanted him to comfort me.

I think you should move – he said.

For one crazy moment, I thought he was going to suggest I come and live with him, but then he said – I have this colleague who's just bought a buy-to-let studio. He was asking me about builders yesterday. Can't get much for it as it is, and it's sitting empty right now. He's got a lot on at work, don't think he's planning to do anything about it till summer. Maybe he'll let you stay there for a bit. I'll ask him.

But I didn't want him to offer me practical solutions. I wanted him to tell me that things would be ok – or, no, not even that – I wanted him to stop me thinking at all. I wanted him to reach into my brain and switch it off.

I leant over him and kissed him. At first, he was gentle. He kept his hands by his sides, said my name like he had a question, but I didn't want him to speak, so I got on top of him. I pulled my shirt over my head, took his hands and put them on me, made him touch me, and then he sat up and kissed me again, and this time he was different. He put his arms round me, flipped me over so I was underneath him, pulled at the waist of my trousers to tell me to take them off. I lay there and watched him while he stood up, got undressed, and I heard my breath go fast and shallow, the black fear still pooling in my stomach like an oil spill, and I knew that he could make it stop. So I pulled him on me, and then I didn't know what I was doing anymore – biting him, scratching him, telling him to do it harder and harder – not knowing what he'd do next and that it could be anything. He got me on my knees and knelt behind me, one hand wrapped hard round my hair, pulling sharply at my scalp and it still wasn't enough, I could still think, and so I heard my mouth say to him all these things I wasn't sure I meant, that I wanted him to do anything to me, to hurt me, and he put his hand over my mouth. He said – *stop it, be quiet* – and he pulled my head backwards towards him, and then his hand wasn't on my mouth anymore, it was on my throat, still stretched back like that, and I felt it tighten. Little spots of light in my eyes and my mind went blank and my blood streamed hot, and I heard his voice, very distantly, somewhere in my head saying my name, and then all that blackness rushed towards me and I couldn't think about anything anymore, there was just this noise, animal and frightening, something like a scream, but not a scream, I didn't know what it was, I'd never heard it before, and I knew it was me.

When I opened my eyes, he was lying on the bed, and I was still on my knees, leaning my head against my arms on the wall. I could feel blood pounding in my neck. I put my hand to my throat. I tried to swallow, then I started to cough.

Why did you do that? – I whispered.

What? You wanted me to.

I tried to say something else, but I couldn't.

He touched my back, pulled at my arm to make me lie next to him. He stroked my hair. Neither of us spoke for a second, and then he said – I thought that was what you wanted. Wasn't it? Anna? Was that not what you wanted?

At the weekend, Mil had a play on, and her mum came to London to see it. She came round to the house in the afternoon. They'd been for lunch at The Delaunay, and then they'd gone on a shopping trip, and Mil was carrying lots of bags full of clothes her mother had bought her. She'd also had a personality transplant, and was now Amelia, all acquiescent smiles and uncontroversial opinions.

We all came down to have tea with her mother. We said how much we liked the house and thank you very much for letting us stay. We talked about how many tourists there were in London, and how difficult it was to find proper clothes these days without spending a fortune. We ate some organic biscuits, talked about baking for a bit, and then we got the bus to the theatre.

The play was about how all women are victims, particularly the ones who think that they aren't, and everyone on stage was dressed in various shades of drab. I found it hard to concentrate, because Laurie squeezed my knee whenever she found something funny, which was pretty much all the time. It was ninety minutes through without an interval, and afterwards everyone congregated in the lobby. A trestle table, paper cups of warm white wine.

Mil's friends were there, ones I recognised from New Year's Eve, with their bobs and knitwear and big glasses. They stood in a group, talking about a guy one of them knew from uni, who was making a big name for himself in theatre. He'd written a one-man show, which involved him dressing as a parody of a woman – micro skirt and heels, long plaited wig, red cheeks and bright red lips. Half the girls were furious, including Mil, who'd started a petition against the show transferring from the Fringe and, since this had failed, was trying to arrange a protest for opening night. She claimed his get-up was inherently misogynistic and that, as a privileged white male, gender was not something he had the right to profit from deconstructing. The other half were furious with Mil et al, saying that they were reinforcing normative values and denying the validity of his form of self-expression. The conversation was already fraught.

Well, he is gay – one of them was saying.

Yeah, so he claims, but he also went to Eton, so –

Me and Laurie went to get another drink.

Meanwhile – she said to me, once we were out of earshot – the men are laughing. They're all getting on with making theatre, while the women fight amongst themselves.

So, how's your week been? – she asked. – Are you feeling better?

I hadn't been to rehearsals for the past few days, not since the audition on Tuesday. Whenever I imagined singing, I remembered the men laughing at me, that pure irrepressible panic, and I couldn't face it. Said I was ill. I thought I'd be interrogated, but they were mainly doing Act One anyway, the act Musetta's not in, and so the Director said – *fine, whatever, but make sure you're better next week* – and that was it. I spent a lot of time walking aimlessly, sometimes heading south – through streets lined with quiet Georgian houses and on to the fancy bars of Upper Street – sometimes north – where Turkish restaurants displayed trays of buttery pilaf, white bean stews in their windows, and food stores interrupted the grey pavements with crates of colourful fruit. I tried to focus on the feel of my feet on the pavement, the air in my lungs. To wear myself out by the end of each day, and not to think.

Kind of – I said. – I think not singing this week was good for me. I've been run down lately, I think that's what it was.

What are you up to tomorrow night? Want to hang out at home?

Well, actually, I won't be there tomorrow – I said.

Max's colleague had said it was fine for me to have the flat, but Laurie had been out the past few nights. I hadn't found a moment to tell her.

I've got some news actually – I said. – I've kind of found somewhere else to live.

She stared at me, and then she said – I see. Since when?

Not long. I've only known for a couple of days. I wanted to tell you in person.

Well, consider me told.

It's free straightaway, so I thought I'd move my stuff tomorrow. Given that it's a weekend and everything.

Right. That makes sense. Where is it?

Farringdon.

Something to do with him then?

Kind of, yeah.

Makes sense – she said again.

Are you ok? I thought you'd be pleased. You'll have the room to yourself.

This seemed like a logical argument. Max had raised it several times when I'd said I was scared to tell her.

Yeah – she said. – Yeah, you're right. I'm pleased. We should get back to the others.

She walked off.

I was suddenly angry. She had no right to act like I was doing something wrong. I decided I'd go home, leave her to realise she was being childish. I went over to say goodbye.

To say this is all about sex is misleading, isn't it? – she was saying to the group. – Sure, sex is one way men show us they despise us, but it's not the reason. It's a symptom, not a cause. Stopping men from groping us at work isn't going to magically fix the pay gap.

I'm leaving – I said.

She turned round and, for a moment, I thought she might say she'd come too. I really hoped she would. But she just said – *cool, see you later then* – and turned back.

I found my suitcases in the hall cupboard and went upstairs to start packing. It felt like I was always putting my stuff into boxes and getting it out again. The more times I packed it and unpacked it again, tried to arrange it in a new space, the more worthless it seemed. I started folding my clothes, but so many of them were bobbly and worn, I went down to the kitchen and got a binbag. I started to throw things away – things I felt no longer matched the person I wanted to be. I had to make myself stop after a bit, though, because otherwise I wouldn't have much left. Just the stuff I'd bought recently. Some beautiful clothes. The earrings he'd given me.

After a little while, I gave up and went to bed, and then Laurie got back. She switched on the light. I curled up with my face to the wall and pretended to be asleep, but she thumped round the room, throwing her bag on the chair, slamming the wardrobe door. I sat up.

How was the rest of the night? – I asked.

It was fine.

Is Mil still there?

Yeah, she stayed out with the actors.

I forgot to tell you – I said, trying to get her back on side. – You know what she said to me yesterday? She said that she preferred not to date men at all, but when she absolutely had to, she'd only date black men because they understood the struggle.

Laurie gave me a long critical look.

You know what? – she said. – You can say whatever you like about Mil, but she barely knows you and she's let you stay here for basically nothing. She's incredibly fucking kind, and all you can do is be a cunt about her.

Why are you annoyed with me?

I'm not annoyed with you.

She turned away, started looking for something in her bag.

You know we're not together, right? – I said. – You can't get upset about me not wanting to share a room with you. We're not together, and we're not twelve either.

You can live wherever you like, Anna – she said. – I really don't care. But I don't suppose it ever occurred to you that I need you here to be able to afford this room? That you giving me a day's notice before you fuck off leaves me in a really difficult position? Did you ever consider that?

I hadn't.

I'm sorry – I said. – I didn't realise. I'll keep paying for a couple of months.

Yeah, really? We both know what you mean by that. You're not earning any fucking money, Anna, and don't pretend to me you're living off savings. You don't have any savings. I'm not an idiot. And I'm not having him pay my rent too, but thank you very much for offering.

He hasn't been paying my rent.

Yeah? So, you can suddenly afford a flat in central London, can you?

It's not like that – I said.

Max had presented me with the flat as a fait accompli the day after the audition. I asked how much his colleague expected for it, and when Max told me, I was horrified. I said he knew I couldn't afford that, and he said that, yes, he thought I'd say that, so he'd already given Vincent the money. Just for the next couple of months. He wanted the flat empty by June anyway. And I told him I couldn't let him do that, it was too much, and he said it was silly for me to sabotage my career on a point of principle, he wanted to help me out, and anyway, I could give it back to him one day if I wanted. So I said ok, fine, thank you, and I added the money to the list on my phone, even though it was too much, now, to ever hope to pay him back.

Anna – Laurie said. – I'm worried about you. You must know that. The way you are about him, it frightens me. You seem to second-guess everything you do these days. It's like he's taking the person you were and rubbing bits of you out.

You've barely even met him – I said. – You don't know him.

Yeah, but neither do you – she said.

I woke up when I heard the door shut. I thought she'd left but, a few minutes later, she came back with two cups of coffee. She handed me one, sat down on the bed, and said she'd help me pack.

It's none of my business – she said. – You have to do what you want. You know what I think, but I won't interfere.

She put some music on, and we packed the rest of my things. We talked about all sorts of stuff. About her book, about the guy she was seeing, about whether we thought Sash was actually a drug addict or just rich. She didn't mention Max again, but when I'd got everything together and we'd carried it downstairs, she said – I'm sorry we argued. Don't disappear.

I won't – I said. – I promise.

I hate to see you throwing your life away for a man – she said. – That's all.

I hugged her and I didn't say anything. I knew that she cared about me and she was trying to be nice, but she was wrong. He wasn't compromising the life I wanted. He was making it possible.

FIFTEEN

My new place wasn't what I'd expected. It was in an art deco block, mostly studios, and mine hadn't been touched since the twenties. There was a small entrance hall with three doors. A tiny kitchen, ancient microwave I was scared to plug in, cutlery with different coloured handles. A bathroom, lemon-coloured toilet, spotted mirror, dim lights. A studio room, filled with too much heavy furniture – small table, dresser, wardrobe, sofa bed. One window. It looked out onto the blank wall of the building next door.

I spent the evening I arrived unpacking, though there wasn't room for everything, and even when I was done, it looked untidy. At the bottom of my backpack, I found the photo of me and Laurie. She must have put it there when she was helping me pack, and I was sad, looking at it, not sure what she'd meant by giving it to me – if it was a statement of love, or if she didn't want it anymore.

The next day was Monday, and I went back to rehearsals. It had been nearly a week since the audition by then, and I hadn't sung since. I'd tried not to think about it. If I let enough time pass, I thought, I'd forget the fear and everything would be fine – but if I tried to sing while I still remembered it so clearly, there was every chance it would happen again. Last week, I'd told Angela I couldn't come to my lessons because I had a cold. She was concerned on the phone, said I sounded odd and what was wrong, and she'd texted me every day to check in. Her worry made me even more anxious, so I was glad she was now away for a couple of weeks. She'd left at the weekend, was singing in a series of concerts abroad and, focused on her own work, she'd gone quiet.

I arrived at the rehearsal without trying to warm up. I planned to say I was still ill, and to take the first day back slowly. I'd wait until I felt comfortable being on stage again, and then I'd ease back into making sound. As it turned out, though, no one cared, and I didn't sing all week. We were blocking Act Two, Musetta's first entrance – a scene so complex, the Director was having enough trouble following the score, let alone directing us. It was week three, and he was fast discovering that his vision would be impossible to execute. Not in this space, not with these singers. While he was busy doing crowd control, barking at us all to shut the fuck up so he could tell us where to fucking stand, the show he'd imagined – that beautiful, ethereal show he'd dreamed about for months – had slipped away out of Stage Door, unnoticed.

There were lots of issues.

The main problem with Act Two was the sheer scale of the thing. It was set in a Parisian kerbside café, peppered with soldiers, citizens, students, shopkeepers, seamstresses, and a whole load of children, all singing. You needed at least fifty chorus members, plus kids, for it to make any sense at all – but children were a logistical nightmare, so we didn't bother with them, and Marieke could only round up twenty singers – mainly undergrads – willing to devote this much time to rehearsals just for a chorus credit. The ones playing Mothers had to swap to playing Children, and the ones playing Vendors, advertising their wares, had to swap to playing Customers, buying them – all in the space of a few bars, until the scene was reduced to nonsense and the Director got very angry. The more confused the chorus were, the more terse and sarcastic he'd become, until he'd snap and shout – *let's take a break. Take a break. I need a break* – and he'd sit there, looking at the score, muttering to himself – *and what the fuck's a fucking hawker, anyway?*

Then there was the soprano singing Mimi. She'd been cast because of her beautiful voice, but she was fat and she couldn't act, and the Director held her personally responsible for destroying his romantic bohemian fantasies. He'd puff and sigh his way through her bits, and then afterwards he'd snarl – *yes, well, something like that, but maybe next time keep your face still, dear.*

Frankie was also a problem. If there were any other tenors in the Conservatory good enough to sing Rodolfo, he wouldn't have been cast. He'd worked with the Director before and they hated each other, and Frankie was barely even trying to follow instructions, far less look like he was into Mimi. He kept winking at me every time he had to show her affection, and whenever the Director shouted at him about hamming it up like a fucking amateur, he put on his confused, hurt face, and hammed it up even more. He'd do it properly on the night, and the Director knew it and, as far as he was concerned, that made him even worse.

And finally there were, as always, too many male parts and not enough men. Marcello was already working professionally, was allowed to miss half the rehearsals for more important commitments and, whenever he did show up, acted like we should all be grateful. Schaunard had only translated his own part and had no idea what anyone else was singing, just stood there, staring at them, until it was his turn again. Alcindoro was at least thirty years too young to be my sugar daddy, and Parpignol had a voice like a foghorn. Every time he opened his mouth, the Director performatively winced.

So whether or not I was singing was really the least of anyone's worries. Everyone's voices were tired. We were doing the same bits over and over again, and so most of the principals – except for Frankie, who'd pop out his top C for anyone who'd listen – had started marking anyway, crooning it down an octave, singing quietly, and I marked too. I sketched the notes in, not singing out, and no one cared. Every time we got to my aria, the Director said – *and Musetta will just fucking do something here, won't you sweetheart? Let's skip it, skip it. No time.*

It was easy to pretend, and even to believe, that everything was ok. In rehearsals, I was more brash than usual, overcompensating, playing the part of a self-assured singer, and everyone bought it. After rehearsals, we'd go to the pub, and then I was right there in the hot, incestuous centre of show-making, where the actual singing bit seemed irrelevant. All anyone cared about was who fancied whom, and the private jokes, and the bitching about the Director when he wasn't there, and the sycophancy when he was. A bunch of them would always stay late drinking, the performances too far away to bother being careful, but I always left by mid-evening. I spent most nights that week with Max. He'd been affectionate since I'd moved, wanting to see more of me, though he still wouldn't stay at mine – hadn't realised how studenty the flat would feel, he said. Anyway, I was happy to sacrifice a few hours' drinking to please him. Frankie asked me where I kept rushing off to, and when I told him, he said – *oh yeah. Him. I met him, remember? The old guy* – and gave me his most innocent smile, and I was surprised by how much it annoyed me. The next morning, he called me a dirty stopout when I'd forgotten to take a change of clothes and turned up in the same outfit. I pretended to be embarrassed, tried to join in with the banter I'd missed from the pub last night, though I didn't quite get it, and then the Director told us to stop nattering on like we were at a mothers' meeting, and to get the fuck on the fucking stage, and it started all over again. I didn't sing. Two weeks had passed since the audition, and I'd barely made a sound.

No one seemed to notice. Angela was still away. I wasn't expected to go to regular classes in production weeks, so no one missed me. And the other singers in *Bohème* had all started to panic too, now that performances were getting closer. They said their voices were tired, thought they might be getting ill. They catastrophised, and I did too. It was the done thing to catastrophise. I said I'd had this cold, it was awful, sitting right there on my vocal cords. I wasn't getting over it, needed to be careful. I'd keep marking for now, I said, and no one thought anything of it. I didn't sing.

I didn't sing, because it was easy that way to tell myself it was fine. I felt fine. I wasn't ill. I didn't have a sore throat. I felt normal. I told myself that vocal rest was good for me. I'd got over-tired and that's why it had happened.

I didn't sing, because I was afraid that, if I did sing – I don't really know – I suppose I was afraid that, if I did sing, it wouldn't be fine, and then I'd have to do something about it and I wasn't sure what that might be. I was afraid that fear would open its black eyes again, reach up and put its hand around my throat.

A couple of times that week, I thought — *well, this is ridiculous, isn't it? What the hell do I think I'm doing?* — and I booked a practice room. I started to warm up and it was all fine. There was nothing wrong. I didn't need to worry. But then I felt fear begin to wake up, to wake up and stir inside me, and I looked at myself in the mirror and saw that my eyes were wide and my face was pale. So I stopped trying. I left the practice room and shut the door. I called Frankie and we went to the pub instead.

The next week, Laurie suggested meeting. I told her Max really wanted to get to know her better, told him the same thing, and unexpectedly they both said — *well, ok then, let's have a drink*. They'd been wrong about each other, I thought. I needed them to get on. He said he'd pick me up after work, so I avoided being dragged to the pub when rehearsals were finished, headed straight back to mine.

Before he got there, I turned the bed back into a sofa, then I tried to clear up the overspill of my belongings. I chucked my clothes, my scores into the bottom of the wardrobe, arranged my pictures so they looked decorative, not incidental.

As I was putting things away, I sang to myself. Force of habit, not conscious, I barely even noticed I was doing it at first, but then I realised and I was happy. It was like waking from a bad dream. It takes a second, the dread of it still clinging to you, until you open your eyes properly and know that none of it was real after all. Everything's the same, nothing's changed. The relief.

I can't have been singing very long, five minutes maybe, when there was a knock on the door, and it was him.

How did you get in downstairs?

Nice to see you too. Vincent gave me his key. In case you ever get locked out. He's away a lot.

That's creepy — I said, joking, but he didn't seem to get it.

Should we go? Are you ready?

Outside, the City workers were all walking in the same direction, towards the Tube, like we were in a building on fire, and they were heading towards the exit, trying not to panic.

I heard you singing – he said. – When I arrived.

Oh, really?

It's not exactly quiet. I imagine everyone in the building heard.

Is that a problem, do you think?

I don't know – he said. – Doesn't really matter, does it. But were you not taking time off, I thought? Not singing for a bit? Aren't you still ill?

I'd said this to him too. Couldn't think of another way to explain it that didn't sound bad or mad or both.

Kind of – I said. – I've got a few auditions coming up, though. I need to start singing again now, really, or I won't be ready.

Auditions? I didn't realise. For anything good?

Some ok stuff. Nothing brilliant.

We walked for a bit without talking, and then he said – so, is it worth doing them then, if it's not for good stuff? Are you even likely to get them?

Likely? Well, no. Not likely. The odds are always tiny.

He glanced at me. He looked concerned.

Maybe you should give them a miss then? – he said. – Given that you've been ill. You were so worked up over that last one. You should be kinder to yourself. Give yourself time to get better.

I realised that what I felt was relief. I didn't want to do them. Couldn't imagine getting in front of a panel again, and he'd made it seem the reasonable choice not to. I was absolved. His hand brushed against mine as we walked, and I took hold of it, changed the subject.

Thanks for doing this – I said. – For coming tonight.

It's fine. I mean, you owe me. But it's fine.

You'll like Laurie. Honestly. If you give her a chance.

I'm sure.

Just please, promise me you'll be nice.

When am I ever not nice? – he said.

We were meeting in a pub down a backstreet, Max's suggestion. It was one of those very old buildings in the City that makes you remember it was all like that once, dark wooden panelling, oppressively patterned carpet. Laurie was already there when we arrived, and she followed exactly the script of social niceties.

It's so nice to see you – she said, embracing Max, and she hugged me too.

He went to the bar to get drinks, and we were left alone. I couldn't think of a single thing to say to her.

Thanks for coming – I said, eventually.

It was my suggestion.

You know what I mean. With him.

She shrugged.

I thought I probably should. Just to check you're still alive and everything.

Still alive, thanks – I said, and she sighed and said – *look, Anna, you know you can talk to me, right?* – but then he came back with a bottle of wine and three glasses, and she stopped. He pulled up another chair, topped us up, and we all said cheers and took a sip. There was a silence. They both looked at me expectantly. I said the first thing that came into my head.

Have you ever been to this pub before? – I asked Laurie.

No. This isn't exactly somewhere I hang out.

I walked around the City a bit at the weekend, and everywhere was shut – I said. – The streets were totally empty. Like everyone was at a party somewhere else and I hadn't been invited.

My voice was strangely stilted and everything I said sounded dull. Laurie and Max smiled with strained politeness, like they were teenagers round at a friend's house, enduring the mother's attempts at conversation, hoping she'd leave the room.

So, how have you been? – I asked Laurie, but she just said yeah fine, so I asked Max about work, awkwardly formal, and then I trailed off. There was a tiny pause, where I thought maybe I should admit this was a stupid idea and suggest we call it a night, when Max turned towards Laurie and said — *so, I met Mil the other week* — in an *anyway, as I was saying before we were interrupted* kind of way, and they started chatting.

I was half-relieved he'd rescued me, half-irritated that he was so good at making things fine, when I was apparently so bad. He said he'd come over to Mil's place right before I'd moved, when Laurie had been out. *How do you know her?* — he asked, and Laurie talked a bit about university, they swapped stories, and then he asked her how it was in the house, whether it was nice to have the room to herself.

It's good, yeah. Actually Anna's been replaced. We got a pug at the weekend.

A pug? — I said. — Well, thanks.

Sash bought it off some guy she met on Shoreditch High Street. She was too high to remember she hates dogs. Thinks he had it in his coat, though she's not sure. Anyway, so now we've got this fucking pug that no one really wants. All fun and games our end.

I watched her talking and him listening, feeling a bit like I was at a play, and I wasn't quite convinced the actors knew their lines. I couldn't relax and enjoy it. The air was taut and sharp with the potential for disaster. Laurie said that they couldn't agree on a name. Sash liked Boudica. Ella called her Simone. Mil wanted to name her after some Danish feminist writer who no one else had heard of. Max asked her which she preferred and she said she didn't care, she didn't like dogs, found unconditional devotion suspect. He laughed, and I studied his face, wishing she'd swear a bit less.

So, last night, Sash had a bunch of her druggie friends over — she said. — They were all doing coke, and then one of them knocked some on the floor and the fucking dog came and licked it up. It was hilarious. But Sash started crying and saying Boudy was going to die, and that she was the worst person in the world. So God knows how long the dog's going to last in our house anyway. But the coke didn't seem to do it any harm. It was more alert than ever, actually. Thriving.

Then they started talking about drugs, which ones they'd taken and what they thought about legalising them. It always surprised me how many topics I'd never even thought about that Laurie had considered opinions on. I said a few things, but nothing particularly well informed, too focused on following their conversation, poised to smooth over any tension, and before long, they were acting like I wasn't there at all. They were looking at each other, not at me, and then Laurie got that naughty gleam of challenge in her eyes. The one that meant trouble.

I mean, I imagine you're generally coked up to the eyeballs, aren't you? – she said.

Do you now?

Forty-something banker. Are you telling me you're not?

Forty-something?

Late-thirty-something? Whatever.

Aren't you meant to be a writer? Shouldn't you know better than to fall back on cliché?

One of my friends who's an analyst, he said that on their company ski trip, the MDs got all their juniors to use their credit cards for the strip club, so their wives wouldn't see it on their statements. Such a pathetic cliché, you'd really hope it wasn't true, wouldn't you? And yet.

I took a big glug of my wine, thinking God this is a fucking disaster, what can I say to get us out of here. When I looked back at them, though, they were looking at each other.

My wife's pretty chilled about the strippers, actually – he said. – It's the heroin she doesn't like. But no, honestly, I don't take drugs. I like feeling in control.

Oh really? – she said. – That's a surprise. It's just, you come across as so laid-back.

He laughed.

Touché – he said.

You're very quiet over there? – he said. – Are you alright?

I was wrong to worry about either of their performances, I realised. I hadn't needed to worry. They were both having a great time.

Laurie's very against drugs – I said, trying to match her tone. – She had a very conservative upbringing. All those values instilled in her as a child are still in there somewhere.

Laurie gave me a wicked grin. It was stupid trying to beat her at this game.

Anna doesn't like drugs either – Laurie said. – But not for any ideological reason. She's just really uptight. But I'm sure you've noticed that already.

I have – he said. – Puritanical, I'd say.

Oh yes – said Laurie. – She's definitely that.

They were both smirking at me, and I felt like my jealousy was entirely transparent to them, scrawled all over my body, and then Laurie laughed and said – oh, for God's sake, Anna, stop looking at me like that. We're joking.

I know that – I said.

I picked up my glass to drink, and spilled it down my skirt. The fabric spotted red. I swore, and Laurie said I should go to the bar and ask them for some white wine, and Max said I should go and ask for some salt. I ignored them both and went to the bathroom – one of those carpeted pub toilets that smelled of different bodily fluids, all mingled together. I tried to dab at my skirt with some paper towels, but the wine stayed stubbornly there, purple and angry looking, like a bruise on pale skin. *But this was what you wanted* – I thought. – *You wanted them to get on.*

I went back, determined to join in. There they were, sitting together. He was saying something. She was listening carefully, nodding. Suddenly – and it must have been there the whole time, really, for me to see it so clearly like that – but suddenly an image dropped behind my eyelids. Him with other women, in pubs like this, in restaurants. Them looking at him like that. Him reaching for their hands across the table or touching their legs. I blinked, but the image stayed. Because I'd never asked him, had I, I'd never asked him. So concerned about his wife, whether he still saw her in New York, whether he still wanted her, that I'd never said – *so what do you do, then, in London, the nights you don't see me?*

I sat down, and he glanced at my skirt.

Oh dear – he said, and Laurie said – are you sure you shouldn't ask them for white wine?

She knew I was upset, and I suppose she felt she'd punished me enough, because she started paying lots of attention to me then, putting her arm round me and doing the whole double-act thing she liked to do, saying to Max – *did Anna ever tell you about the time when we* – and I felt an intense aching jealousy of her. I hated her. I hated her for how pretty she was. For how confident and funny she was. I hated her for being so scathing about all men, and yet still somehow being exactly the sort of girl all men wanted. But mostly, I hated her because I had no reason to hate her. I couldn't be angry. The only thing she was doing wrong was being more interesting to him than I was.

She started telling him about Mil's vision for the house. How she thought women were conditioned to respond to men – their needs, their demands – and she wanted to free them from that. From a life of one-sided compromise and domestic drudgery. Women shared, they gave, men took and kept. Women could only know what they were, Mil said, what they might become, without men.

Kind of makes sense – he said. – That's what my mother's life was like, our whole childhood. Creating this domestic idyll for us, that's all she did. And you know, I always thought she loved it. My father always said she did, that it was her thing. Organising dinner parties and arranging playdates and writing *thank you* cards. Just a couple of times, I saw that maybe he was wrong. Maybe she didn't love it so much after all. This one time, Pancake Day, she made all these different toppings. Insane amounts. More than we could ever eat. It must have taken longer than she'd predicted, because I remember me and my brother sitting at the kitchen table, all these bowls of toppings in front of us, and her really tense and stressed out, saying it wasn't done yet, and then my dad got home from work, and we should have been in bed. I thought he'd be angry with her, but he wasn't. He was angry with us. I've never forgotten that, how unfair that seemed. He was angry with us because we were falling asleep at the table – it was way past our bedtime, I must have only been seven, maybe. We weren't hungry. We just wanted to go to bed. When it was all ready, we didn't want to eat it, and he said – *look at all the trouble your mother's gone to, you could at least show her you're grateful* – so we did.

He laughed.

Well, I've never been that keen on pancakes since – he said.

Laurie said that, God, families were a nightmare, weren't they? Mil was right, we'd be better off raised in communes.

Perhaps – he said. – A whole range of adults' issues to imitate or react against. Not a concentrated dose of two strains of madness.

Or only one – she said. – Depending on your childhood.

Oh yes – he said. –Yeah. I'm sorry.

Laurie looked confused.

Why? Why are you sorry?

Oh, it's just Anna told me about your mum. I thought that's what you meant.

My mum?

I stared at him with meaning, but he didn't notice.

That she's not around anymore – he said. – I'm sorry.

For a second, it was like Laurie's face had been wiped clean of any front, unguarded, like when you catch someone totally alone – the split-second before they see you, when the outside entirely reflects the in, and it's raw and woundable, and then they notice you and smile. Only for a second, and she recovered it.

Well, that's a very odd thing for her to have said. My mum's very much around. I meant my dad. When I said one person, I meant because it was really my mum who brought us up. My dad was always at work.

I never said that – I said quickly. – I never said your mum wasn't around.

I guess I must have misunderstood – he said.

Yeah, I guess so – she said.

Then she said it had been nice, but she was really tired and she had to go. He went down the stairs ahead of us. She didn't look at me. She was putting her coat on, checking for her phone in her bag. I didn't know whether to say anything, wasn't sure if she'd exactly understood what he meant or if she was angry. But then she looked up at me, and I saw how angry she was.

Well, anyway – she said. – I'm really glad I give you guys something to talk about. It'd be nice if he actually listened to you closely enough to get his facts straight, but hey, you can't have everything.

She started walking out. I went after her.

I'm really sorry – I said. – That was really insensitive of him. I'm sorry.

Really insensitive of him, Anna? Really insensitive of him? Are you being serious?

Then we were out on the street and he was there, so we couldn't talk anymore.

On the way back to his flat, I told him Laurie was angry. He said he hadn't noticed, and I explained.

Oh, I see – he said. – Well, I guess I misremembered what you'd told me. I thought you said she'd killed herself. That she was dead. I didn't really see how that could be a secret.

Tried to. I said she tried to.

Well, anyway. Maybe you should have kept it to yourself? If you knew she wouldn't like it.

We walked in silence. The streets were empty, and the office buildings, lit up, were empty too. No traffic either, just a few black cabs, looking to lick up the City worker dregs. I knew he was right. I couldn't even remember why I'd told him. It was like Laurie had said. I'd told him because I thought it might interest him. To make conversation.

Then he put his arm round me and said – people are sensitive about their families, Anna. She'll get over it. You worry too much.

Back at the flat, he had work to do. He got some papers out of his bag and lay on the bed, reading through them, crossing things out. I was restless. I wandered round the room, looking in the mirror and fiddling with my hair, flicking through *Men's Health* on the bedside table, picking things up off the dresser and putting them down. I felt his eyes on me, and I knew I was annoying him, so I sat cross-legged on the floor by the window. I leant my back on the wall and looked out. There was the world, blooming on the other side of the glass, and it seemed suddenly very far away.

What is it? – he said.

Nothing.

I've seen you on stage. I know you can act, so I can only assume you want me to ask you what's wrong. So, come on, off you go. Tell me.

Coming back from the bathroom, watching him with Laurie.

Are you still seeing other people? – I asked.

Why? – he said. – Are you?

Can you just answer the question?

Oh, right. You're being serious. Um. Well. When do you imagine I have time to do that?

I turned my head back to the world through the glass. Thought about the rest of the cast in the pub still, the intimacies that developed there, the private jokes I wouldn't understand. About Laurie, going back to the house by herself, our little room, and wondering if she was lonely too. Overwhelmed with this petty feeling he owed me somehow. He owed me something. Some compensation, something touchable, solid, something real – for this – for this – for putting me behind glass.

But, so, are we exclusive? – I asked.

He laughed.

I don't think anyone's asked me that since I was a teenager – he said. – I've just said I'm not seeing anyone else.

You didn't actually say that.

He sighed.

Look, Anna – he said. – I, well, I don't really get – I thought you understood that—

Stop it. Please. Don't. Stop talking.

A pause, and then he said – Laurie. You were feeling left out, right? But I thought you said you didn't get jealous?

I don't.

No, I can see that. Anna, darling – he said. – Be reasonable, please. You asked me to be nice. Was that not exactly what I was being?

Very. Exceptionally. Thank you.

He put his papers down on the bedside table, and sat up.

Is it that I wasn't nice enough to you? Is that it?

Something like that.

He started to laugh. Not at me, I didn't feel he was laughing at me, more like we'd been playacting, pretending to be annoyed with each other, all a big joke, and he'd cracked. He couldn't keep up the pretence anymore. It was too funny, and suddenly I found I was laughing too. We were both laughing, and he said – come here, come and lie with me.

Oh, I see – I said. – You're interested in me now, are you?

Yes. Yes, I am. Very interested in you, in fact.

I got up and lay next to him, and he turned on his side and faced me.

So you want me to be nice to you? – he said. – Ok, how's this?

And he told me he liked my eyes and my hair and this bit here, right at the top of my thigh, and how soft the skin was there. He told me he liked how much I hated traffic and pigeons and rush-hour, when I claimed to love London, and how seriously I took all sorts of things that didn't matter. He told me he liked my smile, and how there was always a moment when I smiled at him when he could believe that he'd made me, not just happy for now, but happy forever. He told me he liked that I was jealous, he liked it, and he liked that I pretended not to be. He wished he could make me more jealous, he said. He told me he liked it when I sulked. He found it sweet – how I seemed to genuinely believe that my bad moods were irreversibly bad, and then forgot all about them the second he'd made me laugh.

Well, now you're making fun of me – I said. – I'm not sure that counts as being nice.

Never. I'd never make fun of you. You're far too serious, I'd know better than to do that. I meant all of it. Look, I'll show you. Shut your eyes.

I shut them, and I felt him pull my top up.

He said — *stay still* — and I heard him reach for something on the bedside table, and then there was the sharp tickle of ink.

There. Look. That's for you.

I opened my eyes and looked down at my stomach. He'd drawn a heart.

SIXTEEN

I messaged Laurie on my way in the next morning, and said I was sorry. She replied instantly.

> *I honestly don't know what I expected, so I don't know why I'm angry. I just really fucking hope you know what you're doing.*

I was still thinking what to say, when she messaged again.

> *It's fine, I'll get over it. Just give me some space.*

I replied saying ok, but I'd miss her, and then Angela called.

Anna – she said – where are you?

I'm nearly at college. Why?

Well, we're meant to be having a lesson now. Ten minutes ago, in fact.

I'd forgotten she was due back this week.

Oh God, I'm so sorry – I said. – I'll be there as soon as I can. But, well, actually I'm still a bit ill. I'm not sure if I should be singing on it yet. Should we maybe cancel?

Wait, you're still not singing? But it's been – what? – over two weeks now? And you're not better? Right, I definitely want to see you then. Come as soon as you can.

So I went, telling myself it was time to stop being silly. The performances were less than two weeks away now. If I confronted my fear head-on, I told myself, I'd be pleasantly surprised. It wouldn't be as bad as I thought, like when you stub your toe and you instinctively cover it with your hand – the pain – you don't want to know what you've done, sure you'll see the nail hanging off, blood seeping from the wound. But when you finally force yourself to take your hand away, there's nothing.

I'm so sorry I'm late – I said, and then, with forced brightness, I found myself chatting on about the Director and rehearsals and Angela's trip, trying to delay the moment where she'd want to hear me sing. She interrupted me.

Anna – she said. – What's going on?

Nothing. What do you mean?

I mean you don't sound ill to me. Manic, yes, but not ill. I was expecting you to come in here with a streaming cold. So what's wrong?

Weakness meant being left behind in this industry. I knew that. Asking for help meant saying you couldn't do it.

I don't really know – I said. – I don't know what's wrong. It just doesn't feel right.

Ok, well let's see. We'll warm up very gently. See where the voice is at.

I took a couple of breaths, tried to relax into the familiarity of the practice room. This wasn't a frightening scenario. We'd spent hours together in this room, working on my voice, and Angela had heard already everything it could do. There was no reason to be scared.

She ran me through some exercises. At first it was ok, and she made reassuring noises while I sang – *fine* – *good* – *that sounds great.* But then I started to think about the people walking past the practice room, how bad the sound-proofing was because the building was listed, and how they could all hear me, imagining ears pressed against walls and eyes at window slits to watch. I tried to get back inside my body, inside my voice, to steady the quiver in the sound – to imagine the breath as an expanse of water in the dark, its surface unrippled, but I couldn't make myself see it. Instead, the images that flickered across my eyelids were random, uncontrolled, irrelevant – Spitalfields Market that evening, and him saying – *what do you like?* – the heart on my stomach, still there, it wouldn't wash off – the earrings I was wearing, the ones he'd given me – like two lanes of traffic, these images on one side, and on the other, the sound, me scrutinising each note as it came out, turning back to look at it, to think – *why wasn't that right? What was wrong with it?* – and Angela wasn't saying anything now, she was just looking at me, and then there was a thickness to the voice. Something between my throat and the sound and I couldn't dislodge it, and panic descended on me, like a persistent rain, so light at first you barely notice it until you're soaked, and I stopped.

I'm sorry – I said. – I – it doesn't feel right.

Ok – said Angela. – It's ok. Well, look, Anna, honestly I can't tell too much from what I've heard. It doesn't sound to me like there's anything seriously the matter, but you're protecting it, aren't you? Not singing out. We'll get you to an ENT, of course, just to be sure, and then – well, when are these performances? Two weeks? I'm wondering if we can get away with not telling Marieke just yet. If we can get you to an ENT first and see what we're dealing with. Because assuming there's no real issue – it's just a technique blip we can sort together straightforwardly, maybe quite quickly – it seems silly to risk her pulling you out, and—

I don't want to – I said.

Don't want to what?

I don't want to go to an ENT.

Why not?

Thinking about the energy, the movement, the effort, the struggle it would take to deal with. Something wrong with me or something not wrong with me. It didn't much matter. The result would be the same. Picking myself up, starting over, hours of work, of sacrifice, all leading me to a future of uncertainty, of – *no thanks, try again next year*. It was insanity, this life.

What do you mean you don't want to, Anna? This is your livelihood. You have to—

It's not.

What?

It's not my livelihood.

Hearing the dull, sad truth of my words, I said them again – it's not my livelihood. I barely earn anything from it. I pay more to do it than I earn.

Angela's next student arrived.

Give us a minute – she said. – Can you wait outside? Anna, do you have rehearsals today?

Yes. Now.

Well, you should go, because you've already missed a week, haven't you, and I don't want you getting into trouble. Mark if you can, and we'll talk afterwards, ok? Call me.

Ok.

I'd picked up my bag and turned to go, when she said – what does your man think about all this?

About all what?

Well, about how you're feeling?

I don't really know – I said. – Nothing, I don't think.

Then Angela's next student was peering in through the glass to see if we were done, so I left.

You promise you'll call me later? – she said.

Ok.

I was late to the rehearsal, and the Director was angry.

Bit of professionalism wouldn't go amiss, sweetheart – he shouted, as I made my way down the aisle, through the sad emptiness of the stalls, the ghosts of audiences past.

Rodolfo, Marcello and Mimi were already onstage. My cover was there too. She went and sat in the front row, score in hand.

Tavern scene – the Director said. – Yes, that's right. Remember what opera you're in, dear? Well, get up there then.

The argument. We'd sketched it out a few weeks ago. We started. None of them were marking, so I couldn't either. Marcello began to accuse me of flirting. *You don't own me* I'm meant to be saying *I can do whatever I like,* but he seemed too close to me and, at the same time, much too far away. Loud, and I could barely hear him. I couldn't hear my voice. I couldn't hear the piano. I could control nothing. It was like those dreams where you have to run and your legs don't work, and Marcello had his hands on my shoulders, shaking me, and then the Director was shouting – *stop, stop, everybody stop.*

I could see Frankie looking at me, and I avoided his eye.

Well, great acting, sweetheart – the Director said. – Great acting. But – and believe me, it really fucking pains me to say this – but this is opera, you know. The audience is here more for your pretty singing than anything else, ok? Marieke won't like it if you compromise on that, even if it's a fucking Oscar-worthy performance. So let's not have that emoting thing get in the way of the voice like that, got it?

He realised at the same time as me, and with exactly the same horror, that I was crying for real.

Christ – he said. – Let's take five. Take five and pull yourself together. My rehearsal room isn't a safe space, sweetheart, ok? I'm not going to make this safe for you. I frankly don't have fucking time, ok? Anyway, any art that feels safe isn't worth creating.

Mimi looked delighted. Frankie put his arms round me. I tried to hide my face from the light.

Any art that feels safe isn't worth creating – the Director said again, ponderously, after a pause. – That's good. You can write that down if you want.

The rest of the rehearsal happened and then it was over. Afterwards, I couldn't remember much about it, because when we started up again, the fear – the fear that was stopping me, I'd thought, from getting inside my voice, from reaching that thing in the centre of me that gave it weight and colour and meaning – gave way to something far more frightening. I suddenly thought – this indefinable thing at my core – this thing I've always believed about myself – well, maybe it doesn't exist. And then there I was, standing on stage, singing – and I must have been singing something, though God knows what, because no one had stopped me – pulling off and discarding layers of myself, trying to get hold of this thing of value, finding nothing.

When it was over, I went to get my stuff, and Frankie said – not coming for a drink?

I knew that I should. I should go and be chatty. Say – *God, that rehearsal was a fucking car crash, how embarrassing. I'm so hungover* – or something, anything. Make a joke of it, like someone who knew that it was a one-off and was confident it would all be fine tomorrow. Or, at the very least, I should go and sit there in silence. Be there, so they couldn't talk about me.

No – I said. – I'm going home.

Are you ok? You seem kind of off today.

Off?

Yeah, you seem stressed. Come and have a drink.

I shouldn't. I should rest. I'm still ill.

Sure – he said. – Up to you.

I watched him head towards the other singers. They were solid and real, and I was dissolving.

Then I was on the Tube. People all squeezed close together, pretending not to be. People sneezing. People biting their nails and putting their hands, still glistening with spit, back on the pole. People coughing into their shoulders. Sweat beads on temples, smudged mascara, dandruff on collars, air vibrating with the potential for contagion, the germs of London mating and mingling together, smeared on plastic and glass. I tried to hold my breath, not to touch anything, and then I was standing on the corner of his street, breathing in metallic air, the men in suits swerving round me, like I was an object in their way – a lamppost, a postbox – or like they hadn't seen me at all.

It was Friday, but I knew he had a meeting the next morning, was still in London. As I walked towards his building, I called him. He didn't pick up.

I called him again. It rang and rang and rang.

I called him again, and then I called him again.

No thoughts, just that I had to hear his voice, I had to see him, he must make me real.

I called him again.

233

I stood on the street, outside his building, the noises out there too loud, the traffic, the sirens, the helicopter circling somewhere overhead.

I walked in. I walked past security, they didn't stop me – so they can't see me either, I thought – I went up in the lift. I banged on the door to his flat. No one answered.

I called him.

I banged on the door again.

I stood there, thinking I couldn't go back out there, I couldn't, I'd have to sit on the floor here, wait for him, however long that took. But then I banged again, and he opened it.

Anna – he said. – What the fuck?

He looked awful, like he hadn't slept in days, eyes ringed with red and skin so pale it was like you could see the skull underneath.

Why are you here? – he said. – We didn't have plans.

I'm sorry, I – can I come in?

I'm really not in the mood for this sort of thing – he said, and I remembered how cold his eyes could be.

For what sort of thing?

For the sort of thing I imagine someone who's called me fourteen times out of the blue has turned up to say.

Please – my voice cracked. – I haven't come to say anything, I promise. I just wanted to see you.

For a moment, I thought he was going to tell me to leave, but then he stood to one side, and I went in.

It was a mess. Drawers in the cabinet open, papers all over the floor, like he'd been looking for something and given up. Contents of his bag tipped out on the table, crumbs and receipts and coins spilling over onto the carpet. Takeaway containers littered on the kitchen counters, leaking their juices.

He ignored me, and went back to the sofa. His phone was on the table, flashing with my calls, next to a bottle of whisky, a glass, wet rings where he'd picked it up and put it down again, overlapping, superimposed, like the footprints of someone lost, walking round and round the same old ground.

I stood, not knowing what to do, and then he said – I suppose you'd better tell me why you're here.

I just wanted to see you.

Let's not do this, shall we? I'm not going to play a guessing game with you. What is it you want? Tell me, or you can leave. Your choice.

His voice was empty, like an actor memorising his lines, not trying to imbue them with meaning. I needed to feel his eyes on me, the warmth of his approval, to tell me I was real. But he didn't look at me. He stared out of the window.

I just wanted to see you – I said. – I'm ill. I still can't sing, my voice hasn't come back, not properly, and it's not too long until opening night, and—

You're ill? – he said, and he did this nasty laugh. – That's why you're behaving like a crazy person? Because you're ill?

It's not a joke – I said. – It's not just some stupid thing. It's a big deal. This show's a big deal.

So you keep telling me. But you're ill, and so you can't do it, and you can't be the first person in the history of the world this has ever happened to. I don't know what you expect me to do about it. What is it you want from me, Anna?

For you to look at me – I thought. – I want you to look at me.

Nothing – I said.

Talk to someone at the Conservatory – he said. – You're a student. Sorting this out, finding someone else if they have to – that's their job, not mine.

I can't tell anyone – I said.

And I couldn't. That's why Angela was so reluctant to tell Marieke – she knew how this worked. If I pulled out, if I told them I couldn't do it then, fine, it happens, I wouldn't do it. But I wouldn't be cast again. Not in a role like this, and possibly not at all. That would be it. People remembered. Show people you're weak, and they might be nice to you, but they'll never forget it. Plenty of singers out there, just as good, who don't cause problems.

You think I should drop out? – I said. – You really think that's what I should do?

He finished his glass and topped it up, took another sip.

I have no idea what you should do – he said. – I don't know why you're asking me.

He still didn't look at me. I could see my reflection in the window, transparent, partial, against the bright lights of the city, and I wondered if that was how he saw me too.

He got up, went over to the sink, started washing up.

Is that – is that all you're going to say? – I said. – Do you really not care?

I followed him. He put the mug he'd rinsed on the side, wiped his hands on a tea towel, and turned towards me. He spoke, very calmly.

Anna – he said. – Do you honestly think I don't care? About your career? You think it's ok to say that to me? Really? That I don't care about whether or not you do well? Maybe think about that one for a second. Remember how exactly you've got the time to do all this in the first place, why you're not doing that shitty bar job anymore, hm?

I felt like I had in that rehearsal, like I was dissolving.

I'm sorry you're having a bad time – he said. – I really am. But, frankly, you want me to believe how much you love singing, how it's a vocation and you do a vocation for joy not money, etcetera, etcetera. But I look at you now and I don't see a happy person. You want to know what I think? Do you? Really? Well, I think you're miserable. I think that if you have to pull out and if that apparently means, as you insist, that that's the end of this whole endeavour, well – you want to know what I think? Really? – I think that's maybe not the worst thing in the world.

He sighed.

Look, I know you think this is really important right now – he said. – I know this opera seems really important. But I promise you, in ten years, it won't seem important at all, if you even remember it. You're so young. You'll find something else to do. Most people don't get what they want. They start off with all these big grand ambitions, and then they learn it's better to compromise, to be realistic. To find meaning in other things, you know, in their friends, their hobbies, their children. Learning that's part of growing up, Anna.

I was suddenly enraged.

You'd love that, wouldn't you? – I said. –You'd love it if I gave up on what I really wanted. If I got some mediocre little job that never fulfilled me, stopped working to have kids, and never started again, said to people – *oh well, you know, it wasn't such a big thing for me, because I never really found what I wanted to do.* That's exactly what you think a woman should be like, isn't it? That's your sad little fantasy, isn't it? Which is weird, I think, given that's what your mum did, and you clearly despise her for it.

I don't know what order it happened in.

Him taking a step towards me.

Him saying – don't ever talk to me like that, do you understand? Don't ever make comments like that about my family.

Some movement of his hand, to – what? – to gesture, to grab me maybe, to, I don't know, but me flinching away from him and my voice saying – *don't, don't* – and then he stopped and I stopped, and for a moment we just stared at each other, like we'd both forgotten our next line. His mouth opened and shut again, and then he walked away.

I stood in the middle of the room, trying to slow my breathing down, then I followed him. He'd gone into the bedroom, and he was standing, forehead pressed against the glass. He didn't turn round. I stood there, looking at him, not knowing what to do, and then he said – I'd never hurt you, Anna. Why did you flinch like that? I wasn't going to hurt you. I'm not that sort of man. I've never hurt a woman in my life. I never would. I don't understand why you thought I would.

I'd never heard him sound like that before. He sounded broken.

I went to him, and put my arms round his waist. I rested my cheek in between his shoulder blades.

I'm sorry – I said. – I'm sorry, I'm sorry, I'm sorry.

I don't know how long we stood like that, before he breathed out deeply, turned to face me. Then he put his arms round my shoulders, and drew me to him. It was such an unexpected gesture, loving and warm, that I wondered if I'd imagined his anger. He held me tight against his chest. He kissed my forehead. He murmured into my hair – what will we do with you, my love?

I don't know – I said.

He led me to the bed and told me to sit, gave me a shirt to wear, poured me a drink. I was going to say I couldn't, not with the performances so soon, but I realised that didn't much matter anymore, and he said – *drink it, it will relax you* – so I did. I lay down, and he lay next to me, rested the back of his hand on my cheek. It seemed pointless, now, to pretend. I told him how afraid I was, and he listened. I made it sound, perhaps, even worse than it was, because he was sympathetic, saying *that sounds awful*, saying *my poor love*. I felt empty and calm, like when you've walked for miles and every muscle feels used up.

He got up to get another drink, and I looked at my phone. Missed calls from Angela, a message saying to ring her back.

Don't – he said. – Not now. There's no rush, you're paying her, you don't owe her anything. Take the weekend to think. Talking to her now will only stress you out.

I just don't think I can cope – I said.

Well, no. It seems a horrible sort of life. I'm not sure who could.

There was a pause, where he seemed to be debating whether to carry on, and then he said – but you have seemed – and I didn't want to say anything, I hadn't planned on saying anything, but since we're being honest here – you have seemed incredibly anxious lately. I mean, disproportionately. In a way I'm not sure is normal. Have you thought about getting help for that?

You think I'm crazy?

Crazy?

He laughed.

Not sure that's the PC term, Anna. And no. That's not what I meant. Just it must be uncomfortable for you, that's all. Being this stressed.

I want you to be happy – he said.

We lay for a little bit without talking. A couple of times, he ran his fingers through my hair, or stroked the inside of my wrist, or brought my hand up to his mouth to kiss it. I wondered what had prompted him each time, what he'd been thinking, and then I said — what happened?

What do you mean?

Before I arrived. Why is the flat such a mess?

I was looking for something. Papers. Can't find them.

Work?

No.

Oh.

Personal stuff. I won't bore you with it.

It wouldn't bore me — I said.

A little silence and then — Max? — I said, because he was being kind, and I was feeling brave. — Why do you never talk about her?

I thought he wasn't going to answer, but then he said — why do I never talk about her? Well. I suppose you get to an age where you stop wanting to rehearse your own failures. Where they become less of an interesting psychological exercise, you know. More a reminder of time you can't get back.

Do you still love her?

I could see my face, big, in his eyes.

Love her? No. Honestly, I don't think I've really loved her for a long time.

I moved a bit closer to him, so that our faces were almost touching and I thought, there are so few times in your life when you know in the moment you're happy. I was happy then.

SEVENTEEN

Then it was the weekend, and Max went to Oxford. I did nothing. I didn't call Angela back. I barely left the flat. I was too tired, and the City was a sad place to be alone. It existed only for the working week, and there was nothing there to sustain life, only money. The 3D version of a spreadsheet, rigid grids where numbers multiplied.

On the Sunday, he called me. He was on the train back, and wanted to know if I was free the next night.

Actually, it's my birthday.

Today?

Tomorrow.

You've got plans then?

I didn't have plans. Laurie still wasn't talking to me, and half the people I knew in London were her friends, not mine. The other half were singers, and I didn't want to see them.

I don't, actually – I said. – I went out with some friends last night. It was really nice, a surprise thing. Laurie organised it. But anyway, tomorrow I'm free.

Can you meet early? Around six?

I said ok, even though I dimly remembered an evening rehearsal. He said see you tomorrow, and hung up. He was always like that on the phone, never wanted to chat. I sometimes wondered why he bothered calling at all, when what he'd called to say was always factual, information easily contained in a message. Early on, when I mentioned it to Laurie, she said he probably didn't want to create a paper trail for his wife to see – a text here, an email there, it all got too confusing. Far simpler to always call, keep all your indiscretions in one place, so to speak. When I told her to fuck off, he wasn't married, not everyone in the world was practising some grand deception, she said that well, no, in all seriousness, he probably preferred calling because he was old. This actually didn't make me feel too much better.

The next morning, Mum rang. She wished me a happy birthday.

Are you ok? – she said. – Anna? You sound weird.

I've just woken up. I'm fine.

We didn't know what you'd like – she said. – Your dad's transferred you some money, so you can buy your own present.

That's really kind. Thank you.

I checked my account when we'd got off the phone, and saw how little they'd sent – it would cover the cost of a few days on the Tube, at most. That made me sad, that they thought it could buy something nice.

Laurie messaged me a bit later. She said happy birthday, and did I remember her birthday a few months ago? That underground bar we found. Those men we got chatting to, before we found out they were gangsters, said they were anyway. *That was so much fun, wasn't it?* she said, and I saw this as a sign of forgiveness. I was constructing something to send back, when she messaged again. A card had arrived from my mum. *So you didn't tell her you moved,* she said. *Too awkward to explain where to, I guess.*

I discarded my draft, texted the Director to say I was ill and wouldn't make it to rehearsals that day, then I switched off my phone. I went back to sleep, woke late. Spent the afternoon having a long bath, trying on outfits and discarding them.

I met him at a hotel restaurant in Covent Garden. The walls were painted mottled to look like stone, and the chairs were embroidered.

Why didn't you tell me about your birthday? – he asked.

I don't know. I've never really liked my birthday. I don't like being the centre of attention.

The parties were always failures when I was a child. Mum hated them, lots of people in the house, and I found her embarrassing

– supervising us all the time, so we couldn't play our own games, telling my friends off when she thought they'd been bad. So we gave up on them, and then it was just the three of us. Lots of presents. Them watching me open them, watching me blow out my candles and eat cake.

Is that not a contradiction? – he said.

Is what not a contradiction?

Well, being a singer, and not liking attention.

Him calling me a singer was painful. I didn't know if I could call myself that anymore.

Not really – I said. – I don't think so. You don't think about the audience. You actually forget they're there when it's going well. Like sport, I guess. You're thinking about the rules of the game, not playing to the crowd.

We ordered, and I asked him when his birthday was.

January – he said, and then he laughed.

You don't need to look so offended – he said. – I think there are about five people in the world who know when my birthday is. I was away, anyway.

While we were eating, he told me about birthdays when he was little. How his mum always organised big parties for them, but never acknowledged her own birthday. He said it was sad she'd cared so much about ageing when she was young, and looked the same to them every year. How much she'd worried when there was no reason to worry. I told him a story about one of Tara's birthday parties when we were teenagers, and he laughed at everything I said. I felt sharp and witty without trying. I could just stay like this with him, I thought. I wouldn't have to strive for anything, wouldn't have to worry. It would be easy.

We'd just finished eating when he got a call and said he had to take it. While he was gone, I watched the couple next to us. They were dressed smartly, like this was a special occasion, and they were barely speaking. The woman had these small, nervous eyes, and she kept darting looks at the man, attempting a word or two with a big twitchy grin on her face. He muttered one word back in response or answered with a tight little smile. After every few bites of his dinner, he took a big glug of his wine, then he turned back to his dinner, then back to his wine, methodical, like eating here was the next item on his to-do list and he wanted to get it done as efficiently as possible. And she looked so sad, his wife, she looked so sad. I saw Max through the glass, laughing at what the person on the phone was saying, gesturing, although they couldn't see him. A feeling of contentment, of affection for him, rushed through my veins and spiked in my brain like a drug – thinking that nothing else mattered, if I could have him, there was nothing else I needed.

He ended the call and came back, smiled at me and touched my shoulder as he went to sit down. I smiled back. We're not like that couple, him and me, I thought.

We should go – he said.

Where are we going?

So, I haven't got you a present. You didn't exactly give me much notice. But I got tickets to something through work. I thought you might like it. That's why I called last night. We should go, we'll be late.

He paid the bill, and we started walking through the West End, queues everywhere. Queues for returns outside theatres. Queues for noodles outside noodle bars, indistinguishable inside from the queue-less noodle bars next door. Queues to get down to the Tube. Even the street was a queue, people shuffling with M&Ms and Hamleys bags, waiting for the people in front. He wouldn't say what the tickets were for, but he did say we should hurry up a bit, and he steered me round a group of Chinese tourists, and then I realised where we were headed. Panic began to crawl across my skin, like bugs on a light strip, and I started chatting inanely, determined not to ruin his gift. Not to let him see I was scared.

We arrived outside the opera house.

It's *Bohème* – he said. –That's the opera you're doing, right?

There was a moment where he looked at me, and I thought – *the opera I'm doing? Surely it's occurred to him I wouldn't want to see it now?* – but he seemed so expectant I'd be happy, I said – *yes, yes, it is* – and I thanked him and kissed him, excessively grateful, and he laughed and said – *well, someone can't handle drinking at 6 p.m.* – but he seemed pleased.

The foyer was nearly empty, and the voice over the tannoy said that the performance was about to start, so we went straight to our seats.

Have you been here before? – he asked.

A couple of times.

I'd actually had a ticket for this production, but I'd given it to someone else, hadn't been able to face it. I didn't tell him that. He already looked disappointed enough that this wasn't a new experience for me, like he'd told me a joke and I'd let him get all the way through before saying I'd heard it before. It wouldn't occur to him, I suppose, that you could go for basically nothing if you didn't care where you sat.

I've never been in the stalls before though – I said. – Only right at the top. You can't see anything up there. This is totally different.

I wasn't just saying that to please him, it was different down here, and for a moment the novelty could distract me. This was where everything was designed to be viewed from – you could appreciate the scale of the building, the glittering lights round the balconies, the detail on the ceiling, the perfect line-of-sight to the stage. The audience down here were different too. They looked like they'd dressed up to come – although I suppose it was possible they dressed like that all the time – and the average age had shot up several decades. Up top was almost all students, straight from rehearsals or classes in leggings or jeans. You always bumped into people you knew. There was a party atmosphere, people climbing over the backs of seats before curtain up to shout hi at someone sitting five rows above. I never minded that you couldn't see much on the stage. Sometimes I preferred it, to shut my eyes and just to listen.

Well, I'm glad we've got good seats then – he said.

The noise from the audience muted a couple of times, premature anticipation, re-swelled when nothing happened, and I felt something dart, electric, across my skin. The panic, again. So it hadn't gone away, no, still there, and it was burrowing into my flesh. I kept talking, saying anything, anything to stop myself from feeling it. I asked Max how come he got opera tickets through work, and he said they bought them in advance for entertaining clients, offered them out if they weren't needed.

Actually, there were a few spare, and I think Vincent took two as well. You know, Vincent, who owns your flat. So you can meet him.

And then the house lights went down and real silence fell. The conductor came on and everyone clapped. The curtain went up and the music started, and then I couldn't distract myself anymore. I took some deep breaths, and thought – *well, this is totally stupid, isn't it? It's not like you have to sing it* – and while I knew that was true, it didn't mean much. Max reached for my hand in the dark, but I moved it. My palms were wet.

Act One, the act Musetta's not in. I'd sat through this first scene so many times in rehearsals, waiting for my entry, that I got through it now in a numb stupor. I stared at it, without thought, like I might watch a reality TV programme, just because it happened to be on and there was nothing else to do.

But then it was Act Two, the arrival of Musetta, and from the opening chord, I couldn't look away. I was sitting in this vast space and, at the same time, trapped in a tiny box, running out of air. There she was, there was Musetta, pouting and flirting her way onto the stage. A man with her to make her on/off lover – Marcello – jealous, and the more he feigns indifference, the more OTT she becomes. I sat, staring at this woman in her heels and fur coat, singing notes higher and louder than I could possibly imagine singing, although I knew I had once, and not that long ago – those look-at-me notes, and everyone was looking. That's me, I thought, or rather, I'm meant to be her, and I couldn't imagine being her, far less believe I ever had been.

The interval. House lights came up.

What do you think? – he asked.

It's good – I said, and gave him my most convincing smile. – I'm enjoying it. Are you?

Yeah – he said. – It's – oh, that was Vincent and his wife, I think. We should go and say hi.

I'm just going to the bathroom. I'll find you.

There was a queue, and then I dawdled in the cubicle, determined to avoid small talk, and by the time I'd gone to wash my hands, they were asking everyone to take their seats. I made myself smile in the mirror, and hoped he wouldn't notice how frightened my eyes were.

He was already in his seat.

Long queue? I told Vincent we'd have a drink afterwards.

Oh, ok.

I can't have looked that pleased, because he said – just a quick one, they live far out anyway. He's a useful person for you to meet. He's very into opera, knows everyone.

Curtain up for the second half.

I tried to let it happen in front of me, not to properly watch, to think about other things, but I couldn't. It was like when you walk past an accident, you find yourself perversely drawn to it, even though you know you don't want to see. I stared and stared, and at the end, when I watched Musetta, speechless, get down on her knees to pray – a moment I'd never understood in the opera, it had never seemed to fit with the bold, daring woman I'd seen her as – I suddenly got it. Action felt futile. She was helpless.

The applause, and when it had stopped, Max said – are you ok?

Ok?

You seem very tense.

He was looking at my hands, and I saw I had them clasped together, knuckles white.

I'm fine – I said, and pretended to be very moved by the music.

He smiled.

It's sweet how into this you are – he said, and we went to meet Vincent.

The opera house bar was a cross between an auditorium and a greenhouse. The ceiling was high domed glass and the wall onto the street was glass too, so that the multiple mirrored surfaces reflected the blackness outside. The audience were positioned in the round – tables at gallery level, a viewing box suspended at the back – and the lights were dim, only the circular bar in the middle lit up.

That's them – Max said, and it did feel like walking on stage, going over to the couple at the bar. The scene was set, a bottle of wine on the counter between them, their faces turned towards us, dramatically lit from below.

Anna – Max said. – This is Vincent. And this is his wife, Geraldine.

I'd imagined Vincent would be Max's age, but he was older. Somewhere in his sixties. White hair, quite long, set unmoving across his forehead. Skin that sort of ruddy tanned favoured by the very rich, somewhere between health and skin cancer.

It's nice to meet you – I said.

What are you drinking? – Max asked, putting up a hand to get the barman's attention.

Just wine is good. Red.

Any particular type?

I don't mind.

A girl of true discernment – Vincent chuckled, and I hated him.

Max handed me the wine, and then he started talking to Geraldine. She was younger than her husband, though it was hard to say how young. One of those women wealth would always preserve, like a lemon pickled in a jar. Her ageing was shameful and secret, something that happened underneath her clothes, behind her skin.

Vincent rounded on me.

Enjoy that then?

I tried to think of something intelligent to say, knowing it was unlikely he'd find anything I said intelligent.

I enjoyed it – I said. – The staging was quite traditional, so—

It's *Bohème* – Vincent said. – Know the opera at all? What would you expect?

Well, yes, I do know it. Actually—

What did you think of the girl who sang Musetta? – he demanded.

Yeah, she's got a lovely voice, she—

She got my scholarship – he announced.

Your what?

My scholarship. When she was studying. I support young singers. She's just sublime. Just a sublime singer, isn't she, Gerry? Gerry?

He tapped Geraldine on the shoulder, and she turned away from Max.

Sorry, darling?

Musetta.

Oh, yes – she said. – Oh yes. Sublime.

She turned back to Max.

We go and see her in everything she does – Vincent said. – Such a nice girl too. We've seen this production three times.

He seemed to expect some sort of reaction, though he hadn't asked me anything.

Oh, wow – I said obediently. – That's a lot.

It is.

Do you see much opera then? – I asked, trying to make this at least nominally a two-way conversation.

Nearly every show here. Then I'm on the board for one of the festivals. Know the guy running it well, great guy, lovely man. Great shows, really. You'll be interested in this actually – he said – if you're interested in opera. We were in Mallorca over the summer, out there on the boat – the kids loved it, jumping on and off the deck into the water – and anyway, this guy was there. This festival guy. Such an intelligent man. Kids loved him. And we got into this argument one night about modern staging, which you'll find inter-esting. I was saying I didn't really get this trend for setting all the classics in brothels or in nightclubs in Shoreditch. He was defending it. He was so animated about it. But, as I was saying, it's ridiculous to bastardise beautiful music like that just to make it more palatable to the masses.

I waited for him to finish, but this was the sum of his argument.

Well – I said – I see what you mean. But, I suppose, when people like Mozart or Puccini were writing, they wanted their operas to say something about the world around them then. They didn't set them historically. They were contemporary, you know, often controversial. So it makes sense that directors now want them to have the same impact.

That's not opera though, it is? – he said. – A nightclub in Shoreditch? That's not opera. If I wanted to see that sort of thing, I'd watch television.

Yeah, I suppose. But when these operas were written, they kind of were the equivalent of television.

But what I'm saying is – he said – is that it's ludicrous to bastardise this beautiful music to get more people in.

I realised I'd insulted him. He'd been educating me, not asking for an opinion.

Max saw me looking over at him and said something to Geraldine. They turned towards us.

You two seem to have a lot in common – he said. – I thought you might.

This one's got some strong opinions – said Vincent. – You'll have to watch out for her.

They both laughed, and I made myself smile, but I looked away. I didn't like seeing them together. This man was so unlike Max, but putting them next to each other, it was like holding two different colours under the same bright light, realising they were much more similar than you'd ever have thought. I found myself wondering, suddenly, what Max had said about me. How he'd described me. *My girlfriend*. No. Not that. He wouldn't say that. *This girl I'm seeing*. No, surely not. Those weren't words he'd ever use. Something else, then. Something less flattering and perhaps more true.

You know something else this guy was saying? – Vincent said, determined to have the last word. – He said that the staging makes no difference to sales at all. None. You advertise the show as a new take on a classic or you put everyone in period dress. No difference. You know what makes a difference?

No – I said. – What?

Which opera it is and who's in it – he said triumphantly, as though we'd been playing Snap and he'd just swatted my hand away from the matching pairs and claimed them for his own. – If it's a popular one people have heard of, and if there are big names singing. That's it. That's how you get sales.

Oh – I said. – Right. I see.

I didn't know how to talk about opera like this, like it was a cup of coffee in a chain coffee shop, and we were discussing the colour of the cup and how many beans were needed and how catchy the brand name was. How much, in other words, someone might pay for it, and not the taste. The taste was irrelevant.

Max and Vincent started talking about work, and Geraldine, with the air of someone well practised in smoothing over awkward social situations, began to ask me polite, open-ended questions, responding to my answers more enthusiastically than could ever be sincere. I couldn't get much out of her about herself. She'd been an actress, she said, but she wasn't anymore. She told me about her children and said she hoped I was enjoying the flat, and then Vincent said – Gerry, home time.

He inhaled the last of his wine and said to Max – so are you in tomorrow, then?

I am.

Isn't it tomorrow you're off? – the question was directed at Max, but I saw Vincent's eyes flicker towards me. They were mean and hard.

It is. Evening flight.

Well, it was wonderful to meet you, Anna – Vincent said to me. – It's nice to see Max has such a sweet friend for the time he's in London.

Yes, I like to think so – I said.

And are the talks with New York still ongoing? – he said to Max. – It all went rather quiet on that front, didn't it?

In a way, still ongoing – Max said. – They're still talking, anyway.

They both wished me a happy birthday, and then they were gone.

Max said – shall we go too? I have another little surprise for you actually.

We went out. He hailed a taxi and said something to the driver.

Where is it you're going? – I asked.

It's a surprise.

Tomorrow, I meant. What did Vincent mean?

Just a work trip. New York.

I see.

What did you think of Vincent, then? Was he useful? I gather he's a huge investor in the arts. Very influential, I'd imagine.

He's awful. Why are you friends with him?

Max laughed.

Oh come on, he's harmless enough. We're not friends, anyway. We're colleagues.

I don't understand why people like him claim to care about art. What's in it for him?

The appearance of benevolence, I suppose – Max said. – Anyway, he seems genuinely into it to me. Knows a lot about it.

Paying for things isn't the same as knowing about them.

He took my hand and stroked my wrist. It tickled.

You shouldn't be such a snob, darling – he said. – Who exactly did you think your audience was?

What did you tell him about me? – I asked.

What do you mean?

When you asked him if I could stay in the flat. Who did you say I was?

What do you mean, who did I say you were? – he said. – I said who you were.

But who did you say that was?

He looked confused.

I don't understand the question – he said. – Why? Who are you?

The taxi pulled up outside a hotel.

EIGHTEEN

A hotel right in the centre of town. Doormen in white gloves. Reception, marble-floored and wood-panelled and high-ceilinged. Silent. It was totally silent in there. The reverent hush that accompanies luxury. He'd got us a room for the night and all I could think about, going up in the lift, was how much it must have cost.

You really shouldn't spend this much money on me – I said.

He hooked his thumbs into the belt loops of my coat, and pulled me towards him.

Who do you suggest I spend it on? – he said.

We went down the corridor and he tapped us in. An entrance hall, the bathroom off to the left, the main room at the end. He took my hand and led me round, looking for my reaction, wanting me to be pleased with everything. I could imagine him as a boy, taking his paintings home to his mum at the end of term, demanding she say how good they were, and I played my part and was impressed. It wasn't difficult anyway. The room was designed to impress. Everything in it – the four-poster bed, dark embroidery on the headboard and matching curtains, the carved marble fireplace, the ornate table and glass drinks cabinet, the silk-covered armchairs – was grand, scaled up, oversized, and I felt very small.

I sat down on the bed. There was a bottle of champagne in an ice bucket on the table. He opened it, filled up two glasses, then he came and sat next to me.

Twenty-five – he said, handing me a glass. – So, do you feel like a grown-up?

Have you brought me here to patronise me?

Not exclusively, no.

I was talking to this singer – I said. – Someone a bit older than me. She was saying that everyone always told her how much time she had, how long it took for the voice to mature, how she didn't need to worry at all because she was so incredibly young for an opera singer, still had years before she needed to feel any real pressure to make it. Until the day she turned twenty-five. From then on, it was all *aren't you worried you're not singing in proper Houses yet? What exactly's happening with your career then? Getting a bit old now, aren't you?* So, yes – I said. – I'm feeling pretty past it, thanks.

I'd hoped to make him laugh, but he didn't. He looked at me, very serious, and I thought, oh God, why did I bring that up, idiotic of me.

What? – I said. – What is it?

Nothing. It's just you do look pretty past it, that's all. Now you mention it.

He grinned, and I felt almost stupidly happy. The champagne, I suppose. He took my glass out of my hand, put it down on the bedside table, and he kissed me. I lay back and pulled him with me, his body heavy against mine, remembering that feeling from earlier, that certainty – if I have him, if I can only have him, then nothing else matters. All other thoughts, which even an hour ago had been like jarring tunes stuck in my head, loud and obnoxious and demanding to be heard, were dialled down. There was only one nagging pitch still whining in my ear, a note of discord I needed him to mute.

Max? – I said. – How long are you going away for?

What?

He had unbuttoned my dress. I could feel the tickle of his stubble as he kissed my stomach.

New York. How long are you going for?

There was no reason to be worried. He went away for work all the time. But there was something in the way Vincent had glanced at me – mischievous, trying to cause trouble. He knew something.

Him and Gerry would laugh about it on the way home – *she clearly has no idea, poor silly girl* – they'd say, and they were right.

Do we really have to talk about that now? – he said, without looking up.

Is it a secret? – I asked.

He moved next to me, propped himself up on his elbow.

A month – he said. – It'll probably be a month. Maybe more like six weeks. Whenever this deal's closed, basically.

Right.

I don't really want to go.

So, why are you going then? – I said, making my voice teasing. – Not important enough to get out of it?

Too important, my love. Well, kind of. It's an American client. I worked with them when I lived there, and they basically only want to work with me. They're a huge client for us, stupid sums of money involved, you wouldn't believe it. So every time we do a deal with them, I get roped in.

What did Vincent mean?

When?

When he asked if talks were ongoing?

Nothing really. We'd been going to move back there. The New York office wanted me to transfer. Still do.

Oh. Will you?

He shrugged.

No. I mean, no immediate plans. Can we stop talking about this now? It's depressing me. Bad enough I have to go for so long, without talking about it too. Let's not ruin your birthday with me complaining, ok?

He kissed me again, and then he said – just give me a minute.

He went out to the bathroom.

I lay on the bed and looked at the pattern on the curtains. There were big dark flowers clustered close together. I tried to follow the lines – it looked like loops that joined up – but when you followed them, you saw they trailed off to nowhere.

A month, maybe more like six weeks.

It wasn't that long. It was self-indulgent of me, I knew, to think then about the weekends in the City alone. Self-indulgent to imagine how it would be with him gone, how every day would be like that, the weeks opaque and flat and grey, gathered around nothing.

I tried to make my mind quiet. A few hours ago, I thought, in that restaurant, I'd been happy. I remembered it very clearly. I clung to it, as if it would keep me safe. One image. Watching him on the phone through the glass, standing there in the greying light, how he'd run a hand through his hair, walked a couple of steps one way, then a couple of steps the other, the animation on his face as he'd laughed.

I don't know why. I don't know how it happened. Something about the darkness of the flowers on the curtains. Something about that man, the way he'd sneered at me and said *it's nice for Max to have such a sweet friend for the time he's in London*. Something about the intimacy implied by that laugh – that was what had made me happy, of course. It was a laugh I'd only seen him do with me and I liked it. Something about how he'd looked at his phone quickly, angled away from me so I hadn't seen who was calling – and didn't he always do that, now I really thought about it? – before he'd said – *sorry, I'm going to have to take this*. Something about that. Him laughing through the glass. The image stuck in my throat.

He'd left his phone on the bedside table, and I reached for it. I'd seen him put his passcode in before. I went to his call log, and there was the number that had called him. Five minutes and thirty-seven seconds. It was saved as *Home*.

I locked his phone and put it carefully back on the bedside table. I was surprised by how calm I felt. It made sense. Of course he was still married. Not separated-about-to-get-divorced married, but actually married. Of course he was. I could see her, standing in their huge farmhouse-style kitchen in Oxford, picking up the phone, looking out onto the garden. They would have designed it all together, the patio area where their friends gathered for barbeques, the fruit trees, the screen of bright-coloured flowers you could look at from the sink. Why had she called him? Five minutes and thirty-seven seconds. To say she missed him – no – far too dramatic – the sort of thing I'd say. To remind him to reply to some email about a dinner she'd been trying to arrange, or to say he'd left a work document on the kitchen table on his way out last night, did he need it, or – why not, why not? – if the whole separation had been a lie, then what else had he lied about? – to tell him something funny one of the kids had said that day. Maybe that was why he'd laughed like that, run his hand through his hair – a nervous gesture, wasn't it? – as he'd glanced back at me, sitting there on the other side of the glass.

I looked around the hotel room and saw it, as though through a coloured film, everything altered. It was too expensive, too impersonal, too discreet. It was sordid. A hotel only frequented by tourists and rich people having affairs.

You know – he said, coming back into the room – it's past midnight. Not your birthday anymore.

He didn't notice my silence. He came over to the bed and kissed me, and I let him. A filter had been applied to him too and I saw him differently or, perhaps, for the first time as he really was. Older. More cocky. Eyes that looked straight into mine but revealed nothing. This new face, this new person. It was almost more exciting, knowing now what role I played in his life, still letting him. I let him pull my dress over my head, and slide his hand into my pants, and kiss my breasts. I bit his lip. He moaned and said fuck, and I felt my heart knock against my ribcage, pumped with this odd muted excitement, this having something over him, this knowing who he really was. But then he held my face in his hands, looked into my eyes in this pretence of intimacy and honesty, and I couldn't stand it anymore.

Who called you earlier? – I said.

What?

He sat up and his eyes slid off, away from mine, glanced at his phone.

What? – he said again.

Who called you earlier?

You've — Anna — he said. — Were you looking at my phone?

What? No.

Who called me when? What are you talking about?

In the restaurant. Earlier. In the restaurant. When you went out.

Why the hell are you asking me this now?

Why won't you answer the question?

He sat on the edge of the bed and started pulling his trousers on.

I can't believe this — he said. — I really can't believe this. You're checking up on me? Checking my phone? Seriously? What the fuck's wrong with you?

Why won't you tell me? — I said, quieter this time.

There was a pause, then he said — it was my mother. Not that it's any of your business. What the fuck's going on?

Your — your mother?

That's what I said.

As soon as he'd said it, I knew it was true, but the relief I felt was empty and sad. It was too familiar.

I turned away from him and picked up my clothes where they lay on the bed. I dressed with my back turned to him, and I tried to remember the things I knew.

He was a man with blue eyes, and he had a scar on his shoulder.

A man whose brother's tooth was embedded in his temple, under his scalp. A childhood argument, he'd fallen, there was blood and no one had realised until the skin sealed over. You could feel it if you put your finger there and pressed.

A man who could make anyone like him. Who would start conversations with waiters, taxi drivers, people behind the bar. He needed that, I think — the admiration of strangers.

A man who knew about unexpected things. Antique furniture and Russian literature and flowers.

A man who was fragile, had been disappointed by life. I'd tried to be gentle with him, thought that if I stayed still for long enough, he'd come to me, but he didn't want me. Not in the way I wanted him.

He was a man who wanted a family. Who'd bought a house I wasn't allowed in for, I assumed, this perfect family he wanted one day to have, and yet – and this seemed to me the saddest fact of all – and yet, at nearly forty, still had his parents' number saved as *Home*.

I looked at him, and his face was again the face I knew.

I realised, or rather I articulated it to myself for the first time, a solid irrefutable fact, that I was in love with him. In almost the same moment, it occurred to me that I'd never been more miserable in my life.

I covered my face with my hands.

What is it? – he said. – What's wrong with you?

I didn't realise I was crying until the strands of my hair, trapped under my hands, turned wet. I love you, I thought, that's what's wrong. I love you, and you've never lied to me. You like me. You think I'm pretty and funny and you like talking to me. You like sitting across from me at restaurant tables, putting your hand on my leg in bars and lying next to me in bed. You like my body. You like wrapping your fingers round my hair and kissing my neck and running your tongue up the inside of my thighs. You like me and I love you and everything you've ever told me is true.

I thought my tears would make him gentle, but they didn't.

What the hell is this? Anna? Why are you crying? Stop it.

He grabbed my wrist and pulled it away from my face.

Look at me – he said. – Tell me what's wrong.

You're hurting me.

He dropped my wrist.

Tell me – he said.

It got to him, I realised, it got under his skin, this situation, a woman covering her face and crying over something he'd supposedly done. He'd been here before. He hated it. It angered him. Bored him. It made him tired.

Why didn't you tell me you were going away for so long? – I said.

This wasn't what I meant. I meant that it would carry on like this, me and him – that's what I wanted to say, what I wanted him to contradict. That, for as long as I kept seeing him, it would carry on like this. I'd give him anything he asked me for, and he'd take it, he'd never say no to it, but that meant nothing. I'd keep thinking I'd finally got a hold of him, and he would keep prising my fingers off – ignoring messages, avoiding questions, saying – *I'm just going to New York for six weeks* – as casually as he'd say he was popping to the shops, or thinking about replacing his toothbrush.

Why didn't I – really? – he said. – That's what you're crying about? Look, I'm sorry, ok? It wasn't some big deliberate deception, if that's what you're getting at.

What was it then?

Jesus Christ, Anna. You know this is actually insane, don't you? I wasn't trying to hide it from you. I go away all the time, you know that. I only didn't mention it because you've been crazily stressed lately, and there never seemed a good time. That's literally it.

His voice was calm, measured. He considered himself to be reasonable, and me not to be.

And honestly, Anna – he said. – Honestly? Well, I didn't realise you'd care this much. You've got your show on, haven't you?

My show? But you – you told me not to do it. I didn't go to rehearsals today. You told me to pull out.

What? – he said. – You're not being serious, are you? I never said that. I never told you to do anything. I just tried to show you that maybe it wasn't the grand tragedy you thought it was, if it turned out you couldn't do it. That's all. Fuck. Believe it or not, I was trying to be nice.

I tried to remember what his exact words had been, but I couldn't.

Come on – he said. – Be fair. Let's not get dramatic. I'm really not going for that long.

Imagining him and his wife, some cool restaurant with an incredible view, meeting to finalise the divorce papers, reconciling, him deciding he'd move there after all.

Will you – will you see her while you're there? – I asked.

There was a little pause and then he said quietly, in a weary sort of way – please, for the love of God, Anna, don't be crazy.

I felt very tired. Wanted to go back thirty minutes, an hour, to unstart this. I tried to backtrack.

You could have discussed it with me, that's all – I said.

Discussed it with you? What, like, asked for your permission?

I stared at the pattern on the curtains.

But Anna – he said, gently. – Anna, I'm sorry. I'm a bit confused. I didn't think we had to ask each other permission to do things. I thought – well – I thought that you've got your life, and I've got mine.

And then anger flared up inside me like a match struck in the dark.

You couldn't care less how I feel, could you? – I said. – You really don't care.

I was on the edge of saying words I knew couldn't be taken back. Words that would destroy the illusion I'd spent months creating for him – that he was on the margins of my life, and not the centre. They were flooding into my mouth, and I tried to swallow them back, but then he raised an eyebrow at me, like I was a child, testing boundaries, and he was trying not to lose his patience, and he said – *you do know you're being ridiculous, don't you?* – and then they all seeped out. A confused mess of words.

You don't think I'm good enough for you, you never have, nothing I do ever pleases you, nothing, when you want me to do something I do it and then that's wrong too, you don't even like me do you, you don't even like me, you're just marking time with me, because it's fun and it's easy, I've made this so easy for you haven't I, always, I always wanted to, to make things nice and good for you, and so you're just using me so that you don't have to know you're alone and because I flatter your vanity, and that's all I am to you, and one day you'll meet someone who just knows how to be, who just knows, who's already successful and attractive and nice, who you won't have to tell all the ways that she's wrong and –

The look on his face. He was horrified. I knew I sounded hysterical, I knew why he looked so afraid, but I actually felt very calm. Oddly detached. I was standing back, watching myself destroy our beautiful budding relationship, or so I'd seen it – this thing I'd been tiptoeing around for months and months and months now – *oh yes, I'm busy too – no, sure, I'm easy – whatever works for you* – afraid that if I made any sudden movements, I'd scare it away. This beautiful, precious thing that I'd guarded and protected and let grow until it had become everything to me, and now I was watching myself break it apart. There was power in that, in taking a sledgehammer to the thing I loved. It felt good.

He stood up abruptly and made a movement towards the door, as if to leave, but then he stopped. He crouched down on the floor in front of me and took both my hands in his, kissed my fingers, rested his forehead in my lap. For a moment, we sat like that, neither of us speaking, and then he looked up at me. The light from the lamp made his skin look so pale it was almost translucent, and the hollows in his cheeks were cavernous. He looked so tired.

I'm sorry – he said. – I've been – I've been stupid. And selfish. I'm sorry. I didn't realise you were unhappy. I knew that maybe you wanted things to move a bit faster. I guessed, I mean. Sometimes. Some of the things you said. But this. Honestly. I had no idea. You always seemed to be enjoying yourself. I thought we were – well – I'm sorry, Anna. I really am.

The shame of all I'd said and all he hadn't contradicted bloomed inside me, thick and sharp like a bed of thistles. But he looked so sad. I wanted to put my arms round him and tell him it was ok and I hadn't really meant it. Poor Max. I felt sorry for him. He'd wanted someone to make him happy for a bit. Someone who'd distract him, who'd make him feel good. He hadn't wanted that person to be real.

I am enjoying myself – I said. – With you, I mean.

Well, not right this minute, I imagine.

No, not right this minute.

Things were strangely fine after that. He went to the bathroom and came back with a hot flannel, and I mopped my face. Then we got ready for bed in a carefully choreographed dance of normality. We brushed our teeth, standing next to each other in front of the mirror. I splashed my face with cold water and took off the make-up that was smudged under my eyes. He used the hotel moisturiser, which I said made him smell like a girl, and he laughed. We got into bed and switched off the light. Nothing else was said, and before long, the dark layered up on top of me, heavy, like a weight on my chest.

I lay there, thinking, in the morning, it will be like this never happened. This room. The sheets will be changed. The half-empty toiletries will be thrown away, replaced with new bottles. There'll be more champagne in the bucket. Another couple in here, playing out their little scene.

I lay there, thinking, you build one person up to be the person who can give your life colour and meaning, the person who can save you, but they can't do that, no one can do that.

Thinking, there must have been a moment when I could have walked away from this and it wouldn't have hurt, but I couldn't remember.

Thinking about that time he'd talked about his flat. *It's not a real place* – he'd said, and I hadn't known what he meant. I'd thought he made my world bigger, but now I saw he'd shrunk it down, made it just those four walls, and they weren't enough for him. *It's not a real place.* Not his real life. Temporary. When he walks out of his flat and into the world, he starts to exist. When I walk out, I cease to.

Thinking, was what I said irrevocable, then? Or was it not? And feeling every moment electric with the possibility that I could open my mouth and say something to him that would change things, that would make things ok, but I didn't.

He wasn't asleep either. I could hear him shifting around, turning onto his side then onto his back, flipping his pillow over, then over again. At the loneliest point of the night, the point where I thought I couldn't stand it anymore, he said – *are you asleep?* – and I said – *no, are you?* – and then he found me in the dark, his mouth on my mouth, the warmth of his skin. Bodies remember everything, fit right back together like they always did, so that nothing seems changed. And then we both slept – first him, then me.

*

I woke to find him up already. His hair was wet. He was standing in front of the mirror, tying his tie.

Morning – I said.

It felt strange to be naked when he was clothed. I sat up and wrapped the sheet under my armpits.

Morning.

He sat down on the bed.

Look – he said. – So, I'm leaving later today.

He looked uncomfortable. I tried to think of something that would make a difference, but I couldn't. In the most emotionally intense moments of your life, you never say anything real, start reciting lines you've heard in films. He'd talk in clichés – *not ready, can't do this anymore* – and I would too. I couldn't remember any other words.

So he said his bit, and I said mine, and it was over.

The flat's paid for until June – he said. – So you're fine to stay there until then.

I don't want to stay there.

Well, ok. You don't have to. Just leave the key at the office.

Fine.

Then he said – but Anna, I'm worried about you. Are you going to be alright? Can I give you some money?

I couldn't think of anything to say to that and, shortly afterwards, he left.

NINETEEN

Nice of you to show up, sweetheart – the Director said.

He'd called while I was still in the hotel, a landline number I didn't recognise. I thought it might be Max, so I picked up, and there was the Director's voice at the end of the phone.

Oh, you're alive, are you? – he said. – That's nice.

I was still sitting in bed. I don't think I'd moved since Max had left.

So, I can't imagine you've been checking your schedule much lately – he said. – Sure you've had more important things on. Thought I'd give you a personal call to remind you of the full run with piano today. New service I'm offering for the more flaky members of the cast. You're welcome, sweetheart. Marieke's coming to watch.

The curtains were shut. I had no idea what time it was.

I've told her all about your various ailments and unaccounted-for absences – he said. – So she's very much expecting you to be there. As am I.

I was about to say I wasn't coming – they could give my part to my cover, I didn't care – but he'd already hung up. I got up, dread turning my insides to concrete, and I dressed in my clothes from the night before. I wished I'd brought flat shoes with me. I walked into the theatre and everyone, in their leggings and plimsolls, their trainers and jeans, turned to look.

Break's nearly over – the Director shouted. – Three minutes.

They'd run Act One already, and now it was time for Act Two. The chorus were congregated in small groups, some sitting quietly, checking something in their scores, finishing their coffees, others clowning around, loud and theatrical, trying to attract the Director's attention. One of them, who'd just arrived on his bike, had been wearing a special mask to protect his vocal cords from the London air. He'd taken out the filter, black with pollution, and was going round, proudly displaying it, like a kid doing Show and Tell.

I waved at the principals, standing in their own little huddle, and dumped my stuff in the front row.

Rehearsals had started to feel to me like a party that must nearly be over. You're tired, you're not having fun anymore, and it's too late for anything good to happen. You keep having circular conversations that no one's enjoying. You don't want to be the first to leave. Surely people will call it a night soon, you think, surely they'll go home, why aren't they tired? And then new people arrive, more drinks get brought out, enthusiasm's renewed. It starts up again.

I sat by myself, and pretended to be doing something on my phone. I always knew this, I thought, what it was like here. That the people who managed to stick around longest – who didn't get bored, who could maintain their charm and joy and focus, or pretend at least – were the people who'd make it. Most people would give up eventually and go home. They'd get tired. The party would get too much for them. Because most people can't live their lives like this, in this frenetic limbo. They remember they have responsibilities, bills to be paid and money to be earned. They remember that the years are passing, and that the years matter. They go home, and spend the rest of their lives saying – *God, I don't know how people live like that, it was mad in there.*

Places – the Director shouted. – Bananas and coffees and phones away. That was twenty. That was it. You've had it.

I went to the wings with Alcindoro. There was eight minutes of music before our entry, and we used to chat, make jokes, while we were waiting to go on. Now, he stood there, staring at the stage, arms crossed. He didn't want anyone to think we were friends. I was seen as one of the singers who wouldn't make it, and failure was highly contagious.

The eight minutes passed, and then it was time.

The first thing you hear from Musetta is her laughter. The audience hears it offstage, and then she enters. I opened my mouth for the laugh, but it came out so quiet, it would barely have reached the front row.

We do actually need to hear that, you know – the Director heckled. He didn't seem to get the concept of an uninterrupted run.

I entered on Alcindoro's arm. The entire cast, as they're meant to, turned to look. Tension paralysed my throat and, when it was time for me to sing, I could barely get enough sound out to mark.

Stop, stop, stop – the Director shouted. – No marking. Not now. Too late in the process for that.

Eyes on me. The chorus. The principals. Eyes on me, that looked to pick holes, that wanted me to fail, little glances at each other, the endless speculation in the pub, I knew exactly how it went – *what do you think's wrong with her? And didn't you always think she was a little –.* Marieke's eyes on me too, there in the second row, making notes.

I just, I—

Almost inaudible in that vast space.

What? – the Director boomed. – What's she saying?

I'm still ill – that came out too loud, like I was being sarcastic.

The Director put his hands on his hips and sighed.

Look, the chorus have to hear you, sweetheart, don't they? It's musically fucking complex enough without a fucking part missing. Be a nice colleague, now, won't you?

I'm sorry – I'd slipped back to a whisper. – I can't do it.

What did she say?

She said she can't do it – the chorus shouted.

Right – the Director said. – She can't do it. Right. Well, that's all we fucking need, isn't it? Where's her cover? Where is she, Musetta's cover? Come here, then. It's your big moment.

We started from Musetta's entry. The Director got me to walk through the part, miming – *assuming you'll deign to sing on the night, so let's keep you slotted in* – while my cover sang it from the side.

I was now the Director's particular target. The more he heckled, the more mistakes I made.

I tripped over one of the multiple chorus members' legs on my way to sit down.

Careful – he warned.

I walked in front of the bohemians' table, rather than behind it, blocking them while they sang.

It's not all about you – he snarled. – Have some awareness of your colleagues, come on, we've rehearsed this.

I put my finger in my wine glass – empty for practising – and then sucked the finger on the other hand.

That's the perfect fucking example of why you shouldn't fake it on stage – he shouted. – The perfect example. Take note, everyone. We're having an acting lesson.

Then it was the aria.

For the first part of it, I sat on the bar, surrounded by the male chorus members. Then I got up and walked across it. It suddenly felt very high. I picked my way along, watching the floor lurch, trying not to tread on people's hands or glasses.

Can you just be more sexy? – the Director barked. – It's not like you're actually singing it. You have literally one job. Be more sexy, ok?

I wriggled my hips in a parody of femininity, and the Director sighed to make it clear he did not consider this sexy at all.

We had a break at the end of Act Two. My cover went over to talk to the principals. A final year, I'd overturned the hierarchy by being cast ahead of her. I tried to slouch off to my seat, to make myself invisible, but Marieke intercepted me.

What's going on, Anna? – she said. – You're ill?

This vestigial instinct in me, still, to protect this, to cling onto it, not to give up even though it made sense to, like how someone falling into cold water instinctively thrashes and struggles, which only makes them drown faster.

I've had a really bad cold – I said. – I'm getting better, but I'm trying to look after the voice. Not overdo it. I'll be ok by next week.

She looked at me sternly. She knew she was being lied to.

I had a call from Angela yesterday – she said. – She's very worried. Said you hadn't been able to sing for a couple of weeks, and now she couldn't get hold of you. But you sound fine to me. Your speaking voice is normal. You don't sound ill. What exactly is it that's wrong?

I couldn't think of anything to say.

I don't know – I said.

She took her glasses off and scrutinised me, like I was a piece of furniture she'd just moved, and she was trying to work out if she'd liked me better where I'd been before.

Well – she said, eventually – there's not much time now till opening night, is there? The Director says you haven't been singing at full voice in rehearsals for weeks, and it's *extremely* late to still be marking. The voice needs to build the stamina to tackle the full role, you know that. I did say to you right at the beginning, Anna, that this opportunity was provisional. If you think you're not up to it—she trailed off. – I'm going to have to hear it – she said. – We'll run Act Two again from your entry.

But I haven't warmed up – I said, a final trump card. – And I haven't sung for a few days. I can't do it cold.

We're on a break – she said. – Twenty minutes. That's plenty of time.

I went backstage through the wings. There was no one there, and the corridors felt neglected and sad. I didn't have a plan. I could just leave, I thought. Go out through Stage Door. No one would see me. *You don't have to do it. No one can make you do it.* I could walk out, and then that would be it. Over. I could walk out and never sing again. But something stopped me, some dim flicker of remembrance, I suppose – how much I used to love this party, how alive it had made me feel. Knowing that, if I went home now, I'd always wonder what might have happened if I'd stayed.

I opened the door to the nearest dressing room and sank down on the floor, put my head on my knees. When I looked up again, I saw it was the dressing room I'd used for Manon. There was the costume rack, hung with clothes, ready for us to wear them, to animate them and make them real. There was the strip of mirror, the unlit bare bulbs, waiting for us to switch them on, to sit in their light and make up our faces, paint ourselves as different people. There were the same walls that had absorbed it all over the years – the nervous waiting, the glorious anticipation, the tears, the laughter – and now radiated it back to me. And it started to beat inside me again – that energy, that excitement – remembering what it felt like, to put on a costume and make-up, to zip yourself into someone else's skin and use them to say something you knew to be true and to have people listen. How much I had wanted this. Wanted it and wanted it and wanted it, beyond all reason, and I thought, why shouldn't I have it? He could leave, I couldn't stop him, but I could still have this – amazed that I'd spent the past few weeks thinking it didn't matter anymore, that I could be happy without it.

I started to warm up and, as I sang, I didn't listen to the sound. I thought about Musetta. My favourite scene – cut from the opera, but it's there in the source. The courtyard scene. Musetta has to leave her flat because she's behind on the rent, and her landlord has moved all her furniture outside. She was meant to have a party that night, but she doesn't cancel it. She spreads a rug out on the court-yard, arranges her table and sofa and chairs around it. She gets all dressed up, and she receives her guests outside. She's a show-must-go-on kind of girl. I tried to channel some of that. I remembered everything about her, Musetta, as I started to sing some of her music. The work I'd put into it, weeks ago now, how I'd coloured it. She was like an old friend I hadn't seen in a long time. I'd worried that meeting her again might be awkward, but everything was exactly the same.

Twenty passed, and I went back upstairs. Everyone was annoyed.

We're going from Musetta's entry – the Director said. – It's only fifteen fucking minutes of music. Stop whingeing. Let's go.

I went and took my place in the wings.

Musetta enters stage right, on Alcindoro's arm. She's laughing.

269

There he is, there's Marcello, sitting outside the café with the others, and it's all nostalgia – the heavy smell of jasmine, the endless night sky. He hasn't looked at me, and so I make myself laugh, like Alcindoro's said something funny, though in truth he never does. We walk past the table, and still he doesn't look at me, but seeing his face is like looking at an old photograph. Memory has all the bad bits filtered out. You incinerate the complications, only print off the pictures where everyone's smiling. But I haven't forgotten. I know I was afraid to love him. That old life reduced me, I thought, limited where I could go and what I could be, and I didn't want that. I wanted to be free. Yes, I was afraid to love him, but there were some things I couldn't control – like how my mind was wiped clear and blank when he touched me, or how, when I was waiting to hear from him, I'd catch myself literally – and I do mean *literally*, I'm not saying *literally* when I mean *figuratively* – holding my breath. People say we make choices between the head and the heart, but that's not true. Or not true for me, anyway. The two things I want – him and not him – are both from the heart, two competing desires I can't fit together.

Musetta and Alcindoro sit at a table, centre stage, next to Marcello and the other bohemians. She tries to attract Marcello's attention. She shouts at the waiter, drops a plate.

Some of them are laughing, I can see them. Looking over at me and laughing. I can't stand it. Them looking at me, believing this act – this look-at-me act – and finding it funny. Only Marcello won't look, and he's the one whose look I want. I want to remember what it's like to be under his eyes. I'm tired of this game, want it to be over. I'm tired of us performing it, rehearsing our indifference in front of all these people. These people, whose grasp of subtext is not exactly nuanced. Who see gossip in our performance, but can't read feeling. I'd like to be honest. I'd like to say to him – you know those flowers you bought me? When we first met? I said I'd stay with you for as long as they didn't fade. Do you remember? Well, it was me who kept them alive. I got up each night, while you were sleeping. I gave them water.

Musetta stands to draw attention to herself. Alcindoro tries to shush her.

Does he – did I imagine it? – does he glance at me? Yes. We look at each other, just for a moment, and then excitement quivers through me, because I know, and the game becomes sweet again, not painful. The looks across the bar. The little smiles. Knowing he wants me, and it will start up again. Knowing I'll have his warmth and his love, even if it's just for tonight. And maybe tonight is enough, after all, because I like to be free. I like to wake up in the night alone, to open the window and feel the air on my face and not to worry about disturbing him, to turn on the light if I can't sleep, read my book, watch TV, lie awake and have no one ask me what I'm thinking. The days that are mine and no one else's. Not worrying about another person and what they want. Not muting my colour to match some-one else's. No one there in the morning to know what I look like when I sleep, un-made-up and unguarded.

Musetta goes downstage, and sits on the bar to sing her aria.

He's still not looking at me, but I know him. The way he keeps flick-ing his hair. The chain-smoking. How he's consciously looking away, studied, purposeful. He wants me, I know it, and later, when we're alone together, he'll say – when you came in this evening, I didn't know where to look, I wanted you so badly, I –

Musetta stands on the bar.

I stood on the bar and faced out into the theatre. The lights weren't completely down, and I could see them. The Director in the front row. Marieke staring right at me, looking down, scribbling some-thing in her notebook. The covers having a chat. A prickle of fear – don't – don't look at them – but it had already started, and I stumbled over a note. My whole body froze rigid. Everyone was looking at me. Everyone on stage. Everyone in the audience. I looked away from them, towards the darkness at the back of the theatre.

Then the door at the back opened, and a man came in. He sat in the back row, too far away for me to see his face.

That's him – I thought. – That's Max.

I knew it was crazy. It couldn't be him.

But why not? It could be. He knew where my rehearsals were, he'd been here before. If he'd wanted to see me before he left, tried to call me, went to the flat, couldn't get hold of me, would he not come here? Is that not exactly what he'd do?

I stared at the back of the theatre, trying to see the man's face, but it was too dark. And then I felt myself hurtling into a tunnel of panic, where there was no light anymore. Standing up there on the bar, it was like everyone could see through my clothes, through my skin, right into the empty core of me. Turning back and looking at every note as it came out of my mouth, thinking – *if that's him, then he's listening to this* – examining the sound and finding it lacking, and then a note cracked.

I stopped and looked at everyone, still obediently looking at me, exactly as they'd been directed. I swallowed and tried to restart. I couldn't get a sound out. I stood there.

I could vaguely hear the Director shouting at me.

I dimly registered the faces of the other people on stage, some confused, some pissed off about stopping again, some barely concealing laughter, glancing at each other, looking forward to talking about this in the pub.

I opened my mouth and shut it again.

Then I jumped off the bar, got down from the stage, grabbed my stuff from the front row. I walked out. It was almost exciting, in a nasty kind of way. Grimly pleasurable, knowing how bad it had got. No going back from this, is there? No. No pretending any more that things are ok.

The Director shouted after me, and then there was silence. Dramatic silence for my final exit.

On my way out, I glanced at the man. It wasn't him, of course.

PART THREE

TWENTY

We walked for miles, the baby strapped to Tara's back. Fields full of daffodils, a sky, blue and cloudless, like in a child's drawing. We stopped in the shade and sat in the grass, and she released the baby, held him under the armpits while he bounced up and down.

Look – she said. – Look at that. See? That's an Emperor moth.

She pointed out its dusty orange colour, the spots on its wings that only came in spring. She showed him poppies and orchids, blackthorn, red kites and hares, pink thrift. I didn't know the names of things, but she did, and the baby would understand the world through her.

You're meant to talk to them all the time – she said. – And sometimes I forget that other people can hear me too, so I say things like – *oh, look at those people in their too-tight Lycra, aren't they silly?* – or – *that couple are having a nasty argument, aren't they? Do you think they'll get divorced?*

He seems advanced – I said. I had nothing to measure him against, but it sounded like the sort of thing you should say.

A genius, yes, if my mum's to be believed.

He pulled himself up to standing, using Tara's arm as a crutch.

He's just normal, I think – she said. – Good at some things, not good at others.

We watched him crawl, Tara running after him intermittently to check he hadn't eaten any of the grass in his fist, to bring him back to us. I pulled my top up to my bra and lay back, enjoying the sun on my stomach. It was one of those hot April days that feels like midsummer. Winter had been shed like a skin, and underneath – impossible to imagine, even a few weeks ago – everything was new and fresh.

When I'd called Tara to tell her I was home, she said – *thank God, I'm so glad* – and she sounded like she really meant it. We met for coffee. For a while, I thought it would be like it had been at Christmas, me asking her polite questions about the baby, her answering them in a distant, distracted sort of way.

But then she said – can I tell you something?

Sure.

There was this one night last week when he wouldn't stop crying. And crying in this horrible sort of way. Not like he wanted anything – I don't think there was anything I could do about it – just like he was angry, like he was angry with me, like I'd done something wrong. I'd been up with him half the night, and I – I don't know – I suddenly thought I couldn't do it anymore, I couldn't be in the same room as him, or – I don't know – I don't know what I would have done – I just knew I couldn't. I put him back in his cot and shut the door, went outside – could still hear him screaming, even out there – got in the car.

Where was Rob?

Rob? Asleep. He sleeps with earplugs in. Anyway, I drove around for hours. Or it felt like that. I was too scared to come back. Because I've never done anything like that before, you know, I was terrified. I had no idea what he'd do.

Rob?

She gave me a funny look.

No – she said. – Not Rob. The baby.

What did he do?

Nothing. I don't know. When I finally made myself go back, he was asleep.

He seems so good-natured. I can't imagine him being difficult.

At night, he's different. At night, he hates me.

She said this like it was deeply shameful, and I felt bad then, all those months I'd been in London, how little I'd thought of her.

The next couple of weeks, we saw each other nearly every day. We spent most of the time walking, taking different paths out of town, out into the country, because she was sick of being inside, she said. I got the impression she hadn't had anyone to talk to for a long time. She told me about Rob's family. They lived two streets away and popped by all the time, unannounced. They dumped on her vast quantities of plums and apples from their garden, which mouldered in the fruit bowl before they could be eaten. They did it on purpose, she thought. They commandeered the baby, quietly critical, offering her unsolicited advice. Rob didn't get why they annoyed her so much, but then Rob only had to see them once a week. He loved it here, she said, this town, and he'd set up his own practice now, so they'd never move away.

I was vague when she asked about me. I said I'd come home because I wasn't sure I wanted to be a singer anymore, and I didn't really want to talk about it. This seemed to me like a humiliating admission of failure, but all she said was – *oh right, that's a shame.*

That day, though, with the baby crawling around under the tree, and me lying with the sun on my stomach, she said – so what are you going to do?

I didn't answer at first, and she added – I meant, if you're not going to sing anymore. Have you thought what you'll do?

Not really – I said, in a tone I hoped signalled this was the end of the conversation.

So do you think you might change your mind then?

I felt something crawl over the back of my hand, but I didn't open my eyes to see what it was.

No – I said. – I don't think so.

Over the past couple of weeks at home, I'd told myself that not singing was a choice I'd made. I repeated all the reasons I knew not to sing. The most typical career was a disappointment. A mishmash of teaching, underpaid church and choral society gigs, perhaps an opera or two a year with a fourth-tier company, but only if you were really lucky. That was what it was all for, for most singers – the seven years of training and the four languages you could speak and the however many thousands of pounds you'd spent on lessons. And then there was the fact that if you were successful, genuinely successful, top-of-your-game successful, your life would be spent in hotels, lived out of suitcases. That was what most singers aspired to – and I had too, once – but I wasn't sure I did anymore. Max had once said – *but that's not a life, is it? How do people have relationships? See their families?* – and I'd never thought of that before, not in any real way, it hadn't seemed relevant. It was another reason to add to my list. There were so many reasons, actually, it was surprising that anyone wanted to do it at all.

I repeated these reasons to myself over and over – rationalised my decision – but I didn't believe them. I'd tried to sing a few times when my parents were at work. Rushed down to the piano when I heard the front door shut, guilty-feeling, like I was sneaking in a boyfriend. Always, it was the same. An iron clamp round my throat. Black-eyed terror. I could barely get a note out now.

I don't know what I'll do – I said.

Well, you could have a baby. Then no one will ever ask you again what your plans are. No one seems to expect you to achieve anything. It's quite freeing. Will you not miss singing though?

I don't know.

The weeks at home, I'd experienced none of the excitement, the joy that came with singing, but none of the lows either. Maybe it would be better to live a life that was muted, where experience operated within more limited parameters.

Well, do you have anything to go back to London for? – Tara said. – If you're not going back to the Conservatory?

I guess not. Not really.

So you could just stay here for a bit then? Until you know what you'll do next.

I suppose, yeah. It would make Mum happy anyway.

Is she liking you being at home?

Well, I know she'd like it if she thought I was staying for good. Right now, she's so busy slipping jibes about my lifestyle into every conversation, I can't imagine she's having that much fun.

Anyway, what about that guy? He's a reason to go back, right? The one you mentioned at Christmas.

That's over now.

How come?

I didn't realise I wanted to talk about him, until I found myself telling her the whole story. The last few months. The last time I'd seen him. The phone call. The argument.

And you believed him? – she said. – When he said it was his mum?

Believed him? Yeah, I mean – what? – you don't?

Strangely, although it had seemed plausible to me he'd been lying all along, it had never occurred to me he'd been lying in that moment.

I don't know – she said. – I've never even met him. But it would make sense, wouldn't it, him still being married? What you said about his house, not letting you go, how vague he was about what he got up to, all that stuff.

I guess so – I said.

I wished I hadn't told her. I crawled over to the baby, and he started to race me, me pretending he was too fast, I couldn't keep up, him shrieking with something I supposed was laughter. Tara sat, watching us, pulling up handfuls of grass that made a noise like Velcro.

You know – she said – I do sometimes think it's a good thing there's no one close to my age round here.

Really? Why's that?

Well, when we got married, we promised never to have sex with anyone else ever again our whole lives. That now seems like quite a big ask. Luckily, I never meet anyone, though. No temptation. No opportunity to disobey the sacrament of marriage. It's really no wonder, is it, that there are more Christians in the countryside.

Rob's parents were very religious, which was why her and Rob had married so young. Early twenties, she was just out of uni. I was surprised, when she said they'd got engaged. Tara had never exactly had conservative values. When we were at school, our Religious Studies teacher had refused to answer her question about where exactly in the Bible it said no sex before marriage – said Tara was trying to cause trouble – and Tara had walked out. *She wouldn't answer, because it doesn't say that* – she said to me afterwards. – *Nowhere, and she knows it. It doesn't say that in the Bible.*

The baby stood and fell over. She sighed.

Amazing he keeps trying really, isn't it? An adult would have given up by now. But seriously – she said – it's not normal, is it? That I've only slept with one person. It's weird.

Well, you're not missing much. All men are pretty much the same – I said, though it wasn't true.

She put the baby back in the sling, and we started to walk back. I sometimes felt like we were still teenagers, these conversations, like she was playing at being an adult. But then I'd think no, she really was married – to Rob Faulkner, who'd been two years above us at school, who was prematurely receding and who I'd never liked – she really did have a baby, there he was, he was real, I could reach out and touch him. This was real life. It was happening to her, and there was no reason for it to make me sad.

After I'd walked out of rehearsals, people had called for a bit, but I didn't answer. No one had my new address, so they couldn't get me that way. The performances of *Bohème* started, time ticked on, and then they were just as quickly over. Everything went quiet. I'd done it. I'd disappeared. What I found surprising was how easy it had been.

Other singers I'd known over the years had disappeared. They'd stopped coming into college, stopped replying to messages, and no one had ever heard from them again. Rumours would do the rounds, mock sympathy that barely concealed delight – *anxiety, I heard* – or, even better – *nodules on her cords, has to have an operation, won't be able to sing again for two months – I heard, a year – surely it's possibly never again? Months of speech therapy, anyway.* But sometimes the speculated reason was more disturbing. Hushed whispers. *I heard, well, her teacher said, that she doesn't want to be a singer anymore. She's going to try and do something else.* No one knew how to react to that one. Singing was a cult. The existence of opposing ideologies was a threat. We could speculate endlessly about why they'd left, but we never asked where they'd gone.

The days after I'd disappeared, I listened to music all the time, anything that wasn't classical – Scottish folk and nineties pop and reggae – pre-made Spotify playlists that required no decisions. I pushed the earbuds right into my ears, until it felt like my skull might split in half, and I filled my head with other people's voices. It created a distance that numbed. I walked across the road without remembering to check for traffic, knocked into people in the street, struggled to make myself understood in shops. I needed it, though, the constant noise, because whenever it was silent in my brain, I filled the space with fantasy. Him and me – I put us in rooms and moved us around like puppets. I pulled at his strings, so that his hand was on my face, his lips on my neck, his arms round my waist. I made us speak. Scenes where I confronted him, scenes where he cried and confessed everything – there were all sorts of things, I imagined, that he might have to confess – scenes that ended, always, in reconciliation. Him saying that he loved me. That he'd thought about me, always, the weeks we were apart. That he wouldn't leave me. I'd wake in the night, or first thing in the morning, and I'd already be in one of those imagined rooms, him and me, until I thought, *this is how people go mad, isn't it?*

It felt like a very long time, those days I spent alone in the flat, but it wasn't that long. About two weeks, and then one day I saw my parents' number flash up on my phone, and I felt – entirely unexpected – a longing for home.

Do you want me to come and visit? – I said. – I can come.

But what about your show? – Mum said.

It's not happening anymore. The Director let us down. He got a better offer at the last minute.

This made next to no sense, but Mum didn't question it.

Well, we'd love to see you – she said.

And then home was a reset button, like when you die on a computer game, and find yourself right back at the start. Their house was so neat and so quiet. Nothing was changed. My bedroom was the same as it had always been – stuffed toys on the shelf, single bed, photos of schoolfriends I hadn't spoken to in years – and my parents still wore the same clothes they'd had when I was little. I stuck to my story about the show being cancelled, didn't say there was a problem. They made an issue out of the smallest of things – me wanting to watch a programme they didn't normally watch, or having a shower at what they considered to be an odd time, or saying I might be ten minutes late for dinner. I'd always hated it. Had always wanted to seem the opposite – effortlessly competent, like nothing was a problem for me.

On my first day back, Mum asked me how Laurie was, and I said that we'd had a bit of a falling out, actually. I'd forgotten I never told her I'd moved, and she said – that must be really difficult, living with her. You only have the one room, don't you?

I had to make something up about us taking it in turns to sleep on the sofa, and she said – well, do you think you can make it up?

I don't know – I said. I felt a sick stab of missing her, and changed the subject.

I spent a lot of time with Mum when she wasn't at work. We went to the shops, drank coffee in the garden, cut up vegetables together for dinner. She told me how many months Sally's daughter had been trying to get pregnant, and why my old headteacher was selling up now, and what had happened to Rachel's son who'd married that alcoholic. I asked lots of questions. Normally, I had to try hard to seem interested – I hadn't seen these people in years and couldn't always remember who they were – but now, I liked the stories. They helped to tether me to the world again, and I could see she was pleased. It wasn't that hard to be the daughter she wanted. A few times, I nearly told her about the show, about Max. She'd always been good at comfort. The smallest hint of illness when I was little, and it was a day off school, unlimited TV, endless sympathy, whatever I wanted to eat. I'd exploited her concern, until I realised it came at a cost – the expectation of obedience. Now, I managed to stay quiet.

In the evenings, they always seemed to have activities planned, which was unusual. We went for walks together, or played board games, or they took me to dinner at the Chinese restaurant, still seen as new and exotic, though it had been there ten years. They were treating me like a convalescent, making sure there were nice things in the house for me to eat, leaving me asleep in the mornings. Mum asked me once why I wasn't practising, and I said I was tired and didn't really feel like it, and she didn't press it. I wondered if they knew there was a problem, after all.

After I'd been home about a week, we were watching *Orange Is the New Black* – their new programme of choice – and, after a particularly uncomfortable lesbian sex scene, Mum paused it to get a drink. Then Dad cleared his throat and said, awkwardly, that he was very sorry to hear about me and Laurie.

What? – I said.

He repeated it, glancing at the TV, and I realised what he meant and started to laugh. I laughed until it hurt, and when Mum got back, and Dad explained why I was laughing, she got annoyed.

Well, what were we meant to think? – she asked.

They stopped being quite so nice to me after that.

Sometimes, alone in my room, I listened to recordings of my singing. I had hundreds of them on my phone – lessons and practice sessions and concerts. I was oddly pleased when I came across ones that were bad. They made me think that maybe I never could have done it, maybe I hadn't lost that much. The good ones hurt, though, and I deleted them.

I thought about him, but gradually, the more days that passed, the more those thoughts lost their intensity and power. Of course they did. Things can't stay big like that forever. They shrink away, and it only hurts when you try to make it hurt – when you find it and press on it. It was easier away from London. Away from that flat, where the need to hear from him was like a physical pain. It contained, too much, the memory of him. I'd spent too many nights there, wondering if he might call me unexpectedly. Too many nights, sitting in that flat, on the off-chance that my phone might ring and he'd say – *I'm actually free tonight. Where are you? Are you home?* So my body, in that flat, could not forget the sensation of waiting. The startled excitement at the buzz of my phone, or how my heart jumped, automatic, at the sound of a man's step in the hall outside.

Three weeks had passed, and I still had no plan. The thought of going back to London without one was unbearable, so I decided I'd stay for a bit. It would make Mum happy, at least.

When I came back from my walk with Tara, she was outside, watering the front garden. I got an apple from the kitchen, and went to sit on the lawn.

Nice walk? – she asked.

Really nice.

Say it, say it.

I tried to force out the words. There was a sad inevitability about them, I thought, and perhaps I'd always known it, really – how far I'd go to end up right back here.

I'm not going to be a singer anymore. I'm going to stay here for a bit. Is that ok?

I bit into the apple, and found it tasted of Dettol. She'd started bleaching the shopping.

When is it you're going to France? – she asked.

What?

That festival you're doing. When is it?

Oh right. Not for a while. July.

After the audition, when I'd texted to say I'd got a place, she hadn't replied. It had become something we'd never mention again, I thought.

I don't think I ever properly congratulated you – she said. – I looked it up online. It looks good.

Thanks.

She turned and looked at me, sitting there on the grass.

You sitting behind me like that – she said. – It reminds me of this time – have I told you this? – I was weeding, and you were playing by

286

yourself. You were only just four. And I swear I only turned around for a minute – it wouldn't have been much longer than that, I was so careful with you – but when I turned back you were gone. You were two streets away by the time I found you, and the strange thing was you weren't even scared. You were never scared of much, were you? I always think that when I see you on stage.

It wasn't true, though. It wasn't true. Growing up, I'd been afraid of everything. Of dogs and cracks in the pavement and strangers and bones in meat and losing Mum in a crowd and waking up when it was still dark outside.

I don't remember that – I said.

She picked up the hose, and I pulled a leaf off a bush, started to strip it down to its green bones.

By the way – I said. – I think I'll go back to London on Saturday. So I'll stay two more nights, if that's ok? I'll book my train tonight.

Stop doing that, Anna – she said, as I picked another leaf.

Sorry.

She filled up the watering can from the hose, about to do the pots. Her hair was tied back, but one strand kept falling in front of her eyes, and she'd blow it away.

Is that ok? – I said. – If I stay two more nights, then leave at the weekend?

Ok – she said. – If that's what you want.

TWENTY-ONE

The bar was almost empty by the time I got there, and Laurie had stopped work. She was talking to two guys and, when she saw me, she smiled and waved. I felt like I'd been underwater for a long time and had finally come up for air.

Here she is – she said. – I told them I had a friend coming.

She gave me a big hug, sweet and familiar-smelling – Pomegranate Noir stolen from the Ps, coconut shampoo – and I was happy, thinking she must be pleased to see me, though she hadn't been too friendly when I'd called her. But then she turned back to the guys, arm round me performatively, and said – *Carl, Joe, this is my best pal, Anna* – and I realised she was acting. I was expected to play my role too. I looped my arm round her waist and kissed her cheek.

It's nice to meet you – I said to the guys.

Likewise. I'm Joe – said Joe. – He's Carl.

They were about Laurie's age, maybe a bit older, and they wore the weekend uniform of wealthy men. Boat shoes. Ralph Lauren polo shirts, Joe's red, Carl's plum. Belted chinos. They were both generically good-looking – slightly less attractive versions of actors whose names you can't remember. Carl was small and blonde, and he spoke with the almost-American accent of a rich European. Joe was very English – big and broad, dark hair, pink cheeks.

You're not from London, are you? – Laurie said.

And what makes you think that? – asked Joe, suggestively challenging, like she'd asked if he was into bondage.

You're hanging out in the City at the weekend. No one does that.

Carl, pedantically sincere, started to explain that they'd been at a party round the corner, a colleague's engagement thing, and then Malcolm the Manager came over. I hadn't seen him since I'd quit. He told us he was shutting up in five.

Can we not have a lock-in? – asked Laurie, showing off.

You're in a hotel, you moron. It's open all night. You can sit in the lobby if you like, but I'm going home.

But it's not a lock-in without booze.

Well – he said – I guess it's not a lock-in then, is it?

You're no fun at all – she pouted, and she turned back to the guys, and started saying – so you work together, do you, what do you do, oh wow, how *fascinating* – in that entirely over-the-top-God-I'm-so-impressed way of flirting she had, that men amazingly never seemed to recognise as sarcasm.

So, Anna – Malcolm said. – Long time no see. Want your job back?

Have you not got someone else?

A couple of others, yeah. Haven't found a girl the men like as much, though.

Pretty sure you're not allowed to say things like that to women who work for you, Malcolm.

You don't work for me – he said. – Anyway, my bar, my rules.

Nor that. And it's not your bar.

Semantics. The offer still stands.

Well, thank you – I said. – I'll think about it.

I had no idea how I'd done it – turned up, unrehearsed, un-warmed up, bashed through tunes I knew by ear but had never sung, improvised, added high flourishes, had fun with it. The people listening so close, I could see all their faces. No character to hide behind.

I had to earn some money soon, though.

Are there any waiting jobs going? – I asked.

You can have a waiting job if you'll sing for us too – he said. – Now get out of my bar, ladies and gents.

Hey, give that back – said Laurie.

He'd collected up their glasses, Laurie's still half-full. He ignored her, tipped it down the sink, switched on the main light.

It's not your bar – she muttered.

Let's go somewhere else – said Joe. – What do you think? Is there anywhere open?

Nothing. It's dead round here.

Well, you know what? – he said, like it had only just occurred to him. – We live close. Ten minutes away. Let's take this party to ours. We've got booze, haven't we, Carl?

We have – said Carl.

Party games.

Oh yes.

You live together? – said Laurie. – That's sweet. What do you think, Anna?

I couldn't think of another way to make Laurie like me again, so I said sure. Out on the street, while the boys were walking on ahead, she said – just for a bit, ok? If it's awful, we'll leave.

Ok – I said.

We'll have fun – she said. – Promise. I've missed us having fun – and then a cab went by with its light on, and Joe stuck out his arm.

Get in girls – he said.

Hang on, I thought you lived ten minutes away? – said Laurie.

We do. Ten minutes away by cab.

He sat in the middle seat, me and Laurie either side, and he put his arms round both of us. I didn't really like him touching me, but it would have been embarrassing to make a fuss, I thought, so I stayed quiet. He joked about us having a threesome, and laughed like it was an original thing to say. Me and Laurie laughed too.

What about Carl, though? – she said. – Poor Carl, he's all left out.

He'll cope.

Carl sat opposite on the flip-down seat, watching us and smiling to himself. He'd seen this all before.

Ten minutes passed, and then twenty. We drove along the river – drunk people spilling down from Soho, the landmarks of London all lit up, like in a postcard – then on, past deserted stretches, the shadow of parks, and I didn't know where we were anymore. Maybe I'll look back on this one day, I thought, and wonder what the hell we were doing, Laurie and I. Why we didn't ask the driver to stop. But it didn't feel like we were in danger, even though this was exactly the sort of thing you were told never to do. Joe was trying too transparently to impress us to seem dangerous. He kept up a constant stream of conversation – about his colleague who'd got engaged and about how much they'd drunk already that day and about all the cool places they hung out in London and how expensive they were – in a way that seemed self-conscious, like he was scared of silence, or scared that, if he didn't keep reminding us how great he was, we might laugh at him. Anyway, I was too distracted by the meter to think about much else. I'd only ever got black cabs with Max, and I was transfixed by it, watching it go up and up and up and hoping they wouldn't expect us to contribute. Laurie kept looking at it too, and I knew she was thinking the same.

We didn't need to worry, though. The cab stopped and Carl passed the driver a bundle of notes through the hatch. The guys got out first, and we followed.

Joe said – here we are, girls.

So where the fuck's that then? – said Laurie.

We'd stopped on the edge of a little harbour, stains of light on the water and the outline of boats. It felt empty and purposeless, like a holiday resort out of season. Streetlights illuminating deserted pavements. White apartment blocks, their windows black.

Thought you said you were from London? – said Joe. – Never been here? Chelsea Harbour. We're this way. Come on.

As he turned to walk, Laurie glanced at me, and it made me uneasy. She was uncertain too. I thought she might say we were leaving, or else that she wanted me to say it, but Joe said – *come on, this way* – and the moment passed.

He took us into one of the white buildings, into the lift, used his key fob to press the penthouse button. Once the doors had slid shut, he relaxed. He stopped the incessant chatter, looked at us and smiled. He'd thought we might leave too, I realised, and now he knew he'd got us.

The lift doors opened right into the flat.

Fuck me – said Laurie.

We were in an entrance hall, circular and triple-height, like a cathedral. Polished marble floor. Glass ceiling. You looked up and there was your reflection, small and far away, swimming in the black sky.

Laurie walked into the middle of the room and turned round slowly.

This is where you live? – she said. – Really? How?

It's Joe's – said Carl. – He's very rich.

I am, it's true – said Joe, holding his hands up as if to say *you got me.* – This way to the bar, girls. Follow me.

There were six doors, all shut. The one Joe opened took us into a corridor, softly lit and lined with more doors. He led us down to the one at the end, through to a room with glass walls, a view over the harbour. There was a bar on the back wall and, set into it, an illuminated aquarium, colourful fish flitting around with expressions of mournful surprise. Laurie put her face up close to the glass.

I've always wondered how you feed them in tanks like this – she said. – How does it work?

Oh, there's a hole – said Joe, vaguely. – Now, make yourselves at home, girls. Take your jackets off. Sit down. That's right.

He gestured over to a seating area – leather beanbags, positioned to face the view over the harbour – and me and Laurie sat with Carl.

Right. Drinkies – called Joe from the bar, at a volume appropriate for addressing an entire conference, not three people in his living room.

He made cocktails theatrically enough to stop us having a conversation without him, and then brought them over on a tray, handed us one each.

What is it? – asked Laurie.

Try it and see.

He pressed a button to turn on some music, did a brief little shimmy to it, and then he sprawled on a beanbag and grinned, first at me, then at Laurie. His features were hard and adult, but he had a mischievous, boyish look, as though the pencil lines of twenty years ago had been rubbed out of his face, but their imprint still remained. There was always something threatening, I thought, about that look in adult men. It's like when puppies don't realise how big they've got, and hurl themselves at you and knock you over.

So? – he said.

Rum – said Laurie.

Very good. What else?

She took another sip and swilled it around her mouth to taste.

Something Christmassy.

Christmassy?

Cloves. Something like that.

Oh right. I think so. Yeah. Maybe.

What do you mean, you think so? What is it?

A Zombie. Rum. Falernum – that's got cloves in it, right? Absinthe.

Absinthe?

Absinthe? – he mimicked, doing a breathy take-off of her voice, which wasn't even close to what she sounded like. – It's not really a hallucinogen, sweetheart, worse luck. Don't believe the hype.

A pause where we all took a sip.

You know, the woman in the flat below me? – Joe suddenly said. – She only has one arm.

With the breezy air of a child blithely rehashing an irrelevant pre-prepared essay, assuming he'll get away with it, he launched into the anecdote. It wasn't particularly funny, but it was well rehearsed – an excited tone of voice to show we were meant to be interested, pauses at appropriate moments, so we could fill them with laughter. He told us that this woman was with a different man each time he saw her, and the men were all very different, so either she had very varied taste – *or* – *well*——. He smirked over the phrase *varied taste* with a look of hungry disapproval. I wasn't sure if he considered this, or sex work, to be a clearer indicator of a woman's poor character.

I don't believe you could afford a flat like this through prostitution, though – Laurie said. – If that's what you mean. I just don't believe it. You wouldn't earn that much. She must have money anyway and do it for fun.

It's niche prostitution though – said Joe. – Amputee fetish. It's a thing. Can charge a fortune.

I suspected that, if Mil had been there, not me, they both would have told him off – explained that sex work was work like any other, nothing to smirk about, or else informed him that *consensual objectification* was more PC than *fetish* – but Laurie just giggled. Then she said she couldn't picture exactly where we were on a map, and Joe moved her over to the window. He started pointing to where various places were, laughing at her when she said that knowing which direction north was didn't help. *Bloody women,* he said and she didn't punch him in the face.

Actually – I said. – I read that somewhere. That men navigate by compass points and women by landmarks.

Neither of them were listening to me.

I took the hint, and turned my attention to Carl. He asked whether I was from London, and I said that no, I actually hadn't lived here for very long, and he said he hadn't either.

Ah – he said – it is a unique loneliness, being from elsewhere. When your surroundings don't recognise you. I moved in here for that reason – he said. – To be with Joe. Because it is bad to be alone.

Carl's English was so precise it sounded sarcastic. I don't think it was, though, because his eyes were kind, looking at me with interest, but not with expectation, and we talked a bit more and I started to have fun. I finished my drink, and we went over to the bar, topped up our glasses from the jug Joe had made, and I felt unexpectedly light, enjoying the cold cleanness of the alcohol burning down to my stomach, and the chameleon skin it gave me – the feeling I could be anyone.

But then Carl said — so, what do you do? — and I found I couldn't remember the answer.

For work, I mean — he said, as if I might have misunderstood the question. — For your job. What do you do? Or are you a student?

Oh right, yes, I'm a student — I said.

What do you study?

Singing.

You sing? What sort of singing?

Classical. Opera.

I have a cousin who's an opera singer — Carl said. — A very beautiful cousin. She does all those ones, like, hmm—

He thought for a bit, and then, in a surprisingly rich baritone, broke into song. Madama Butterfly's aria. The one where she imagines her husband coming back to her.

What's this all about? — demanded Joe.

She's an opera singer — said Carl. — I was telling her about my cousin.

Not your fucking cousin again — said Joe. — Carl's obsessed with his cousin, it's actually quite weird. So, you're a singer, are you? — he said. — Sing us something, then.

What? No.

Fear made the room hard and sharp, where drink had softened it.

No — I said again.

Come on — said Joe. — If you're a singer, prove it. Sing us something.

Yeah — said Laurie, her eyes glittering with disloyalty. — Go on.

I shook my head.

No — I said.

Why not?

I can't. I've drunk too much.

I'm not asking you to drive, am I? What is there, a drink and sing limit? Come on.

I should've hated him, but I didn't. He was too forceful, too cheerfully domineering, like he was trying to persuade us that he believed we'd obey him.

I said no again.

But then he said to Carl — *whatever, she's clearly lying* — as if I couldn't hear him, and I was about to get annoyed, when I suddenly thought, well no, he's right, I suppose I am lying, aren't I, and I said — *I – I, um* — and I saw Laurie looking at me, confused.

Oh, leave her alone — she said. —You're just jealous. We can't all be rich, talentless fucks like you.

Worse luck — sneered Joe, and then he said — come now, ladies, let's all calm down, shall we? Loosen up.

He went back to the bar, got a bottle of vodka and four shot glasses, handed us a glass each, and topped us up. Laurie was trying to catch my eye, but I pretended not to notice.

Let's play a game — Joe said. — Never Have I Ever. Me first. Never have I ever gone home with two strange men I've only just met. Drink, girls. Come on. Downy downy.

Laurie did her shot, so I did too. It tasted like nail varnish remover.

Glasses filled up, and suggestions poured out. Never have I ever had sex in a public place, looked through someone's phone, had a threesome, slept with someone within an hour of meeting them, had sex at work — *doesn't count if it's with yourself* — Joe said, when Carl drank. Years of experience translated into soundbites for mockery or stories of triumph.

After a bit, I started pretending to drink, but was still finding it hard to do sentences.

Never have I ever had an STI — I said, only thing I could think of, forgetting that Laurie had.

She drank and said — thanks for that, Anna.

Well, you didn't actually have to drink.

Really? What game are you playing? — she said. — My turn. Never have I ever been a kept woman. Go on, Anna. Drink.

What? No.

Anna was a kept woman, you know — Laurie said to the guys, as she topped up my glass. — Like, actually. Like in the nineteenth century.

Never have I ever – I said – claimed to be a feminist, but also had no problem letting random men, just, you know, random men I meet in bars buy all the drinks and take me out for expensive dinners so I never have to spend any money myself and can afford to keep writing my book, which is, wait for it, about how much I hate all men.

What? – she said. – What are you talking about? What does that even mean? Anna has a very narrow view of feminism – she said to the guys. – She thinks that women who like violent pornography or who make the informed choice not to have any pubic hair can't be feminist.

I couldn't think of anything clever to say. I felt like I was watching a poorly dubbed film, my comprehension always a little behind the action.

You were a kept woman? – Carl said, with interest. – Is that really still done in England?

No. What? No. I wasn't a fucking kept woman. She's just, she just didn't like this guy I was seeing, that's all, but anyway, it doesn't matter, it's all over now.

Well, thank God for that – she said.

You shouldn't diminish your friend's feelings – said Carl to Laurie. – It's not nice.

Yes, very naughty – said Joe.

You guys probably know him actually – Laurie said. – He's in finance too. Don't you men all know each other?

Yes – said Carl. – All of us.

Where does he work, then? – asked Joe. – And what does he do?

I told him.

But he's in New York at the moment, I think – I said. – He's been there five weeks.

Why?

Well, work.

What sort of work?

Something to do with a client. American client. They asked for him.

Oh really? – said Joe. – Doesn't sound likely.

What?

He shrugged.

I mean, not impossible. Just doesn't sound likely. Someone that senior? Allowed to drop everything and fuck off for that long? I mean, it's plausible, sure – he grinned at me. – Carefully plausible. But it's unlikely, my dear, I'm afraid.

It took me a second to work out what he meant. Its implications. I stared at him.

What? – I said. – What do you mean? You mean, you think he was lying? You don't think he went?

But Joe had already lost interest.

He said – what? Hm, yeah, maybe. No idea – and then him and Laurie disappeared into the next room.

I drank some more vodka.

The next few hours are partial, big holes eaten out of them like spots of rot through an apple.

Joe calling us next door. A dining room. Long glass table. Beer pong, he said, ten plastic cups of beer each end, and a ping pong ball, held between finger and thumb. Joe saying *it's boys against girls, throw the ball to our side from your side, if you get it in one of our cups, we down it, if we get it in one of your cups, you down it.* Tripping up on the downing, and the who downs what when, so keep drinking things I don't have to, Laurie saying she doesn't like beer, Joe saying, *that's fine, we'll do strip pong instead,* and Laurie, *but I'm only wearing about three things,* and him, *well, you should have thought of that earlier, shouldn't you?*

Joe telling Laurie she's cheating. Tights and one of her shoes, and him saying that both shoes are one go. She has to take them both off. *But they're separate shoes,* she says.

Joe taking his top off. The body of a man who played rugby as a teenager, then stopped. Spent all his twenties drinking too much. Bulky and soft.

Laurie and Joe still playing, but I'm on the sofa with Carl. I notice I'm not wearing my dress. He's saying, *it sounds like you've had a really hard time,* and I'm looking into his face, and thinking, *now, what the hell did I say for him to say that?* Trying to tell him something else, because I've remembered that my body and everything in my head are mine to give away, but words are difficult to bite down on. To squash into place with my tongue. Too big for my mouth. Him, confused-looking, saying – *sorry, can you say that again?*

Laurie's hand on my arm – *find the bathroom with me* – Joe trying to stop us going together, asking why we need to, and Laurie saying she needs my help, she needs to do her bikini line, she says, if we're going to keep playing, she's just in her skirt and her bra, and me saying *what?* and her saying *come on.*

Through corridor. Laurie kicking open doors then shutting them again. Hall. Another corridor. A bathroom. Dizzying silence.
    You're doing your bikini line?
    What? No. I'm rescuing you.
    Then her laughing.
    God, you really are wasted, aren't you? You really are fucking wasted.
    Sits down to pee, still laughing, and me, *stop it, stop it, stop laughing at me,* and her saying *it's just I'm normally the one who's the mess you're never the mess it's refreshing I wouldn't expect you to under-stand,* then opening my eyes, I'm curled up in the bath, cheek against its ceramic coldness, and she's there next to me, trying to get me to sit up, and it's like the drink is an acid that's been applied to my skin, stripping me down to my nerves, saying how I'm sorry I've ruined everything I'd hurt her I'd thought he was real life and everything else had got small but really he should have been small and everything else stayed big, and she's saying, *shh, I get it, it's ok, it will never be like this again, do you understand, you'll never feel like this again. It will be ok. You'll come back and live with us. Things will be exactly like they were before.*

How long passed? – I don't know – a film on fast-forward, maybe everything was said, and maybe nothing was.

We'll get our clothes – said Laurie. – And then we'll say we're leaving.

Back through the corridor. The entrance hall. Another corridor. But they were all the same. All looked the same, I mean. We opened doors. Bedrooms. Bathrooms. A laundry room. God-knows-what-else rooms.

The music – said Laurie. – Let's listen for the music.

We listened and heard nothing.

I sat on the floor.

Don't sit down. Stand up. No ok. Sit. Wait. Wait here.

Head between my knees, and the world rushed towards me.

Suddenly, Laurie.

Come here – she said. – Come and look.

Pulled me up.

Look in there – she said.

Lights twinkling from the room, like a toy shop at Christmas.

I flicked the main switch – she said. – Thought it was the light.

Go in – she said, and I went in.

There was London in miniature. Everything had shrunk and I was suddenly big.

Can you see it too? – I said. – What is this? What's happening?

It's a model, you idiot – she said.

A perfect replica, raised on a platform, eye-level, you could walk round it, look into the buses and see the passengers and read the street signs. Thames looped, peppered with London landmarks, a mini Houses of Parliament, the Gherkin. Electric. Lights lit up in houses and streets. Trains running on tracks. London Eye spinning. I crouched, looked at the Christmas lights down Regent Street.

Like being God – I said to Laurie, and then there was Joe, shouting – girls? Where are you? What are you doing?

We're here – Laurie shouted back. – This is incredible. Seriously. Who made this?

There it was, the City. Barbican towers. Office blocks of glass, ancient graveyards. Hours I'd spent there with him, but the City wasn't there for me anymore, or not with him in it – it was blasted away, gone, replaced with nothing, just the space where it should be – and then Joe was at the door. Naked, face heavy with anger. Nothing more silly than a naked, angry man. I started to laugh.

You think it's funny, do you? – he shouted. –You think it's fucking funny? What are you doing here? What the hell are you doing here? Sneaking around my house? Looking at my private things? Get out. Get out. Go on. Both of you. Get the hell out of my house. What's wrong with you? What the fuck's wrong with you both?

We're very sorry – I said. – Very very very sorry.

Well, can we at least have our clothes back first? – said Laurie.

Joe went to get our clothes.

He's very sensitive about his village – said Carl, mournfully. – It's a shame.

TWENTY-TWO

I could hear my voice going on and on about him, and I knew that Laurie was bored.

Three weeks had passed since I'd got back to London, and it was early May by now. Another day of unseasonably slick-palmed sunshine. Laurie cried about climate change, and then we put our bikinis on and went to the park. This was British Summer Time – here, and who knew for how long – and people were trying to inhale as much of it as possible. Grass dotted with clusters of picnicking Londoners, blistering across its surface, like an aggressive rash. Ponds half-empty with heat, swans wading through stagnant water, their feathers stained with scum. Air thick with traffic, the jingle of ice-cream vans, the smell of hot meat and overripe bins.

London's ugly – I said. – I don't think I like it anymore.

Really? I'm too used to it to see it, I guess. It's like looking in a mirror. You think about what you look like on a particular day, but never really about what you look like in general.

Well – I suggested – maybe it's because of Max?

I'd become skilled at shoehorning him into every conversation. Topics I couldn't bring back to him, I'd discovered, no longer interested me much.

It was hard, I went on, knowing he'd probably lied about how long he'd gone to New York for. Knowing that even if he hadn't, he was probably back in London now at any rate. And maybe that's why it had started to seem ugly to me, I suggested. Because of him.

And then I kept talking. I couldn't make myself stop, even though Laurie was looking at her phone, no longer even pretending to listen. I was like a toddler who'd only just learnt to speak. I was obsessed with the sound of my own voice, but seriously limited in what I could do with it.

She'd been patient at first. After the model village fiasco, I'd stayed at Mil's with her, and the next day she'd come with me to the flat.

So what the fuck happened in here? – she said.

It was worse than I'd remembered. The air was pre-breathed, close and stale. The sofa, still set up as a bed, occupied half the room, unmade. The kitchen sink filled with water, the dark shape of plates and mugs submerged, greening with mould, like a ship sunk long ago. Drawers were open. Curtains were shut. Clothes, books, bracelets, empty ready-meal boxes, shoes were scattered, sparsely punctuated by scraps of carpet. I stood in the doorway and stared. It was like looking at a map of the time after he'd left, and it led me right back there – those empty days, the heart of my loneliness.

But Laurie helped me. We cleaned the flat and packed up my stuff, brought it back to Mil's. I said I felt bad, coming back when she'd got used to having the room to herself, but she said not to be silly, and that was the end of it. She explained to the other girls what had happened. She cleared space for me in the wardrobe. She went to Max's office and left the key in an envelope at reception, no note. And then she let me talk about him. She indulged my speculation and, God, I could speculate for hours. Of course, he'd been married all along, hadn't he? A million signs I'd blithely failed to spot. Never letting me come to his house in Oxford. Being so bad about reply-ing to messages, particularly at weekends when, it seemed obvious to me now, he would have been with her. Not telling me about the New York trip. Well, if he'd actually gone to New York, which no longer seemed that likely. An easy excuse to leave me. I was becom-ing – what? – too needy? – too suspicious? – too samey? He clearly liked variety after all, didn't he? Or, if he had gone, it'd been some-thing to do with her, hadn't it, not about work at all? Like Joe had said, it was hardly a plausible story. They'd been visiting her family, perhaps. Or maybe they were actually still planning to move there. Talks were still ongoing. A partial truth he'd told me.

Honestly? – Laurie said. – I did always think it was weird how you just believed him. I thought that you didn't actually, you were trying to convince me that you did, or to convince yourself, or whatever.

He became like a school project for us, and Laurie was enthusiastic about research. You could apply on the Land Registry to find out who owned properties, she said. I asked her if they'd notify him but she said no, she didn't think so, so we filled out the form and, a week later, we got the letter. The house in Oxford was registered as having two owners: him and a woman. I didn't think that really proved anything either way, but Laurie said, *oh, really? Come on*. We looked her up online, but there were too many results – the name wasn't distinctive – and it was impossible to say which of these women, if any, she was. Laurie said then that she'd find out if he'd really gone to New York. She'd find out definitively. She called his office and asked to speak to him, but he wasn't available, they said.

She encouraged me to analyse him. Lying wasn't his only character flaw, after all. Perhaps not even his worst. He'd undermined me. Diminished me. Belittled what I did. *Classic* – she said. – *Dissatisfied with his own pathetic life. Trying to make himself feel better.* He'd disliked anyone I'd ever introduced him to, facilitated my isolation. *Classic controlling behaviour.* He'd told me to pull out of the show, then claimed he'd never said it. *Classic gaslighting.* Sometimes, the things I told her really did shock me, and other times I knew I was exaggerating, because I liked the reaction it got from her. Not only that. It absolved me, this version of our story. I was purely the victim. I wrote out anything that made me feel ashamed. Because I was ashamed. There were days when I was embarrassed about everything I'd ever said to him. Every time I'd ever expressed an emotion, and the need he must have read there. Sometimes, lying awake at night, or walking down the street, I was overcome with my own idiocy. The stupid things I'd said to him. The needy way I'd been with him. It made me bite my lip hard or dig my nails into my palm. It stopped me short, the embarrassment, thinking, *well what exactly did you think it was? Did you think he was falling in love with you? Is that what you thought?*

Together, Laurie and I nailed him down into a coherent narrative. It was a damning character study, but it made sense, this version of him. It was like seeing a word you've never really understood in a new context, suddenly knowing exactly what it means.

A week passed, then two, then three, and Laurie had lost interest by now. There was no new information. He was a puzzle we'd solved, and we could put him back in his box, except I couldn't, because I couldn't stop talking about him. Laurie was making a daisy chain, stabbing a clean incision through each stem with the methodical precision of a surgeon, and I was talking about him.

There was this one time – I said – where we met outside his work. This was quite early on. We'd planned to have a drink, but when I saw him, he said he wanted a flapjack and I thought this was so charming. That a grown man was insisting on getting baked goods after work, not booze. He was so whimsical and eccentric, I thought. God. I was an idiot. I followed him round trying to find a flapjack for what felt like hours. It was raining and all the cafes were shut, and the ones that weren't didn't have any flapjacks so we went in, looked at the counter, then he made us leave, try somewhere else. It makes me sick, thinking about it now. How taken in I'd been by that, thinking it was so sweet, when it was obviously a power move.

Fuck – Laurie said.

What?

It broke.

She started pulling the petals off the daisies.

Look – she said. – Don't think I don't get it. I get it. There's nothing a woman loves more than a doomed project. A man who gives her nothing, so she can fill in the blanks herself. But most men lack the imagination to actually be evil, you know. I think you might be giving him too much credit.

I knew I was annoying her, so I stopped talking, but it was all still there in my head. I felt, often, like I was watching the world on TV, not in it myself anymore. In the weeks since I'd got back, I'd spent my days looking for jobs I didn't want, and going over and over all the ways he'd ruined my life. I was still living off the last envelope he'd given me. I didn't have much choice at that point – it was all I had – but every time I paid with his money, I felt ashamed. Sometimes I'd think about calling him. I'd consider turning up at his flat. I'd draft emails I wouldn't send. I wanted him to feel my anger which, I knew, was so strong and heart-breaking and all-consuming that it was close to love. The only parts of London that interested me were places I related to him. I'd take circuitous routes, past bars and restaurants we'd been to together, wondering if I might bump into him. Sometimes, the remotest possibility I might see him was the only thing that could force me out of the house. The hope he represented that was no hope.

We walked back. Children cartwheeled. Teenagers sucked at each other's faces. Squirrels threatened the weak.

You know what your problem is? – Laurie said. – You've been in too many operas where men are mean to women, and then they have to kill themselves or get TB. That's not how the world actually works, you know.

I didn't say anything.

Oh, well, maybe you're right – she said. – Maybe he is evil. Like, just actually evil. Hey, maybe he murdered his wife. Do you think that's why he's renovating the house? She's under the patio.

That night, I dreamt about it. The garden. Layers of wet concrete. A mouth filled with mud.

When I woke in the morning, I thought – *enough. Enough now.*

It was a few weeks into term already, and Marieke was taking performance class with the undergrads. A girl was doing Rusalka's aria. Body floppy, two singers from her class led her round, tipped her between them, coaxed her to lie down on the floor or pulled her back to standing. One of Marieke's favourite exercises. It was all about psychological barriers, she said. The way we allow our own bodies to get in the way of our voices. Realising that and letting go.

I stood at the back, waiting for the girl to finish, listening to the sound spill out of her like juice from an overripe peach. I knew every note of that aria, every word, both in Czech and in the English translation, and I didn't like how she was doing it. She was pulling the tempo round too much, taking it too slowly, self-indulgent, I thought. I noticed I was squeezing one hand hard in the other. She had a nice voice and she was clearly enjoying herself and I couldn't bear it. That she could see the world with an extra dimension, while to me it was flat.

When the class was finished, I went up to Marieke. I decided to be direct. I wanted to come back, I said.

Oh, you do, do you? — she said. — Well, where exactly was it you went?

I don't know what I'd expected. That she would see my decision as brave and congratulate me for it, I suppose. I quickly realised that was absurd. She was looking at me impatiently, like she was waiting for me to understand I should leave.

Nowhere — I said. — I mean — what? — nowhere. I didn't go anywhere.

She picked up her handbag and a score from the piano, and I thought she was going to tell me to go, but then — maybe the crack in my voice as I spoke, she felt sorry for me — she said — I've got fifteen minutes, Anna. That's all. Walk back to my office with me and we can talk.

As we walked, I delivered the speech I'd prepared. I told her that I'd been going through a difficult time. I was having vocal problems. That's why I'd walked out like that. I hadn't known how to deal with them. I still didn't. But I wanted very much to sing again, I said. More than anything.

I realised, verbalising it like that, that it was true.

Can I come back? — I said. — What would you need me to do?

She opened the door to her office, and gestured for me to go in first.

But I'm not quite sure I understand — she said, when we were sitting down. — Why didn't you tell me you were having problems?

I didn't – I don't know – I guess I didn't want you to pull me out of the opera.

She raised an eyebrow as if to say – *well, that went well, didn't it?* Then she flicked through her address book, and found me the number of an ENT doctor. We couldn't talk about how to proceed, she said, until we knew exactly what we were dealing with. She told me that the Conservatory would pay. I called the doctor and made an appointment while she watched.

Mind you – she said, when I'd done it – you sang in that rehearsal. I didn't think there was any reason to be concerned from what I heard. A bit of tension, maybe. But it's best for us to be cautious. We don't want you singing on it if there's a problem, do we? Can get yourself in an awful mess that way.

On the way home, I Googled vocal cord damage. Lesions and nodules. Polyps. Paralysis. Greek-sounding medical words always concealed something nasty. I clicked on the images tab, and scrolled through all the possible growths that could cling to the cords, hefty fruit just about ready to drop. There was something pornographic about the images. The plump pinkness of the folds. The mucus glistening. I noticed the man next to me glancing over at my screen and, embarrassed, I shut the tab.

It didn't feel like a doctor's surgery. The walls were decorated with signed photographs of opera singers, and a bay window looked out over a leafy garden. The ENT sat behind a vast mahogany desk, like you might find in the headmaster's office of a posh boys' boarding school. Reassuringly paternalistic in a *let's get this all sorted out for you, dear* kind of way, he showed me a small camera and said he would put it down the back of my throat. He'd get me to sing a little, and then, he said, we'd see exactly what was going on.

Sing? – I said. – I can't sing. That's why I'm here.

I'm not looking for perfection – he said. – It doesn't even need to sound nice. Something gentle, please. An *ee* vowel's probably best once this is in. It's a little uncomfy, I'm afraid. Really – he said. –You don't need to feel self-conscious, my dear, I've heard it all before.

He put the camera in my mouth, and I choked some notes out. The image transmitted to the screen in front of him — my vocal cords fluttering like a butterfly trapped in a glass — and he looked at them without speaking. They hurt, these fledgling notes, and I felt dull with hopelessness.

That's enough — he said, and removed the camera.

I knew what he'd say. Nodules. An operation. Months of recovery, but there wouldn't be much point in going ahead with it, anyway. They wouldn't hold my place at the Conservatory. Too much hassle, particularly after how I'd behaved. I'd be left behind.

Look at this — he said.

He played the video back slowly, and paused it.

That's a clear shot there — he said. — See? There's nothing wrong with you.

I stared at the screen.

Nothing wrong? — I said. — There can't be nothing wrong.

Physically, I mean. Everything's physically fine. Some closure issues, you see here? The cords aren't fully closed. See the chink at the top? But that's about technique. It's not a physical problem.

But I can't sing. Why can't I sing?

The voice is so tricky, isn't it? — he said. — We can see it on the screen here, the mechanics of it. We know it's all there. I can explain to you how sound production works. Your teacher can tell you how to put that into practice. But the voice is a fickle beast, that's why it takes so long to train it, I suppose. It's not like a violin — you can't put it in its case and then get it out the next day, and nothing's changed. A while back, I saw a patient whose husband had left her, and from that day on she had a stutter. No physical reason whatsoever. And there was a *very* famous soprano in here once. Had lost all her money notes and, let me tell you, there was nothing to see in her throat to explain that. Turned out she'd heard the tenor who played opposite her be unkind about her top C. An indelicate comment to another colleague right after they'd come off one night. The voice has a fragile ego, you see, a delicate constitution. Even if we think we don't.

He gave me the number of a speech therapist.

Now, don't go to anyone else – he said. – Some of these people do more harm than good. She'll sort you out. Everything will be exactly as it was before. You'll see.

How much is she? – I asked. I still had some of Max's money left – enough for my rent that month, a bit left over – but it wouldn't last long.

Well she's not exactly cheap – he said. – No, I wouldn't say she's cheap. But she's worth it. So don't go seeing someone else for the sake of a few quid. Promise?

I went back to Marieke. She said that I was to see the speech therapist – as many sessions as she saw necessary – and to follow her advice exactly. The Conservatory could give me a little money towards it, she said, at least for a while. If all went well, there was no problem with me returning. With a little creative licence, she could pass me for the year on the basis of Manon, a good report from Angela, the classes I'd sung in, but I'd have to re-audition for my scholarship. I'd missed Musetta, and I hadn't auditioned for anything this term, never mind not going to all the classes. The bursary committee didn't take kindly to their singers not being involved in the life of the Conservatory. She'd have to make a strong case for keeping me. It was out of her hands.

And you got a place on the Martignargues Festival, didn't you? – she asked. – Will you still be going?

I suppose so. If I can. I haven't said I'm not.

Wonderful, that'll be good for you. You can come and sing for us when you get back. End of August, is it? Plenty of time.

May always promised a lot. A flirty month. Brilliant sunshine some days, and others, like being trapped in a close room with the walls painted grey. The sunshine made me happy, though. When the summer's just getting started, you could believe it might last forever.

I saw the speech therapist twice a week. She had me blowing through straws. Reciting nursery rhymes. Sirening up the scale on a rolled R. Eventually, coming into real sound. A note. A string of notes. An arpeggio.

One day, sitting at her kitchen table, I thought our session was over, when she said – sing me something.

Now? Here?

Yes.

Like what?

I don't mind. Whatever you like.

So I sang her the first thing I could think of. A few phrases of a Fauré song, the one about the men going off to sea and leaving behind the cradles. I could feel my knees shaking under the table and, when I'd finished and she said it was nice, I found I was crying. She said it was very normal and most people did.

After that – something that scared me almost as much as singing – I made myself call Angela. I told her I was sorry. I hadn't known what to do. It had got out of control. Using the sort of phrase I thought she'd respond to, I told her I'd had my heart broken.

But Anna – she said. – I don't understand why you didn't come to me. I'm on your side, you know that. Why didn't you say you were having problems? What exactly do you think my job is?

I'm sorry – I said. – I was – I was ashamed, I guess. I didn't want to make it real. I was stupid. Do you not want to teach me anymore?

Let's not be melodramatic – she said. – This singing business is complex enough as it is.

She had a month free in her schedule, and she invited me to her beautiful house in Kensington for whole afternoons. She fed me, played me recordings of her favourite singers, lent me autobiographies of famous sopranos who'd had vocal problems. And she stripped my broken voice back to its foundations, built it up again, brick by brick. She said it was better than it had been before. There was a quality in it she hadn't realised was missing. A new depth to it, she said. A sadness.

We can't sing without life experience – she said. – It's our bread and butter. It would be like trying to paint without a brush.

There were songs I'd crooned through before, enjoying their harmonies and textures. Now sometimes, I found their words almost unbearable. *Only you who have felt desire can understand my suffering* or *I want the morning not to know the name I told to the night* or *my peace is gone, my heart is heavy, I will never find it again, no never, never again.*

May bled into June. The days got longer, with all the unbridled optimism that brings. I practised singing in front of people. I sang for Angela's husband. I sang for Laurie, and for the girls in the house. Angela took me for a walk in Hyde Park one afternoon, and got me to stand on a bench and sing, and people stopped to stare. The terror began to lose its grip on me. I learned to go inside again, to open the door to the music, and it was all still there – like coming home after a long trip away, finding everything exactly as you'd left it.

In mid-June, Max's money ran out.

I'd paid Angela. I'd started paying the speech therapist, now that the Conservatory had stopped. Everyone I spoke to had a suggestion of something else I could pay for. Acupuncture and meditation apps and laryngeal massage and Pilates. I paid for it all. I started to feel like I was leaking money – like I couldn't go anywhere without leaving a mess of it on the seat behind me.

So I went to Malcolm and asked for my job back. The first evening, my legs shook and my voice quavered, but everything carried on as it always had – people talked over me and after I'd finished each song, they clapped. It became routine. I did jazz three nights a week and, the other nights and a few afternoons, I waited tables. I started teaching singing too. Laurie recommended me to one of the families she tutored.

Let us know how much you charge – the mother said. – We're flexible.

I asked Laurie – what does *we're flexible* mean?

It means *we're unspeakably wealthy* – she said.

I spent three hours a week with Freddie, more singing tuition than I had myself. He was twelve, and preparing for a music scholarship to boarding school. He wanted to be Prime Minister, and I imagined he probably would be. He told me in our first lesson, alarmingly adult – *it's not about the money, Anna, of course. The scholarship, I mean.*

We're not poor or anything like that. It's about the prestige. Easier to get into Oxford if you've been a scholar, Dad says.

At the end of each lesson, Freddie's mother would approach me with a fistful of notes and ask me to remind her how much I charged. I could have said anything, and she would have given it to me. Money was only paper, and it circulated endlessly. She paid me in notes. Malcolm paid me in notes. I held onto them for a bit, then I gave them away – Angela, speech therapist, Mil – and so it went on.

Not all of them though. Each time I got paid in cash, I'd take a note or two off the top, put it in my drawer. I still had the list of what I owed him, and I was determined I'd pay it back. I would not have him own me. It was a fantasy I had. Whenever my mind was inactive or when I couldn't sleep, that was what I thought about. Not him curled around me in the dark, not him whispering into my hair things he would never say. No. I'd see myself going into his building. Up in the lift. Knocking on his door. His face, when he saw me – what? – shock – yes – shock – admiration, sometimes – sometimes, yes, sometimes even love. But I would be cold and distant. Successful. In my fantasy, I'd become somehow, in quite a short space of time, wildly successful. He'd be able to see it in my eyes. *I can't stay* – I'd say. – *I've got a concert tonight* – or something like that. The dialogue needed work. Then I'd hand him the money in an envelope. He'd look at my outstretched hand. I'd say to him – *here, Max. Take it. It's for you.* He wouldn't understand at first what it was, then he'd get it.

June and into July. The Northern line became too hot to legally transport cattle. It shouldn't be this hot, England. The world was ending but, in the meantime, everything went on the same as before, and I got ready to go to the festival. Learnt my repertoire. Packed my case. I felt like I hadn't inhabited myself for a long time, and I developed a new interest in my body. I started to care about what I ate, cut down on caffeine, alcohol, cooked everything from scratch, bought more fruit. I started to run. Short jogs around the park at first, and then I got more confident. I found I could cover longer and longer distances, end up in different parts of London just through the movement of my limbs. I was making myself strong, I thought, unbreakable. Looking at my body, I saw the outline of muscles and the brightness of my skin. I was becoming more solid, less conditional. I realised I'd always believed what other people said about me. What he'd said about me. We remember everything other people say about us, I think. Wear a skin made of all those words, so that when we look at ourselves in the mirror, that's what we see. I was starting to pick that skin away, and I was happy. I liked what I found underneath.

It was only sometimes. Long days in the practice room, nights in the hotel. Coming back to the house alone. I was often alone. Laurie had started seeing someone new. It was serious, and you're not allowed to be jealous of your friends' boyfriends – the attention they get that you think, by rights, should be yours – but I was. I'd go into our room. There were her papers, piled up on the floor, and every surface lined with her books and the back of the chair heaped with our mixed-up clothes. Sitting on our bed, eating, for the fifth night in a row, the vegetable-stew-kind-of-thing I'd made on Sunday, I'd be punched in the stomach by loneliness. It would catch me by surprise. *Is this it?* – I'd think. – *Is this what it takes? Success. To be completely alone. No one's voice in my head but my own.*

Sometimes, those nights, I'd look at the money in my drawer and I'd think about spending it. I could buy myself something nice. Make myself feel pretty. Other nights, I'd get out the things I'd collected that reminded me of him. Matchboxes from restaurants. Corks from wine bottles. Notes he'd scribbled, left on the bedside table, which never had any emotional content, but sometimes ended with a kiss. A jumper he'd lent me once. These would seem to me, on those nights, like magical objects. I'd line them up on the bed. I'd smell the traces of him left on the fabric, citrus and wood and some-thing indefinable that was him. I'd trace with my finger the X. I'd watch these objects stir, glowing and luminescent, like creatures in a rock pool, pulsing underneath the water with life.

*

Frankie was going to Martignargues too, and we got the train there together. I hadn't seen him since I'd walked out of rehearsals. I told him I was embarrassed about going back.

Don't be – he said. – Everyone just thinks you're really highly strung, and you're a soprano. The more of a diva you are, the better they assume your voice will be.

I don't remember too much about those weeks because I was happy. The sun was hot and the air was thick with music. Long days in air-conditioned studios, working on the voice. Singing every day in front of people – lessons and concerts and public masterclasses in shady squares – so that it became a part of me again. I could have fun with it, laugh when it went wrong. In the evenings, the heat still rose from the cobbles, panted out of the walls, and children played in the streets until late. We always went to the same place. A restaurant with a courtyard garden, trees strung with lights. Jasmine and cigarette smoke. We ate cheap food and drank too much cheap wine. I felt healthy, slept deeply, however much I drank, and classes rarely started before the afternoon anyway – too hot. So we sat there night after night, having intense, pretentious conversations – about how the voice is the most visceral, the most fundamental form of human expression – about how opera had to be made living art, a living, breathing object, to have any meaning – about which works, which composers could still speak to us, and which couldn't. Frankie and I were the only English singers. Everyone was from different places. We spoke in English, combined with the other languages most singers could get by ok in – French, German, a bit of Italian. The world expanded. My career could take me anywhere. No one ever went home until well past midnight, when the air was starting to cool.

The festival's academy took composers and writers, as well as singers, and we were grouped together to collaborate. We spent a few weeks creating short work, and I realised I was bored of repeating the same old tropes. Of being the raped woman or the too-slutty woman or the murdered woman or the spurned woman who went crazy and killed herself or her husband or her children. Of saying:

He did X to me.

He did Y to me.

I never got over it.

It didn't seem true to life to me, or I didn't want it to be, anyway. I rejected it. I realised that this art I loved could say anything I wanted it to, not just the same things over and over again.

Late one night, Frankie and I were walking back to the apartment we shared with a Danish bass and a French soprano. The streets were quiet and empty. We'd done a concert that evening, and had the next day off, so everyone had stayed out drinking. I didn't want to go home. In a little square, I wandered over to a fountain and dipped my hands in it, and then Frankie came up behind me. His hands on my waist, and when I turned round, he kissed me. He smiled, like this was the culmination of some secret understanding between us and, because it was nice and the evening was balmy and rich with potential and the unhidden excitement in his face touched me, the fact I could feel his heart beat fast against my chest, I smiled in the same way. I put my arms round his neck and kissed him back, like I'd been thinking it too.

After that, we acted like young people in love. It was hard to say if that's what we were or not. Frankie was a good actor, and so was I, and the props of romance presented themselves so nicely to us. We drank coffee together on our balcony in the sunshine, and walked to rehearsals. There were concerts every evening as part of the festival, and we joined the crowds in the open air to watch. On our days off, we hired a car and drove to the seaside. We walked through cobbled streets with colourfully painted houses, like the ones you see in tourist brochures. We sat on the beach and watched children building sandcastles and other couples having arguments. He swam and then came up to me, wet, put his arms round me. We had lunch in shady squares, where the trees made lattice patterns on the ground and on each other's faces, and we told each other the trivial details of our lives. He was nothing like Max. I could read him exactly. When I asked him questions, he thought very carefully before answering, made sure to give me all the information I could possibly want. He enjoyed talking about himself. He was theatrical.

Whatever he thought about anything, I could see straightaway in his face.

It wasn't that I forgot about Max, more that he belonged to a different time. To the winter months. We'd never been warm together. We'd never wandered through streets hand in hand, and not been in a hurry to get inside. I suppose sometimes on those evenings with Frankie, I wished I'd been with him. In bed, Frankie was exactly as he always was. Easily excitable. Transparent. Sometimes I'd think about Max then too, I'd shut my eyes and think about him, and afterwards I'd feel ashamed. Other times, I'd be with Frankie and the other singers, and he would be gregarious, loud, and I'd like being seen next to him. Then I'd think, is this so different to Max, after all? If you hold me up to different men, I take on their colour. Become more like them, less like myself. Maybe Frankie didn't let me be me, it was more that he was closer to me in the first place. The skin he draped me in was one which more closely fitted my own. He only asked me once – *what happened with that guy? The one you were seeing* – and I just said – *nothing much. It didn't work out.*

We were there for six weeks. My skin went brown and my hair turned light in the sun. Frankie's grew to his shoulders, so that he looked like a proper bohemian, or like the impoverished Chevalier I'd first known him as. He tried to get me to cut it for him, but I said no because I liked it.

PART FOUR

TWENTY-THREE

A hotel room in Paris. A woman smokes. Her lover sleeps.

My room has the form of a cage, but there are big, high windows. Dawn. He sleeps, but I don't. Sit, feet up on the sill, watch as the sun reaches its arms through the glass, and sky turns to white above white rooftops. Whitens body, picks out gold in hairs on arms, caresses and bleaches skin, and I watch it. Don't dress. Day's starting, and people have things to do, people think, but I don't, or I won't. I want to smoke. Sit here, above the rooftops, and smoke. Create my own pictures in the air. Hotel room behind me, clothes mixed up on floor, and messed up sheets, and smell of skin and sex and hair, and still he sleeps, but he doesn't matter. The light matters. The sun that passes its arms through the glass, and I reach towards it. Light my cigarette on its fire. I don't want to work. I want to smoke.

Silence. Still, in my head, in a hotel room in Paris, and then the clapping starts, and I'm back. Bow, gesture to pianist, she bows too. Looking out at the audience, then, and knowing, or hoping, they got it, and then it's back to the dressing room. This moment afterwards of being alone. Total silence. An hour ago, I was here, excited, stretching to calm, doing my face, walking through the piece again to check it was still as I'd left it. Now, I put my make-up bag away, change out of concert dress and heels. Elation gives way to tiredness, and then there's a knock. Someone comes in, and says

— congratulations — and someone else pops their head round and says *— we're going for a drink, are you coming? —* and someone else *— lucky you going last. I hate singing first. But, fuck, that piece of Poulenc you sang's so beautiful, isn't it? Well done. Are you coming? —* and I say *— yes, I am. I'm coming. Give me a minute —* and then I'm alone again, just for a moment. I put my music back in my bag — those songs are over now, but there'll be more — and then the room's a normal room again, and I'm a normal person, and the whole night's mine.

So I head out to join them, a group from my year. Some bar under the arches at Charing Cross, full of artsy types, a white grand piano, pianist playing songs from musicals, people crooning along. That was our last commitment before Christmas — fund-raising event for the Conservatory, a few of us got roped in — and now it's the end of term, no need to worry, no need to think about tomorrow, let's just enjoy tonight. The bar's packed, everyone shouting over each other, wine you have to drink fast so you don't taste it. We have intimate conversations we hope that no one will remember. When we can't find words anymore, we dance. We get home too late. A few hours of restless sleep, and then suddenly it's 5 a.m., and I'm awake, heart thrumming against my ribs, convinced that what I've seen is real. I'd turned up at Max's house in Oxford. Door answered by a girl — long shiny hair, perfect skin, early twenties, late teens, even — and I thought, fuck, he really does like younger women, doesn't he? *I'm here to see Max —* I said, and she turned and shouted *Dad,* and he came down the stairs, and I saw he was old, much older than me — how had I not seen this before? How had I not realised? — much older than he'd ever said he was, and he was angry, he hated me, he said — *Anna, what the hell are you doing here, get out before —.*

I've been thinking about him all week. Ever since I realised that — finally, after all these months — I had the money to pay him back. It was a week ago now. A jazz session at the hotel. I'd finished my shift, was waiting at the bar for Laurie to finish hers, and a City worker came over. Late fifties, early sixties maybe, and visibly drunk — red cheeks, tie off, a few shirt buttons undone. He was out with a big group of banker types, a work Christmas thing, I guessed. I'd noticed them earlier because they were making so much noise. I steeled myself to be nice enough not to offend him, not to give him cause to complain to Malcolm, though I really wasn't in the mood, but all he said was – *that was lovely, this is from all of us, happy Christmas* – and he handed me a fistful of notes. People didn't tend to give me tips for singing, it wasn't the done thing. I wasn't even sure I was allowed to keep it, but I looked around me and I couldn't see Malcolm, so I put it in my bag. I counted it when I got home, found it was more than I normally got for a whole week of jazz, and then that was it – I had enough. I could pay him back.

The next day, money in an envelope, I went round to his flat. I headed straight for the lift, but the man on reception stopped me.

Where are you going?

Flat 192. I'm a friend of Max. He's expecting me.

A stupid lie, and he knew I was lying.

There's no Max there – he said.

Maybe it's 193? The nineteenth floor.

No Max on that floor.

I suppose my expression must have matched the wrong-footed horror I felt, and he was sorry for me, coming up with his own version of events – who I was and why I was there and what the relationship between me and this Max had been – because then he said – I'm new here, but I think Flat 192 changed tenants not too long ago. I guess he moved.

I guess so – I said. – Thanks – and then, taking in properly what he'd said – but what do you mean tenants? Like, renting?

He re-evaluated me, then, as a crazy person, and said self-importantly that he couldn't share information about his residents and I'd better be leaving.

Out on the street, I Googled the flat. It hadn't changed owners since the block had been built eight years ago, when Max had still lived with his wife wherever it was in the suburbs they'd lived. So he'd been renting it, then, he hadn't owned it like he'd said. I felt a smart of anger, like the familiar twinge from an old injury that's never quite healed. I hadn't known him, not really. A version of him he'd wanted to present, that was all.

And then I couldn't stop thinking about him. That insistent tune I'd worked hard over the past few months to mute started up again, and I lay awake at night, speculating endlessly about why he'd left the flat, where he'd gone, circling round and round the same spot obsessively, like a bluebottle buzzing round a bin lid, hoping for the chance to get in, until I knew I had to see him. It was because of the money, I told myself, knowing that, while this wasn't the whole truth, it wasn't untrue. I didn't want to keep the money. I felt compromised, having it in the house. Lying in bed with Frankie, I was uncomfortably aware of it – how much cash there was stuffed into my drawer and who it really belonged to.

It wasn't just the money, though. I knew it wasn't just that. It was that I'd always thought I'd see him again. The money meant I'd see him again – all I needed was to save enough, and then I could go to him. It made me calm, knowing that. It meant I could stop thinking about him. I didn't need to speculate anymore, to try and work out what exactly he'd been lying about – whether he was still married, whether he'd gone to New York, why he hadn't wanted me. It didn't matter. Someday soon, I'd see him again and, seeing him with distance, it would all become clear. After going to his flat, though, after finding him gone, I had to confront the fact that I might never see him again, it was actually quite likely I wouldn't, and then I found myself right back there – that unreal world, imagining scenes and scenarios, things he would say to me, endless speculation and doubt.

I'd deleted his number, but I did have his email. His work one. I knew his secretary got copies of everything he was sent, so I crafted a message that was as neutral as I could make it. I had something I wanted to give back to him, I said. Could we meet? I sent it, and straightaway got a message back. The email had bounced. I looked him up on his company's website, but nothing came up. He didn't seem to work there anymore. That night, I found myself suddenly awake, remembering how the man on reception had said *there's no*

Max there, thinking insanely — *was that not his real name, then?* But that was stupid, mad, and as soon as the world had sharpened, I knew it. I'd seen it on his business card, his bank card, on the backs of envelopes.

At the weekend, Laurie got a Christmas tree. No one wanted to invest in decorations, though, so we improvised, hanging its branches with necklaces and bangles and cutlery tied onto pieces of string. Sash cooked a vegan Christmas dinner, and we spent the evening together, bickering about climate activism and Instagram feminism and whether Ella was cheating at Articulate. Mil's experiment in communal living had worked, Laurie said. We were exactly like a big family, with all the dysfunctional squabbling that entailed. I thought we might descend into a proper argument then, an ending-the-evening sort of argument, but everyone got sentimental instead.

It's four days till Christmas, and they've all gone home now. Frankie's going this morning too. He's often away — singing work — he's doing well — and when he's not here, I don't really think about him, but I'm always happy when he's back. He lives in a huge house with other singers, more than I can keep track of. They reuse teabags and no one ever does the washing up, and Frankie has a sheet pinned over his window because the curtain rail broke and he doesn't want to pay to replace it and so, in his room, it's always a grubby sort of dusk. He tells me he loves me when he's drunk, which is often, and I don't say anything, because I don't love him — or not in the way I used to understand love, anyway. He doesn't come near my inner life. Is that love, if he can't hurt me? If he can't reach in and grab hold of that essential part of me, squeeze it in his fist so that he's all there is? Can this be the stuff of centuries' worth of poetry, films and opera, tears, suicide — going to the supermarket together and watching TV in bed when we've got the day off and arguing about where I leave my shoes and why he recounts my anecdotes at parties as if he was there too when he wasn't?

He's still asleep next to me. I find my phone, scroll back in my gallery. The picture I'd taken of the bank statement, address at the top. I'd considered this before, dismissed it as impossible. The house has taken on mythic proportions in my fantasies, like a medieval castle, high walls, moated, unbreachable. I decide I'll go there. I'll see him again. I'll fix a final image of him in my head and it will be one that won't haunt me. His real context – no potential for deception – he can't hide from me there.

Frankie wakes. Says he has to go, he's going to miss his train. Kisses me goodbye and says he'll call me, wishes me a happy Christmas. He goes, and I get the money out of the drawer, put it into stacks of a hundred, and lay them out on the bed to count. I've never told Frankie about the money. A little bit about Max when he's asked, but never about the money, and he's never asked much. I'm glad, because when I talk about him, I can hear my voice become bitter, vitriolic, and I don't like it. Frankie doesn't seem to notice or, if he does, he isn't bothered. He's not a jealous person. He takes my affection for granted in a lazy sort of way that's charming when I want him, irritating when I don't.

I look at mine and Laurie's bed, transformed by a bedspread of cash. It's taken me months to save it up. Months and months. A little bit each week, hidden in a tin in my underwear drawer, while the days got shorter and shorter, and the air outside turned gradually cold, like bathwater left to sit for too long. I count it, and it's the right amount. I knew that anyway, but the ritual was soothing. I put it back in its envelope, check the train times on my phone.

Outside, it's beautiful. The sort of crisp, bright, cold December day they put on Christmas cards.

I get the train to Oxford, then find a cab, give the driver the address.

Going home for Christmas? – he asks.

Not yet, no.

No more information offered, make myself unfriendly, but he still wants to chat. Desultory conversation. Politics. Spanish food. The price of pool cues.

People don't think of it as an expensive hobby – he says – but –

We turn out of town.

A big road, lined with identical boxy houses, some strewn with festive cheer, flashing with lights or hung with plastic snowflakes or decorated by a Santa's bum and legs stuck out of a window.

The driver's still talking. Grandkids. Pool, again. The man who once sat exactly where I'm sitting now, the back of his cab, and pulled out a knife. I make the polite responses required, *oh really, no way, wow, I can't believe that*. It feels like being at an audition. Getting into the headspace. Your rival, to break focus, makes casual chat.

I try to concentrate, to enforce clarity, because in my mind, the house and all the people in it are pixelated, like someone on the news whose image can't be shared. *In fifteen minutes,* I tell myself, *in ten minutes, in five*. I feel for the envelope in my bag, check my face with the camera of my phone – *in three minutes* – but I can't make it real. I've imagined it so many times that, even though I'm in it now, it feels made up.

We turn a bend, and then there are no more houses. Fields either side of the motorway. The driver's still talking, and I keep making listening noises in the wrong places. A smaller road, a smaller road – further and further into unreality – and then a narrow country lane. I recognise it. It's where Google Street View stopped.

He takes me right down to the end, stops at a gate, tree-lined drive beyond, so you can't see the house.

It's fine – I say, not wanting anyone to hear the car. – I'll get out here.

Sure?

Thanks.

I pay him and go through the gate, up the drive. Turn the corner to this house that had seemed inviolable, and here I am, violating it. The image sharpens.

Nothing like what I'd thought.

Long, low, L-shaped, flat roof, brick, long windows all along. I couldn't name the type of building. Couldn't even guess when it was built.

I walk right up to the front door and ring the bell. It's so different to what I'd imagined, I can't believe that him or her or anyone could answer. I don't even know if I believe in him anymore. There's only a very brief moment – after I've knocked, a little silence, then foot-steps in the hall, someone fumbling with the latch – when I start to feel afraid.

Is Max in? I've got something to give him. Is Max in? I've got something to give him.

I don't need to say it, though, because when the door opens, it's him. Having him there again, right up close, it's like being confronted with someone I've only ever seen in a photograph – finding him intensely familiar and, at the same time, entirely strange – wondering whether I really know him, or just think I do.

He smiles.

Anna – he says. – Hi.

Any advantage I thought I'd have by turning up unannounced disappears with the smile.

Hi – I say.

If he's surprised to see me, he doesn't show it. I'd imagined a moment of shock, a moment of panic before his brain caught up, and then he'd try to get me out of the house. But, no. He opens the door wide, nothing to hide, and he smiles. There's something else odd, and it takes me a second to work out exactly what it is, but then I do. He's wearing jeans. Blue jeans. A red knitted jumper, a bit too big for him. Bare feet. Drained of imagined menace. I've never seen him in jeans. I've never seen him look normal.

Do you want to come in? – he says.

I walk into the hall, and he takes my coat, puts it in a cupboard. I take off my shoes, and he disappears them as well. He doesn't say anything as we perform this ritual of welcoming – no questions, no asking what the fuck I'm doing there – and it throws me. I find myself apologising.

I'm really sorry to turn up here like this – I say. – Sorry. It's just, I needed to see you. And I broke my phone a while back, so I didn't have your number, and I went round to your flat but they said you'd moved out and, well, I've got something to give you, so – sorry, I hope I'm not interrupting anything, I couldn't think of another way to see you, I –

He waits for my apologies to run out. Looks at me with an expression that could be amusement. I'd forgotten his stillness. How he makes me aware of every unnecessary movement I make.

Really, don't worry about it, Anna – he says. – It's nice to see you.

We stand in the hall. He doesn't make a move to go in, doesn't speak, just smiles, like I've inadvertently said something funny, and to fill the silence, I fall into social niceties. Cocktail party conversation. I tell him the house is lovely. I admire the hallway. And it is beautiful. Long and very light, a low-slung bench along the window to the left, sliding doors to the rooms on the right. A light wooden floor merging into the wooden staircase, which curves up the wall at the end. Bright flowers in vases.

Thanks – he says. – I like it too.

What have you been up to?

Today? Putting up the tree. In here.

The first room on the right, a sitting room, two walls of timber-framed windows. The tree's at one end of the room, almost to the ceiling and real. A woody pine smell, and the floor's covered in green needles where he's dragged it in. A couple of boxes of decorations, baubles, a string of lights on the floor. He's midway through detangling. There's a saw, and a ring of trunk, a couple of branches he's hacked off to make it fit in the stand.

He stands close to me in the doorway. I can smell his sweat. A tug of wanting.

Are you going to decorate it then? – I say, to say something.

I'll save it for the kids to do.

What?

More hysterical than intended. He looks at me sideways.

My brother's kids – he says. – They're coming on Monday.

Get a fucking hold of yourself.

Oh right – I say. – That's nice.

It is. The whole family's coming actually. We're having Christmas here.

That's nice.

It is.

A pause.

It's a mess in here – he says. – Let's go upstairs.

Down the corridor, he points out the rooms as we pass, has me look in. Dining room, antique table, blue chairs. White kitchen, charcoal grey tiles. Everything is light and neat and quiet. He tells me about it. Built in the thirties, he says. But this is new modernism, not your white cube box kind of modernism. Same fundamentals – simple elevation, functional design – but traditional materials, he says. The proper stuff. He names the architect, as if I should have heard of him, and I haven't, but I nod. Owned by the same family since it was built, he says. Passed down from father to son. Falling apart when he bought it. He loves it, he says. He's put it back together.

We go up the stairs, him still talking. I feel like I'm in one of those dreams I sometimes have, where I'm on stage and I know I'm meant to be singing, but I can't remember what opera I'm in. It's not exactly a nightmare, though, because he's carrying it so nicely by himself. All I have to do is go along with it.

In here – he says.

Another sitting room, more intimate than the one downstairs. Sofas arranged around a brick fireplace. One wall, all bookshelves, neatly lined with books. Flowers in blue vases. A timber-framed sliding window, floor to ceiling. A balcony that looks out onto green – lawn, trees, pink blossom. There are no other houses.

We sit on the same sofa, him on one side, and me very far away on the other.

So you've left the London flat? – I say.

I'm renting it out. Might sell it. Haven't decided.

Why?

Well, I'm not really sure it's such a good investment anymore. Not in this climate.

No, I mean, why have you left?

I don't need to be there anymore. In London. I quit.

Your job?

Yes.

Seriously? Why?

He shrugs.

Various reasons – he says.

Like?

Well, they were still putting pressure on me to move to New York. And I was kind of considering it, but six weeks there made up my mind not to. And, well, yeah. Various reasons.

What are you going to do instead?

I don't quite know yet – he says. – Something meaningful.

He smiles, like he's making fun of himself, or possibly me. That old familiar sensation – he knows something I don't, I can't keep up, always staggering, stumbling a few paces behind. I can't think of anything else to say, so I say – can I use the bathroom?

End of the corridor – he says.

Hallway, glass-dazzled. The bedrooms along it have neatly made beds, empty otherwise. The one at the end is his, the biggest, ensuite. A pile of books on the bedside table. A couple of shirts on the back of a chair. I go into the bathroom at the end. Try to remember why I'm here. Wash my hands with some expensive smelling soap – no other toiletries, nothing on the side of the bath, this bathroom's not used. Look in the mirror. Smooth my hair. And I can't help but imagine him here alone, wonder how he fills his time. The weekends when I was in London, obsessing over what he might be doing. And what exactly had he been doing? Reading his books? Walking in his garden? Pulling up his floorboards to see the pipes underneath?

When I get back, he's looking out of the window, and he doesn't turn round straightaway. It's late in the day for December, and the cold sinking light paints him gold. His hair's longer than it used to be. He doesn't look tired anymore. I have an urge to go to him, to put my arms round him, but I didn't come here to be weak.

I've got something for you – I say.

He turns. The familiar movement of his smile.

You said. What is it?

I get the envelope out of my bag and hold it out to him.

What is it?

The money I owe you.

He looks confused.

What money?

The money you lent me.

There's a pause. He looks at the envelope, then at me.

Oh – he says. – Oh right. You really didn't have to do that.

I said I'd pay you back.

I know – he says. – Well, thanks.

He doesn't take it, though. I put it down on the coffee table, and he doesn't say anything, and I start to feel embarrassed. What I'd imagined to be a *fuck you* sort of gesture now seems in quite poor taste. I've written the amount on the front too. I wish I hadn't.

So, you've got a job then? – he asks.

No. Well, yes. Kind of. I'm back at the Conservatory. And singing jazz again. Some teaching too.

That's good – he says. – I'm glad you're doing well. I was worried about you.

I want him to know, then, just how well I'm doing. I start to tell him about the festival back in summer. The concert last night. The show I was in last month, *Les mamelles de Tirésias*. The new opera I've been collaborating on with some people I met in Martignargues, how we've recently got funding. There's lots that I'm proud of and I want to tell him. While I'm talking, he listens, he nods, he smiles. I feel like he's not quite getting it, though, so I tell him that I sang the title role in the Poulenc, there were some really good reviews – maybe he's seen some of them? That the director's cast me in his production of *Manon* next year, the full role. He asks questions. I tell him about the competition I won in October, how I've had offers of representation from it, am doing a recital series off the back of it next year. He seems interested. So I don't know why it feels like the more I try to impress him, the further away he moves. Why I feel self-conscious, like I'm showing off. Exaggerating. I still want him to like me, and so I stop talking.

I'd glad you're doing well – he says again. – Maybe I could come and see you in something.

Maybe.

There's a little silence, and I say that I might need to go soon, check the time on my phone as something to do with my hands. He looks at it.

Isn't that the same phone you've always had? – he says.

What?

You said it broke.

Oh. Yes. I got it fixed. It was wiped, though.

Right – he says.

Then, as if he's suddenly realised an inconsistency in a story I didn't tell, he says – how did you say you got this address?

The guy on reception gave it to me. In your old building.

Well, that was unprofessional of him – he says, mildly.

It also doesn't sound true, I don't think, but if he identifies it as a lie, he doesn't say so.

Do you have to rush off? – he says. – Let's have a drink. Wait here.

He goes downstairs.

It's almost dark outside. I start to think about the journey home, how long it'll take, and how cold it is outside. The broken curtain rod and the reused teabags. Wondering how you could fail to love someone in this house, how easy it would be for things to stay unbroken. Not for her, though. Them on this sofa together, diarising, drinking wine. Her curled up on that armchair opposite, flicking through work documents, saying – *can you just be quiet for a second? I'm trying to think.* Looking at the blackness beyond the window and seeing nothing and feeling – what? – and feeling lonely. Did she? And feeling trapped. Stupid to imagine it. She never lived here, I don't think.

He brings a bottle of red and pours us both a glass. He lights the fire. He sits back down on the sofa, next to me.

Did your friend tell you I came to find you? – he asks.

What? No. Laurie?

A few months ago. Right before I left London. I went to the bar. Thought you might have started working there again. Well, I was right, as it turned out, but you weren't there that night.

What did she say?

She said you were fine. That you were with someone else and really happy and I should leave you alone. I respected that.

I'm still trying to process what this means, when he says – and are you still?

Still what?

Still with someone.

Yes.

Well, I'm glad you're happy – he says. – Kind of.

What do you mean *kind of*?

Just it's a shame, that's all – he says. – That you're with someone, I mean. Tell me about him.

There's nothing much to tell.

Who is he?

You met him actually. He's a singer. Frankie.

Oh. Him.

He raises his eyebrows, as if he finds the idea amusing.

Are you jealous? – I ask.

Well, you're with someone else – he says – but you thought you'd come all the way here to see me. Rather than, you know, posting a cheque. It's an interesting choice. So – he says, his voice heavy with irony. – Is it love?

Why are you asking me that?

Just making conversation.

There's a silence. I've drunk my wine, though I barely tasted it. He tops it up. His bottom lip's stained red.

Then he says – look, do you want the truth? I had to see you. That's why I came to the bar. I'd started thinking about you again. Couldn't stop thinking about you, actually. When I heard you were with someone else, I, well, I don't know – he says. – I'm sorry.

I stare at him. I can't think of anything to say, and so he starts to talk.

It was when it got cold again, he's saying, when autumn came. That's when he started thinking about it. Regretting what had happened, how it had ended. Not his finest hour, he says, with work and with the divorce and, well, with everything. He behaved badly, he says, he knows that. But when it started to get cold again, something about it being the time of year when we'd met maybe, and –

His voice went on and on, smooth and soothing, teasing my defences out of my fingers. He could always do this. Articulate suddenly, entirely unexpectedly, what I'd been thinking and I'd never imagine he'd think it too. Because it'd been the same for me, when summer ended, when autumn came, looking back and thinking, that was a year ago – and wondering if it would be like this always – if this time of year, always, would be infused with his colour. Thinking, this is useless, useless, this nostalgia, which makes beautiful forever times you know were complicated, a mess, that made you unhappy – it serves no purpose, surely, you think, this longing always for the past.

He looks right at me, his eyes into my eyes, and I remember what it's like, when nothing else matters but this second, and then this one, and then this one.

And what's the point, anyway? – he says. – In doing – what? – the right thing? In doing the right thing? What does that even mean? What is the right thing anyway? Isn't being with the person you want to be with the right thing? Because what's the point otherwise?

I don't know – I say.

I wanted to see you again – he says. – That's all.

Well, now you have.

Yes, now I have.

There's a moment where we both look at each other, and I think, this is why I came, isn't it? He's right. If I stay very still, if I just stay still, it will happen.

But he breaks it. He looks down at the envelope on the table.

Anna – he says. – Honestly, I had no idea I'd given you that much money. I didn't notice it. It hasn't made a difference to me. You should keep it. I don't need it.

The window's black now, his face hollowed out by the light of the fire, but the room is unexpectedly cold.

Take it – I say, and my voice sounds oddly detached, not like my own.

Take it – I say again. – Please. Take it. I want you to take it.

He looks down at it.

Ok – he says. – I'll take it.

But when he reaches for me, he leaves it, lying there between us.

ACKNOWLEDGEMENTS

Thank you to my agent, Emma Finn, for her enthusiasm for this story, and her unfailing and generous support. To Allegra Le Fanu, Kerry Cullen and Amy Einhorn for being such brilliant editors. To Hillary Jacobson for championing this book so wholeheartedly in the United States. To the wonderful teams at Bloomsbury and Holt for looking after it so well.

I started writing this book on a Curtis Brown Creative course, and I am grateful to everyone there for their thoughtful feedback. Particular thanks to Alicia Kirby, Helen Barham and Ed Moustafa for the numerous hours they spent discussing early chapters with me, and for their encouragement and friendship.

Thank you to Holly Braine for our inspiring conversations. To Eleanor Braine and Georgie Glen whose kind hospitality gave me the space and peace to write. To all the singers who talked to me while I was working on this novel – in particular, to Charlotte Richardson and Kirsty McLean, who were hugely generous with their time. To Daniel Ekpe for encouraging me to pursue this project, and for his patience in answering my questions about banking. To Val Hudson for her early support of my writing and her very wise advice.

And finally, huge thanks to Maggie, Martin, Catherine and Lucia – for listening to me talk endlessly about this book, for reading multiple drafts and for their optimism and support.

A NOTE ON THE AUTHOR

Imogen Crimp studied English at Cambridge, followed by an MA in contemporary literature at UCL, where she specialised in female modernist writers. After university, she briefly studied singing at a conservatoire. She lives in London.

A NOTE ON THE TYPE

The text of this book is set in Perpetua. This typeface is an adaptation of a style of letter that had been popularised for monumental work in stone by Eric Gill. Large scale drawings by Gill were given to Charles Malin, a Parisian punch-cutter, and his hand-cut punches were the basis for the font issued by Monotype. First used in a private translation called 'The Passion of Perpetua and Felicity', the italic was originally called Felicity.